TIM WICKENDEN

ANGEL AVENGER

A MAX BECKER THRILLER

BOOK ONE

[signature: Tim Wickenden]

SLUGADO PRESS
Cymru Independent Publisher

First Published by Slugado Press in 2019
Fishguard, Wales

❖❖❖

Amazon Paperback edition © 2023
ISBN 978-1-9161048-3-9

❖❖❖

© Tim Wickenden, 2023
All rights reserved
Tim Wickenden has asserted his right under the Copyright, Designs and Patents Act 1988 to be identified as the author of this work.
All rights reserved. No part of this book may be reproduced, or stored in a retrieval system, or transmitted in any form or by any means, electronic, mechanical, photocopying, recording, or otherwise, without express written permission of the publisher.
This book is a work of fiction and except in cases of geographical or historical fact, any resemblance to actual persons, living or dead, is purely coincidental.

❖❖❖

For more information on
Max Becker and Tim Wickenden visit:
www.timwickenden.com

❖❖❖

Cover design by Creative Covers
ccovers.co.uk

❖❖❖

Book design by The Naked Designer
Printed by Amazon POD

Foreword

Angel Avenger is set in Berlin, Germany. To keep the geographical flavour I have used some German terms and language. Where possible I have provided in text translation, but for other instances a glossary of translations and other information is given in Appendix A.

T.W. 2023

For innocent victims of war

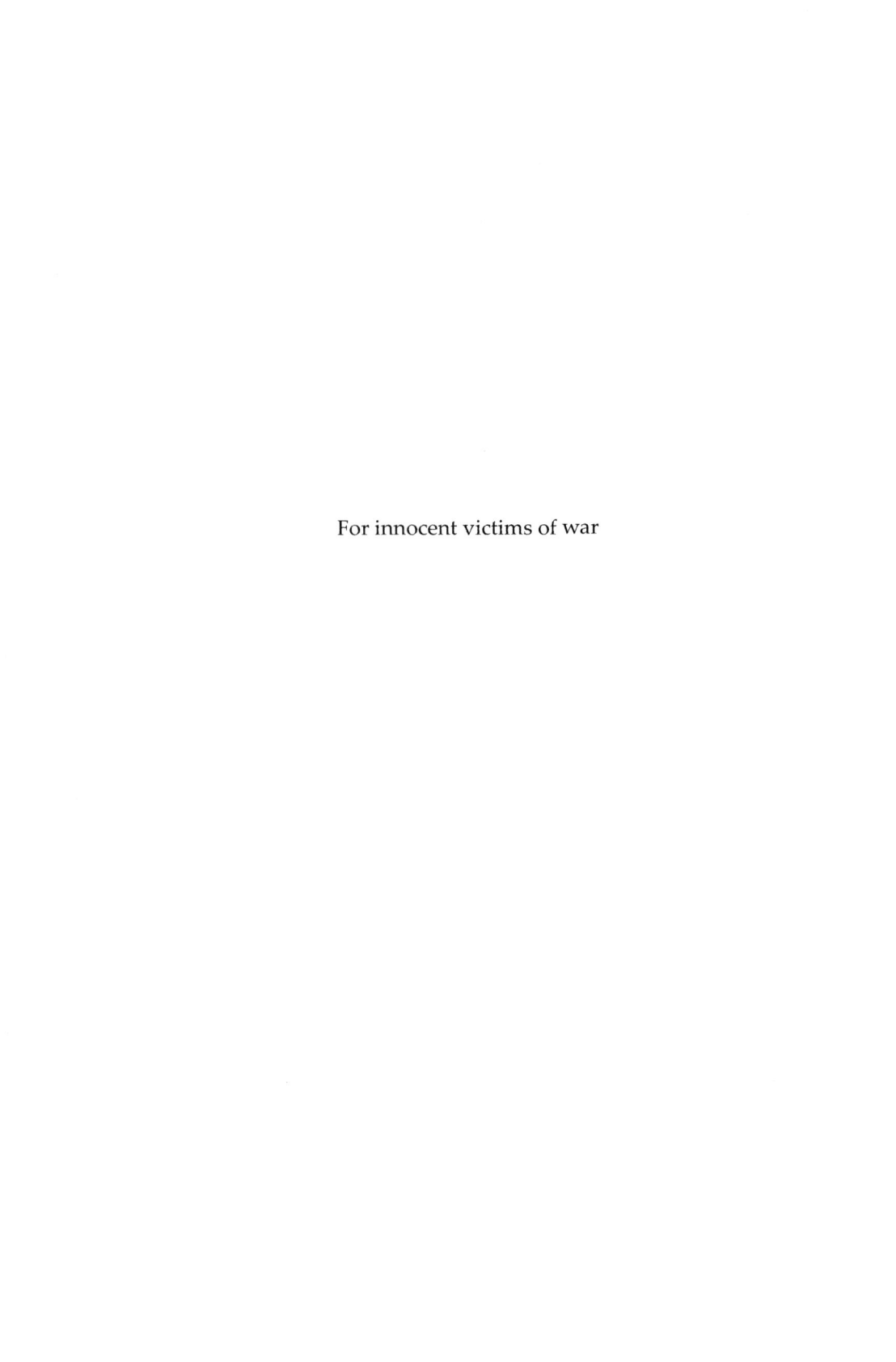

1

What's past is prologue

Berlin: Thursday, April 26, 1945.

The night brings a mighty thunderstorm, the rain so heavy that it has put out fires burning around the city. The air hangs dense with the pungency of sweet decay, acrid, damp smoke, and a stench so thick that it stings eyes, coating nose and throat.

There's banging on the barricaded door. A frantic voice. 'They've shot him. Are you there, Dr Mann? Let us in! Let us in! For pity's sake! Help, he's dying!'

In the cellar, the haggard, fearful people, lost in the folds of their misery, make scant response.

Dr Mann turns to his wife as if for approval. 'Gerda, I must go look see.'

She pushes him forward. 'Yes, go, go quickly, before she attracts attention with all that shouting. Manfred, use your bulk and go help Horst with the dresser.'

The two men go up the stairs and drag the furniture away from the door. They throw the bolts and remove the cross-planking, open the door a crack, and peep out.

Mann recognises the girl but does not know her name. She's distraught and looks badly beaten. In a cart is a boy; it's hard to tell his age. Mann sees severe wounds on his head and upper right leg.

He looks around. 'You got him here all alone?'

She shakes her head. 'No, I had help, but they wanted to get away before…' she hesitates, looks away, 'before they come back.'

Mann says, 'It's usually safe in the early morning. Ivan sleep off the excesses of the night. I take it you mean Ivan, yes?'

She nods her head, shivering.

He beckons to her. 'Let's get you inside. Come, come.'

He ushers her in. He and Manfred carry the boy downstairs.

He says, 'Quick, Gerda, clear that space, we need to stop the bleeding.' He turns to another woman. 'Take the girl and see what you can do for her.'

Mann inspects the boy's wounds. The head looks bad, but it's superficial; he can come back to that. The leg is worse, and the boy has lost a lot of blood. He has few dressings, and none of them are sterile: there is no water spare for boiling instruments and bandages, just some cheap spirits.

He begins his work, relieved that the boy is unconscious: there's no morphine. He stops the bleeding, tying off the leaking veins. He uses spirits to flush the wound and searches for the round. It has buried itself in the muscle. He retrieves it. He has seen too many bullets and knows this is a nine-millimetre round from a handgun. For a moment, he examines it. The boy has been lucky: no arterial bleed and no shattered thigh bone. If he avoids infections, he may survive. Completing his work on the leg, he turns his attention to the head wound. A bullet has cut a deep gash as it grazed passed. Just a few millimetres the wrong way, and the boy would have died instantly. He flushes the wound with some precious spirit and stitches it closed but does not apply a bandage, it's better to leave it open.

The girl, now cleaned up, comes over. 'How is he? Will he be all right?'

He looks into her wide, darting eyes. 'Maybe yes, maybe not.' He looks away. After the last few months, he never sugar-coats it. Life has become cheap and death routine. 'He's lucky, but he must fight and then, if... if he survives, it will take time to recover. Honestly, I'm not sure what time any of us have anymore. What happened, anyhow? And where are your parents?' He stands and throws a bloody rag into the corner, stretching out his sore back. 'No, on second thoughts, don't tell me. I don't want to know.'

He turns to her and grabs her by the shoulders. 'Right now, there is no past and no future; there is only now, this second, you understand?'

Trembling, she stares back at him, her pupils like saucers. She nods slowly.

Dr Mann softens his voice. 'We live second-by-second, but we live, you hear?' He lets go of her. 'Now get some rest and look after him; he's your responsibility now.'

'Thank you. I'll take good care of him.'

Going over, she lies down next to her brother. He is clammy, his breathing ragged and shallow. She whispers to him, 'You must fight, you hear me? You must live, for mama and papa and me.'

She recalls the horror and weeps quietly, shaking. Holding him, she whispers, 'I will never leave you, you hear?'

At last, sleep takes her, but it's into a world of dark dreams where pain and fear stalk her.

2

The serpent's egg

IN THE EARLY HOURS OF Sunday, September 11, 1960, Manfried Bikart lurches out of his favourite Bierkeller on Gottschalkstraße in the Wedding district of West Berlin and staggers off down the quiet street to walk the one-and-a-half kilometres home. Turning right into Wilhelm-Kuhr-Straße and just before the bridge over the railway, he passes the warning sign: *"Achtung! Sie verlassen nach 40m West Berlin"*. The East side of the footbridge marks the open border between East and West. It's a pleasant night. He pauses for a few moments, leaning on the bridge railings and lights a cigarette. Taking a few deep drags, he looks out along the railway line then, belching loudly, stumbles off and rejoins Wilhelm-Kuhr-Straße, where another sign reminds him he is now in *"Das Demokratische Berlin"*. A little further along, the street skirts Bürger State Park, where Manfried turns off, heading along a footpath.

Even sober, it's doubtful he would have noticed the figure trailing him: it's not the first time they have followed him from the Bierkeller back to his rooms in Pestalozzistraße. They've shadowed him several times, and on each occasion, he's taken the same route home. As he passes the historic landmark of Freidhof Pankow in the south-east corner of the park, a colossal figure emerges from behind a tree, clubbing Manfried on the head, and he slumps, unconscious, to the ground.

The night is deathly quiet, the half-moon and broken clouds casting deep shadows. Moments later, the assailant is joined by Manfried's follower.

With a glint in her eye, she looks at Manfried's stricken figure. 'Good job! Pick him up and wait where I told you. I'll get the van.'

He nods, and hefting Manfried onto his shoulder, heads off and waits in the shadows close to the park entrance. It has been a good idea to strike on the East side, much quieter and less traffic. There is the issue of driving back to the West, but they have rehearsed travelling around the area and between the two sides at night. Günther Alsbach, whom the large man does occasional work for, has been happy to lend them his old and battered 1950 Citroën van as, recently, he's purchased a year-old Volkswagen vehicle for the building firm he runs. Lights appear down the road. He makes sure that it is the van, before once more shouldering the unconscious Manfried. The van pulls to a stop, and she gets out and opens the side door. He bundles Manfried inside and then follows and sits on the floor, guarding. The door bangs shut, she climbs back in, and they set off down Wilhelm-Kuhr-Straße, then go right following Am Bürger Park. They have decided to cross back over on Klemkestraße, but should they encounter any problems, they have an alternate crossing further north. The way is clear, and soon they are back over in the West of the city, where they drive the remaining two kilometres to Teichstraße. They pull up at the back of the abandoned buildings. The driver checks all is clear, then opens the side door.

'Bring him out, quickly. Take him straight down,' she whispers.

He hoists the unconscious Manfried on his shoulder and carries him down a small alley, across a bit of rough ground, to a row of derelict buildings. They have carried out some alterations to one, refurbishing the basement, fixing old factory, stout metal doors they have purchased from Günther. He heads straight down to the prepared room. She locks the van, has a last look around, then follows.

The big man lays down Manfried and then throws a switch. Two super-bright spotlights clunk on, giving off a distinct buzzing noise. They've positioned the lights on stands about half-way across the room and pointing directly toward the wall furthest from the stairs, where a sturdy, planked-board fitted with straps to hold a body at wrists, ankles, waist, chest, and forehead is attached. In the darkness, behind the lights, is a table with a portable reel-to-reel tape recorder with a built-in speaker. They have rigged up electric cable via the old ceiling light, providing power to the spots and the tape machine. In a corner, by the table, is a doorway that leads directly to concrete stairs up to the ground floor.

The top door bangs shut, and there is the scrape and tap of two bolts engaging. She descends, shutting the lower door and throwing the bolts. She places her bag on one chair behind the table, then goes over to inspect Manfried, checking his pulse and breathing.

She looks at her accomplice. 'You hit him so hard, I thought you might have killed him.'

He grins back. 'Sorry, don't know my strength sometimes. It was simpler than I thought it would be.'

'Yes, it was; you did good. He'll come around soon. Let's put him on the board, then wait. Strip him off and put his clothes in the corner; we'll burn them later.'

They go through his pockets, removing a small bunch of keys on a ring with a cheap copy of a religious icon titled *The Raising of Lazarus*—she looks at it for a moment, then says, 'Let's hope not, eh?'—a greasy old wallet, a crumpled pack of Nil cigarettes with a book of matches from a bar called Dagmar's, some assorted coins, a filthy handkerchief, and a knife with a knuckle-duster handle; all go in the bag.

The big man lifts him to the board and holds him in place as she tightens each strap. The body, now fixed, is powerless.

They step back and inspect their work. She nods and collects the bag. 'That's it; he's not going anywhere. I'll get the torch, then we'll turn off the lights and wait.'

They sit and switch off the lights. In the pitch dark, they drink water, eat sandwiches, but they do not talk. They have planned every move to the last detail. She can hear her heart beating, feel the adrenaline pumping. From now, nothing will ever be the same. The room smells damp, earthy and of decay. They are patient for time is nothing to them. Having eaten, he dozes while she stays alert. In the room, it's impossible to tell day from night, rain from sunshine, the passing of time and nature indiscernible: this space is theirs.

The hours pass, and sometime later that morning, Manfried wakes up. His head throbs, and he feels nauseous. He thinks that on his way home, he must have fallen and passed out. He is confused, seems to be upright and bound uncomfortably. His arms spread out as on a cross, his legs akimbo, tied at the ankles; the bindings dig in painfully. His hands and feet have little feeling. As his mind clears, he realises he is naked and bound tight to a wall or board. He thinks he has gone blind, as the world he's woken up to is pitch black. Held tight across his forehead, he cannot look about; his eyes dart uselessly, straining and searching this nightmare world. Perhaps it is a nightmare, and he might wake up. He shouts into the dark. There is a clunk, and a penetrating light floods over him, burning his eyes, which he shuts tight. Slowly, blinking them open, he understands it is a nightmare, but not one from which he can awaken.

There is no sound other than his heavy, gulping breath and an electrical buzzing. Gasping, he yells, 'What the fuck's going on here? Is anybody there?'

Nothing. He tries to calm his breathing, but the effect of a large intake of alcohol, the concussion, and the stress of his predicament makes him heave painfully, vomiting down himself. The lights go out.

'No, put the light back on. Who's there? Why are you doing this?'

A few minutes pass and the light returns. He peers, trying to look beyond the blinding light, but it's impenetrable. He calms down. Being sick has made him feel marginally better, and his breathing slows. Feebly he asks, 'What do you want?'

From beyond the light, he hears a metallic click and a whirring noise as the tape machine starts. A moment later, a deep male voice says in Russian, 'The People's Court finds you guilty and sentences you to death for your crimes. You sick, filthy, Soviet pig!' There is a click and the whirring sound stops.

He shouts back, 'What? What are you talking about? Go to hell! I'm not even Russian, you stupid fucker! You've got the wrong man. I'm Manfried Bikart. Does that sound fucking Russian to you?'

For a while, he continues shouting. Again, they extinguish the lights. He holds still and listens. He hears footsteps and senses someone approaching. He feels the heat from a face as it comes close to him, smells the breath. A deep voice hisses, 'Squeal pig.' A huge hand grabs his testicles and squeezes harder and harder. Manfried resists, but the pain becomes unbearable. He screams, but it brings no relief to the crushing pressure, and the agony becomes so intense, he passes out.

The big man releases his iron grip. She joins him. 'Get the bucket and throw water over him, then we'll switch off the light.'

Retrieving the bucket from the corner, he dashes cold water in Manfried's face, then turns out the light. Manfried comes around, feels sick, the pain in his groin a raging, aching fire, the area swelling up. He can sense a person, another person, smaller, and tenses, expecting more pain, and praying they do not start again on his testicles.

Quietly, he asks, 'Who the hell are you? Why are you doing this?'

There is a sharp, metallic click. He feels the prick of a sharp point on his left side, halfway down his ribcage. Slowly the pressure builds until, with a pop, the point punctures the skin sinking in, pushing deeper, then with a swift flick of the razor-sharp blade a wide gash opens. The pain is excruciating. He yells, feeling the blood flowing thickly down his side.

A female voice shouts, 'What is my name?'

Pain shocking his mind, Manfried is confused. He shouts, 'I don't know you! I don't know you!'

Again, the voice, insistent. 'What is my name?'

There is silence. He racks his addled mind. 'Is it Navlova? Yes? You've got it all wrong; it wasn't me who tipped off the Stasi…'

The voice interrupts him, right by his ear, and he feels the air as the words spit at him. 'Not Navlova, someone worse, much worse. Time for another lesson.'

A flashlight clicks on, its beam in Manfried's wild, staring eyes, the pupils shrinking back to pinholes of black fear. He feels the cold barrel of a pistol dig hard against his genitals. 'God no, what are you doing?'

'What is your real name?'

'It's Manfried Bikart.'

'Wrong answer! One more time, or you lose your cock. What is your real name?'

For a moment, he breathes hard, bewildered. He feels the cold barrel dig harder, a shot of pain surges through his testicles. 'Okay, okay, stop. I'll tell you.' He swallows, gulping in air. 'It's Dedov Damir Olegovich.'

'There, that wasn't too hard, was it? Now, I have a little something for you, Dedov Damir Olegovich.' She squeezes the trigger; the gun goes off. He screams, gulping in air, shock and adrenaline kicking in.

She shoves the hot, smoking barrel under his chin, pressing hard. 'Yes, scream, you sadistic animal. What does it feel like?'

He moans, losing blood, and drifts. They dash another bucket of water over his face, reviving him.

Her voice whispers in his ear, 'Have you any last words, Dedov Damir Olegovich?'

Coughing and choking, his voice feeble, he gasps, 'Who the fuck are you?'

She slaps him around the face. 'You know, you and your friends should have killed us all.'

'Killed who, when?'

She grabs his the chin. 'Have there been so many you can't recall?'

He gabbles, 'I don't know what the fuck you're talking about.'

She lets him go, lightly slapping his cheek twice. 'Well then, no need to chit-chat longer, is there? Besides, I don't wish to talk to you anymore; you make me sick! Now, time to get back to where you came from.'

Once more, he feels the still warm, sticky barrel of the pistol pressed into the soft flesh under his chin, and in a last show of bravado, he shouts, 'Fuck y...' He does not hear the gun go off or feel the bullet travel through his head, tearing out his life. The round, designed to penetrate body armour, embeds itself in the concrete ceiling, its energy spent. Manfried's eyes, pupils blown wide, stare out lifelessly at the torchlight. For a moment, she regards him through dark, hollow eyes, then turns off the torch. The spotlight returns, bathing the grisly scene in stark, white light.

Without turning, she says, 'Go to the van and get the canvas. We'll move him later tonight.'

The Makarov pistol hangs down from her hand, a wisp of smoke still leaking from the barrel, and the smell of cordite, blood, and vomit imbues the room. While he's gone, she applies the final touches. Taking a hammer and stout nail from a bag, she makes holes through the hands and feet. Finally, she wraps tightly around Manfried's broken head a coil of barbed wire.

A few minutes later, he returns. He looks at the body. 'I thought you'd forgotten.'

She looks over at him, her face drawn. 'Somehow, I could not bring myself to do that part while he was alive. The rest was enough, he died afraid and weak.'

He nods solemnly. They take down the ruined body, wrap it tightly in the canvas, and stow it to one side. From a corner, they retrieve another bucket and begin cleaning the worst of the mess.

He looks across at her. 'Are you all right?'

'Yes, I'm fine. I can't quite believe it. No going back.'

'He deserves what he got, right?'

'He got off lightly.'

'The bastard will go to Hell, won't he?'

'I think that's where he came from, he and all the others.'

He nods, returning to his work. 'Maybe this time he'll stay there.'

3

On the dank and dirty ground

BEFORE RETURNING HOME TO SLEEP, Christian and Angelika drive to a café and sit outside in the warmth. The day slips away and in the dead of Monday night, they return to thier grisly business. They load the body, now in a state of rigor mortis, into the van. Nervously, Christian asks, 'Have you got everything?'

'Yes, stop worrying, will you? Everything is going to plan. Let's get on.'

They start the engine and head off in a westerly direction, skirting south of Tegel Airport and out toward Spandauer Forest. They drive along the east side of Friedhof In den Kisseln cemetery. The half-moon gives off a soft, chromium light that fluctuates with passing, broken clouds.

Laughing, Angelika turns to Christian, nodding her head toward the cemetery. 'People are dying to get in there!'

For a moment, he frowns, thinking. He shakes his head. 'That's not funny, not funny at all. You shouldn't laugh at your jokes.'

She gives him a playful nudge. 'Sorry, it's nerves.'

At the T-junction, they turn left into Radelandstraße, drive along the north side of the cemetery, turn into Grünefelder Straße, enter the forest, and stop. Set back from the road is a lodge, but it is quiet, with no lights or signs of life. Killing the headlights, she creeps the vehicle past the house. Dense woodland flanks the road; they drive to the end and park.

They dismount, open the back and retrieve the still rigid body and, carrying it between them, set off for a small clearing down a path they selected a week earlier. There is just enough light from the moon to guide them along, though the forest presses in on them, and to any observer, they would make a macabre spectacle.

They disturb an owl, hooting it flies off, and for a moment, they freeze, listening. She whispers urgently, 'Come on, let's get on with it. This place gives me the creeps!'

A few minutes later, they arrive at a railway line across which is a clearing. Unrolling the body from the canvas, they try to set it against a tree facing back out to the track, but it is still too rigid, and for a while, they struggle with the awkward, heavy corpse.

Angelika mutters, 'Crap, this isn't working. I'll get some rope from the bag, and we'll stand him up and tie him to the tree.'

For a time, they wrestle with the uncooperative corpse before securing it. They stand back. The horror of it shocks her. For a moment, she doubts herself. She says, 'God help us, Christian. I hope we're doing the right thing.'

'Like you said, no going back now. How long will the body stay stiff like that?'

'I don't know. Remind me to find out. Get the sign from the bag, will you?'

Passing it over, he asks, 'Where will you find out such a thing?'

She scowls. 'The library, of course. Come on, we need to hurry; this is a well-used track.'

The last act is to hang the sign from his neck, and once again, they stand back. She collects the bag. 'Check around and make sure we have dropped nothing, no clues, okay?' He nods, and they spend a few seconds checking.

'That's it; let's go,' she says.

❖❖❖

By 6:30 a.m., daylight pulls the darkness away with the promise of another pleasant day. Alda Bendik sets off with her two-year-old German Shepherd, Flik, on their morning walk. She crosses Hubertusstraße and enters the forest, following the path along the railway line. The dog has gone on ahead, bouncing and sniffing through the undergrowth. Alda is looking forward to a visit from her niece, Lise, whom she has not seen in a while. They plan to go to the city to have lunch and visit some shops. After a few minutes, Alda loses sight of Flik. She calls her name a few times, then hears her barking. Alda hurries forward, homing in on the sound, and coming to a crossing sees what has agitated her pet.

Alda gasps, raising her hand to her mouth. 'God in heaven! Flik, here, heel, come!'

The dog carries on barking for a moment, then trots over to Alda, all the time looking behind and growling.

Alda clips on Flik's lead. 'It's okay, girl, okay,' she says, petting the dog.

She crosses the line, cautiously approaching the body. Now close enough to see, she shudders. Once again, she covers her mouth with her hand, screwing her eyes shut. She takes a deep breath and opens her eyes. Tied to the large oak tree is the mutilated body of a man, the head broke open like a topped, boiled egg, its face and upper body a bloody mess. He is naked, an open wound to his side, and the area where his genitals should be, a pulpy mess. Hanging from his neck is a sign. Transfixed, she stares. She says, 'Dear me,' a few times. The dog is hyper-alert and growling. Horrified by the sight, she turns, saying, 'Come on, girl, off home. We must telephone the *Polizei* at once!'

It does not take long for Alda to make her report, and at 7:15 a.m., two officers arrive: one experienced with fifteen years' service, the other a rookie, attending his first suspicious death.

Alda rushes out to meet them.

The senior officer, Kurt, asks, 'Morning, are you the lady who reported the body?'

'Yes, yes, it's quite horrible. I've never seen such a thing.'

'Can you show us, please?'

She takes them. Approaching the crossing, she stops, not wanting to see it again, and pointing, says, 'It's over the other side, against a tree. You can't miss it. I mean, who would do such a thing?'

Kurt nods. 'No problem. Can you wait here for a minute while we go look?'

She nods, turns away, and remembers Lise will be here soon, the thought of lunch and shopping now far from her mind.

The officers cross over the line and stop. 'Like she says, hard to miss.'

The young officer, Alds, stares at it, at once fascinated and horrified. 'Bloody hell! What a mess.'

Kurt glances at Alds. 'Let's keep this professional, shall we? We need to report this. Go back to the car, get on to dispatch, and tell them to inform KD1. Then bring back the rope so we can cordon the area. Take the woman with you and ask her to stay at home; they'll want to get a statement. I'll wait here.' Alds pauses. Kurt says, 'Well, go on, get on with it, lad.'

'Yes, sir, right away.'

His colleague gone, Kurt spends a few moments scanning the ground, being careful to keep well clear of the crime scene. He walks up the path beyond the tree and spots a man approaching, a Dachshund tracking along slightly behind, engaged with exciting smells.

The officer stops him. 'Been out walking long?'

The man looks beyond Kurt. 'What's happening? What's going on?'

'Can you answer my question, please?'

'I've only been here fifteen minutes. Waldi and I come here often, you know.'

Taking his notebook out, Kurt asks, 'Who's Waldi?'

The man points to the still distracted Dachshund. 'My dog, of course.'

'Name and address please, sir?'

'Why? What's going on?'

Kurt writes and, without looking up, says, 'There's been an incident, and as you are here, we may wish to ask you some questions. It's just routine; I'm not accusing you of anything.' The man gives him his details, Kurt tells him to leave, and watches him go before returning to the scene.

Alds returns. 'Backup are on their way. What do we do now?'

Kurt sighs and shakes his head. 'Didn't they teach you anything at basic training, Alds?'

❖❖❖

Max wants to make an early start to the week, but it does not surprise him to see Bastian already at his desk speaking on the telephone. Replacing the handset, he says, 'They've found a male body out on the south side of Spandauer Forest. Uniform is on site and has secured the scene.' He hands over a note with the details.

Max glances at it. 'Get the car. I'll call through to Lutz and Paul.' Max scribbles a note, leaves it on Tobi Klein's desk, then makes his call requesting his colleagues to attend the scene.

From the Kripo office on the corner of Kurfürsten and Baggranfen Straßen, Bastian steers the light blue Mercedes Ponton 220S westward. He glances over at Max. 'Should be about thirty minutes.'

Max reaches for the car radiophone and connects to dispatch. 'This is KHK Becker. Put me through to KR Dehler.' He can hear the system connecting to his boss's desk phone. After a few rings, it's answered. 'Dehler.'

'August, it's Max. I'm en route to Spandauer Forest, report of a body, white male, gunshot. I've left a note for Tobi.' He listens for a few moments. 'Yes, will do. I'll brief you later.'

Arriving a little after 8 a.m., a young officer meets them. They make their way up to the clearing, the immediate area now cordoned off around the body with Kurt standing guard.

Max and Bastian know the officer. 'Hey, Kurt, how's it going?' Max says.

'Hey, good thanks. It's a nasty one, looks like a close-range shot to the head, but I'm sure they didn't kill him here. I've had a look around, but there's nothing obvious. Spotted a man walking his dog; here are his details.'

'Thanks. Who discovered the body and what time?'

'Frau Alda Bendik, out walking her dog just after 6:40 a.m. She's back at her house waiting.'

'Okay, thanks Kurt, we'll take it from here. Can you wait for Lutz and Paul and call the wagon?' Max points over his shoulder. 'Who's the rookie, by the way?'

'Alds Gümbel, been with us for a month. He's shaping up alright, for a rookie.'

Max likes to put names to faces and, once placed, rarely forgets one. 'They seem to get younger and younger.'

Kurt laughs. 'No, you're just getting old, Max!'

Max scoffs, brushing the remark away with a wave of his hand. 'Send him up, anyway.' He turns to Bastian. 'Ready?'

The two follow the path, taking gloves from their pockets and putting them on. Approaching the body, they spend a few moments absorbing the scene.

Max turns to Bastian, who's scrutinising the body. 'What do you make of it?'

Aged thirty-eight, standing at six-two, lean, fit, and swarthy, dark-haired with touches of grey, and hazel eyes that carry a sadness about them, *Kriminalhauptmeister* Bastian Döhl is a dedicated, experienced detective who joined the *Polizei* straight after the war. A born and bred Berliner, decorated, former paratrooper, and hard worker. At nineteen, he married Lara, his childhood sweetheart, who, early in 1945, died in an air-raid, and since then there's been no one serious. A lynchpin of Max's team, he is loyal and savvy but speaks his mind, which has found him out of favour with some of his superiors. An office rumour tells that during the war, while waiting for transport, he went to the aid of a Russian prisoner being abused by a young SS officer, and it was only the intervention of Bastian's company commander and his exemplary record that saved him a court-martial and banishment to an SS punishment squad.

He looks up at Max. 'You don't miss from that range. They placed the weapon right under the chin and, goodbye Vienna. The puncture wounds to both hands and feet, the cut to his side, and the barbed wire are interesting. Remind you of anything?'

Max nods. 'It's not subtle, is it? Let's hope this isn't some religious crazy. The fact he's naked, his tackle torn off, and tied to this tree like a trussed chicken, seems like an obvious attempt at humiliation. Plus, there's the sign.'

Bastian frowns. 'Has the flavour of a crazy. What do you think?'

The sign is crude, a dirty piece of cardboard about thirty centimetres long by twenty high, with two letters and five words hand-written in red marker.

M - THE BLOOD OF THE SIN - C

Max scrutinises the message. 'Question is, what sins and who decided this was the judgement? They must have tied him hand and foot. Look here, and here there are distinct marks, plus there's a lack of blood and other matter. I mean, with these injuries, he must have bled like a stuck pig, so I agree with Kurt; they didn't kill him here. Anyway, you'd need time to do all this stuff, wouldn't you?' He stands and looks around.'Far too public here.'

Bastian circles the body. 'Interesting tattoos and looks like some old scarring. I'm getting a smell of booze and vomit, and what looks like nicotine staining on his left hand. What age is he, do you think?'

'Forty to fifty, maybe. There's greying hair around the temples, and he's not in great shape by the looks of him, carrying extra around the middle. It would have been hard to move him unaided.'

Bastian nods. 'Perhaps if it were a big fellow, it might be possible, someone used to heavy loads?' He casts his gaze around. 'Can't see any tyre tracks, so they must have carried him here. Alone that would have been tough, and then securing an uncooperative corpse to the tree? Got to have been more than one person.'

'Let's wait for Lutz's and Paul's reports. We'll go over to Frau Bendik and see what she's got.'

Max calls over Alds. 'Touch nothing, keep watch. If you see anyone, keep them clear but get their details, and you don't speak to anyone about what you have seen here: no one, all right?'

'Yes, sir, of course.'

Bastian goes on ahead. For a few moments, Max looks up at the trees, soaking up the quiet of the forest and says out loud, 'Why here?' He ambles after Bastian, smelling the smoke from his cigarette. It is at times like this that Max misses the diversion of a smoke and recalls how a cigarette once saved his life. He smiles at the memory of it. Sometimes Max misses those days, just a little. Unlike his job now, they were brutal, exhausting, uncomfortable, but also uncomplicated. They had no responsibility other than to do their duty and keep themselves alive. Max still carries the marks from that day, a small V-shaped scar on his right cheek and an indent above the right eye: head injuries went with the job. He catches up with Bastian waiting by the car, who drops his cigarette, and grinding it out, says, 'You all right, Max?'

Max smiles. 'Yeah. Let's get her statement.'

4

Adam's sons are my brethren

MAX WALKS WITH PATHOLOGIST, PAUL Schmidt, to the scene; they have been friends since the war. Alds sees them coming and unhooks the rope cordon. Paul places his bag down and begins his examination. 'Someone didn't like this chap one bit, did they?'

Max laughs. 'Nicely understated, as ever, Paul. Can you give me a time of death?'

'Probably not. Of course, as ever, I'll do my best.' He looks up at Max. 'Get anything useful from the woman that discovered the body?'

Max shakes his head. 'Not much. She's in shock. It's not how she planned to start her day.' He sees others approaching. 'Look, I'll leave you to it; Lutz is here.'

Max meets forensic expert Lutz Jensen and his photographer.

Lutz smiles and extends a perfectly manicured hand. 'Morning, Max. Perfect day for a jaunt to the forest.' They approach the body. Lutz and Paul exchange greetings. Lutz stops and regards the scene. 'Well, well, this fellow must have pissed someone right off.'

'Quite,' replies Max. 'Look, I'll leave you all to it. I'll call later and get your initial reports.' He walks back to the car, and Bastian drives them back to base.

'So, what are you thinking?' Bastian asks.

Max glances at him. 'I'm thinking, our victim crossed someone important, maybe a gang boss. Before he died, they made him suffer. It's public and messy, just the way they like it. The only things that don't sit right are the location and that cryptic message.'

Bastian lights a cigarette. 'Yes, that and the genital mutilation.'

Arriving back at HQ, Max says, 'You go bring the others up to speed while I go see August.'

Max enters August's outer office. Department administrator, Lisa Engel, sits behind a busy but tidy desk, efficiently tapping away on an imposing electric typewriter. Looking up and removing her glasses, she smiles. 'Max, my dear. How are Anna and the kids?'

'Good thanks. Anna's working hard, you know? Heike and Markus are great. I can hardly keep up with them anymore, particularly Heike; she's a dynamo. How's your lot?'

'Max, my darling, I cannot complain. Rudi is much happier now he has retired, though our Daniel is a little, how shall I say, adrift at the moment.'

'I envy him; he's young. Back in our day, we didn't have time to breathe: but we don't want to go back there, do we? Is he in?'

'Yes, go straight in. Coffee?'

'Please.'

'A *Krapfen* too?'

'If it's not too much trouble?'

'For you, Max, no trouble at all.'

He goes to the door, pauses, and turns back to her. 'Oh, just one thing, perfume?'

She frowns. 'Perfume, what about it?'

'Do you have just one perfume or others, say everyday wear and something special?'

'Yes, I have my everyday scent, but I also have something for special occasions. Rudi usually buys it for my birthday or at Christmas. Why?'

'Oh, nothing much, just something I noticed this morning at the scene.'

'Ah, intriguing. Was there a hint of perfume?'

'Yes, exactly, a hint. The fact it has stuck in my mind makes me think it might be important.'

Max knocks and walks in. He's known forty-five-year-old August Dehler since late 1944, when they served together on the Eastern front in a heavy Panzer battalion. By the time they met, the war was in its final violent throes; lost, and they knew it.

Afterwards, they had parted friends and gone separate ways until a chance meeting in '52. Max, by then a seasoned young detective with the Lower Saxony *Polizei* based in Hannover, had arrived in West Berlin in pursuit of a suspect fleeing to the East. Visiting the Kripo office to meet a colleague, he had bumped into August. There had followed a joyful reunion. August, who at that time had Max's job in the newly formed KD1, urged him to join them, and as a born and bred Berliner, he was eager to go back. Initially, Anna had not been keen, pointing out that Berlin was stuck in the middle of East Germany, surrounded by the Red Army, of which she'd had quite enough during the war. However, there had been an excellent opportunity for her at the Zehlendorf hospital, and Max said it would be good for the kids to grow up in a city full of possibilities, and that it needed people like them to rebuild. As always, Anna had succumbed to his enthusiasm and powers of persuasion. That summer, they moved and never looked back.

'Good start to the week, eh Max?' says August, pointing to a seat. 'What have you got?'

'Not much, yet. Paul's carrying out the autopsy this afternoon.' August arches his eyebrow.

'Yes, he's doing us a favour and bumped us up. I left them at the scene, but not sure how much we'll get, as it looks as though the victim died elsewhere. No ID, of course. He was naked. They had tortured him: genitals removed, wounds to the left side, hands, and feet, and barbed wire wrapped around the head crucifixion style. Death most probably caused by a shot to the head. They also hung a sign from his neck that read: *M - THE BLOOD OF THE SIN - C.*

August sighs. 'Just what we need, another one leaving cryptic notes. Any ideas of what that refers to?'

'Not yet.'

'Who are you putting on this?'

Lisa enters with coffee and *Kuchen*, inviting-looking doughnuts. August says, 'Thanks, Lisa. How's the report going? Director Grob needs the stats by the end of the day.'

'All in hand, it'll be ready by lunchtime. Enjoy your coffee.'

Already Max has started on the *Krapfen*, a bead of jelly squeezing out of the side.

August nods. 'Thanks, Lisa.'

Max wipes his mouth with his handkerchief. 'I'll team up with Otti and put Jürgen with Bastian, who was at the scene this morning. For now, we'll leave Tobi with Udo picking up. I'll go to the autopsy this afternoon, then catch Lutz at the same time. Meanwhile, Bastian and Jürgen are going to interview a dog walker seen near the scene, call at the lodge beside the access road, and go door-to-door in the housing area where the finder, Alda Bendik, lives. They left the body sometime overnight, as Alda confirmed she had walked there last evening. So, we have a time of death between 6 p.m. and noon Sunday and body left between 5:45 p.m. Sunday and 6:45 a.m. Monday.' Max takes a sip of coffee.

'You sure Otti is ready?'

'I'm sure. She did great work on the Grünpeter case. She needs the experience, and we need her.'

Smiling, August slides a formal document across the desk. 'The good news is, I've got clearance for her weapons training. Here.'

Max takes up the document. 'Good, about bloody time. I thought Julius would never give in.'

'To begin with, he was dead against it, but I persuaded him. Let's say I got him to see it your way.'

'Well, we better not screw up then, eh?'

'Just don't get her killed, Max.'

❖❖❖

Ottilie Jäger has been with the team just over four months: the first female front-line detective in the Berlin Kripo. Commonly, women *Polizei* officers carry out administrative or back-office roles and are unarmed. Max does not care about gender, knowing only too well what women are capable of.

He first came across Otti when he had given a lecture at the detective training college. As she was one of only two women attending the talk, she had stood out. He would not deny that her striking features, pale skin, jet black hair, and piercing blue eyes attracted his attention, nor her insightful questions and observations during the lecture. Back at base, he'd requested her file.

She graduated second in her year. Max knew there was a need for more women in criminal investigation and wanted her in his unit. It had been easy getting August to back his selection, but Julius Grob required convincing.

It surprised Otti when the call had come for her to report to Berlin's KD1 for an interview. She had assumed it was for a worthless administrative role, such as data collection or evidence handling. The meeting had been short. Max told her he was looking for a new member of his team to carry out the same duties as the others. He would get her the clearance to carry a firearm, and she would work on the front line with the rest. The position was hers if she wanted it.

She never imagined that she'd get a chance like this, and without hesitation, accepted. He had tried to put her off, told her she would experience "attitude", he called it; that right or wrong, she'd have to work harder and shout louder to get noticed and, as he put it, she was attractive and was going to get unwanted attention.

She remembered her first day entering the KD1 office, a room that reeked of testosterone. The two younger detectives, Udo Popp and Jürgen Zeigler, had bounced over to her. Shaking hands, they had not been looking at her face, and it had taken less than five minutes for them to find out if she was single and ask her out for a drink.

The novelty wore off. She fitted the team's dynamic and realised that, despite their shortcomings, Udo and Jürgen were professional and capable detectives. She would happily partner up with any of the team, though she wasn't sure that worked the other way around.

For the first few weeks, Max teamed her with Bastian, whom she liked from the start. He'd been doing the job a long time, was good at it and contented with his lot. You didn't get any bullshit or front with him, and he didn't stare at her tits or treat her differently. He told her that their lives may depend on the actions of a colleague, and you could only make those decisions if you kept things professional.

She was a quick learner, and Bastian had been thorough. Including training in the team's practical and procedural business, he'd added which of the department bosses were arseholes. She'd only met Julius Grob twice and hadn't warmed to him. He had dark, well-groomed hair, an oval, pasty face seemingly devoid of stubble—squeaky clean—a pair of gleaming, rimless spectacles perched on a small nose, and elegantly manicured hands, which when they shook, had an iron grip, surprising her. His manner gave her the creeps, dark eyes probing her head-to-toe as if they were undressing her. Bastian said he was, without a doubt, the biggest shit ever, and it was odious little Nazis like him that had fucked everything up. But he told her not to underestimate him, his exact words being, "Slimy turds like him always float to the top," which had made her laugh out loud. She'd heard no one else speak quite like that about the boss.

She had to hand it to Bastian; he'd a way with words, and her "frontline" vocabulary was developing nicely. To begin with, she thought he was doing it to impress her but soon realised he had no front or pretence; it was just his way. Her mother, tutting disapprovingly, had been shocked when Otti had cursed a wayward driver with the word "dickhead". Her sister giggled, saying, "Wait until they give her a gun, mama, then they better watch out."

Otti sits at her desk, completing admin. Max leans out of his office calling her in.

She sits.

'Along with Bastian and Jürgen, I'm assigning you to this case. Ever been to an autopsy?'

'We had to attend one at college, but to be honest, it was lame, not the real thing.'

'Today you get to see one performed by the best, a chance to meet formally the talented Dr Paul. After, we'll see Lutz and get the preliminary forensic and crime scene report. I want you to coordinate with him in this case and handle evidence.'

Smiling, she says, 'That sounds great, thanks.'

'The icing on the cake is your firearm's permission has come through at last. When we get back, I'll take you down to the range commander, and we'll get your training sorted. I'm sure you'll have it knocked off in no time. I suggest you practice with Bastian; he can shoot the snot out of a flea's nose.' They stand. 'We leave at 2 p.m., we'll use the white Ponton, you drive.'

5

All that lives must die

AT 2 P.M., OTTI IS WAITING outside, the Mercedes idling. The door pulls open and Max shrugs into the passenger seat.

'Let's go. Left out of the yard, then left again. To the end of the street, then right into Potsdamer Straße; I'll give you more instructions as we go.'

Nodding, she steers the car and, joining the traffic, speeds up. She enjoys driving. The *Polizei* Mercedes is smooth and comfortable, the column shift precise. Max sits quietly, his finger tracing the scar on his cheek. She's noticed him doing this whenever he's thinking.

She glances at him. 'Bastian tells me you're a keen biker.'

He laughs. 'Oh God, don't get me started on bikes. That's one subject about which I could bore the arse off anyone. Anna would say just one of many subjects.'

'No, go on, I'm interested, really.'

He looks at her for a while. 'Okay. I have three bikes. I recently took delivery of a brand-new model BMW R69S, and I have a '57 Triumph Trophy, but my pride and joy is a 1936 Brough Superior SS80.'

'Is that British?' He nods. 'Nice. I've never been on a bike. Is it fun?'

'Bloody exhilarating. You feel so connected with the elements and the machine. Riding makes me feel free, like I want to keep going and going. You should try it.'

'I'd love to.'

He smiles. 'I can see you on a bike. I'll introduce you to Gus Brück; he runs the *Polizei* bikes. If you want to try, that's where to start.'

She smiles warmly. 'I'd like that, thanks.'

'By the way, we are having dinner at ours this Saturday. The monthly do, you know? Like last time.'

'I'll have to check my diary.' She laughs. 'Only kidding. Look forward to it.'

'Bring a friend, if you like? It will please Heike you're coming; you made quite an impression on her.'

'In a good way, I hope?'

'For sure, but don't let her bother you. Oh, straight on to Boelkestraße here, then right to Tempelhofer Damm.'

They park up in the lot of the Polizei Technical Institute (PTI), which houses both forensic and pathology labs. They push through the inner doors, a strong chemical smell hangs in the air: sweet and a little oppressive. Save the gentle hum of distant refrigerators; it is silent. Further down, a bright light is coming from one room. Looking in, they see three metal operating tables standing in a row, each with a bank of powerful lights and a microphone above. Along one wall is a counter on which stands scales and other equipment. Trolleys carry surgical instruments. Their victim, bathed in an intense pool of light, lies naked on the far table, and Heinz, the lab technician, preps the area. 'Hey, Heinz, Paul about?' Max asks.

He points down the corridor. 'Oh, hi there, he's in his office. We're starting in a few minutes.'

'Thanks.'

The door is open. Paul sits behind a chaotic desk, drinking from a mug with the slogan *'Väter! Selbst wenn sie sich irren, haben sie recht!'*—Dads! Even if they're wrong, they are right!—waving to them, he says, 'Come, come, it's been a day, my God. And you have brought with you the famous trailblazer, *Kriminalmeister* Ottilie Jäger,' he says, thrusting out his hand for her. 'Very good to meet you, my dear. I'm Paul Schmidt, butcher and worker of miracles. At least that's what this man wants all the time, eh?'

Shaking hands, she says, 'Call me Otti, and it's good to meet you, Dr Schmidt.'

'Oh, pah to all that, just Paul, please. Now, are you ready? Death waits for no man or woman. Come, let's see what secrets this fellow hides, shall we?'

Donning protective gear, they enter the room. Paul, who has put on special gloves, begins examining the body. 'This is your first, Otti?'

'It is.'

'Well, if you're feeling queer or want to puke, don't stand on ceremony; just sit down or get out, all right?'

She smiles and nods.

He lends her a paternal look. 'Good, well, let's begin.' Reaching up, he switches on the microphone. 'These are new, bloody handy too, saves a lot of damn scribbling, doesn't it, Heinz? Damn good idea. So, this is case number MZ578832/S/B present at the procedure are Dr Paul Schmidt attending pathologist, Heinz Güber, Pathology Technician, and from the Berlin *KriminalPolizei* KD1 are KHK Max Becker and KM Ottilie Jäger. I'm starting with a full examination of the exterior of the body…'

Paul covers every millimetre of surface, inspects every orifice, and photographs every noteworthy mark, including the various tattoos and scars, most notably, the wounds. And from the nostrils, ears, under fingers and toenails, and from the mouth, he takes samples of all stains, fluids, and powder residue. Max and Otti watch in silence.

Turning off the microphone, Paul says, 'Well, the cut to the side and the holes in the hands and feet aren't very subtle, but they're interesting.'

'How so?' Max asks.

'They did the cut on the left side premortem, but I think the feet and hands, post. See, there's a good deal of bleeding from the cut, but the puncture wounds hardly anything, which means…'

'His heart had stopped pumping, ergo not much blood,' Otti says.

Paul glances at her, a flash in his eyes. 'Yes, yes, precisely. Had they made these wounds when he was alive, there would have been a good scarlet stream. Question is, why? Particularly as there is further evidence of torture. Save one testicle, his genitals are history.' He looks up and chortles, 'Ouch!' Heinz laughs out loud. Max looks at Otti and rolls his eyes. She smiles. Paul continues, 'Looking at the wound, I'd say they put a gun against the area and fired. Must have hurt like blazes. So, if torture was the name of the game, why inflict damage postmortem?'

'Good question,' Max says.

'Maybe something or someone disturbed them, and they had to finish later?' Otti suggests.

'Or perhaps they ran out of steam?' Max adds.

'Let's have a look inside, shall we?' Paul switches the microphone back on.

He opens the body with a Y-incision running three to five centimetres from the tips of the shoulders across to and meeting just below the suprasternal notch and running vertically down to the navel. He peels the skin away and cuts the ribs allowing access to the organs, each of which he examines and removes. Heinz then weighs and extracts samples for analysis.

Paul inspects the stomach contents and extracts samples to determine the victim's last meal and approximately how long before death he consumed it. He collects samples from the gallbladder, ocular fluid, and urine. Finally, he turns to the head, accessing and removing the brain and examining and photographing the damage.

Two hours later, they are back in Paul's office. 'Well, what did you make of that, Otti? And more importantly, what did you observe?'

'Well, I'd say it's obvious what killed him, massive trauma to the head and brain caused by a gunshot.'

'Agreed,' says Paul, 'though be careful about using terms like obvious. I've learnt in this business that nothing is ever obvious. I've seen gunshot wounds used to cover up other injuries. Proceed.'

She crosses her legs. 'He has historical injuries on his side that you said look like shrapnel wounds. So, given his age, can we also conclude that he saw action in the war? Though was he fighting, and if so, on whose side? The tattoos are fascinating; they seem graphic. By that, I mean are they telling a story, or are they just doodles, you know, body art, for art's sake?'

Paul nods. 'Good, very good. Where would you say he's from?'

'No idea, do you know?'

'I believe he's Russian. First, there are the tattoos. I remember seeing similar ones on a Russian soldier I treated during the war. I was going to ask him about them, but he didn't make it. Lost too much blood. Anyway, I don't know what they mean, so that one is down to you, Max. He looks Eastern Slavic, prominent pointed nose, dark hair and eyes, a round, flat face. Anything else you noticed?'

Otti nods. 'He had a lot of staining on his left hand around the index and first fingers, presumably from nicotine, so was he left-handed?'

'Yes, agreed. You may have noticed that he had more calluses on that hand, and the muscles of his left arm are more developed, and though not a hundred per cent, it is most likely that he was left-handed. There were a fair amount of non-organic dust fragments embedded in the head, hair, and brain. My best guess now is that when the bullet exited, it struck a surface above, causing debris to fall back and contaminate the wound area, and for that to happen, I'd say he was most likely in a standing position. A heavy smoker, you could see that from the tar in the lungs, also his liver was shocking, cirrhotic, badly diseased. He was overweight too, but his muscle tone was quite good, so he could probably handle himself. Other than the blows he took to the hands during the assault, there is evidence of recent marking and bruising on the knuckles, so it's possible he was in a fistfight.'

'Could that have happened during the assault? I mean, did he put up a fight?' asks Otti.

'Possibly, but these look historical, so unless they took him and held him for a while, I wouldn't think so. There was a fair amount of damage to the mouth; his teeth were poor, with little sign of any dental care. In short, this man didn't take care of himself. If someone hadn't killed him, he probably would have been dead within a few years. We'll get more when we get all the test results back. I'll have the report transcribed and biked over to you in the morning.'

As they rise to go, Paul says, 'Oh, one last thing, your killer is probably right-handed. The wound on the torso was to the left side and cut front-to-back, and the angle of the shot travelled left to right.'

They shake hands.

Making their way back to the foyer and taking the stairs, they climb to forensics. The wide corridor is spotlessly clean, with a lingering smell of polish. They hear distant typewriters clattering out technical reports. Lutz's office, a double-aspect corner room, is at the end. Light floods in, and along one wall are exotic plants that he nurtures. Max taps on the open door, saying, 'Knock, knock!'

Lutz sits behind an immaculate, ordered desk, holding an expensive-looking fountain pen and is busy writing notes. 'Ah, comrades, come and sit. Some coffee?'

'Yes, to that,' says Max. He turns to Otti. 'Lutz is famous for his coffee. It is the best to be had, anywhere.'

Lutz beams. 'You're too kind, but even if I say so myself, it is first class.' He holds out his hand to Otti. 'Lovely to meet you again, and Max tells me you are my liaison on this case.'

'Yes. Good to see you, too. I look forward to working with you.'

'Yes, now, sit yourselves down, take the weight off.'

Lutz busies himself with an elaborate coffee maker, which soon vapes a rich, nutty aroma about the office. 'Smells devine,' Otti observes.

Lutz looks across. 'Wait until you taste it. The aroma and taste together, that is the thing. So, Max, to business. As you know, we've had little time to compile reports, but I've got back a set of the photographs we took this morning and our initial observations.' He picks up a folder from his desk tray and hands it over. 'As you can see, the scene was clean, no decent shoe prints, though there were many light impressions, but it's impossible to say if they were from the party or parties of interest or members of the public. As a guess, and I stress, guess, I'd say that at least two people were at the scene placing the body. I retrieved a long blond hair from the rope, and there was a smeared thumbprint on the sign. The sign will need further investigation but it looks like cardboard roughly cut with a knife from a box, and the lettering looks like they wrote it using a red Magic Marker. The point is, if you can find a pen and similar cardboard, we can see if it matches. The rope has gone for tests and analysis but seems to be a three-strand hawser-laid or twisted natural fibre type, with an 'S' twist, which is left-handed. Again, find some rope, and we can have a good stab at matching it. Alas, it does not seem to be anything fancy, so there's probably lots of this type of rope about, such as on construction sites, in factories, and so on. The string used to hang the sign is a similar product, probably made from hemp and sold widely from hardware stores, again nothing fancy.'

As Lutz speaks, Max flicks through the file, and Otti makes notes in her pocketbook. 'Did you notice a strange smell at the site?' Max asks.

'What sort of smell? The body didn't smell great, and there was an odour of alcohol and vomit and a distinctly metallic smell from the blood mixed with powder residue. That what you mean?'

'No, it was sweet and spicy, like some perfumes. I may have imagined it; it was just a trace.'

Lutz sits back. 'Perfume, intriguing. No, can't say I detected anything like that, but interesting. We'll sample the rope and other material to see if we find anything, though it could have been from one or more trees or even something drifting over from one of the nearby houses, and is it possible he may have died in one?'

Otti makes a note in her pocketbook: *Perfume, long blond hair*: *A woman?* But keeps that thought to herself.

'I've got Bastian and Jürgen going house-to-house, so we'll see if anyone has heard or seen anything suspicious. I'm not holding my breath. Well, Lutz, it has been illuminating as ever, and your coffee, wonderful.'

'Yes, thanks,' says Otti, 'I know where to come when I need my caffeine fix.'

Lutz smiles. 'You're always welcome here, Otti. Great to have you on the team.'

Max didn't need to give directions for the return journey, and a little after 6 p.m., they park back at HQ.

'There's always range practice on Mondays, so we'll nip down and get you signed up, shall we?'

'Great, can't wait to get started,' Otti says.

Max nods. 'Good, and by the way, excellent work today.'

The range is in the basement, and as they come down the stairs, they hear the pop of rounds firing. Max introduces Otti to Bern Schoenbeck, the range commander, then leaves them to it. The rest of the team is in the office, and as he enters, Bastian and Jürgen stand. 'We have something interesting.'

Max ushers them into his office. 'Okay, fire away.'

Jürgen flips open his notebook. 'The owner of the lodge, one Hans von Gretz, says he was having trouble sleeping on Sunday night and had got up to take a leak. Going back to bed, he noticed a vehicle stop by the lodge. It waited a moment, then the headlights went out, and it drove on past. He thought it odd but said that it isn't unknown for weirdos and poachers to use the forest at night. Anyway, he heard the vehicle drive out again some forty minutes later.'

'Did he give us a time?'

'About 2:20 a.m., which puts the vehicle leaving about three.'

'Did he recognise the vehicle, or even better, get a registration?'

Bastian shakes his head. 'No to both, also it was too dark to get a colour. However, he said it was a light van, square back, with a protruding bonnet, and he said it had the same look as the Junkers Ju52. Apparently, he worked ground crew at Tempelhof and was proud to tell us he was on the Führer's personal transport. Idiot! At first, I thought he was a bit nuts, but he meant it had the same type of corrugated skin as the Ju52. Jürgen suggested it might be a Citroën H van, which uses the same style of bodywork. On the way back, we stopped at the Citroën agents and asked. They had one in for servicing, and it seems to fit the bill. Here, they gave us this brochure. It began manufacture in '47 and is a good seller.'

Jürgen passes Max the copy. 'Great work! This is good. On your way home, can one of you run this over to von Getz for a positive? Otti's handling evidence and forensics, get a picture of the van to her. We'll all meet back here at 8 a.m. tomorrow.'

As they leave, Tobi puts his head around the door. 'How's it going?'

'Actually, not too bad. We're building a picture and have a couple of leads to follow.'

'Fancy one on the way home?'

Max glances at his watch. 'Sure, it'll give us a chance to catch up; give me fifteen.'

6

If the devil bid you

SHE WAKES UP SCREAMING AND thrashing. Sitting up, gasping for breath, she clicks on the bedside light. The clock shows 3:45 a.m., always about the same time. There will be no more sleep tonight.

For a while, she sits in bed, calming herself, shedding the fear. It isn't just the nightmares, she gets flashbacks that come at unexpected times, and panic attacks, particularly when she gets into situations where she feels trapped. Getting up, she goes through to the small kitchen, lights the stove and puts the kettle on. She yawns, looking out of the window; a cat sits on a neighbouring roof, master of its universe. The Spree River a silvery ribbon cutting through the city and beyond the Soviet sector. The kettle hisses and bubbles. She makes the coffee and goes to the small lounge, sitting by the window in the dark. From the other bedroom, she hears his snoring. She never wakes him; he sleeps through anything. His curses lie elsewhere.

She leaves a note and is gone before he rises. They have stepped up the surveillance on Ernst Bärmann, splitting it between them and working around their jobs. It is not difficult, as Ernst goes to the same bar as his late friend, Manfried. A group of them going back a long time, meet most weekends.

The big man asks to borrow the van, which the affable Günther is happy to do. The builders return from their work a little after 6 p.m., ready for a few drinks. Handing him the key, Günther says, 'Are you coming for a beer with us, Christian?' Günther always asks, but Christian has gone with them only once, finding that his beered-up workmates had taken the piss, showing their true colours, which he had not enjoyed and had struggled not to lash out at them. He was happier keeping a low profile. He knows the nickname they have given him, but it doesn't bother him; he's had worse. Work is tolerable, and Günther, whom he likes, keeps him busy running errands and tidying up.

He is not a confident driver, but taking his time, he navigates the few kilometres to the meeting point. As she comes into view, he smiles, and as she opens the driver's door, he slides across to the passenger seat. 'I missed you this morning, Ange. Have you had a good day?'

'Not bad, though I did not sleep well.'

'Are you all right to carry on?'

'Yes, yes, I'll be fine, don't you worry, really, I'm good. How was your day?'

'Okay, I guess. Günther says to bring back the van on Monday.'

'You've done well. Shall we?'

He nods, and Angelika steers the van into the evening traffic, and they head for the basement in Teichstraße.

※ ※ ※

Saturday evening is fair, and the pleasant weather continues. Ernst leaves his drab apartment on Trienter Straße and walks down the Esplanade taking the path under the railway line that forms the border. Someone has defaced the warning sign with the slogan, *Für die Soziale Revolution*. The underpass is dark, smelling of urine and decay. He lights a cigarette, and humming a folk tune, crosses a bit of scrubland that cuts through to Steerger Straße.

Ernst's real name is Viktor Radoslav Ivanovich. He came to Berlin, a soldier in the 3rd Shock Army that had gone to the heart of the Reich. He hated the Soviet government as much as he did the Germans, and not wanting to return to the mother country, where they were likely to send him to a Gulag or work him to death, amid the confusion following the German capitulation, he and five comrades had deserted. They kidnapped and murdered suitable victims, dressed them in their uniforms and dog tags, and burned their bodies, hiding them among the rubble. Rifling and looting their way through the ruins, they had stolen the identities of Germans — some of whom they murdered — and began a new life.

Being cheaper, he'd chosen to live in the East. It had not taken him long to master the language, and within a short while, he and his friends had made new and comfortable lives for themselves. Before the war, he had been part of a criminal gang. During the summer of '41 he had, to save his neck, joined the RONA, an SS brigade. As soon as he was able, he deserted, and after being picked up by a Soviet group, was made to re-en-list. Now, he is a fixer, supplying whatever people want, mostly weapons. Within a few years, two of the original six deserters were dead, victims of their criminal lifestyle. Naturally, he kept in touch with the others. None of them worked legitimately.

Most Friday and Saturday nights, they meet up at *Die Rosa Muschi* on Gottschalkstraße, an inexpensive, shabby bar, its only attributes being its excellent pork knuckle, *Liebesmädchen,* and discretion. The owner, Franz Krippner, himself a shady character, occasionally avails himself of Ernst's services.

Twenty-five minutes after leaving home, Ernst pushes open the door into the already bustling, dimly lit bar. Spotting his friend Rolf sitting in their usual booth, he shoves his way through the crowd and sits down. Rolf has ordered four steins of frothy lager, and scooping one up, Ernst drains it in one, slams down the empty pot, belches and shouts, 'Prost! Comrade!' The two men laugh loudly and summon a barmaid to replenish his stein. Rolf grabs the poor girl, pulling her down on his lap, groping her roughly and trying to kiss her. Used to it, she shrugs him off. A few minutes later, they are joined by Johann.

He sits, his eyes dark, a deep frown on his craggy face. 'Have either of you seen Manfried? We were supposed to meet on Tuesday, but he never showed.'

'No, that old bastard will be shacked up with some dirty, old whore. He's about as reliable as Adolf's cock.' Rolf bangs the table and roars with laughter.

Johann takes a long pull from his drink and wipes the froth from his mouth with the back of his hand. 'Yeah, you're probably right. Still, not like him.'

'Stop worrying, have a drink; he'll be here.'

At a table across the bar, Angelika and Christian sit, watching. He's tucking into a large helping of *currywurst mit pommes frites.*

She nudges him. 'Is it good?'

'Mmm,' he says, shovelling in a forkful of chips dripping in sauce. 'The food's fantastic here.' He takes a mouthful of beer.

'That's good, but don't drink too much, okay?' She sips her glass of Mosel. She isn't hungry.

With Christian's meal complete, and satisfied that all is going to plan, they leave. Strolling to the end of the street, they turn right into Wollankstraße, where they've parked the van. From here, they can see which of the two potential routes Ernst will take home.

Just after 1:30 a.m., Franz gets the last customers to leave, and the three men, now drunk, spill out onto the street and, for a while, smoke, slurring loudly at one another. After a few minutes, they head off to the end of the road. Rolf turns right, Ernst and Johann go left, and at the junction with Steerger Straße, they part.

Angelika starts the van's engine. 'Okay, we know which way he's going; let's go.' They drive straight ahead and, a few minutes later, cross the border and turn right, now running parallel with the route Ernst has taken. By the time they stop, just north of the community park on the Esplanade, he is still some minutes away. Getting out, Christian hides in the shadow of a tree at the edge of the park. Ernst stops in the tunnel, relieves himself, lights a cigarette and stumbles on. He walks along the road and, drawing level with a van, hears a voice. 'Excuse me, *Mein Herr*, I'm lost. Can you help me?'

Stopping, he lurches over to the van and leans in, leering at her. 'You're a pretty little thing. What's it worth…' Christian looms over Ernst, and his world turns black. Leaping from the van, Angelika opens the side door. 'Get him in, quick.' Twenty-five minutes later, they are in the basement at Teichstraße.

They place Ernst on the board against the wall. When they go through his things, it surprises them he is carrying nearly thirty thousand Deutsche Marks, which will come in handy. Killing the lights, they sit and wait, drinking coffee from a flask.

'Are you sure you're all right to do this?' she asks.

'Yes, this one is all mine.'

She takes the Makarov out of the bag, offering it.

He shakes his head. 'No, not that way.'

She tucks the pistol away. 'I understand.'

After some half-hour, Ernst regains consciousness. He moans a few times. 'What the…' he says, 'What the hell, what's going on?'

They click the switch, bathing Ernst in light. His lean body adorned with skilfully executed, vivid tattoos, most notably, a pair of eyes inked just above his hips that, strangely, make his genitals look like some grotesque nose. He carries a few scars, and under his left arm, a small tattoo detailing his blood group. Still intoxicated, he tries to turn his head to one side and, screwing his eyes shut, moans, 'What the fuck is happening? You…'

'Silence!' Booms Christian. The authority in the voice halts Ernst.

The tape clicks, and the message plays: 'The People's Court finds you guilty and sentences you to death for your crimes. You sick, filthy, Soviet pig!'

'Is this a fucking joke? Who are you? What the fuck do you want, you cocksucker?'

Before he can utter another word, Christian strides across the room, standing before him. He sees the surprise in Ernst's eyes as they lock on the hefty club.

Christian places the end of the club against Ernst's chest. 'What is your real name?'

'What are you talking about, you big cunt?'

Raising the baton, the big man smashes it into Ernst's right hand. He screams.

'I don't like the way you speak! Once again, what is your real name? Your Russian name.'

Despite the searing pain from his shattered hand, Ernst is defiant. 'Fuck you!'

Once again, the club swings, smashing the other hand. 'One last time or the next place I'll hit you will be between your legs.'

At last, Ernst sees the seriousness of his predicament, and his bravado slips. 'All right, you fucker,' he breathes deeply, his hands throbbing. 'I'm Viktor, all right?'

Christian places the bat against Ernst's genitals, making him wince. 'Victor, what?'

'Victor Radoslav Ivanovich. Now fuck off!'

'You have a filthy mouth; I can fix that for you.'

Ernst opens his mouth to launch into more profanities, but before he can utter another word, the club swings in a mighty arc and strikes Ernst across the jaw, shattering bone and teeth. A shower of crimson blood flies across the room. Pain screams through his head, his jaw flapping hopelessly. His eyes stare wildly as Christian paces back and forth. He stops, looks Ernst in the eye and with another colossal swing, he thuds the handle into Ernst's groin, destroying his testicles and smashing his pelvis. A pain so intense engulfs his body and he loses consciousness. Moments later, he comes to, but with such burning pain, he is having trouble focusing. His eyes watering, he does not see the lump of wood as it strikes first his right kneecap, then the left, shattering them. Ernst's world collapses in on him, blackness reaches out and, for a few seconds, takes away the pain. Christian throws a bucket of cold water over Ernst's mangled face, and the world of agony and light reclaims him.

For a few minutes, nothing happens. The intensity of the pain seems to lessen, or perhaps his body is shutting down, protecting him from the suffering. Christian brings his face within a few centimetres of Ernst's and whispers, 'Do you remember me? You forgot. Kids grow up.'

Ernst tries to form words but cannot. He moans and mumbles but cannot make sense of what is happening to him. He knows he is an evil man. He knows that sometimes for evil men, this is how it ends. He has ended lives himself, many lives, in many terrible ways. Christian stands before him and says, 'You should have killed us all.'

For a split second, Ernst sees his fate and the distinct look in the eyes of his assailant as the club crashes down on his skull with devastating force. There is a sickening, dull thud and crack; the blow so violent that the handle breaks. There is no need for more. Breathing deeply, Christian drops the broken end of the wood and turns away. Angelika comes over and checks Ernst's pulse. A trickle of blood leaks from his nose and one ear.

Christian turns back to face Ernst. 'Is he gone?'

She looks at him, eyes wide. '*Mein Gott*, yes! You made me jump when you hit him. It was bloodcurdling. I saw terror in his eyes. Come on, it's early; let's shift this worthless pig. He is nothing now.'

Impassively, Christian nods. 'Good idea.'

❖❖❖

Parking close to woodland and the cemetery near the Olympic Stadium on Trakehner Allee, they carry the body a short distance to the memorial tower built as a folly in the mid-19th century. By the building is a bench, where they seat Ernst, head bowed, his broken hands lying in his lap, as though he is sleeping. About his bloodied neck, they hang the sign.

'Are you sure about this place?' Christian asks.

'Yes, quite sure. Don't worry.' They hear an approaching vehicle, and as it drives by, beams of light shine and move through the trees. For a time, they freeze, listening. The car passes and disappears. 'Come on, we're done here, let's get going.'

They make their way back to the van, momentarily waiting in the shadows before climbing aboard and setting off.

'Home, or shall we clean up?' Christian asks.

'I'll drop you at the apartment. Get some sleep. I'm on a late shift, so I'll go back. When I'm done, I'll bring the van back.'

'You sure?'

'Yes, you did well tonight. Are you okay? I mean after…'

'After killing him?'

'Yes.'

'I'm not sure how I feel, but I am glad that he's gone; better that way.' She touches his arm. 'You know we can stop anytime, if you want…'

He pulls away from her touch. 'No, never, never. We must finish it. We can't let them…'

'It's okay, I know. I didn't mean to upset you; I just want you to know that we make the decisions, okay? That's all.'

Looking straight ahead out to the dark, he says quietly, 'We must complete what we've started.'

Placing her hand on his, she whispers, 'And we will, don't worry.'

It is just after 6:15 a.m. when she drops him at the apartment and makes her way back to the basement. As she picks her way across the broken ground, the first glimmer of morning breaks through. Huddled away under an old carpet that someone pulled into an abandoned outbuilding lies a vagrant. Hunger and the early morning chill have awakened him. He is thinking of making a move when, just a few metres away, he hears approaching footsteps. His eyes, well-adjusted to the dark, peep out from a hole in the wall and observe a passing figure. Not tall, it moves with the loose-limbed gait of a youngster. Hooded, it carries a kit bag, like the type favoured by servicemen. To see better, he cranes forward, watching where they go. He does not think anyone lives in the abandoned buildings. Perhaps, he thinks, there might be some better shelter he can use.

Stopping by one building, the figure pauses, looks around, then goes through the broken doorway and disappears. He can hear the metallic sound of a lock and creak of a door. A moment later, there is a dull thud and the sound of bolts closing. Cautiously, he approaches the building, enters, and finding the doorway, presses his ear against it, listening. To no avail, he tries to open it. He scouts around the ruins, but there is nothing to see or hear. Returning to his shelter, he collects his things and sets off in search of food and, if he is lucky, some paid work. He wonders about the figure and what they are doing. Perhaps they were coming back from a night shift or maybe a cat burglar back from a night's pilfering? His interest aroused, and with little going on in his life, he decides he will return to find out more.

7

Where there is true friendship, there needs none

MAX'S HOUSE IS IN THE Zehlendorf district on Schwarzer Läufer Straße. A pleasant locality, close to Anna's work, the schools, and a twenty-minute drive for Max. It is close to the largest green area in the city, Grunewald, large bodies of water, Wannsee, Nikolassee, and the Havel, where there are beaches, water sports, and great walking: the sort of neighbourhood anyone would be content to live.

Otti rings the bell. From within, there are sounds of running footsteps and youthful voices. The door bursts open. Heike, with Markus close behind, greets Otti. 'Oh, *Fräulein* Jäger, it's so good to see you again. Come in. Mum, dad, it's Ottilie.' Grabbing her hand, Heike pulls Otti inside. In the background a Nat King Cole song plays.

'Please, call me Otti.'

'Otti, yes, may I? That's so much better.'

Doe-eyed, Markus stares at Otti. 'Otti, may I take your coat?'

She reaches out and places her hand on his face. 'Ah, what a gentleman, thank you, Markus.' He takes her coat and touches his face where she had placed her hand.

Heike steers Otti to the lounge. 'August is here, and Uncle Tobi, he's not really our uncle; we just call him that. He and dad trained and were in the force at Hannover together. Bastian's always a bit late, well, always last to arrive, anyway. Do you like music? Mum loves Nat King Cole. Ugh, old people's music! Dad likes Bill Hayley and Elvis Presley, which is much better. Did you know he was in Germany until recently?'

Otti laughs at the storm of information. 'Well, I love music, particularly Nina Simone, though I do like Nat King Cole too, and I'm not old, and yes, I knew Elvis was here, and who doesn't love Elvis? What music do you like?'

'I like that new song, "Itsy Bitsy Teenie Weenie Honolulu-Strand-Bikini" and "Chantilly Lace". Do you know them?'

Otti laughs. 'No, I think I'm behind the times.'

'Oh, you must, they're great to dance to!'

Markus joins in. 'How about, "I Only Have Eyes For You" by The Flamingos?'

Heike scoffs. 'Oh, Markus, no, that's so soppy! He knows all the hit parade; such a cram.'

Anna comes to her rescue. 'Come on you two, give Otti a chance to catch her breath.' She gives Otti a hug and a peck on the cheek. 'So lovely to see you again. How are you?'

She hands Anna wine and chocolates. 'Good, thanks, and you?'

'Fine.' Anna looks over the chocolates. 'Oh lovely, what girl can resist?' She ushers Otti into the living room. 'I'm busy, you know? Time poor but very well and looking forward to a lovely evening. I'm not on call and no work tomorrow. How are you finding it working with this lot?' she says, pointing at the men.

Otti grins. 'Oh, they're great.'

'Well, I must get back in the kitchen.'

'Can I help with anything?'

'No, no, relax, enjoy. Max, Otti needs a drink?'

Handing Tobi a beer, Max says, 'Glad you could come. What will you have?'

'White wine would be great.'

There's a loud knock on the door. 'That'll be Bastian,' shouts Markus. 'I'll go.'

Markus opens the door. 'Hey, kid,' says Bastian, stepping into the hallway, 'when are you and Heike coming shooting again? We need a rematch.'

'Soon, I hope. I'll ask dad. Wow, I like your tie, hilarious,' says Markus, pointing at the tie depicting vividly coloured, laughing clowns.

Bastian looks down at his tie and smirks. 'Oh that. I won it off a Yank at a competition, a kinda bet. It's really tacky, don't you think?'

Markus giggles. 'That's why I like it.'

As the meal is served, the kids, complaining loudly, get sent to bed.

'I'll come up later to say goodnight,' Tobi says.

'Otti, you come up as well?' Heike pleads.

Otti nods. 'Of course.'

It's a wonderful evening. Drinks flow. They rifle through the eclectic record collection, swap stories, tell jokes, and relish poignant moments of silence from memories clawing at them from the past.

At the end of the evening, Otti gives Bastian a lift home. For a while, they drive in silence.

'That was fun,' Otti says.

'Yep, good company, booze, and the best of welcomes. They always put on a decent spread. Anna is one of a kind. Max sure is lucky.'

Otti glances at him, a twinkle in her eyes. 'Bastian, do you hold a candle for Anna?'

He waves his hand dismissively. 'No, nothing like that. She's just, well, who wouldn't be happy to have a partner like that?'

Otti scoffs. 'Partner?'

'Fuck, this isn't the Middle Ages. Women aren't chattels, you know. Leastways, not in my book.'

'From where I'm standing, most women are pretty much like that.'

Bastian laughs. 'Oh crap, I feel this is one argument I won't win.'

Otti grins. 'No, you're okay, but seriously, they've been very good to me, and the kids are great, too. I was a bit like Heike when I was her age, you know, tomboyish and full of adventure. Truthfully, I'm still like that. I don't just want to be a stay-at-home wife and mum. I'm very grateful to get this chance.'

'So, you want to get married and have kids sometime, then?'

'Perhaps. But right now, this is all I ever wanted.'

Bastian gives her a playful nudge. 'Oh, you'll do fine.' Then, more seriously, he says, 'But you need to watch Udo.'

She glances at him. 'Oh?'

'Yeah, I think he's jealous and, maybe, threatened by you. He's had a moan to Tobi about you being put on the case; feels it should have been him. He's a good detective, but he's got a bit of a chip, you know? And, in my opinion, he's immature. Anyway, just watch him; that's all.'

'Has he said anything to you?'

'Not directly, just been gobbing off behind your back.'

She grips the steering wheel tightly. A surge of nervous acrimony spreads through her. 'Kinda cowardly, isn't it?'

'I guess he feels vulnerable with your status with Max.'

'What about Jürgen?'

'Oh, Jürgen is fine. He keeps his head down, likes the intellectual challenge, but it's possible Udo may influence him.'

'Does Max know he spoke with Tobi?'

'He has said nothing to me, but my guess is, yes. He and Tobi don't have secrets, least not professional ones; they go way back. But I know Tobi likes Udo. He got him on the team, kind of his protégé, so he'll have his back.'

'Any words of advice?'

'Just be yourself, be professional, don't rise to the bait, and…' He looks at her, 'don't fuck up. If you're unsure about anything, ask me, okay?'

Nodding, she says, 'When he hired me, Max said that this might happen. Said that I'd have to be twice as good and work twice as hard. I'm as good as any man.'

Bastian smiles. 'Oh, sure, I can see that, but the *Polizei* are like the military: a safe male-dominated, testosterone-fuelled, hierarchical, obedient manfest.'

Otti looks at him. 'Isn't everything?'

'I guess. The Kripo's home to people having extreme views: right-wing, racist, homophobic, chauvinistic. You name it, they're here, and it's always been a safe place for them. Some are in senior positions. It's going to be hard for you. There are plenty of arseholes who don't want the place filling up with women in front-line roles. They'll say one thing to your face and quite another behind your back. Point is, if you're here to stay, you'll have to grow a thick skin, or it'll eat you up. Be the best you can, and you'll win by just staying the course. I know it's wrong, but that's the way it is.' He cracks the window open. 'Hey, you've done the hard part, you're in the club now with the support of Max and August, both of whom carry respect, and that means something. Honestly, you don't need to prove yourself to anyone but your team, and from where I'm standing, you're doing just fine. Everyone is watching though, so as I said, don't fuck it up.'

'Are we all right?'

Bastian looks across; she is staring out, concentrating on driving. She glances at him. 'What?'

He grins warmly. 'Not that it should matter much what I think, but yeah, we're good. Thing is, you're one of us now, and we look out for each other. It doesn't mean we have to love one another, but professionally, well, it's us and them, if you know what I mean? For me, I learnt a long time ago not to underestimate women.' He pauses a moment, turning in his seat. For and instant, he closes his eyes and sighs. 'In late '41, at the Leningrad Front,' he pauses and shakes his head, 'shit, that was fucked up. Anyway, command tasked a small group of us to hunt down a crack Soviet sniper team that had been causing havoc in our lines, killing dozens of officers. Usually, they worked in pairs, you know, one spotting, the other shooting. It took three weeks to pin them down, and when we caught them…'

She turns to him, a glint in her eye. 'They were women?'

'Yes. Two beautiful young women. I've never seen such defiance and strength in a person. You know, most men we took prisoner just looked resigned, some even relieved, but the look on those young women's faces lies forever etched in my mind: beauty, hate, fear, and dignity.'

'What happened to them?'

'Their war was over. We took them prisoner, but I don't expect it was good. Our treatment of Soviet prisoners is a shame we must all carry, and by all, I mean those of us who were part of it. I've still got the rifle she was using, not as a trophy, but as a reminder. For me, it was a defining point of the war. I questioned things, you know, what we were doing and why…' He stops speaking for a moment. 'Shit, listen to me going on; I've probably had too much to drink.'

Otti looks across. 'No, it's okay. You know you should talk about it more, the war I mean; bottling stuff up isn't healthy. That's the trouble with you men, all that macho crap. It's not very endearing, you know?'

'Yeah, I know, but it's easier said than done. And anyway, the lot of us are in denial about what happened, you know, what we did and was done in our name, and that stuff isn't going away, no matter how much we wish it to.'

'I get that, but it is easy, you know? Just find someone you trust and talk; they'll listen. Sometimes that's all you need.'

Bastian thinks about it, shifting uncomfortably in his seat. 'Changing the subject, how goes the shooting?'

Otti sighs and rolls her eyes. 'Okay, though I got a lot of stick down the range Monday and Wednesday. By the end, I was doing all right.'

'Have they issued you a P1?' She nods. 'Ask Bern if you can try a Walther PP; it might suit better.'

'Okay, sounds good. Anyway, I like it; it's kind of relaxing and I'm getting used to the spectators.'

'Apart from those three women *Polizei* cadets we trained a couple of months back, I can honestly say that you're the first woman *Polizei* officer they've seen down there. Come and have a practice with me. I go in on a Sunday afternoon when it's quiet. I can give you some tips and show you some of the other weapons we have in the collection. The more you handle and try, the better, okay?'

'Yes, Max told me to shoot with you. He said, what was it? Oh yes, that you could shoot the snot out of a flea's nose or something daft like that.'

Bastian holds up his hands, laughing. 'Guilty as charged. I am a great shot. See, I told you we're all arrogant arseholes.' He points. 'Oh, this is me; turn left here.'

The Beetle pulls over. He hops out. 'Hey, thanks for the lift. See you on Monday or tomorrow. If you want some target practice, call me. Hey, and don't worry.'

She smiles. 'Thanks, Bastian, and thanks for the heads-up. You're a mate. Oh, and by the way, that tie is horrible.'

Smiling back, he shoves the door closed. Gunning the engine with its distinctive sound, the VW wails off down the road. For a while, he stands watching the receding lights. Sparking up a cigarette and inhaling deeply, he feels for the first time in years that there might be more to life than work. He's told no one else his sniper story. He hardly ever talks about his war but carries it with him like a bad habit.

8

Cowards die many times before their death

THE TELEPHONE RINGS. MAX, SITTING at the table drinking coffee, glances up at the kitchen clock showing 7:55 a.m. He glances at Anna, who raisers her eyebrows. 'This won't be good.'

He goes through to the lounge and picks up the receiver.

'Becker.' He listens.

'Okay. When? I'll be there in thirty minutes. Do me a favour, will you? Call Jäger and tell her to meet me there. If she doesn't answer, call Zeigler.' He listens as the caller speaks. 'No. that's okay, I'll do that.' Hanging up, he redials and calls both Paul and Lutz.

He goes back to the kitchen and drains his coffee. Anna is relieved it was not an emergency call out for her. 'Another body?'

He nods. 'Looks like the same MO. I'll see you later.'

Getting into his '59 Mercedes 220SEb Fintail, Max heads north, joining the autobahn through Der Grunewald. He puts his foot down, the speedo climbing to one hundred and thirty kph. At 8:35 a.m., he arrives and parks up behind the patrol car where a uniformed officer waits. It is a peaceful spot, much of it parkland, with a cemetery and crematorium at the south end. The first responders have cordoned off the areas around the folly and bench. Another officer waits by the access path. Max doesn't recognise him; he shows his badge. 'I'm Becker. Who found the body?'

The officer looks at the proffered ID and, with a faint air of disdain, answers, 'The cemetery caretaker, Herr Fellner.'

'Time?'

The officer sighs, and taking out his notebook, consults it. '7:40 a.m. He said he wouldn't normally be in so early on a Sunday, but he couldn't sleep and decided to take a walk through the park before going to tidy up.'

'Where is he now?'

'Over at the cemetery office; I told him to wait there.'

Max nods. 'Okay.' He walks off down the path.

Otti parks up behind Max's car and gets out. The same officer comes over. 'You can't stop here, Fräulein, this is *Polizei* business. Move on.'

She shows her ID. 'I am *Polizei*, KM Jäger.'

The officer looks confused and takes her badge, turning it over. He hands it back and smirks at her. 'Down that way, darling.' As she walks off, she hears him say, 'They must be fucking desperate.' For a moment, she thinks about turning around and confronting him but remembers what Bastian said. *Don't rise to the bait.* Seeing Max talking with another officer, she joins them. 'Morning, sir. Thanks for the call.'

'Morning! No problem.'

She's dressed in running clothes, her hair held back by a fuchsia bandanna. 'You look like you had other plans?' They walk together. 'Get Bastian home all right?'

'Yes, and I was just off for a run in the Tiergarten when they called.'

Max hands her a pair of gloves. 'The Tiergarten, eh? You remember what it looked like in '45? Back in the day, it covered a much greater area, right into the Wedding district and beyond. Anyway, they've done a great job restoring it. Here, put these on and touch nothing; you know the drill.'

As they approach the body, already they are scanning the site, the grotesque figure still in its sitting position.

'Okay, tell me what you see,' Max says.

She regards the sickening spectacle and is glad she hasn't eaten. 'Hell, I've seen some things in my time, but that is not a pretty sight.' She looks closely, forcing herself to detach. 'We have a naked, white male, maybe forty to forty-five, well built, lean, dark hair, head wounds, badly smashed jaw—lots of blood and gore. Blood from his nose and one ear?' She looks at Max. 'I guess that's from the massive head trauma that has left such a deep impression? There's a noticeable smell of alcohol. Both knees and hands smashed, as well as genitalia… well, let's say… terminal. Someone really didn't like this guy, did they? As with the other victim, he's got some interesting tattoos. The eyes above his hips are creepy, don't you think?'

Max nods. 'Go on.'

'Also, I see he's missing the index and first finger from his left hand. Then there's the sign, like the last one; same type of cardboard and red ink.'

Max reads it out.

M - THEN BECOME CORRUPT - X

'Just as cryptic. What or who become corrupt? And the M and X? A person or a reference? What do you think of the location?'

She looks around. 'Well, you can't see it from any road, but clearly, they intended the body to be found and quickly, just like the last one. It's peaceful, don't know whether the cemetery is significant. There was one not too far from the other site, wasn't there?'

'Yeah, quite close. What about the method?'

'It looks similar enough to the last one. I'd say it was the same offender or offenders,' Otti says.

'Agreed. Interesting that they chose a unique weapon, but in both cases, there's huge trauma to the head and genitals.'

'Could they have ditched the weapon used last time or, perhaps, a different assailant?'

'Like they were taking turns, you mean?'

A voice from behind. 'Hope you haven't been touching,' Paul says, joining them.

Max turns and smiles. 'Morning to you too, Dr Grumpy.'

'Well, you'd be grumpy too if you'd planned a pleasant day's fishing. Criminals have no bloody consideration; didn't even have time to get a coffee.' He drops his bag and wearily regards the corpse. 'Let's see to this poor sod, shall we?'

They leave Paul doing his stuff and walk over to the cemetery building. Just inside the entrance, there is an office, the door ajar and a plump, middle-aged man wearing a bemused expression, with cup of coffee in hand, sits behind a small desk.

Max and Otti show their badges and introduce themselves. The man gets up and, taking two chairs from the stack in the corner, places them in front of the desk. 'Please, sit.' Sitting, Otti takes out her notebook.

'How long have you worked here, Herr Fellner?' Max asks.

'About twelve years, I think. Give-or-take.'

'Do you always come in on a Sunday?'

'Usually, unless I am on holiday. I live alone. My wife died three years ago. I like to come in because it is quiet, and I can get things done. Also, I like to chat with people who tend to the plots. My Eva is here too.'

Max enquires, 'Your wife, yes?'

Herr Fellner nods.

'Sorry for your loss. Can you tell me exactly what time you came in?'

'Yes, I got here by 7:40 a.m., though normally I come in about nine, have a little sleep in, you know, and a substantial breakfast. But today, I had woken unusually early and felt the need to get going.'

'How come you came up past the tower? Isn't the car park for this building on the other side?'

'Ah yes, yes, it is, but I live just on the other side of the park, you know? Insterburgallee ends with a path that leads directly here. I walk up through the park. I often stop to feed the water birds on the Sausuhlensee, and the primary route goes by the tower and the spot where I found him. Are you going to move it soon? I mean, it will upset the visitors.'

'Don't worry about that.'

Otti looks up from her notes. 'Were you here last evening?'

'I was until 3 p.m., then straight home as Saturday I go out and play *Skat* with my friends at the club.'

Otti stops writing and looks up. 'My dad loved playing *Skat*. He tried to show me once, but I was only six and didn't understand the attraction.'

Herr Fellner laughs. 'I wouldn't miss it. It is the highlight of my week.'

'Was anyone else here when you left?' Max asks.

'No, I locked up, but there may have been people in the park. As I left, I saw no one.'

'Have you seen anyone around in the last few weeks that looked out of place, say if they were taking a lot of interest in the tower and bench or routes into and out of the park?'

He shakes his head. 'Nothing comes to mind.'

'Thank you, Herr Fellner.' Max hands him a card. 'This is my number. Please call if you think of anything, even if it seems insignificant.'

They saunter back to see how Paul is getting on. 'You said your father enjoyed playing *Skat*. Is he dead?' Max asks.

She glances across at him. 'They arrested him in '42 and sent him to Sachsenhausen. There was no trial, no defence. He refused to fight for the Nazis, who he hated with a passion. He was the political opposite and held strong to his principles. They forced him into slave labour at the Klinkerwerk brickworks, where they worked him to death. We never got a body; I've no idea where he is.'

Stopping, Max takes Otti's arm and gently pulls her around to face him.

'Shit Otti, that's just awful. What the hell? I'm so sorry...'

'It's okay, really. I think it was from him I found my independent spirit. I thought, if he felt strong enough to die for his belief, then I could do something, well, something single-minded. Let's put it like that. Luckily, you saw fit to give me a chance.'

Max sighs. 'Oh, you didn't need me, and I'm sure he would be very proud of you.'

She nods. 'Thing is, I need you and this opportunity. I must ensure those terrible things never happen again, then my father won't have died in vain. He and all the others.' For a while, they walk on in silence. 'Oh, by the way, please don't tell the others, if that's all right?' she says.

'Yeah, of course, and I hope you didn't mind my asking? Can't keep my nose out of it, at least that's what Anna says.'

'She's wise.'

'That she is, and so much more.'

They walk through the park, stopping for a while by the lake.

Otti says, 'Bigger than I expected. It always surprises me how many lakes and green spaces the city has.'

'Yes. Did you know Berlin is geographically nine times the size of Paris?'

She shakes her head. 'No, never thought about it. I've never been to Paris.'

'Do, it's beautiful. Come on, let's walk down to the road Herr Fellner uses to access the park.'

At the end of the park, the path carries on under the railway line before joining Insterburgallee where there are houses and a school.

'Do you think they brought the body this way?' Otti asks.

Max shakes his head. 'I doubt it, too far, and there are all these houses with more chance of detection. All the same, we'll still have to go house-to-house. It's much more likely they parked up where we did and came in that way. Wouldn't you?'

She agrees. On their return, Max times the walk. 'Nine minutes, say about nine hundred metres, at a leisurely pace, like if you were carrying a body.' He thinks a while. 'No. It wouldn't make sense coming this way.'

Returning to the scene, they see Lutz has joined Paul, the two deep in conversation. They join them. 'Well, how's it looking?' Max asks.

Paul glances at his watch. 'Still a chance of some fishing, so I'll be off;

Lutz will fill you in. I'll do the autopsy tomorrow afternoon at 3 p.m. See you there?'

Max nods. 'Sure, see you then.'

Lutz smiles. 'Just the way to start a peaceful Sunday, isn't it? And two grizzlies in one week, eh? That's not good. Now let's see. Paul and I agree they killed him elsewhere and moved him here during the night, sometime between midnight and 6 a.m. There is rigour setting in and liver mortis showing in the thighs and buttocks. We think he died, and they moved him soon after death, unlike the other fellow, who they left lying up for a time. Cause of death is most likely the bump to the noggin. As far as we can tell, one blow only. The rest is self-evident.'

'They killed him with one blow. Isn't that unusual?'

Lutz shrugs. 'Yes, I'd say that most people would have another whack, just to make sure. I would, wouldn't you? There are some splinters of what looks like wood in the scalp, so something hefty, maybe a bat or stout batten, though my guess is a baseball bat. Here, see the rounded depression in the skull?'

'If they hit him hard enough to break the wood, maybe that's why there was just

one blow?'

Lutz smiles. 'Yes, but what a blow. It would have hit the ball clear out of the park.'

Max shakes his head. 'Would that have left those splinters?'

'Most likely. If we had a similar piece of wood, we could run some tests; hopefully, we can find out more when I examine the splinters. I've got a range of bats and handles back at the lab that we can check against the shape of the wound. By the way, have you got an ID for victim one?'

'Not yet. Jürgen's been looking into the tattoos, and we're looking at missing persons, but somehow, I don't think it's going to give us a name. If nothing springs up by midweek, we'll release details to the press. There was a small article about a body in the forest published in Tuesday's *The Berliner World*, but so far, we've kept press interest down. Fortunately, the papers were distracted by that Soviet Bloc leaders' attendance of the meeting at the National Congress in New York. Though I suspect, with this second body, that's going to change.'

'That New York jolly is just a load of old waffle and Soviet propaganda if you ask me, but if it keeps the journos off your back, all good. Anyway, seems to be similar here, no obvious ID, fortunately not my department. I wish you happy hunting.'

'Quite. Look, we'll pop in tomorrow to get the photographs and whatever else you've got.'

Lutz packs up his bag. 'Well, Max, Otti, a pleasure, as always. Until tomorrow.' He strides off.

Max calls over to the uniformed officer. 'You can take the body now, Dagmar. Oh, by the way, what's your colleague's name?'

'Mosinger.'

'Not seen him before.'

'He was in Munich and transferred here a couple of months back. Between you and me, he's a lone wolf and a bit of an arse.'

'Okay, thanks.'

Otti makes a mental note of Mosinger's name. She won't forget it or his comment.

The lab recovery team pass by, pushing a gurney.

Max and Otti walk back to their cars. 'To the office?' Otti asks.

'Yup, get the report typed up and let August know.' Max looks at his watch. 'Tell you what, let's go to Malinda's for coffee and kuchen first.'

It's just after 2 p.m. when Max heads home. Otti's still at her desk. 'You should go home; it'll be a long week. We've got to track down that van and try to get names to faces.'

She looks up. 'I'm just finishing up.'

'Okay, see you bright and early. Good work today.'

Fifteen minutes later, Otti heads out. As she's getting in her car, Bastian arrives. 'Hey, what are you doing here?' he asks. She tells him about the body.

'Same MO, then?'

'Yep, pretty much.'

'Crap, I hate the weird ones. I've come in to shoot, fancy it? You can bring me up to speed.'

'Yeah, I could do an hour, let off some steam, hey?'

'In that case, we'll have to break out the shotguns, too.'

She grins. 'Now you're talking.'

9

By that sin fell the angels

ANGELIKA FINISHES UP IN THE basement. Not sure what time it is, she has a last look around, kills the lights, locks up, and goes out into the watery autumn light. She crosses the waste ground, climbs aboard the van and, sitting back, closes her stinging, dry eyes. It's nagging at her. There's been nothing in the papers about a body or a murder. Have they found it? Perhaps the forest was less well used than she had thought? She wrestles with her conscience, and deciding, opens her eyes, turns the key, and drives.

There's not much traffic, so it's not long before she is back in Spandauer Forest, which looks different in the light: a haven of green tranquillity against the stark grey of a city still emerging from the terror and destruction of war. Daily, lorries transport the Third Reich's memorial to its people, dumping tons of rubble in an ever-growing mountain of smashed concrete, steel, filth, and decaying matter that Berliners call *Teufelsberg*—Devil's Mountain. Tumour-like, it grows on the foundation of a never completed Nazi military technical college that proved so challenging to destroy, the allies buried it.

She drives on by the lodge and parks up. She does not walk directly to the clearing but takes a detour, fearful that anyone she meets will know about the body and suspect her. She tells herself that it's crazy, but guilt plucks at her, and she is sure it shows as though written across her face in bold, black ink—*Murderer*! After thirty minutes of following paths through the woodland, she comes to the clearing. It looks as it did the first time they saw it. The large tree where they had tied the body stands sentry, mute witness to the deed. For a moment, she doubts they were here, then a gentle breeze takes the end of a light-green rope clinging to a branch. It catches her eye, and walking over, she touches it. Carelessly left, it is unmistakably from a *Polizei* crime scene cordon. They have found it. So why no press? It hits her that now the hunt has begun, and it fills her with fear and a strange feeling of euphoric power. All they must do is keep to the plan and then disappear. She's been through it in her head repeatedly, and even with the messages left on the bodies, she can't see how the *Polizei* will ever link them to their victims.

They have killed twice. It felt good to make those men suffer, though it shocks her how easily she had exacted such violence and brutality on another and thinks it must be because she does not consider them as human, and they deserve her and Christian's justice. Startled by the sound of a snapping twig, she turns. A young deer looks at her before moving on. Angelika shivers and, lingering no longer, crosses the railway line, but instead of heading straight back to the van, turns right, heading parallel with it. The path ends at a road across which lies housing. It surprises her there are so many homes close to where they left him. For a while, she stands watching. Then, turning to leave, a German Shepherd bounces up to her. Momentarily thrown, she dodges past the inquisitive hound and, head down, hastens back up the path, hardly noticing the dog's owner. Alda calls Flik to heel. The obedient dog returns, and Alda clips on a leash and watches the retreating figure.

'I should not have come. It was stupid,' Angelika says out loud. Hurrying back to the van, she realises how tired she is. She feels out of control, panicky and lurching over to a tree, vomits. She is trembling, sweating, her head pounding, and thinks she is going to pass out. She leans against the tree, calming herself, but a voice from behind startles her. 'Are you all right, my dear?'

She freezes. Then, recovering some equilibrium turns around, saying, 'Yes, yes, thank you. I think I must have eaten something bad. I'm so sorry.' She is mindful to keep her face away from them, pulling the hood further over her head.

They look concerned. 'Are you sure? We live nearby. Do you want to come back and rest a while, have a glass of water, perhaps?' The woman asks.

Angelika shakes her head. 'No, really, I'll be fine, but thank you; you're very kind.' Without another word, she hurries away. Ten minutes later, she drives the van passed the lodge and, turning left into Radelandstraße, heads back to the city.

Glancing up from his Sunday paper, Herr von Getz notices the van and, returning to his reading, thinks nothing of it. But something niggles at him. '*Mein Gott*!' he exclaims, standing up. Going over to the telephone and taking Bastian's card from the drawer, he dials. The phone rings and rings, no answer. Frustrated, he hangs up and dials again. Of course, he thinks, it's Sunday, they won't be in. For a moment, he hesitates, then dials the *Polizei* emergency number.

It's nearly forty minutes later when a patrol car draws up outside. Two uniforms get out, and von Getz is at the door before they knock.

'Come in quickly. I saw it, I think?'

'The van?' queries one.

'Yes, yes, of course, the van. What else would it be?'

'Can you describe it?'

'Yes, the same type of body as the one on the night of the murder,' he says dramatically. 'You know, like *Tante Ju*.'

The officers look at one another, frowning.

'Detective Döhl came back later and showed me a picture of a van, and I am sure it was of the correct type.'

'What make was it?'

'A Citroën. On the night, I couldn't tell the colour, but when I saw it earlier, I could.' He pauses, revelling in his sense of importance.

'Well, what colour is it, then?'

'Blue, sky blue, I'd say, not too light, not too dark. Yes, a sky-blue Citroën H van, that's it.'

'Did you get the registration?'

Herr von Getz shakes his head. 'Oh, no. Sorry.'

One officer says, 'I'll get on to dispatch and get an alert out to stop and question all vehicles of that type.'

The other officer asks, 'Did you get a look at the driver at all?'

Von Getz ponders. 'No, it was just a fleeting glance, you know?'

'Could you tell how many passengers there were? Was it a man or woman?'

'No, sorry.' He says, his voice flat, annoyed at himself for not realising earlier.

'Anything else you can add? Anything at all?'

'No, that was it. But if it was the same van, why did they come back?'

The officer shrugs. 'Why indeed, sir, why indeed? Thank you for reporting it. We'll look around. I'll make sure that a report goes through to Detective Döhl. I expect he'll contact you tomorrow.'

'Ok, I'll be on the lookout, you know, if they come back, and I'll be sure to get the registration.'

Von Getz stands at his door as he watches the officers return to their vehicle.

※※※

Angelika parks the van a couple of streets away, and it is almost lunchtime when she gets home. The apartment lies in the Kreuzberg district. Housing is shabby, but rent's cheap and she and Christian have a small, two-bed flat that is tidy and looks out toward the Spree and East Berlin. She checks the mailbox before climbing to the fourth floor. Closing the door, she leans against it and breathes a sigh of relief. For a moment, she stands, eyes closed. She can hear him moving about the kitchen. She gathers herself and joins him. 'Thought you might be asleep. Are you all right?' she asks cheerily.

He is heating soup. 'Yes, I'm fine. You've been a long time.'

'Sorry, needed to have forty-winks.'

'Yeah, I slept for an hour or two, but then I woke up feeling hungry. There's plenty; do you want some?'

She realises it has been hours since they have eaten. 'Yes, please, soup is a good idea. I'll go to the bathroom and clean myself up.'

On her return, he has laid the table in the lounge, setting down two steaming bowls of soup, a loaf of black bread, and a jug of water. They eat in silence. After, she makes coffee, and they sit by the window, each in their chairs, like an old married couple set in the comfort of routine and physical surety.

'What time are you going to work?' he asks.

'I'm in at six, should be back by 2 a.m.'

'I don't like it when you work late.'

'I know. Look, after we've finished this business, I'll look for something else. We've saved enough money. Perhaps we could move away…'

'No, I like it here. I know where things are, and I have my job with Günther. We don't need to move. Here is just fine.'

'It's okay, I know. I'll tell you what, I promise I'll get a better job, just working days, like you. Maybe we could buy a small café or a shop selling toys and books.'

He smiles. 'Yes, that would be good. I like books and toys. Could we have train sets?'

'Yes, and toy cars, and puzzles, and wooden blocks, dolls, and costumes for parties.'

For a while, they talk animatedly, a moment of lightness.

'Ange?' he asks.

'What is it?'

'It'll be good. We'll be all right. Won't we?'

'Course we will, you'll see.'

For a minute or two, they sit silently, thinking of a future free from fear and repression. At last, Christian places down his cup and looks over at her. 'When are we going to do the next one?'

'I've been thinking about that. They already missed Manfried, so I guess this weekend, when they meet and discover that he's still missing, and now it's only two of them, they'll know something is up. Plus, there's bound to be something in the papers, surely. Do you think we could take them at the same time? If we don't strike quickly, they may disappear, and we'll never get a chance. And remember, we do Johann last. I want to see him suffer the most. Perhaps we could make him watch as we kill Rolf, then hold him for a while and make him sweat.'

He thinks about it. 'Yes, it would be good to get them both. Then, as you say, we can decide when. I agree, Johann, last. Question is, how can we get them at the same time?'

'Well, we know where they both live, don't we?'

'Yes.'

'So, what we do is...' They spend the rest of the afternoon making and refining a plan, and a little after 5:30 p.m., Angelika leaves for work, satisfied and feeling back in control. She works at a lively *bierkeller* in the mostly blue-collar district of Wedding, and it was there some six months earlier she had first encountered the man she came to know as, Johann. He was at a table with other men. They were a hard-looking bunch, deep in discussion. As she came to take their order, they broke off the conversation, but it was unmistakable; they were speaking Russian. He had looked right at her. She almost gasped. It was him, no doubt. Older, but a face etched deep in her memory. For a moment, she gazed at him, feeling sick and dizzy. The world had stopped; it felt like the crowded room had vanished, and it was just the two of them.

'Did you hear me, you dozy bitch?'

'What... oh, sorry, what can I get you?'

Johann had scrutinised her, his dark, soulless eyes roving over her body. It had made her shudder, and, for a moment, she thought he had recognised her. 'As you're so pretty, we'll let you off. Now get us six large beers and bring vodka too, quick, quick!' As she had turned to go, one had grabbed her ass, saying, 'You come sit on my face later, whore.' The others laughed loudly. Delivering their order, she endured more abuse and longed to snatch up a knife and plunge it into them. But she knew now she had an advantage, and the seed of a plan was growing, as was her determination to deliver to this animal the justice he deserved.

Telling her boss she was feeling unwell; she left early. Near to the bar was an alley, and tucking herself out of sight, she'd waited. The men did not leave together. First, a couple came out, then Johann emerged on his own. He stopped to light a cigarette, then sauntered off. There were people about, which made it simple for her to follow. They walked for fifteen or twenty minutes, arriving at a bar in Gottschalkstraße, which he entered. She waited a while, then glanced in through a window and, seeing that it was bustling, followed him in, choosing a table in the corner. He had gone and sat with three other men and it dumbfounded her: she knew them all. Her blood ran cold. Ordering a brandy, she'd gulped it down in one. For a while, she felt confused, her mind urging her to run, but she sat, and watched, and plotted. She needed to pee, and seeing the men had plenty to drink, risked using the filthy toilet. Soon after, she left and found a dark spot with a view of the door and waited.

They left together, clearly good friends. They were drunk, loud, and lurched off down the street. One went one way, the others headed down to the junction where two turned left, and one went right. She stuck with Johann. A few metres on, his friend turned right, leaving him alone. It was quiet. Apart from her and Johann, the roads were empty. He meandered along, and heart pounding, she'd tailed him, keeping her distance. She hoped it would not be far; she was exhausted. They passed a border crossing sign. The road led under the railway line, and at the next junction, he turned right down Brehmestraße. Within a few minutes, he turned off again and fifty metres down Gaillardstraße, stopped, fumbled about in his pocket, unlocked a door and entered. She waited and watched, and a few moments later, came lights from the top floor. Briefly, he appeared at the window, looked out, then closed the faded curtains. She waited another five minutes before walking up to the door. There were three doorbell buttons, each with a nameplate: Johann Kleeman lives on the top floor.

Over the following weeks, she had followed all four men and found out their names, where they lived, and their general routine. The one consistency was the bar where they met frequently. They all walked to and from it and, at least for part of the journey, were alone. She had found the amateur detective work to be thrilling; feeling for once, she had some control, and her life seemed to lift from the mundane ritual of survival to one with purpose and a future.

To begin with, she did not know precisely what it was she wanted to do. But stalking these predatory men, she realised there was but one course of action, and truthfully, she had known it from the moment they came back into her life. Initially, she had planned to kill them herself. But she knew that to attempt this would end in failure and her death. She had been reluctant to involve Christian. His strength and size would be an asset, but he was gentle, and she felt he would make too many mistakes, and the last thing she wanted was to get him caught, or worse, killed. In the end, there had been two options: let it go or use Christian, but unable to let it go, she had laid out her plan to him. He had thought about it for a few moments, then smiled and nodded, and a weight lifted from her shoulders.

It surprised her he proposed changes to her plan, suggesting they find a place to take them and to use Günther's van. As many people did, she had underestimated his abilities. He seemed to come alive, the plan animating him in a way she'd not seen before. And it drew them closer. And it strengthened them and their resolve.

10

Tongues in trees

ANNA TAKES A BREAD ROLL. 'Pass the butter, please, Markus.' Sliding the butter across, Markus asks, 'Dad, is Otti the first lady detective?'

'No, there have been women in the Kripo for years. The difference with Otti is she is the first front-line detective doing the same work as the men on my team.'

'Why did you pick her rather than a man?'

'What sort of question is that? Why wouldn't dad pick a woman?' Heike says.

'Well, isn't it a job more suited to men?'

'Why?'

'Well, it's sometimes dangerous, and there's firing guns and stuff.'

'Well, I can shoot as well as you can, if not better, can't I?'

'Yeees…'

'So, are you saying that only men should do dangerous things?'

'I… I… guess, yes.'

Heike makes a face. 'Well, that's just dumb.'

'You know, I chose her because I thought she was the best person for the job, and that's it,' Max says.

'To be fair though, Max, it is unusual, and you've had to break new ground to get her into an active role,' Anna counters.

'True, but the thing is, times are changing and I don't see any reason women can't do my job.'

'Well, I agree with dad, and I think Otti is super cool,' Heike says.

'Well, I like her too,' Markus returns defensively.

'Anyway,' continues Heike, warming to her task, 'look at mum, she's only got one leg, and she's a doctor and fought in the war.'

'Well, I didn't actually fight; I was a nurse.'

'Yes, but you were in the front lines and wounded, so it must have been dangerous, mustn't it?'

Max interrupts, 'There is no reason men and women can't do the same things, Heike. It's just that some parts of society see things differently. So maybe it is down to Otti and mum and girls like you to change things. You know that whatever you want to do, me, mum, and Markus will support you, all right? Now it's time we were off. Get your things; we leave in two minutes.'

The kids go off. Max and Anna embrace, Max asking, 'What sort of day have you got?'

'You know, the usual, all those sick people to fix.' She pulls away. 'Will you be late tonight?'

'I don't think so unless something comes up.' He shrugs on his coat and holsters his pistol.

'We'll eat at seven, shall we?'

'The autopsy is at 3 p.m. I can come straight from there.'

'I'll see you later and… oh, give my love to Paul, will you?' She pecks him on the cheek. As an after-thought, asking, 'Why didn't Udo come to the party?'

'Ah, he's got the hump about Otti. He's from the school that thinks women should be at home. Honestly, I think he's probably threatened by her, which is silly because he's well able to hold his own. I'm monitoring it. They'll sort it out.'

'How's Jürgen's mother?'

'Not good. I've told him he could take some time off, but he wants to keep busy, and frankly, with the current workload, that's a relief.'

Heike and Markus come thumping down the stairs. 'Better get off.'

Max is sure the killings have not yet finished, that there's a purpose, no matter how twisted, to what is happening. Berlin is a divided city with a chequered and turbulent past; it harbours extremes and holds secrets. He sips his coffee, deciding where next he must direct their enquiries. Bastian arrives, heads over to Max's office and taps on the open door.

'Hey, boss. Saw Otti yesterday and she brought me up to speed. Anything new?'

Max indicates a chair. 'This isn't over yet, of that I'm sure. How many vans have we still to check?'

Bastian flicks open his notebook. 'There are fifty-seven registered, but we don't have access to records in the East, and it's possible that this is a cross-border job. We've ruled out thirty-one.'

'Leave the East to me. Put Jürgen on the van; August has organised two uniforms to help him. After the briefing this morning, I'm putting the rest of you to check the houses nearest the park and see if anyone saw anything Saturday night or Sunday morning. We'll meet back here at 2 p.m. Grab a coffee, soon as the others are in, *Stammtisch*, okay?'

'You want another?'

Max shakes his head. 'No, I'm fine, thanks.'

KD1 has a large open-plan office. Along one wall, partitioned off from the main room, are three smaller spaces: Max's office and two conference/interview rooms, and in the far corner opposite is a walk-in kitchenette. The back wall carries notice boards where they display evidence and case information. Pictures and data from the first murder are there, alongside an unrelated case Tobi and Udo are working on. The daily *Stammtisch* is an informal, open-forum meeting, rank put aside, and all encouraged to speak their mind.

Bastian returns. 'There's a message from uniform to say that von Getz spotted a similar van pass his house yesterday, late morning. They got a description, including colour, and put out an alert, but no further sightings. You want me to go over later and have a word with him?'

'Interesting. Wonder what the chances are of two similar vans being there in the space of one week? Coincidence? I don't think so. Yeah, go see him. Oh, and what colour was the van?'

'Von Getz said sky blue.' The phone on Max's desk rings. He picks up. 'Becker.'

'Ah, hello, this is Frau Alda Bendik, the person who found the body last week.'

'Yes, of course. How can I help?'

'Well, I know this might seem silly, but I was coming back from a walk with Flik yesterday, and there was this strange person. They were wearing a hooded jacket, and when Flik went over, they dodged past her and headed off in a sort of semi-run, scurrying almost, and they kept their head down. They unsettled me, like they were watching. At first, I thought nothing of it, but it nagged at me, so I thought I'd call. I hope that's all right?'

'Yes, definitely. About what time was this?'

'Hmm... let me see... I suppose, late morning, say about 11:30 a.m., give-or-take.'

'Was it a man or a woman?'

She thinks for a moment. 'A woman. You see, the person wasn't very tall and they, well, they didn't walk like a man, and I noticed the feet were quite small. So yes, a woman. Now I think about it, I'm sure of it.'

'What was she wearing?'

'Let me think. A blue hooded top, like a light raincoat; dark boots, and those awful trousers all the young people seem to wear these days, you know?'

'Jeans?'

'Yes, that's it, blue jeans.'

Makes takes notes. 'Anything else?'

For a moment Alda doesn't speak. 'Well, I can't explain why, but I'm sure this person is involved somehow. I know that's not very helpful, but…'

'No, no, I understand and I appreciate you calling. If you think of anything more, call again, okay?'

'Yes, Kommissar Becker, I shall.'

'Listen, If you see her again, under no circumstances should you tackle her, okay?' He terminates the call and shouts out to Bastian.

Bastian sticks his head around the door. 'What's up?'

'I've just had a call from Alda Bendik.' His phone rings. 'One sec, let me get this. Becker.'

'Hey, Max, Lisa. I've had a call through from dispatch. A lady called Brenda Faust said that she and her husband were walking in Spandauer Forest yesterday and saw a young woman behaving suspiciously.'

'Ah, really, that's not the only sighting. Do you have the address?' He scribbles down the details. 'Okay, thanks, Lisa.' Bastian stands in the doorway. Max looks up. 'Interesting, looks like another witness. As I was saying, Alda spotted a stranger hanging around the forest near her home yesterday. She didn't get a good view, but she's sure it was a woman. The time ties in with the van sighting. In addition, we have this sighting of a young woman behaving suspiciously. Leave the other three to do the houses and get down there straight after *Stammtisch*. Have a good sniff around.' Max passes over the details.

The team sits at a round table by the evidence wall. 'We've got two bodies: both tortured premortem. A key element seems to be the removal of their genitalia. It seems likely that one killer is a woman, and given the physical demands of abducting and managing the victims, I suspect the other is a man. You know I don't enjoy jumping to conclusions on scant evidence, so what do you all think?'

'She obviously hates men, or at any rate, these particular men. The question is why?' Udo asks.

'Rape or some other form of sexual assault or abuse?' Otti suggests.

'Yeah, I had wondered about that,' says Bastian. 'I mean, you cut a guy's nuts off for a reason, right?'

'Could be to lead us astray, you know, about motive. In the war, I saw guys from both sides cut off the tackle as a warning. I remember one marksman who got caught, had his *Schwanz* cut off and shoved in his mouth; then they shot him.'

Inwardly, Max shivers. 'I agree; we should be careful not to assume anything. If a woman is involved, then we must keep sexual assault on the table, right?'

'Seems extreme as revenge for rape, doesn't it? If someone attacked her, why not just report it to us and have the men arrested?' Jürgen asks.

'The thing is, you have one woman and, so far, two dead guys. If she comes to us, it'll be her word against her attackers, so maybe she's reasoned that she'll have no chance of proving it. And then, maybe she's not the active killer. Perhaps her husband, boyfriend, brother, or uncle is settling the score?' Otti says.

Max drums his fingers on the table. 'Good. We need more to see where this is heading. So, Jürgen, go meet up with the uniforms August has organised and find that van, blue ones first. You three do the door-to-door on scene two; Bastian's going back to Spandauer to chase up some sightings of our suspect woman. I'm off to see my CI about the tattoos and a lady about some perfume. We'll meet back here later for a debrief.'

The meeting breaks up. Max turns to Tobi. 'Got a sec? In my office.' He closes the door. 'Put Otti with Udo today; we'll see what pans out, agreed?'

He nods. 'Agreed.'

❖❖❖

Over the years, Max has built up a useful network of informants, go-to people, and other less than desirable individuals in touch with the rough underbelly of Berlin life. Max drives over to see an old acquaintance known only as *Der Fuchs*—The Fox. He runs a shop selling army surplus, bric-à-brac and what he laughingly calls fine antiques. But his principal business is a behind-counter operation handling stolen goods, weapons, pornography, and other contraband. Max pushes open the door, a bell tinkles. A voice from the back calls out, 'I'll be there in a minute. I'm armed, so don't think about pinching stuff!'

Max goes past the counter, pushing through the metal string curtain into the back. 'Hey, wait out front!' shouts Der Fuchs. He looks up. 'Oh, it's you, Herr Kommissar. Long time no see, as they say. Here, park your arse, take the weight off.'

Max brushes the seat, sits and crosses his legs. He scans the room. 'How are you keeping, Fuchs?'

Der Fuchs takes a drag from his hand-rolled cigarette, blowing the smoke out through his thin, crooked nose. 'I'm well enough, Herr Kommissar, well enough. What can I do for you?'

'Where were you last week? I was looking for you.'

He chuckles. 'Oh, that. I had to go away for a few days, urgent business. What was it you wanted my help with?' His thin, livid lips crack a smile, revealing a few blackened stumps.

'What do you know about Russian tattoos?'

Der Fuchs grimaces. 'Russians, eh? Evil bastards. What have you got going with the Russians, Herr Kommissar?'

Max pulls out photographs and drops them on the table. 'These, I want to know if they're Russian, and if so, do they mean anything?'

Der Fuchs flicks through the pictures. 'So, got yourself a dead Russian, have you? If I were you, I wouldn't bother chasing it, save to give the killer a big shiny medal. The tattoos look Russian, criminal gangs, you know, prison ink. I don't know what they mean, but I know a man who might.'

'Can I meet him?'

'No, he isn't the kind who will want to talk to *Polizei*. You'll have to let me have the pictures; I'll show him, then tell you. They'll be expenses, of course, with my time and the inconvenience, and I'll probably have to grease a palm or two. Say fifty Marks.'

'Here's twenty now. I'll give you another twenty when I get the information, provided it's worth it. I want those photographs back and don't show them to anyone else.'

'All right, Herr Kommissar, you're the boss.'

Max stands. 'Call me. Soon. And open a window, this place stinks.'

Soon as Max goes, Der Fuchs picks up the receiver and dials a number. He waits while the line connects. At the other end, a chunky hand, fingers like sausages, picks up. '*Da…*'

11

That sweet odour

AFTER THE GRIME OF MEETING with Der Fuchs, Max drives over to Charlottenburg and a shop specialising in perfumes called *Duftender Garten*—Fragrant Garden. The owner, from an old Prussian family, Gabrielle von Eichhorst, had helped him on an earlier case; Max pops in from time to time to buy Anna a gift, and over the years, they have become friends.

Gabrielle had given Max a crash course in perfumery. It had been an education and, having tested Max on a sample of scents, declared he had a good nose. She had told him they believed smell to be the oldest evolved sense and that the earliest recorded perfume chemist was a Tapputi woman living in Mesopotamia over three thousand years ago. Max harvests facts like these, squirrels them away, often amazing his children with his extensive general knowledge.

He parks up in Herderstraße; it is quiet, with few shoppers about on a Monday morning. Entering the shop, a heady smorgasbord of floral aromas accosts him. Gabrielle, sitting behind an elegant, late 19th-century Italian rococo desk, glances up; her face breaking into a broad smile. 'Max, darling, my favourite detective in all of Berlin.' Lightly, they embrace, a peck on each cheek. 'Come, take off your coat, sit down. To what do I owe this pleasure? A little gift for your beautiful Anna, perhaps? Or maybe the lovely Heike is in the market for a first perfume. How old is she now?'

'Oh, she's twelve, thirteen next month, but no, I'm sure perfume isn't high on her list of wants right now, though you could tempt me for Anna.'

'So, she and Markus have become teenagers, though it seems like only yesterday they were tiny.'

He shrugs off his coat. Gabrielle takes it from him and effortlessly spirits it onto an elegant, padded hanger.

'Gabrielle, you look amazing, as ever. How are you?'

'Oh, darling, I am in a whirlwind of organisation and arrangements for my Sophia's upcoming nuptials; my dear, you have no idea the detail and work of it all. You, Anna, and the children must come, of course.'

'Well, that's splendid news. Who's the lucky fellow?' He had once met Sophia in the shop, her beauty and elegance striking him.

'Ah, she has done well and is to marry Otto Puschat, a fine young man from a great family. They match most excellently, and I couldn't be more pleased. Bernhardt is, of course, complaining bitterly about the spending, but as I told him, he has one daughter, so push out the boat that she may set sail on her life in grand style, no? Anyway, listen to me going on. So, Max, I sense perhaps that this is not just a social call. You have, possibly, a little detective work for me, no?'

'Yes, you read me like a book. It's a murder case; the victim discovered in Spandauer Forest, and at the scene, I detected this faint but significant odour I suspect may be perfume. At least that's what I'm here to find out.'

Marie smiles. 'So, a murder and a fragrance, intriguing. Please go on, tell me all.'

'Yes, it seemed out of place in the forest, and it's been nagging me, so here I am to pick at your brains and see if I can give this smell some definition or, even better, a name.'

'What did you smell?'

'It had a sweet element, but also something spicy, aromatic, and heady. I think that was why it had lingered. It struck me as being a smell out of place in a Berlin wood. Sorry, not much to go on.'

Gabrielle goes through to the back, returning with a small wooden case inside of which nestles a selection of vials. 'So, Max, you remember this box, of course? What we'll do first is to get you to identify a few notes and match them to the four categories: floral, oriental, fresh, and woody. Once I have those, we can look at the stock and see if we can find it or something close.'

They spend the next twenty minutes sampling, by the end of which Max has chosen. They have four fragrance notes: bergamot, jasmine, sandalwood, and rose. Gabrielle takes a list from the top left drawer of her desk and begins flipping through it. After a while, her face lights up. 'Hmm, that's good, we have two strong contenders: *Arpège* by Lavin and *Shalimar* by Guerlain, interestingly, both fragrances come from the 1920s.' She looks up and smiles. 'I have both in stock, shall we?'

In the back, Gabrielle has what she calls olfactor rooms for sampling.

Going into each room, she sprays a tiny amount of the product on a card, wafting it about, then leaves, closing the door. Max waits outside, not knowing which perfume is which. 'All right, Max, we'll give it a few minutes so that you get a background of the scent, then go into each room and see if anything clicks.'

The fragrance in the first room has something of the Orient about it, and almost immediately, Max picks up similarities to the smell from Spandauer. There is the hint of jasmine, rose, and patchouli, harmoniously linked to leather and spicy sandalwood. It is almost masculine but with enough floral lightness to remain feminine. As he emerges, she says, 'Anything?'

'Yes, similar. I'll wait a minute, then try the other.'

He repeats the process a few times. 'The first scent is a good match,' he says confidently.

Returning to her desk, Gabrielle shows him a pretty bottle, offering it like a precious gem. 'An interesting fragrance, the crown jewel of House Guerlain's catalogue. Created by Jacques Guerlain himself in 1925. His brother Raymond designed the bottle with its fan-shaped blue stopper and stylish stemmed, crystal glass vessel. I believe *Shalimar* means Temple of Love, and it is most definitely an oriental fragrance inspired by stories of the Indian Emperor, Shah Jahan.'

Max smiles, examining the elegant bottle. 'He of the Taj Mahal, if I'm not mistaken?'

'Yes, he was, and one of the great romantics. I see why it inspired such a heady creation. You mentioned that the scent has a masculine quality. Well, my darling, you might be interested to know it is much favoured by French dandies.'

Max laughs. 'A French dandy killer stalking the forests of Berlin, that would be a first. Is it a good seller?'

'Yes, it is well-liked.'

'So, a result. I can't thank you enough. Of course, in the interest of science and detection, I shall buy a bottle. Now, let's see about something for Anna.'

By the time Max makes his way back to the office, now quite a few Deutsch Marks lighter, it is nearing lunchtime and finding Bastian at his desk, they decide to go across to Malinda's for lunch.

As always, it is busy. Seeing them come in, Malinda waves, pointing them to a booth. They order a hot meal and beer, and Max relates his morning's work.

'It's funny about that perfume. I detected nothing like that, but then again, I'm a smoker and, when it comes to perfume, something of a Luddite. Why are you so bothered about it, anyway?'

'Don't know, really, other than it helps me to form a complete picture, and it's been bothering me. I don't like it when things like that niggle. Of course, it might be totally irrelevant, could just have easily been from someone unrelated to the murder, though not Alda; she was wearing something else, much lighter.'

'Could have been the dog,' quips Bastian, laughing.

Max laughs, and for a few minutes, they joke with one another. 'Anyhow, seriously, what did the witnesses have to say?'

'All seems to tie in. Alda said the woman was standing staring at the houses. The dog went to the suspect, and she hurried off. Alda identified they were wearing jeans, ankle boots—that's when she noticed the small feet—and a blue hooded coat that seemed a little too big. She didn't get a look at the face but said that there was a little hair visible and it was fair or blond. She told me the jeans were well fitted and that her legs were, as she put it, very shapely and muscular, like a dancer or gymnast. She took me to where it went down, and I had a good look. But nothing. I went to see the old couple who saw a young woman vomiting against a tree and seemed quite distressed. She tried to hide her face from them, but they got a quick look and said that she was attractive, fair-skinned, blond hair, quite a sporty build. They guessed her height at about five-two-or-three. She said little, but had a Berlin accent. They offered to take her to their home while she recovered, but she wanted to get away and made her excuses, hurrying off.'

'Hmm, interesting. And von Getz?'

'Oh yes, the pompous windbag! He saw the van pass by his window. At first, it didn't click, but then he realised it looked similar and rang it in. Said the van appeared battered, well used, and that the blue paint faded.'

'If it was her, I wonder why she went back? Perhaps they lost something? I think we'll get some uniforms back to the scene to carry out another search, just in case. We must find that van; it's our priority.'

Finishing, they walk back to the office. As they enter, Lisa is just leaving a note on Max's desk. 'Oh, Max, Tobi has just rung in. They need another hour, but so far, they've drawn a blank. Jürgen also called, said he's got a van matching the description and is chasing it up this afternoon. Also, can you call Lutz? Something to do with perfume.'

'Well, not all bad news, then. Actually, I'm just going over to PTI. Would you call Lutz and tell him I'll pop in to see him then? Thanks, Lisa.'

Max scribbles a note to Jürgen to call him when he gets back to the office and, checking his watch, calls out to Bastian, 'Come to the autopsy. We'll leave in fifteen. I'm home straight after, so separate cars. I'm just popping up to see if August is in; I'll catch you downstairs.'

12

Suit the action to the word

THE TEAM GATHER FOR THE Tuesday morning *Stammtisch*. Max drops copies of the postmortem report on the table. 'The autopsy has identified two interesting facts. Under the left arm, near the armpit, Paul found a small black tattoo identifying Ernst's blood group.'

'He was SS, then?' Tobi says.

Bastian takes a copy of the report and shakes his head. 'Not necessarily. We had a couple of guys in our unit had that type of tattoo; given it when treated at an SS hospital.'

'Okay, so it points to him being SS or, at the very least, he was fighting for us,' Max says.

'Then we have the other tattoos, which are most likely Russian prison-related, giving us an Ivan, who was fighting for us?' Jürgen says.

'The RONA?' Max suggests.

'What's the RONA?' Asks Otti.

'It was a Russian SS unit formed around '41 and involved in many atrocities. They were a hellish lot and had a habit of recruiting Soviet deserters.'

'Ergo, our man could have got his tattoo that way,' Tobi adds.

'All right, maybe that or something else. Either way, it can explain why he's in Berlin. Paul has identified that the killer in the first case was right-handed, but a lefthander killed the second victim, as the blows seemed to come from the victim's right and that the person who inflicted them must be powerful. The blow to the groin that virtually eradicated the genitals also smashed his pelvis—smashed being the operative word. The killing blow to the head caused catastrophic damage to the skull and brain, and by all accounts was a savage and passionate beating.'

'So we have a man and woman team; she's small, sporty, attractive, and he's powerful. It is extreme, isn't it? I mean, beating someone to death. Do you think they're taking turns?' Udo asks.

'The fact is, they're both actively involved suggesting it's a shared motive. It could be what Otti suggested: girl gets raped, and her man helps her to get revenge. It would explain the extreme methods,' Tobi says.

Max nods. 'Okay, let's keep an open mind about motive. The fact is, we don't have enough yet. We must find the van. It's the key; we find that, we find them.' He turns to Jürgen. 'Where are we on the vans?'

Jürgen opens his notebook. 'I've chased down all the blue vans, and all have clear alibis for the times. I'm still working through the rest of the colours, mostly white and grey. As grey is most likely to be confused with blue, we're checking those first. Of course, it might be an East Berlin vehicle.'

Max nods. 'I've got my VoPo guy checking; he'll let me know. Let's get those vans cleared today. I want everyone on it and, in case he was wrong about the van, have a look at all makes and see if it's possible to confuse any other with a Citroën. I'm off to see our leader and sort out press interest, which is hotting up. Questions?' There's a collective shaking of heads. 'Okay then, good hunting!'

Max heads up to see August and Julius. Many of the papers have already latched on to the story of the murders. In Monday's late editions, some released sensational reports, dubbing the killer—*Der Waldscharfrichter*—the Forest Executioner.

Julius Grob's office is on the top floor with a commanding outlook north over the Zoological Gardens and the Tiergarten. His secretary ushers them in. He is standing looking at the view and, without turning to face them, says. 'Please, gentlemen, sit.' I took my niece to the Zoological Park last week. It is remarkable how they have restored it after those barbarians rampaged over our glorious city, no? Have you been, Max?'

'Yes, Herr Director, I have. As you say, remarkable.'

'Did you know that less than one hundred animals survived the war? I believe that originally, there had been some three thousand eight hundred. Of course, Ivan ate some of the unfortunate survivors. As I said, barbarians. But, out of chaos comes light, and in rebuilding the park they have used the most modern facilities, which have improved the lot of our new residents. But it is senseless being emotional about such things, no?' He turns to face them. 'Now, gentlemen, I have read the reports, and I understand you wish to organise a press release, no? Though, of course, I see that some papers have printed childish fantasies and given an unfortunate sobriquet to our perpetrator.'

It was typical of Julius to begin a meeting with some inconsequential chit-chat. It was said he'd picked up the technique from Himmler, who had a reputation for being charming and supportive: lull your audience before issuing the death warrant. One of Max's comrades from his Panzer regiment had gone to receive his Knight's Cross from Himmler, who wined and dined him, gave him a private audience, sought his counsel, and although he hated the Nazi regime, Himmler's charismatic charm beguiled him and he saw how easy it was to be deceived.

'Herr Director, it will be useful if we can establish the identity of the victims, so we need to get names to faces and perhaps rattle the killers. We will, of course, keep much of the information to ourselves, only release what is necessary,' August says.

'So, you are certain it is two killers?'

August nods. 'It's not one hundred per cent, but all the evidence leads us to that conclusion.'

Julius regards them critically. 'Is it possible this is gang-related and, thus, there enters the possibility of multiple perpetrators?'

'If I may, Herr Director?' Max asks.

Julius gestures. 'Max, please, proceed.'

'The murders don't have the mark of gang killings. Those usually involve an execution-style shooting, and then they dump or hide the body. Here, it has a feel of planned revenge, a message is being sent, but we don't know whether that message is for us, other targets, or indeed just an act of closure for the killers. I'm sure this isn't gang-related.'

As Max speaks, Julius removes his glasses and, taking a large handkerchief from his pocket, polishes the lenses, holding them up to the light and checking. Satisfied, he replaces them on his shiny nose. 'Well, Max, that is good enough for me. So, what is your next step?'

'We are pursuing the vehicle, which is crucial and the principal item for the press conference. It's a possibility that it's registered in the East, so I'm having my VoPo contact run a search on their side. I have one of my CIs asking around about the unusual tattoos, and we are still making local enquires at both sites regarding possible sightings. We've run missing persons but come up empty-handed. If these men are who I think they are, then their associates or families probably won't be *Polizei* friendly.'

Julius leans forward. 'Who do you think they are, Max?'

'Most likely Soviet, and I suspect from the criminal ranks. The tattoos were probably from prison culture or the old Russian Mafia. It's possible they're not living in West Berlin.'

Julius's face flushes red. He stands and places his hands on the desk's polished surface. 'If it proves that they are residents of the East, I don't want a lot of ignorant communists muscling in. We keep this in-house, understand?'

'Yes, Herr Director.'

He sits, an almost imperceptible creak from the chair's rich leather, and critically regards his manicured fingernails. 'How's the lovely young Fräulein Jäger doing? I hear she can handle a weapon, no? I look forward to her first kill.' Then, placing both hands on the edge of the desk and gently sweeping them outwards along the edge, he concludes, 'Very well, I agree, proceed. Please let me have a copy of your proposed statement for approval.' Smiling, a glint in his eye, 'If it proves we have vigilantes cleaning criminal communists, perhaps we may have a job for them, no?' Chuckling, he stands. 'Let me know if there is anything I can do to facilitate your enquiries. Thank you for your time, gentlemen. Good day.'

Max and August stand. 'Herr Director.'

They walk down the corridor. 'He's in a good mood today,' August says.

'I can never really tell, but yes, he seemed agreeable. What the hell was that zoo stuff all about?'

'Search me, still, always an education, eh?'

'Yeah, shame though, about the animals. I've never thought about it before. Not sure I really approve of zoos, anyway.'

'Let me know if you need additional resources, particularly tracking the van, all right?'

'Thanks, see you later.'

By the close of business, they wire a press release out to all major news organisations. The first reports go out on the evening radio and TV broadcasts, and by Wednesday morning, all major newspapers run the story.

13

He that dies pays all his debts

AT A SMALL BAR IN the district of East Berlin's Pankow, Der Fuchs meets the man he knows only as *Der Oberst*—The Colonel. Der Fuchs hefts open the door that leads into the dark, rough interior, the air heavy with the smell of strong Russian tobacco. A few men lean on the bar, drinking in silence. Der Oberst sits at a table near the back, a bottle of vodka by his side. Seeing Der Fuchs, Der Oberst snaps out a command, clearing the room. 'Sit. Show me the pictures.'

Der Fuchs places the photographs on the table, and the large, sausage-fingered hand picks them up. Der Oberst flips through, his face impassive. After a few minutes, he puts them down. 'Where did you get these?'

'A friend. He wants to know what they mean?'

'And is this friend filthy *Polizei*?'

'No, nothing like that. As I said, he's an old friend, a fellow dealer,' and tapping his nose, adds, 'if you catch my drift.' Moistening his lips, he indicates the bottle. 'May I?'

Nodding, Der Oberst pushes it and a thick shot glass toward him. Der Fuchs rolls himself a cigarette.

'Why is he so interested in these tattoos?'

Der Fuchs sits back and lights his cigarette. 'He suspects the man might be a *Stasi* spy, that there's something phoney about him, so he's just asking around.'

'But, comrade, clearly this man is dead, so what does it matter?'

Der Fuchs shrugs. 'He's worried what he might have been up to, just wants to know, that's all.'

Der Oberst pours himself another drink and nods. 'These tattoos are genuine. The one on his back shows the story of Prometheus tied to a rock, and in the background, you can see ships. It means that he is damned, but he is a criminal traveller who is prone to escape. The tattoo of the knife piercing his neck means he has committed murder, probably in prison. The skulls and religious buildings also denote murder and thievery. The rose on his chest shows he was in prison when he turned eighteen.' He pushes the pictures back across the table. 'I know this man. I had wondered what had happened to him. Now, thanks to you, I know. So, Fuchs, who killed him?'

Taking out a ten Mark note, Der Fuchs places it on the table. 'For the drink, comrade. My friend didn't say who, but he said it was probably the Lithuanians. Who is this man, anyway?'

'His name is Dedov Damir Olegovich, also known as Manfried Bikart. I've known him for twenty years. Who the fuck are these Lithuanians?'

'They're a group running arms between the American sector and the East, mostly working with the Mafia.'

'Funny, I've never heard of them. I'll ask Viktor. If anyone is running arms, he'll know about it. You better not be making it up, Fuchs.'

'It's what I heard, that's all. Thank you for your time, Herr Oberst, most generous.' Gathering up the photos, he stands.

'Wait, before you go. I have a minor job for you. I want an Armalite with ammunition, must be U.S. military issue.'

Der Fuchs smirks. 'With or without optical sights?'

'It does not matter, but I need it quickly.'

'I can have one by tomorrow. 10 p.m., my shop. Use the back door and bring fifteen thousand.'

Der Oberst nods and waves his hand dismissively. '*Da*. Now fuck off!'

Der Fuchs, relieved to be out in the open, climbs into his battered Opel and heads off to make a deal with his American contact. Back in the bar, another man joins Der Oberst. 'Tomorrow, you collect the merchandise. Make sure Der Fuchs gets a bonus and leave a message.'

The man nods. 'Yes, sir.'

Waving him away, Der Oberst lifts his glass, chucking the harsh spirit down in one and slamming it on the table, drums his large fingers, thinking.

Getting up and going over to the bar, he picks up the phone receiver and dials. 'Rolf? It's Johann. That weaselly shit, Der Fuchs, has been over. He has *Polizei* pictures of Manfried. He's dead.'

'How's that cunt-bastard got involved in this?'

'I've suspected for some time that he is a *Polizei* rat. I'm sending over the ratcatcher.'

'Have you seen Ernst? I've tried calling him, but he's not answering.'

'Hmm, interesting. Have you heard about Lithuanians running arms across the border with the American Mafia?'

'No. News to me.'

'Okay, as I thought. Leave Ernst a message, and we'll meet tonight at mine, 9 p.m. Make sure you're armed. Somebody is after us, but I don't know who or why.' He hangs up.

❖ ❖ ❖

Der Fuchs secures his package and hurries back to his shop to call Max. Unable to get through to him directly, he leaves a message. It has been a good couple of days. He will make a profit of five thousand on the rifle and a bit of walking around money from the Kripo. He thinks they're all dumb arses, like taking candy from babies. Chuckling, he climbs the narrow staircase to the flat above the shop and, selecting one of his special, homemade magazines, he drops his trousers and, lying on his bed, celebrates.

When he wakes, it is dark. The clock shows 8:30 p.m. Getting up, he goes through to the kitchen and makes a sandwich and a hot drink. He switches on the radio, sits at the small table, and eats his food. He is a little nervous, not sure who Der Oberst will send to collect the goods. He rolls a cigarette, lighting it as he goes downstairs to make ready.

At precisely 10 p.m., visible through the obscured glass of the back door, looms the silhouette of a man. The figure knocks, and Der Fuchs throws the bolts and pulls open the door.

The man steps in. 'Do you have it?'

'Yes, of course. Do you have the cash?'

The man nods. 'Show me the rifle and ammo; I want to check it over.'

Going over to a cupboard, Der Fuchs takes out a canvas-wrapped package, handing it over.

The rifle looks new, though serial numbers and other identifying marks have been ground off. The man works the action, looks down the barrel, operates the trigger, and, taking a magazine, deftly locks it into position. He looks as though he has spent his whole life handling firearms.

Der Fuchs looks on nervously. 'It is an excellent weapon, my friend, no?'

The man nods solemnly. 'It is what we wanted, but I'm not your fucking friend. Now show me that dagger hanging on the wall there. I like it.'

Der Fuchs goes to the wall display and, taking down the dagger, hands it over. 'It's a real beauty, top quality SS dagger, as you can see from the maker's mark on the blade…'

'Shut up with the sales spiel. I'm not interested. How much is it?'

'For you, one thousand.'

The man peels off some notes. 'I'll give you eight hundred, no more.'

'Agreed.'

The man takes an envelope and hands it over. 'This is for the rifle and ammo.'

Der Fuchs' eyes light up. Greedily, he snatches the packet. 'Pleasure doing business with you.'

The man turns to go. Stopping, he says, 'Oh, Der Oberst says to give you a bonus.'

Der Fuch's hesitates, frowning. 'That's most…'

Suddenly, the man turns and thrusts the SS dagger deep into Der Fuchs' chest. Shock swamps his face, which instantly pales. Leering, the man extracts the blade. 'With the compliments of Der Oberst, *Ratte!*'

Der Fuchs gasps, blood bubbling from his mouth. He collapses to the floor and stares, wide-eyed, as his life ebbs away. The man retrieves the money and packet. He extracts the knife and, wiping away the blood, returns it to its scabbard. He snatches up the photos of the tattoos and scatters them over the body. Finally, dipping his finger in blood, he stoops and writes *Polizeiratte* on Der Fuchs' forehead. Standing, he takes a last look around, and leaves.

❖❖❖

Getting the message late, it is the following morning. Max makes his way over to see Der Fuchs and, surprised to find the shop door locked, Knocks and waits. Seeing a light on in the back, he goes to check the rear entrance. The door is unlocked and ajar. Pushing it open, he steps inside and curses himself. '*Schieß!* Max, you idiot, you should have had him watched.'

14

To thine own self be true

GÜNTHER, JUST BACK FROM HIS firm's latest project, new housing in the south of the Reinickendorf district, is happy with the progress. There is a knock on his office door. Maria, his daughter-come-secretary, tells him a detective is outside.

'Oh, I wonder what he wants? Show him in.'

Entering the office, Jürgen shows his badge. 'I'm *Kriminal Obermeister* Zeigler. You are on record as the owner of a white Citroën H van; is that correct?'

'It's blue, not white. It is a Citroën, though.'

Jürgen frowns. 'Oh, that's odd. It states clearly here in the records that it is white, registration KB 4165; is that not correct?'

'The registration is, but not the colour.' He smiles and nods. 'Of course, that was stupid of me. You see, a couple of years after I bought the van, it was involved in an accident. I asked a friend to mend it, and he had plenty of blue paint and said he'd do me a good deal and respray the entire vehicle. I just forgot to correct the documentation.'

'So, are you saying that currently the vehicle is blue?'

'Correct. Sorry, amiss of me.'

'Where is the vehicle?'

'In the yard.'

'And where was it on the night of September 10th/11th, say between 8 p.m. and 8 a.m.?'

'What day was that?'

'The night of Saturday/Sunday, ten days ago.'

'The vehicle was here, locked up in the yard.'

'You sure of that?'

'Of course, I saw it Saturday when I left, and it was still here Monday morning.'

'Is it possible someone may have had access to it without your knowledge?'

'No. Look, what's this about?'

'What about the night of the 17th, Saturday last, between midnight and 8 a.m.?'

'Same answer.'

'And you're sure no one else had access to it?'

'Not without my permission.'

'And did you give anyone permission to use it?'

'Detective, if the van was here, it follows that would not have been the case. As I said, what is this about?'

'Just routine enquiries, sir. Would it be possible to have a look in the vehicle?'

'I suppose so, though I am very busy. Here are the keys. Maria will go with you.'

She shows Jürgen to the van. He pokes around inside, noting that the original white colour is still visible. The back is tatty but clean, almost too clean. After a few minutes, he locks up and hands the key back to her. 'Do you ever drive this van?'

'I have, but not for a few years.'

'Who else drives it?'

'I wouldn't know; you'd better ask my father.'

'Oh, I didn't realise he's your father. How long have you worked for him?'

'Since I left school.'

'So, you'd be loyal to him, then?'

'I'm not sure what you mean by that, detective?'

Jürgen looks at her for a while and shakes his head. 'Nothing, just curious, that's all.'

'Is there anything else we can do for you?'

'No, not for the moment. Thank you both for your time. Good day.'

Maria watches him go and returns to the office. 'Hey, pop, wasn't Christian using the van then?'

Günther smiles. 'Yes. He was. I wonder what he's been up to?'

Günther has a good reason he has not told the truth. During the war, the Kripo picked up his brother, who had learning difficulties, and under interrogation, forced him to confess to raping and killing two women. It was convenient for the National Socialist Party to pin serious crimes on foreigners, Jews, and people with mental disabilities. Good Germans did not commit such crimes; they were the acts of *Die Untermenschen*—subhuman creatures. A few days after being sent to prison without a trial, they executed him. On first meeting Christian, Günther had seen in him something that reminded him of his beloved brother.

'Maria, my darling, if you see Christian before me, tell him I want to speak with him, but don't tell him about our visitor, all right?'

'Okay, pops. Coffee?'

'Yes, my darling, thanks.'

Returning to the office, Jürgen feels frustrated. They have eliminated all but two vans, which are proving tricky to find. While it is possible that one of these is the vehicle of interest, he has a feeling about Günther's colour-shifting Citroën. He senses that both Günther and his daughter had been evasive, and the van, for an old builder's vehicle, had seemed too clean. Admittedly, the yard and office had been spotless, but something did not feel quite right. He resolves to sleep on it and discuss it during the following *Stammtisch*. At the end of a long day, he heads down to the range to fire off a few rounds and clear his head.

As he descends, he hears small arms fire, and pushing through the thick double doors into the range, the *pop-pop* sound increases to loud cracks as 9 mm rounds spit down the range. It does not surprise him to find Otti and Bastian here. They've set the target at twenty metres. He stands behind her watching, and with her Walther PP beautifully balanced in her confident grip, she is nailing every shot. Her clip spent, she makes the weapon safe and presses the button that moves the target back up to her position. 'See you've gone with the PP. Nice grouping,' he says amiably.

With ear defenders on and concentrating on the range, she does not at first spot him. 'Oh, hey, Jürgen, you startled me. How's it going?'

'Okay, boring day chasing vans. You?'

'Pretty much the same, so ditto, dull. Are you shooting?'

'Yeah, sure.'

Bastian, having finished, joins them. 'Positive day, Jürgen?'

He shrugs. 'Okay, I guess.'

'How about a bit of fun?'

'What have you in mind?' Otti asks.

'All right, three clips, ten, fifteen, then twenty metres against the clock. I'll shoot left-handed.'

'I'm in, but how about we blindfold you, too?' Jürgen jests.

'All right, sounds fun, I'm game,' Otti says.

Taking turns, they shoot. Inevitably, even using his weak hand, Bastian fires more quickly and accurately, and while Jürgen is quicker than Otti by three seconds, she is more accurate. Looking at the targets, Bastian says, 'Well, that's hard to call. How about you both buy me a beer?'

'How about us two go again, best of three?' Jürgen says to Otti.

In the next round, on the last two shots at the twenty-metre target, Otti deliberately shoots wide, and Bastian gives it to Jürgen.

Later, after they have left the bar and Jürgen has gone off to take the underground train—*U-Bahn*—home, Bastian walks with Otti back to get their cars. 'You threw that, didn't you, on the last target?'

'Yeah, seemed like the right thing to do. Do you think Jürgen noticed?'

'I don't believe so. But I'm not sure about your motive.'

'You know it's no skin off my nose if I don't win. So long as I know I'm good enough, that's sufficient. I've been in a men's world all my life; it's just politics.'

'See, that's my weakness, I'm crap at politics. But be careful, don't make yourself look weak, not in the lion's den.'

Otti smiles, a glint in her eye. 'I think you'll find in the lion's world, it's the lioness doing all the hunting and killing.'

'True, but the lion always gets to eat first, doesn't he?'

They get back to where they parked their cars. 'Ask Max to put you in for the test. You're ready.'

'I will, tomorrow. See you then. Bye.'

15

Death will have his day

METICULOUSLY THOUGHT OUT, THE PLAN is simple. They'd spent the Monday making ready and in possession of the funds from Ernst, have purchased two used vehicles, a Ford van and VW Beetle. By Tuesday evening, all is ready, and they set out in the hope an opportunity will present itself.

Rolf, a man of habit, invariably uses a shortcut through a small, wooded park, either when he's going to the bar or across the border to see one of his friends. Angelika has parked the van with a view of Rolf's apartment and, positioning herself in the back, watches from the rear window. Stationed at the park end of the road, Christian will spot Rolf coming, run ahead and lie in wait.

A little after 8:30 p.m., Rolf leaves. Entering the wooded park, he is unaware Angelika is following. Running to catch up, she calls out to him. '*Hallo bitte, hilfe, hilfe!*'

Hearing the cry for help, he stops, and turns seeing a young woman running toward him, waving, and now distracted, does not notice Christian appear from behind. A moment later, Rolf is down. Angelika stands over him, her heart racing, eyes wide and glowing. 'Huh, that was easy! Nice work, Chris. One down, one to go. I'll get the van; wait by the gate.'

They tuck Rolf in the back, restrain him and, as a final touch, gag and hood him.

'Okay, that should do it. Let's get over to Johann's; we might get lucky.'

They had no way to know that Rolf had been going over to meet with Johann, but luck is quite a thing, and for once it was working full force for them.

When they arrive at Johann's apartment in Gaillardstraße, they drive on to the end of the road and park. They can see lights from his window. Angelika turns to Christian. 'That's good; he's in; are you ready?'

His brow knitted, Christian nods. 'I'm ready. It's now or never.'

Slipping the Makarov pistol in the back of her jeans, she walks down the street and rings the bell. As expected, Johann appears at his window. Looking up, she waves to him, mouthing that Ernst has sent her. He disappears, and Christian joins her. Alert to danger, Johann picks up his Luger, cocking it as he comes down the stairs. As he opens the door, Christian pushes violently, knocking Johann off balance and causing him to fall back and bounce heavily off the stair rail. Recovering, he raises his pistol, but Christian is already upon him, ramming his elbow into Johann's face, breaking his nose, and knocking him back against the wall. The Luger clatters harmlessly to the ground, and now blinded by the blow, Johann flails hopelessly as Christian lands a devastating punch to Johann's stomach, doubling him over, gasping and retching. Christian finishes the job by bringing linked fists down onto the back of Johann's head, rendering him comatose. Scooping up the fallen weapon, Angelika runs to the van, and a minute later, they are aboard and away.

Growing up the frequent victim of bullies, Christian learnt how to handle himself and though his fighting moves are unorthodox, his swiftness and agility, together with his strength, prevail.

Frau Hilde Bach lives in the ground-floor apartment. Hearing the commotion, she stands by her front door, peering out of the peephole. After the melee has abated, she waits a minute and, opening her door a crack, peeps out, sees the hallway empty and the outer main door open. Leaving her home, she pushes the door shut and, turning, notices blood on the floor. Pausing a moment to consider, and aware that Johann is a man of low character, who keeps bad company and likes to drink, she locks her door and, returning to her cosy lounge, takes up her needles to resume knitting, saying to the cat asleep by the gas fire, 'None of our business, is it, Moritz?'

❖❖❖

In the holding cell, down in the basement, Angelika checks over the still unconscious Johann. They strip and chain him tight to the wall. When he comes to, he will be in complete darkness. They go back to the main room where Rolf is lying. He stirs, moaning.

'Shall we risk it?' Christian asks.

Angelika nods. 'Yes, we need him compliant.'

Christian smacks him over the head, and Rolf loses consciousness.

'Anyway,' she continues, 'it does not matter much if he has a head injury, does it?'

They strap Rolf securely to the board. Going through his and Johann's possessions, they find another thick wad of banknotes. Angelika raises her eyebrows and lets out a low whistle. She looks at Christian. 'These men carry a lot of cash, don't they?'

He nods. 'None of it honestly earned, I bet, but a handy bonus for us, eh?'

As before, they kill the lights, sit at the back and wait. It is a welcome moment of calm after the danger and tension of the previous hours. She closes her eyes, feeling a sense of dominance that is alien. With Rolf and Johann are at their mercy, the perilous part is done. She shudders, longing for it to be over, hoping that it will be a new start, and the past laid to rest. She has seen a side to Christian she did not know existed. She had assumed his slow wits protected him, but now she can see that he suffered but did not, or could not, show it. Together, they will be free.

The sound of moaning breaks her reverie. Beside her, she feels Christian tensing, senses his power. Rolf regains consciousness. He opens his eyes but cannot see. He is upright, his arms and legs akimbo. There is a terrible pain in his wrists and ankles where he is bound. He cannot move his head, which throbs terribly. He feels panic rising, his unseeing-eyes darting.

'Hey!' he shouts into the darkness. Nothing. He shouts again and listens intently. He hears a muffled voice shouting back, 'Rolf, is that you?'

Confused, he calls out, 'Johann? Where are you? I can't see anything. They've bound me to the wall and taken my clothes. It was a young woman. Someone hit me from behind.'

'A woman lured me down, and this massive brute laid into me. I'm chained to a wall by my neck, hands, and feet. It's too dark to see. I think we might be underground, perhaps in an old bunker or basement.'

Angelika squeezes Christian's arm, and he flicks the switch, bathing Rolf in bright white light. For a moment, his eyes shut tight, then blinking, he opens them, trying to see. Adrenaline pumping, his breathing comes in short and intense gasps.

'Is that you, girly? Are you there? Fucking whore!'

'If I were you, I'd be nicer. Otherwise, we'll have to cut out your tongue,' Christian says.

'Who are you? What do you want?'

The tape machine starts, the message plays. 'What court? What crimes?' Rolf yells.

Appearing between the lights, Angelika stands before him, defiant. He stares at her. 'You don't remember me, do you?'

'I can't see you properly, you cowardly bitch. Who are you?'

'Truth is, there were so many of us; you wouldn't know if I told you.'

'Go on then, if you're going to kill me… whore… do it!'

'Don't be in such a hurry to die, little man. First, have some contrition, beg me for forgiveness, and I'll make the end of your pitifully insignificant life less… traumatic.'

'Fuck you!'

She moves closer and pliers grab his right nipple, yanking it away from his chest, and with a quick flick of a cut-throat razor, she slices it off. Shocked, his eyes wide open, he yells, but before he can recover, the other nipple is gone. Blood streams down his chest, the pain excruciating.

Her face right in his, she says calmly, 'Shall I cut your filthy little cock off next? Or perhaps, yes, I know…' and with a swift movement, she sticks the blade into his left nostril, slicing it open. He winces and yells, the pain from his injuries screaming and burning, his brain unable to function.

Angelika has detached herself, and a strange, malevolent empowerment flows through her. Even her voice sounds alien: cold, and glassy. 'We don't want to get ahead of ourselves, do we?'

As his yells subside, they hear Johann shouting and swearing. When he quiets down, she whispers in Rolf's ear, 'As a foretaste, your friend is going to listen to you die in excruciating pain.' She lays the blade just under his right eye. He winces. 'But we've got something extraordinary planned for him. Alas, sadly, you won't be around to see it. Tell me, what's your real name? If you tell me, I won't cut off your cock. Promise!'

For a moment he gulps air. 'My name is Rolf Cahnheim.'

'Oh, Rolf, no, no, no, that's the wrong answer. Look, I'm feeling generous. I'll give you one more chance.' She places the blade on his penis, applying pressure. 'So, what is your name? Your Russian name? Surely, you haven't forgotten?'

'Okay, okay, stop, stop for fuck's sake. I'll tell you. My name is Boris Artur Vyacheslavovich.'

'Boris. Hmm, I like that. Well, Boris, I'm sorry, I lied.' With a flash of the blade, she eviscerates his manhood and holds it up in front of his flickering, pupil-wide eyes. He screams. Then blackness. A short while later, raging pain drags him back, blinking in the light. She holds the dripping razor in front of his pain-racked, fear-stricken face. 'You know, someone should have done that a long time ago.'

He passes out. Christian comes forward and throws cold water over him, bringing him back. He stares in wide-eyed terror. 'Please, please, I don't know why you're doing this to me?'

'That's the trouble with people like you. You're so evil and have done so much wrong you can't remember any of it, can you? In fact, I'd say that you don't even think that what you did was wrong. The thing is, Boris, unless you kill us all, one of us might come back and get you. People like him and me.'

The fight and tenacity leak away from him. 'I don't know what you're talking about,' he says pitifully.

'Well, in that case, there isn't much point in carrying on with this conversation, is there? Time for you to leave.'

'No, please, wait, wait…'

She goes to work with the razor, culminating in a deep slash at the join of his leg near his groin, laying open the femoral artery, and in just a short while, Rolf's life ebbs away.

Christian joins her, his eyes wide. He lets out a huge breath, puffing out his cheeks. 'Now I see why you wanted us to wear the coveralls. That is a lot of blood.'

They roll up Rolf in canvas and take him to the van. They clean up the mess and themselves and remove their outer clothing, placing them into a bag with Rolf and Johann's things. They put on new coveralls, and before leaving, she goes over to Johann's cell and, banging on the door, shouts, 'We'll be back!'

'I'm going to get free and fuck you up, bitch!' he yells, hopelessly pulling and thrashing at the chains. They had considered blocking up all the doors to the basement and leaving him there to die slowly, alone in the dark. But they want to be sure he is gone.

They take just under thirty minutes to drive to Wilhelm-von-Siemens-Park, just south of Tegel Flughafen in Charlottenburg-Nord. Parking up in Dihlmannstraße, they carry Rolf to a small clearing near the west end of the woods. They unroll the bloodied body, laying it on the ground, arms and legs spread-eagle. They nail the sign to a wooden stake, driving it into the ground by his right arm and point his finger toward it.

Retreating a few yards away, they take off their protective clothing, place them in another bag, return to the vehicle, and drive away. An hour later, they are back at their apartment.

After Christian has gone to bed and hearing his snoring, she pours herself a glass of the brandy left over from a previous Christmas and, sitting by the window, gulps it back and cries uncontrollably.

16

Every tale condemns me for a villain

THE MORNING OF WEDNESDAY, SEPTEMBER 21, is wet. On the way in, Max stops to pick up the morning papers. Most have put the story on the front page, the artist's impression of the two victims staring out under the headline: "Who Will Be the Next Forest Executioner's Victim?" Max has withheld details about the signs and the torture but included information about the mystery van.

The team sits at the briefing table for the morning *Stammtisch*. Max drops the paper on the table. 'All the papers are covering the story, so we're in the spotlight now. I'm sorry to say someone has carried out a little wetwork on my CI, Der Fuchs. He took the photos of the tattoos to a contact, and it got him killed. Lesson is, I should have had him followed, but hindsight is a great thing, isn't it? I've found a perfume to match the aroma I detected at the first scene. The details are in your briefing document. So, that's my news; what else have we got?'

Jürgen opens his notebook. 'I visited a builder, one Günther Alsbach, and it turns out his white van is in fact blue and fits the description perfectly. However, he says that it was in the yard both weekends. He and his daughter, also his secretary, were not exactly welcoming or helpful. There's something not quite right there, and I think it's worth another look.'

Max nods. 'Agreed. Udo and Otti, you get over there and check it out. Get a list of employees and, including Günther and his daughter, check their alibis. Jürgen, do a background check on Günther to see if there might be a reason he wasn't more accommodating.'

Lisa leans her head around the door. 'Max, we've got another body.'

❖❖❖

Max and Bastian stand by the corpse. The rain has re-hydrated the blood, macabrely streaking the body and ground. By the left hand lie the eviscerated genitals, lips, and nipple, while the right hand points to the sign:

EVEN WHAT THEY HAVE WILL BE TAKEN FROM THEM - L

'Things seem to escalate,' Max says.

Bastian squats down to get a better look. 'Yeah, I've seen plenty in my time, but that's fucked up. They've butchered him and, once again, specifically mutilated the genitals. Wonder why they removed his lips? What do you think about the severed parts by his left hand and the right hand pointing to the message?'

'Seems to further support the rape and revenge motive. Perhaps he and the others raped someone close to the killers? Maybe a child? As to the placement, I really don't know, and we might interpret the message in many ways.'

A voice from behind, 'Ugh, foul day.' Lutz joins them and regards the scene. 'Hell's teeth, that's not what you wish to see before lunch or any time, frankly.'

'Morning, Lutz, you well?'

'I was until…' He makes a face, then smiles. 'By the way, come over to the office after; I have something you'll want to hear on the tattoos.'

He opens his bag and begins. Max and Bastian go back to the car to speak with the man who found the body and is now sitting, badly shaken, in the back of a squad car. Max and Bastian join him. 'Sorry to keep you, sir. We won't be long,' Max says.

By the time they have completed their brief interview, they see Paul has arrived.

As the two detectives join him, he looks up. 'Max, Bastian, interesting one this. The killer has used a very sharp blade, possibly a scalpel. They removed cleanly the eviscerated bits. The killing cut was to the femoral artery, which they have sliced expertly, suggesting at least a modicum of anatomical knowledge. Whoever did this knew not to sever the artery but lay it open. You see, a severed artery can constrict into the muscle, and this reduces the flow and can aid clotting, though without treatment, it would still have done the job. But in this case, the bleeding would have been swift and he would have succumbed within minutes. Mind you, he'd probably have bled to death from all the other wounds, eventually. Quite shocking, really.'

'Do you think a nurse would have such knowledge?' Max asks.

'Oh, yes. However, the person who executed this did so with a zealous prejudice. Death occurred during the night, he was most definitely not killed here, and they moved him shortly after giving him the chop,' he pauses, chortling at his joke. Max and Bastian glance at one another. 'The rest, my friends, I will reveal at the PM. Along with all the usual customers, we've got that CI of yours to autopsy today, so we're looking at tomorrow, late morning for this one. Keep this up, Max, and I'll get you a season ticket, eh?'

❖❖❖

Otti and Udo arrive at Günther's yard. Udo looks at Otti, narrowing his eyes. 'I'll do the talking, okay?'

She shrugs. 'Sure, whatever.'

They open the office door and enter. Smiling, Maria looks up. 'How can I help you?'

'We're Kripo. We want to ask you and your father some questions, and we want to look at your van,' Udo orders.

Her smile turns to a scowl. 'Have you any identification?'

They show their badges. She scrutinises them. 'Do you have a warrant?'

Udo leans on the desk. 'We don't need a warrant, *Fräulein*. Now, is your father in?'

'You need a warrant to see the van. Anyway, we've already kindly allowed your colleague to inspect the vehicle.'

Otti comes round the side of the desk, commanding Maria's attention. 'Look, we'd be grateful if you'd allow us another quick look. This is a murder investigation, and you'll find that where we suspect a vehicle is used in the execution of a crime, we can examine it without a warrant. And right now, that's precisely what we think.'

Maria returns Otti's steely gaze. 'You already have, and we answered your question regarding its whereabouts on the specific dates. We confirmed the van was here over both weekends. In answer to your other...'

Udo loses patience. 'Listen, *Fräulein*, either cooperate with us, or we'll place you under arrest on suspicion of murder and take you down to the station and question you there.'

The door to the inner office bursts open, and a red-faced Günther appears. 'What is going on here? Why are you harassing my employee? We have been most cooperative. This is a place of business, and we have a lot to do, so what is it you want?'

Before Udo can continue, Otti says, 'Can you tell us, please, where you and your daughter were on the last two weekends?'

For a moment, Günther considers. 'All right, all of you, come to my office; we'll talk there.'

They troop in and sit down. 'Now, on the first weekend, we were both here on the Saturday until lunchtime. We went to a restaurant for lunch, left about three, and went home. Maria was out on Saturday with friends, and my wife and I went dancing. Sunday, we were home and then had lunch with friends. We had a quiet evening at home, watching an American film on television. I was back here first thing Monday morning. No one had moved the van.'

'What about you, Maria?' Udo asks.

'As my father told you, I went to a friend's house on Saturday, and we went to a party. I stayed the night. I returned home Sunday for lunch and then stayed home, all right?'

Günther leans back. 'On the other weekend, I was away with my wife; we went to see relatives in Brunswick. Maria had a friend stay to keep her company; that's it.'

For a moment, Udo scrutinises Günther. 'Names, please? So we can check. Also, I need a list of all your employees.'

'We'd like to have a quick look at the van once more. It will avoid us coming back with a warrant and causing you further inconvenience,' Otti says.

'Well, detective, as you put it so politely, yes, you may have a look. Maria, show the detectives, please?'

Twenty minutes later, they're back in the car with the list of employees.

Udo grips the steering wheel, the white of his knuckles showing. 'Don't you ever undermine my authority again, understand?'

Otti bites her tongue. 'I was only trying to help. At least now we've got what we came for, right?'

'I told you I was going to do the talking. You're still on probation.'

'Why are you being such a dick? Also, I didn't realise you were my boss now.' She regrets saying it as soon as the words come out, cursing herself for being so petty.

'No, it's not okay because I wanted to show them they can't piss us about, but you made us look like a pair of idiots. I'm the ranking officer here, so if I fucking say I'm doing the talking, you keep it shut, right?'

'Okay, look, we've got what we came for, and I apologise if I misread your intentions. I don't want to sit here and argue with you, all right? Anyway, what did you think about the van?'

For a moment, Udo sits smouldering silently, then starting the engine and driving off, says, 'I agree with Jürgen. I think the van looks too clean. Also, they're both lying to us.'

'Let's check their stories, but yes, I agree there's something not quite right.'

Udo gives her a look. 'Oh, I feel so much better you agree.'

Otti looks out of the windscreen, Bastian's words echoing in her head—*don't rise to the bait*—and keeps her counsel.

❖ ❖ ❖

Lutz goes over to the Cona vacuum coffee maker. 'I don't know about you boys, but I need a good, strong coffee.'

Max smiles. 'You won't get an argument from us.'

They sit. Lutz pushes an ashtray over to Bastian and fishes out his pipe. 'So, I've been asking around to see if I could get something on those intriguing tattoos and scored a result and found someone. One of my old *Kriegsmarine* buddies came up with a Russian sailor, and yesterday, they came over and had a look. It's fascinating, really. You know, you get to a time in life when you think you know stuff, when actually you know nothing at all. Lutz lays out some photos. Let's begin with victim number one. The tattoo on his back tells the story of him being a traveller or thief who is available for hire, but the Prometheus side shows he is perpetually damned.'

Bastian laughs. 'How prophetic.'

'Yes indeed. Second, those epaulettes on his shoulders with two stars denote rank, in his case, a lieutenant. Obvious really, but still, you never know. Three, the knife through the neck shows he has committed murder while incarcerated and is available for hire. The rose on his chest shows they convicted and sent him to prison before he turned eighteen, and it's likely he was the victim of sexual abuse. I understand that the sodomy of the young and weak is quite common in such places. Apparently, it's a power thing.' Lutz grimaces.

'The cathedrals denote prison sentences: the more domes or towers, the more sentences served. The skulls atop show his badge as a murderer. So, all-in-all, a jolly, likeable chap.' He pauses, tamping down his pipe and relights it, blowing out a cloud of fragrant smoke.

'Now, victim number two. He taps his finger on one photo. The picture of Stalin on his chest was there to protect him: the theory being that authorities in a firing squad would not shoot at an image of their leader. The tattoo of the tiger shows a hostility toward authority, so too does the tattoo of the skull with teeth bared. Now, the eyes just above the waist can have two meanings: they're homosexual or a paedophile. The point is, by placing the eyes just above the hips, the penis becomes the nose. Either way, they'd also have been victimised in prison.'

'That may have been so,' says Max, 'but I'm sure they stopped being victims and became perpetrators somewhere along the line. These are not good men, and their killers dispatched them in a way that suggests a payback. Whatever they did, it wasn't pretty.'

Bastian stubs out his cigarette. 'So, we've got two victims who have been in the Russian prison system, and one of whom was also, at some time during the war, in the SS. Our man this morning did not have tattoos. Is there anything else that has come up in forensics?'

'Not long prior to death, both ate and drank well: a good meal of pork and potato, washed down with copious beer and vodka. There was no sign of drug abuse other than alcohol and cigarettes. Both had damaged livers. Of course, smoking seems to be an essential part of all men. Save you, Max.'

'Well, you're not married to a doctor, and besides, anyone can see that sucking in lungfuls of smoke can't be a good thing, surely? I admit, however, that I sorely miss the habit, which, as you both know, I imbibe only on the very odd occasion in memorial to the time a cigarette saved my life.'

Lutz laughs out loud. 'Oh God, not that story again.'

Lighting another cigarette and holding out his coffee cup, Bastian says, 'I'll smoke to that.'

Lutz replenishes their coffee. 'By the way, Max, I've had the sample tested against that perfume of yours.'

'And?'

'Surprisingly, a match. You're pretty good at the old perfumery thing.'

'Well, well, is it now? A woman with taste, eh? Gabrielle told me that most customers who purchased that perfume were older women, and so far, the description of our suspect is that of a young woman. And what makes a person splash on perfume before they go out for a spot of murder?'

'Perhaps,' says Lutz, 'they work in a place where they need to look and smell good, you know, like an expensive hotel or high-end fashion shop?'

'Perhaps,' Max muses.

'Maybe she's on the game and has taken against some of her clients and is having some pay-back?' Bastian suggests.

Max nods and sighs. 'The more we know, the more we don't. One question simply brings three more.'

❖❖❖

Some thirty minutes after Otti and Udo have left, Christian arrives at the yard. He enters the office. 'Hi, Maria, what does Günther want me to do today?'

'Oh, hey Chris, actually he wants a quick word with you. Are you all right?'

'Oh, yeah, tired, didn't sleep well.'

'Go on in.'

As the door opens, Günther looks up. 'Chris, my boy, come in, sit down.' Christian slumps down. 'You look pale; are you sick?'

'No, I'm fine, just tired.'

'So, my young friend, I've had the *Polizei* here asking about the van, you know, where it was the last two weekends.'

For a moment, Christian looks nervous, shifting in his chair. 'What did you tell them?'

'I told them it was here. Look, I'm not cross, but if you are mixed up in something, tell me. I don't like or trust the *Polizei*, particularly those Kripo bastards, so if I can help, I will.'

Christian frowns, wishing Angelika were here; she'd know what to do.

Günther sits back and smiles. 'The woman detective said that their enquiry was in connection with a murder,' he pushes a newspaper across the desk, 'and interestingly enough, these two evil-looking ruffians got theirs on those dates. So, Chris, if you know anything about these or are involved, tell me, okay? You can trust me.'

Christian struggles, perspiration beading on his forehead, and begins rocking back and forth. 'No, Günther, I couldn't kill anyone. I have nothing to do with this. Me and Ange just used the van to move some furniture for our flat, honest. It must be some mistake.'

Günther thinks for a minute. 'It's okay, Chris, okay, calm down. I believe you. Look, I want you to go to the merchants and pick up this order and take it up to the site. After that, you can go home, get some rest. Now drive carefully, and I'll see you later.'

As he leaves, Maria says, 'See you, Chris, take care.' She watches him go and joins her father. 'What do you think? You believe him?'

'I think so; it makes little sense. Why would he kill men like that? And what about Angelika? I mean, she wouldn't say boo to a goose, would she? No, it's absurd. The *Polizei* are barking up the wrong tree. I mean, how many more vans like ours are there?'

'What are you going to do?'

'Nothing, I believe him, not them.'

Maria sighs. 'Are you sure, pops?'

'What do you mean?'

'Well, okay, let's just say that he is involved, and you cover up for him, and, you know, it goes bad?'

'You forget what they are capable of, Maria. Chris is a good boy.'

She shrugs. 'Okay, I hope you know what you're doing; that's all.'

17

Oft my jealousy shapes faults that are not

UDO LOOKS ACROSS AT OTTI. 'It'll be better if we split up and cover the ground more quickly. I'll check out the alibis while you interview Günther's men, okay?'

For a moment she scrutinises him. 'All right, I guess. If you drop me back at base, I can pick up my car.'

Arriving back, Udo stops the car. Otti hops out and is about to lean in and say something, but without a word, Udo drives off. Watching him go, she wonders what she's going to do about him. Climbing into her VW, she sets off to the Reinickendorf district. She is glad to be off on her own but unsure whether Udo has suggested this to trap her into making a mistake. She counsels herself to stop being paranoid, but she thinks about what Bastian said—*If you're not sure, ask, and don't mess it up*—she thinks, I'm a big girl and if I make a mistake, I'll take the consequences. Better just make sure I do it right. As she drives, she runs through the questions she'll ask. But worry nags at her, believing that Udo has done this on purpose, that interviewing a load of builders might put her on the spot. She shakes her head and laughs, saying out loud, 'To hell with it, get a grip, girl, and don't take any shit.'

She parks up and goes off to find the foreman. Conrad Schmidt is sitting in the site office; knocking, she enters and takes out her badge. 'I'm *Kriminalmeister* Jäger, are you, Herr Schmidt?'

Looking up, the striking detective takes him aback. 'Yes, yes, but please call me Conrad,' and removing a stack of files from the spare seat and dusting it off, says, 'please, detective, sit down. What is it I can do for you?' She remains standing.

Her fears are unfounded. Conrad and his crew are both cooperative and polite, though one or two of them behave sexually, one of the younger guys sits, his legs wide apart and his eyes flitting between her breasts and her groin, but regardless, one by one, she questions them. All except one have an alibi for at least one of the last two weekends. Erich Thiel tells her he was home both weekends but lives alone. He is a slightly built, fifty-seven-year-old electrician with a prosthetic leg. A radio operator in the war, he tells her he had stepped on a mine, blowing his leg clean off. His outlook and demeanour impress her.

'I was lucky. It didn't blow off my manhood, eyes or arms, though of course, it's my hands and eyes I need, and the best part was it didn't kill me,' he'd said, smiling disarmingly.

Finishing the last on her list, she goes off to find Conrad. 'These are delightful houses.'

'Ah, detective, thanks. We take pride in our work. I trust that you have got everything you need?'

'Yes, thank you. I appreciate your time.'

She's about to turn and go when she spots the blue van driving out of the site. At the wheel is a powerfully built man whom she has not interviewed, and as the vehicle passes by, he stares right at her. She turns to Conrad. 'Who's that?'

'Oh, that's Christian. He's just come up with some supplies and dropped them off.'

'He isn't on my list; does he work for Günther?'

'Well, yes, I guess so. You know, he runs errands for him. He's the boss's pet, if you know what I mean? Only works part time, and to be honest, he's not all there, if you know what I mean, a bit of a village idiot.'

'What do you mean by that?'

'Simple, you know?'

'But he's fine driving, and he can carry out work tasks?'

'Oh, yeah, sure, all that, but he's slow-witted. I don't know why Günther keeps him on, but he seems to have a soft spot for him.'

'He looks kind of big in the van, is he?'

Conrad laughs out loud. 'My God, he is fucking enormous. Excuse my language, we all call him Golem, you know, like the monster of Prague?'

'And is he? A monster?'

'No, not really, it's just his size, plus he can be a little scratchy, you know, sullen.'

'Do you know if he's married or got a girlfriend?'

'Married? Girlfriend? Oh God, I doubt it, but hell, I don't know, never even crossed my mind. I mean, what sort of woman would want that…' he stops, checking himself, 'anyway, I can't imagine he's going around murdering people in the forest, can you?'

She ignores the question. 'You don't happen to know how old he is, do you?'

'As it happens, I know exactly how old he is: twenty-six, going on twelve, if you know what I mean? We all have a whip round come birthdays, so it is hard not to know.'

'Any reason you can think of why he's not on my list?'

'You'd have to ask Günther that, sorry. Look, I don't want to be rude, but I really must get back to work, so if there isn't anything else?'

'Just one more question: do you know where Christian lives?'

'No, sorry. Günther will have his address.'

'Okay, thanks.'

Conrad watches as she returns to her car and drives away. As she leaves, one of the other men joins him, a dark twinkle in his eyes. 'I bet she looks terrific naked. I wouldn't mind giving her a good seeing to, eh, Conrad? If all *Polizei* were like that, I'd get myself arrested every weekend.'

'You've got a grubby mind, Brandt. Anyway, she's way out of your league. Come on, let's get back to it, shall we?'

❖ ❖ ❖

When Jürgen gets back from the archives, he finds Max and Bastian making coffee and chatting in the kitchenette. 'Hey, boss, I've found something on Günther Alsbach that may explain his hostility.'

'I'm all ears?'

'Have you heard of the S-Bahn murders?'

'Sure, the Paul Ogorzow murders, back in what '40, '41?'

'Correct. Anyway, seems that in Jan and Feb of '41, he raped and killed two women, both of whom turned out to be pregnant. Anyway, at the time, there was a lot of pressure to find the killer, and they hauled in a twenty-five-year-old man by the name of Klaus Alsbach. According to the record, and I quote: "the subject is of limited intellectual ability yet displays a demonic aggression that predisposes him to unnatural acts", end quote. Apparently, after a weekend of interrogation, he confessed to the murders. With no trial, they sent him to Plötzensee Prison and two days later, they had him guillotined! It wasn't until eventually they caught Ogorzow that they realised the mistake. The trouble was, it made no difference and despite efforts from his family, the authorities never granted a pardon.'

'Let me guess. Günther's his brother?'

Jürgen nods. 'Correct. One Günther Heinrich Bernhard Alsbach, then aged thirty-five, and serving in the Pioneers.'

'I thought there might be something. Back in the day, I think our lot rattled many a cage and not in a good way, and that would certainly cloud your view of the Kripo, wouldn't it? Good work. I think we need to have a formal chat with Günther Alsbach. You two arrest him for obstruction and bring him in.

Otti puts her head around the door. 'Who's obstructing?' She tells them about her chance meeting with Christian.

Max smiles. 'So, this Christian might be simple or retarded somehow, just like Günther's brother, and he has a soft spot for him, eh? And you say he is a big guy?'

She nods. 'He's huge, and they said he could be sullen and, in their words, scratchy.'

Max smiles again. 'Hallelujah, things are happening. You most definitely did right coming back to report. Where's Udo, anyway?'

'We thought it would be better to split up, so he went to check alibis.'

'Hmm, okay, fine. You have any problems interviewing a bunch of builders?'

'Save some wandering eyes and not very subtle comments; they were fine, really. Apart from one, they all had alibis for the dates, which I'll follow up.'

'Who's unaccounted for?'

'Guy called Eric Thiel, amputee, electrician who lives alone.'

'What was your take on him?'

'He seemed pretty straight, and I got the feeling he was telling the truth.'

'Okay, put his name on the board until we can rule him out.'

Jürgen and Bastian set off to haul in Günther. Max takes Otti to his office and goes through the tattoo evidence, asking her to annotate the pictures and put them up on the board. He briefs her about the newest victim and message.

She flips through the disturbing images. 'God, they seem to build in confidence, don't they?'

'Yes. It's possible that they're taking their victims in order of importance, maybe? Paul says that this time the killer was most likely right-handed.'

'So, they're alternating? Or perhaps the killer's ambidextrous? Or are they both victims, and they're killing the ones who hurt them or just sharing the burden? Questions, questions.'

'Let's say that this Christian fellow is the guy working with our unidentified woman.' He pauses, thinking, 'How old did you say he is?'

'Twenty-six, why?'

'Hmm, I'm not sure, but I'm wondering about something. Anyway, don't worry. He's young and big, which fits with the suggestion that one of our two is powerful. Trouble is, all we have is circumstantial, but my gut tells me there is something here. I wonder if anyone else is in their sights? If this Christian fellow is involved, and we can get his address, perhaps we can shut this down quickly?'

Otti nods. 'When he drove by, he looked directly at me, you know, had a long look as though he knew who I was. He seemed confused, looked stressed and worried, scared even.'

'Have you eaten?' She shakes her head. 'Come on, let's grab a bite. I've got a feeling it's going to be a long day.'

They head over to Malinda's and settle into a booth. 'Actually, I'm starving,' says Otti, laughing, 'all those fit young builders have given me an appetite.'

They order. 'We haven't much on Günther, so why are you getting him in?'

'I want to rattle his cage. I expect he'll stall for time, you know, get his lawyer in, be evasive. I don't expect him to cooperate. I haven't got enough to get a warrant to search his house and office, but I may get something. In my experience, if you poke hard enough, you'll get a reaction.'

'Do you mind if I ask you a personal question?'

'Yeah, of course, shoot.'

'Sorry, it's silly really, but I'm curious. The scar on your cheek, which you always touch when you're thinking, how did you get it?'

'Ah, my little cigarette story. It was late on in the war, and we'd been flogging it out for days. I was in Hungary then. Anyway, we had a bit of a lull, and I was sitting on the turret of my tank, took out a smoke, but I couldn't get my lighter to work. So, I jumped down to get one and just as I hit the ground, BOOM! a Russian 100 mm armour-piercing round hit the turret practically ripping it off, and if I'd been sitting there, it would have been the end of old Max.'

'So, a cigarette saved your life?'

'Yes, exactly, but that's how it was: you got lucky, you lived, when your luck ran out, you died. Trouble is, as it got to the end, the odds stacked up against us. Did you know that four out of five dead fell fighting the Russians and most of those in the final year?'

'No, I didn't. What a waste.' She raises her glass. 'Anyway, here's to your luck never running out. Speaking of luck, I heard there was an armed robbery here recently, and you got shot at but a helmet saved you or some such... actually, sounds a bit nuts, doesn't it?'

Max laughs. 'Oh, the office chit-chat. Yes, it was just before you joined. Now that's a story for another day. Ask Markus when you see him next, he was there and I'm sure he'll tell it so much better than I. Changing the subject, you feel ready for your firearms test tomorrow?'

'Yes, looking forward to it.'

'You'll walk it. Your scores are impressive and Bern, who is seldom one to give praise, said you're outstanding, adding that you've got some guys worried, and there had been a lot more practising going on.'

'Thing is, shooting at targets is one thing, but what's it like shooting at a person?'

Max leans in. 'When it comes to the time when pulling the trigger means you save yourself, a colleague or members of the public, you'll make that decision. Remember the training and don't hesitate, that is what gets you killed. I know you've got what it takes. I wouldn't have taken you on if I wasn't sure about that.'

'Well, let's hope it won't be soon, but I'll be ready.'

'So, are things all right with Udo? I mean, you split up today. Really, it's better to stay with your partner, that would be my preference. So, whose idea was it to go it alone?'

Without hesitation, Otti replies, 'Things are fine, and we just thought that there was so much ground to cover, it would be better to do it that way. I'm sorry if we messed up.'

'No, it's okay, no one messed up, but for safety's sake, it's better to avoid solo policing. Most cops that get killed are alone. After tomorrow's test, we'll issue you a weapon, which will give you an edge. Ultimately, I like my team to be free to make operational decisions for themselves, you know, as things develop, so from that point of view, what you and Udo did today made sense...'

'I feel a "but" coming.'

'No, not really. Just this is your first case assignment, you're still on probation, unarmed, and this is a murder investigation. If you were in my shoes, which hopefully one day you will be, what would you advise?'

'Good point.'

'You did a good job today, and all is well, and we're making progress. So enough said, life is learning, well, it is for me. We all make mistakes, like me not putting a tail on Der Fuchs, which ended badly, and I lost a useful CI. He was a rat, but he didn't deserve that.'

Otti smiles, her dark eyes twinkling. 'Poetically put. Do you think we'll ever catch his killer?'

'Doubt it. I'm guessing he took the pictures to a Russian with some clout, probably organised crime; it was the world Der Fuchs moved in and stupidly gave himself away as an informant. One thing criminals hate is a stool pigeon.'

'Thus, the warning scrawled on his forehead in blood.'

'Yes. His execution ordered, and the killer back in the East. I've put out what we've got to the VoPo, but it won't come to anything. Usually, with this type of crime, somebody brags, and word gets around and back to us. We got good fingerprints from the photographs and one from the writing in blood, so if we can get a body to match that, we can make it stick. In the meantime, the file will remain open. If you like, I'll assign it to you, and in your rare down moments, you can keep it on the simmer?'

'Sure, that would be good; my first case. Anyway, that was the most subtle bollocking I've ever had.'

He smiles, a flicker in his eyes. 'And there was me thinking I'd covered myself. I think little will get past you, will it, Ottilie Jäger?'

18

Who speaks not truly, lies

DRIVING BACK TO THE YARD, Christian wonders who the woman was speaking to Conrad? She must have been *Polizei*, mustn't she? Günther said there was a woman detective asking questions. Now she is nosing around at the site, looked right at me and would have asked Conrad who I was, wouldn't she? They know who I am, and they know about the van. Panic rising, he drives more quickly, hurrying back to the yard so that he can get home and warn Angelika.

After the long night, she has managed some sleep and is feeling better but is unsure when to deal with Johann. Should they proceed tonight or wait and see what happens? They can't keep him too long, having to keep visiting to give him food and water. No, it is best they get it over with, and the sooner, the better.

Hearing heavy footsteps out on the landing, she tenses, relaxing when the key turns and Christian enters. He looks stressed. 'Ange, the *Polizei*, they have been to see Günther, and they talked to Conrad at the site. The detective saw me; she looked right at me like she knew. She'll know who I am; they'll be coming for us; we must go.'

'Chris, Chris, calm down; you're not making any sense. Who are you talking about?' Steering him to a chair, she sits him down. 'Now, slowly, tell me what happened.'

After relating the story, he calms down as though the passing of the problem, like a confession of sins, has absolved him. For a few moments, she stalks around the room thinking. Then, she turns to him, her eyes sparkling. 'Okay, this is what we're going to do.'

❖❖❖

Maria opens the office door. 'They're back, pops. It's the one who came first time, and he's with a big, older guy, probably the boss.'

Günther sighs. 'How tiresome. All right, my love, send them right in.'

Entering the office and showing their badges, Bastian says, 'Günther Alsbach, I am arresting you for obstruction. You may consult with a lawyer...'

Grabbing his coat, Günther snarls, 'Yeah, yeah, I know all that crap. Let's get this over with, shall we?'

Maria watches them leave. Going over to the old filing cabinet, she takes out Christian's employee card, carries it over to the sink and burns it. Calling Conrad, she tells him that there won't be anyone in the office for the rest of the day and, locking up, she drives over to Christian's flat and knocks. There is no answer. She scribbles a note, sliding it under the door.

Thirty minutes later, Bastian, Jürgen, and Günther are back at the station. Bastian takes him down to the sub-basement and puts him in a cell. 'We'll call your lawyer; can I get you any water?'

Günther looks at him, his eyes glaring. 'No, I want nothing from you, Kripo man.'

Bastian shrugs. 'Okay, whatever.' He closes the door and throws the bolt.

Günther is a patient man, happy to play their games, and they won't be able to trip him up like they did his brother. He still doubts that Christian is guilty of anything. He's sure they have little; otherwise, they would have arrested him for something more specific. Obstruction sounds to him like clutching at straws. He lies back on the bunk bolted to the wall and closes his eyes.

❖ ❖ ❖

With Angelika following in the Beetle, Christian drives their van over to the Teichstraße. She parks the car a few streets away and, cutting across the rough ground, takes a shortcut to the basement. Huddled away, with a view of the building, is Wolfgang the vagrant. He has watched an enormous, tall man, arrive and is just thinking of breaking cover and going to have a peek when he spots the other one. He's sure it is the same person as before. He's also sure it is a young woman. A shot of blond hair visible from under the hood, which annoyingly covers her face. She walks, head down, to the house and disappears inside, followed by the clang of the heavy door shutting. Waiting a few minutes, he goes to investigate and, standing by the basement door, he listens. Nothing. As he turns to return to his hiding place, he knocks over a plank of wood, which thuds heavily to the floor. Without delay, he takes off to hide.

Angelika stands looking at the piece of wood. A cat jumps down from a broken wall and prowls, purring around her legs. Bending down, she says, 'Hello, kitty, was that you knocking the wood, or was it a nosey parker? Shall we see?' For a moment, she strokes the cat, then she cocks her Makarov pistol and goes outside and has a good look around.

Wolfgang has hidden in an old outbuilding. From within, he can watch the comings and the goings, but if danger threatens, he can crawl into a void beneath the floor, covering the entrance with an old piece of carpet. Now hidden in the void, he cannot see Angelika as she comes out of the house, her hooded eyes scrutinising the area. For a while, she watches in silence, but there is no one about; there never is; that's why they chose this place. Satisfied the cat caused the plank to fall, she goes back inside.

'What was it?' queries Christian.

She makes the pistol safe and tucks it into the waistband of her jeans. 'It was just a cat. Is he awake?'

'Yes, he's lost some of his fight, though. He wants to lie down.'

'Tough. Soon he can lie down forever.'

'He drank some water. Said he was going to kill us.'

'Is that the best he's got? Pathetic! Anyway, we won't give him the chance, will we? Let's settle down. We'll wait for dark.'

'Did you bring the stuff?'

'Yes, I've got it.'

Soon after she started all this, Angelika had spent hours poring over medical books, enhancing her limited knowledge of anatomy, drugs, and surgical procedures and had laid in a few select items; one of them being an anaesthetic drug, Sodium Amytal, and the other Amphetamine Sulphate; both bought, for a fee, from a fellow waitress's brother, who works at a hospital pharmacy and has developed a useful black market sideline supplying prescription drugs.

❖❖❖

In the interview room, Max and Otti sit across the table from Günther and his lawyer. Otti has a pad and pencil ready.

Max regards Günther, who stares back at him with leaden eyes. 'So, can you confirm your full name, please?'

'Günther Heinrich Bernhard Alsbach.'

Max strokes the scar on his cheek, then standing, walks over and leans against the wall. 'So, Herr Alsbach, we have an eyewitness that saw your van in Spandauer Forest at the exact time a body was left there and a witness who saw your van at the scene the following morning. Yet you say your vehicle was in your yard, correct?'

'That's correct, so it can't have been my van, can it?'

'Well, there's the problem. We've checked all vans of that make and colour, and it's only yours that we're not sure about, particularly since the colour has changed and you failed to report it. Also, you failed to tell us about your employee, Christian, whom my colleague here spotted earlier today, driving the same van. What do you say to that?'

'He's not my employee, and the colour business was an oversight; anyone can make that sort of mistake.'

'Who is this Christian to you, anyway? Why protect him?'

'I help him out by giving him a little casual work from time to time. It's nothing permanent, and he is most definitely not an employee. And as far as I know, he needs no protection.'

Otti stops writing and looks up. 'That's not what your site foreman, Conrad, says. He said he works for you, and he didn't know why you kept him on, which implies he works for the firm, does it not?'

Günther scoffs. 'Semantics. I think, detectives, you are playing games. Keeping someone on is not the same. Besides, Conrad does not run the business. I do.'

Otti drops her pen and leans back, holding open her arms and hands, palms open. 'But he works for your firm and uses the vehicle we're interested in, so it is odd, at least to us, that you would not put him on the list or, at the very least, mention him. Unless that is, you are covering for him.'

Günther is about to speak when his lawyer stops him. 'Listen, detectives, it sounds very much to me as though you are on a fishing trip. Either come up with some concrete evidence or release my client immediately.'

Max sits and leans across the table. 'Okay, Herr Alsbach. I put it to you, you are lying about the whereabouts of your van. You know it was not in your yard on those days, and you know Christian was driving it, wasn't he?'

Günther looks away and holds up his hands. 'Sorry, detective, but you have the wrong van and the wrong man. What else can I tell you?'

Max sits back and drops a file on the desk. 'I know why you won't cooperate with us in this matter.'

Günther feigns interest. 'Oh, why would that be, then?'

'You have been obstructive right from the start, which is quite telling. In my experience, people who have nothing to hide are usually accommodating. But you, Herr Alsbach, are not.'

The lawyer leans forward. 'Where's this all going, detective? From where I'm standing, you have absolutely no grounds to have detained my client, other than some circumstantial evidence regarding a van analogous to his spotted at one scene.'

Getting up, Max walks behind Günther and, leaning over his shoulder, says, 'Tell me about your brother, Klaus.'

Günther's face turns bright red, his eyes smoulder, and he clenches his fists. Max, his face close to Günther's, can feel his passion, his growing rage.

Max returns to his seat. 'Did you think we would not check? You have a perfect reason not to assist us in our enquiries, haven't you?' Günther remains silently defiant. Max leans closer, his intense eyes fixing Günther's like laser beams. 'Haven't you, Herr Alsbach?'

For a moment, Günther's lawyer looks concerned. 'I wish to speak with my client for a moment. Alone.'

Max stands. 'Very well, you have the room. Call us when you're done talking. Take your time.'

The door closes, the lawyer waits. Getting up, he goes and checks no one is outside. 'Günther, is there something you want to tell me? I mean, they seem to have something. Do they?'

'It's nothing. It has nothing to do with this matter.'

'That's not what they seem to think, so if you want my legal advice and help, you need to tell me.'

'All right, all right.' He tells the story.

'So, are you lying to them?'

'No, I'm fucking not. They've got it all wrong.'

'Listen, from the evidence they've presented, they don't have any reason to hold you. But I advise you don't obstruct them either. From what I know about Becker, he isn't anything like the old Kripo.'

'Ah, don't let them fool you with their Nazi charms; they'll shoot you soon as spit.'

Opening the door, the lawyer calls them back.

Otti and Max sit. 'So, let's stop playing games, shall we, and start again? What do you know about the van and Christian?' Max asks.

'Nothing, I stand by what I said. I should have told you about Christian working odd jobs for me, but he and the van are not what you are looking for.'

'Okay, in that case, you won't mind if we take it in for examination, will you? Then we can rule it out, once and for all, can't we?'

Günther sighs. 'Very well, all right.'

'I want Christian's address.'

'I don't have it. I only know he lives in the Kreuzberg district.'

'I want your permission to search your office records.'

'Fine, but I want to be present.'

'One more thing? Does Christian live alone?'

'As far as I know, yes. He's mentioned no one else.'

'No girlfriend, sister, wife?'

'As I said, as far as I know, he's a loner.'

Returning to Günther's yard, they conduct a thorough but fruitless search. Günther, a satisfied expression spread across his face, says, 'See, I told you I don't have his address.'

'Please, let me have all the keys to the van.'

Günther opens his desk drawer and, taking out two keys, hands them over.

'Thank you. A recovery vehicle will be here in the morning to collect it.'

'When will I get it back?'

'Assuming it is clean, a few days.'

'How do I know someone won't plant evidence in it?'

'Listen, Herr Alsbach, we're not in the business of planting evidence. We want to get to the truth, nothing more. I'm sorry about what happened to your brother, but those were different times, different men. We'll be in touch.'

Fixing Max's gaze, Günther's eyes narrow to darkened slits. 'You aren't worthy to mention my brother. He was a good boy, and so is Christian. Go bother someone else, Kommissar Becker.'

Max and Otti get back in the car and drive off. Max says, 'Did you notice the smell?'

She nods. 'Something had been burnt. Also, did you see his face when you searched the filing cabinet? It was a smug expression, like he had one up on us.'

'He's lying, I'm sure of it. Trouble is, what exactly is he lying about? Is it Christian, the van, or is he involved in the murders? What colour hair does his daughter have?'

'Blond.'

'So, that fits too, doesn't it? And why wasn't she at the office?'

'You think he, Christian, and Maria might be in this together?'

'It's a distinct possibility. But if they destroyed Christian's employee record, and he saw you this morning, maybe they're buying him some time. Let's get back and see if Udo has checked the alibis. Meantime, I've left a tail on him.'

'You have?'

He nods, smiling. 'I never make the same mistake twice. Bastian's sitting on him as we speak.'

19

In time we hate that which we often fear

GÜNTHER SITS AT HIS DESK, thinking. The last couple of days have brought back memories, things he has buried deep and never dealt with. He has never forgiven himself for not being there when his brother needed him. At the time of his arrest, Günther had been in France carrying out engineering works for the *Wehrmacht* and the Führer. He had not wanted to go into the army, but when called, the Pioneers were a natural choice, and he thought that at least he'd be doing useful things and not much killing. How wrong had been this assumption.

He remembers almost word-for-word the letter his mother had sent with news of Klaus's arrest, confession, and execution. It had been short and cold, and even though his parents knew, in the eyes of the Nazis, people with failings like Klaus's could never become good Aryan Germans and were disappearing, they had believed what the authorities told them. She had told him how ashamed they were to have such a child, useless, now a murderer and enemy of the state. But Günther knew his brother, gentle and loving, could never do that to anyone. He had considered deserting and going over to the other side. Instead, he stayed, botching engineering works, sabotaging wherever he knew he'd get away with it. He didn't care if he died, so he'd be first in to repair a bridge, rig explosives, clear mines and last to leave as the enemy came. Ironically, his acts earned him promotion and an Iron Cross First Class; he embodied what a good Aryan should be: brave and heroic, at least that is how he appeared to his superiors. On one occasion, late in the war, he had been alone in a bunkhouse rigging explosives to destroy a bridge. A young, strutting peacock of an SS officer had come in shouting at him to hurry. Günther had stood up, saw that the man was alone, pulled his pistol and shot him between the eyes. The expression on the man's face was priceless.

After the French released Günther in late 1946, he returned to Berlin. His parents, wife, and young daughter had survived the war. The city was in ruins, so it seemed logical that, together with his father, they begin a building business. To all intents and purposes, Klaus slipped into the dark past, another innocent victim of the Third Reich.

Günther remembered the day Christian had come to his yard looking for work, struck by how much he had reminded him of Klaus. Not physically, but in his manner, the way he viewed the world as an innocent. At first, Günther had given him a full-time job as an apprentice bricklayer, but it had become clear that Christian was unsuited to such work. If it had been any other person, he would have let him go, but he felt that by helping him, he might atone for not being there for his brother. He paid well and allowed Christian to work as he was able. The business did well and life was good.

But now, history seems to repeat itself. The Kripo, which he believes is still a Nazi hotbed, has latched onto Christian; easy prey, who, with a little pressure, will break and tell them what they want to know. Günther cannot let that happen.

With hatred burning in his heart, he opens his desk drawer and, taking out a bottle, pours himself a measure, gulping it down in one. Picking up the phone, he calls Maria. 'Hello, my darling, can you come back to the office? There's something I need you to do.' He listens to her reply. 'Yes, thanks, see you soon.' Hanging up, he goes to the window and looking out at the light slipping away, knows what he must do and, taking a few items from a secure locker in the yard, goes out to prepare the van.

A while later, Maria arrives. 'Hey, pop, what do you want me to do?'

He hugs her and looks into her anxious eyes, a moment. 'If I were that detective, I would have someone watching this office, wouldn't you?'

She shrugs. 'I don't know, pop, where's this going?'

'I'm going to take the van and drive around for ten minutes. I want you to watch and see if anyone follows me, okay?'

'I thought you'd given the keys to Becker?'

He smiles and places his hand lovingly on her cheek. 'Oh, darling, no, I have another key, naturally. Your papa is a smart man, no?'

With a censorious look, she shakes her head. 'All right, go, go. I'll watch.'

Bastian has a good view of the yard and, seeing Maria arrive, notes down the time. A few minutes later, the van drives out. Bastian starts the engine, saying out loud. 'Here we go, just as Max predicted.' For some minutes, they drive around making random turns, and ten minutes later, they are back at the yard. Parking up, Bastian knows what's going down, and there's nothing he can do about it. Günther knows he's being watched. Looking at the time, he hopes Max will soon return, as with two cars, they can probably fool Günther.

When Max and Otti get back, the rest of the team are at their desks typing up the day's reports, a busy clatter from the Olympia SM3 typewriters. He calls a quick meeting. 'So, Udo, bring us up to date on the alibis for Günther and Maria.'

'Yes, boss, they check out. I've either seen or spoken to all but one on the list, and that was the couple they had lunch with that Sunday.'

'Okay, either we're barking up the wrong tree, or Christian, the van, and an unidentified woman are our targets. Günther is going to a lot of trouble to cover for Christian. He has motive and reason: revenge for the death of his brother and his protection and fondness for Christian. It is possible that he is involved and is using others to carry out the murders. But my guess is he's just buying them time. The question is, how far will he go? Any thoughts?'

'Shouldn't we be watching him?' Udo asks.

'We are. That's where Bastian is. We're going to watch him round the clock. I'll go back up now. Otti, Udo, and Jürgen go home and wait by your phones; we'll call you to take over later. Tobi will stay here and coordinate communications and provide backup. Questions?'

They all shake their heads. 'Okay, let's synchronise watches, check weapons and get to it.'

Five minutes later, Max drives north through the Tiergarten, past the Victory Column through Hansaviertel and on into Moabit. Günther's yard is on Sickingenstraße, close to the main railway line, heading out west between the British and French sectors.

Günther turns to Maria and hugs her. 'After I'm gone, make sure the bull is following, then go over to Christian's flat. If they're there, tell them to get out. Give them the money and tell them to go to this hotel.' He hands over an envelope and a note.

Maria hesitates a moment. 'What if they're not there?'

'Wait for a bit, then go home. I might call you later to come and fetch me.' He kisses her on the cheek. 'Okay, you be careful and, Maria? I love you, my girl.'

She frowns, and replies, 'Okay, I love you right back, pop.'

He smiles, his kind eyes twinkling. 'See you later, then.'

In his Opel Olympia, Bastian sits watching, wishing he was in a squad car with a radio. Now dark, he can see the lights in Günther's office, shadows moving about. A little after 7:15 p.m., the lights go out. He curses. Alone, this will be tricky, but he must stick with him.

The Citroën drives out of the gate, turns left, heading west. Bastian follows. They join the main road south into Charlottenburg, then west again, heading toward the Olympic Park. Soon after passing the stadium, they head north to an area of abandoned warehouses and factories. They drive for about twenty minutes, and coming to an abandoned arms factory, the van turns in. Bastian, who'd killed his lights some distance back, follows.

The van disappears behind a building. Stopping, Bastian switches off the interior light, gets out and goes in pursuit. Taking out his Walther P1, he flicks off the safety and cocks the mechanism. He peers around the corner of the road where the van turned. It is dark, and he waits a minute for his night vision to improve. All is clear. Staying close to the building, he stalks down the road. He checks through broken windows. Stopping, he listens. From inside the building, he hears the van stop; a squeak of brakes and a handbrake applied; the engine dies, a door slams, and there is the sound of metal scraping on metal. He moves on, comes to a broken side door, pulls it open and slips in, keeping his back to the wall. For a moment he stays still, listening.

The building smells of the acidic tang of rusting metal and neglect, and there's a faint noise coming from within. Retrieving a torch from his pocket, he clicks it on; the small beam cuts through the still, dank interior. Holding out pistol and flashlight, he sweeps the room and moves toward the van. Every so often, he stops and listens, feeling exposed. There is a faint glugging sound. As he nears the vehicle, he smells petrol and panning the light around, sees a growing pool on the floor. Fully alert and snapping off the torch, he ducks away from the van, but a voice stops him. 'Hold it right there, you bastard.' A beam of light falls over him. 'Lose the weapon and the torch slowly. Throw them over there and keep your hands where I can see them.'

Bastian throws his firearm and torch to the ground. They clatter away loudly; the torch rolls in a lazy arc and comes to rest, its beam casting shadows on the far wall. 'What now, Günther? You won't get away with anything; killing me is a waste of time.'

'Shut up. I've heard enough from you and your friends. You're all corrupt, and you want to frame Christian because he's slow-witted and you'll have no trouble getting him to confess to anything you want. Now, take your cuffs and shackle yourself to the handle of the door.'

'Fuck that! You must be mad if you think I'm going to handcuff myself to a van you've soaked in petrol. If you want to get rid of me, you'll have to shoot me, arsehole.'

Günther fires, the bullet ricocheting off the floor by Bastian's left foot; bits of cement dust spit into the air, the 9mm round whining off, lost in the dark. 'The next one will be between the eyes; my favourite place to shoot SS scum. Now handcuff yourself to the van. I will not ask you again.'

Taking his cuffs from his coat pocket, Bastian moves toward the vehicle. As he clicks the first cuff on the handle, a light shines over Günther. Reacting with surprising speed and agility, he grabs Bastian round the throat, pulling him back close to him, and holds the pistol to his temple. He shouts, 'I know you bastards like to hunt in pairs. Move, and he dies. Throw down the torch and weapon now!'

The light stays on, the beam steady, nothing happens. Günther fires, the round thudding into a concrete pillar; a cloud of dust kicks up across the beam of light, swirling in the glare. Surprised, he realises the torch is a decoy, left abandoned. Quickly, he forces himself against the van and scans his torchlight fruitlessly around the cavernous building. Pushing Bastian and taking a step forward, and with panic rising, he shouts, 'Is that you, Becker? Hear me, you shit, move closer or try anything, and I'll blow us all to hell!' Sensing his moment, Bastian tenses up and, kicking back, pushes Günther hard against the door. As he slams against him, he jerks his head back into Günther's face. There is a dull crack as his nose breaks. With his eyes watering, blood flowing, and pain smothering him, he loses his grip, and Bastian dives away, shouting, 'Now Max, now!'

Just as Max levels his pistol to shoot, Günther pulls a cord, setting off an igniter rigged to the fuel tank. There is a blinding flash as it explodes, the air wrought with petrol vapour erupts with a whomp, and a blast wave followed by searing smoke and flames rushes outward. Bastian dives low, turning as the burning fingers catch up with him, and for a second, he disappears inside the rolling inferno. His jacket and trousers catch fire and desperately, he rolls over and over, damping the cruel licking flames. Seconds later, Max, yanking off his coat, smothers the flames before they get hold.

Looking up, they see Günther, now a human torch, staggering forward, hands held up on either side of his blazing head, his mouth moving, but there is no sound save the crack-n-pop and roar of the heat and flames gripping both man and vehicle. Standing up, Max takes careful aim and fires twice. Gunther drops and is still.

For a few moments, they stare, then retreating well back from the intense heat and smoke, they sit leaning against a large column near the entrance.

'*Scheißekuchen-mit-Senf*, my God, I'm getting too old for this shit.' Tucking his pistol away, Max glances at Bastian. 'You all right?'

'Yeah, I think so. My ears are ringing, and some of these sting a bit, but I've had worse.'

Max, the tension easing, places his hand on Bastian's shoulder and laughs. 'Oh, don't worry about it. Us tankers were always being cooked; you get used to it. At least now we know we're not barking up the wrong tree, eh?'

Reaching into his pocket, Bastian retrieves his cigarettes and taking two from the crumpled packet, lights them, passing one to Max, who takes the smoke, saying, 'Oh yeah, this is one of those times, for sure. Don't tell Anna, though.' He takes a deep drag and closes his eyes, laying his head back on the column's cold concrete. 'Good thing, with all the burnt clothing, she'll never smell it.'

For a while, they sit silently, side-by-side, smoking and watching the flames.

Bastian breaks their reverie. 'I didn't see you. How come you found us? Which I'm bloody glad you did.'

'I drove up to the street just as your taillights disappeared around the corner. Another second or two, you'd have been on your own.'

Bastian waves the air with his hand dismissively. 'Argh, no worry, I had him. Though it is true, I may have burned to death. What I can't work out is why he didn't just shoot me, burn the van, and get out. He didn't know you were there, did he?'

'I think his emotions clouded his judgement; anger and passion can do that.'

Bastian flicks his cigarette end into the dark, a blaze of sparks jumping up as it hits the ground. 'Well, thank fuck for that.'

'Shame, though, we still lost him and the van. Could have been crucial evidence. Perhaps he was more involved than I thought?'

'It was all his choice. You can't predict the illogical mind, can you? Anyway, my head hurts, and these were my favourite work trousers. I'll have to put in a claim, eh?'

Standing, Max offers his hand and, pulling up his friend, says, 'It wasn't your time.' He looks at the mess. 'This is going to take some explaining and a lot of paperwork. Let's call for support, then go get a beer.'

Bastian looks down at his tattered trousers. 'Better swing by my apartment first.'

As they walk away, Max says, 'Takes me right back, and not in a good way.'

'What does?'

'The smell of burning flesh, ugh!'

Bastian places his hand on Max's shoulder. 'The smell of war, my friend. Never forgotten.'

20

His tongue is a stringless instrument

ANGELIKA HAS MANAGED SOME SLEEP. She wakes feeling good and is a little excited to get going. In the far corner, Christian slumbers. Switching on the lights, she goes over, gently nudging him awake. 'It's time. Let's move the vehicles first. You follow me.'

Locking up, they head out. Wolfgang, positioned in his hideout, is drifting in and out of sleep. The sound of the basement door banging shut brings him to. Peering into the dark, he makes out the shape of the powerful man coming up the path toward him, heavy footsteps passing by. The woman disappears off the way she came. He hears a vehicle door close and an engine start. Venturing out, he crosses the rough ground to the alley and, seeing it clear, goes down and looks out to the road. A few meters away, he sees a dark-coloured van, lights off, the V8 engine burbling, and on the back large white letters spelling out the make—Ford. From the end of the road, he hears another sound, the unmistakable noise of a VW flat-four air-cooled engine. Lights flow down the street, and he ducks back. As the VW closes in on the van, he notices the dull red colour. The car slows, draws level and then speeds away. The Ford follows; lights and noise soon lost to the night.

Wondering what they are up to, he goes and takes another look in the building to see if he can access the basement. There is a sliver of moon, the sky sparkling heavy with stars, but there is insufficient light to break the darkness on the ground. His night vision, as good as it will get, enables him to see enough to continue.

The building has a quiet stillness of its own; the sounds, secrets, and memories of countless former occupants lost in its shattered fabric. Access to the basement is from the gutted kitchen; where just an old sink and broken tap by the partially boarded-up window remain. There is another door, then a hallway and the remains of the stairs, a broken cupboard underneath. Looking up, he sees starlight and remembers sitting out at night in their small garden with his two young children, pointing out Canis Minor, Cassiopeia, Orion and other constellations. He wonders if such things have happened here, too. As he turns to go back, he spots in a corner an old rag doll, and, bending down, picks it up. It is in excellent condition, just a little grubby, and similar to the one his daughter used to have. He wonders what has become of his family, who last he saw over sixteen years ago. After his release from Russia, he had tramped the city searching, but they, like countless others, had vanished into the violent vacuum of war-torn Berlin. Now, they travel with him, pockets of joy and sadness, as comforting memories. Tucking the doll in his pocket, he goes back to the door. A heavy padlock secures it, and without the key or right tools, is impossible to open. He bangs on it, listening. Silence.

The loneliness and darkness press in on him. He leaves, going around the back, checking at ground level for any basement windows or hatches, but there are none. He follows the path the woman took, within a short distance, coming to another road. Following it around, he's soon back at the alley and, deciding he can do nothing more, returns to his hideout. He sits and takes the doll from his pocket and holds it. A tear forms at the corner of his eye as he remembers his girl sitting on his lap after she had bathed, smelling of soap. He liked to touch her soft hair and be close to her. Now he waits, time and emptiness his constant companions.

And in his vigil, he tries to remember the name his daughter had given her doll. Was it Lotti, or Lilly, or something like that? In the end, he decides it should be Lotti. Wolfgang does not have a watch, but years of practice have taught him to sense the passage of time, so he judges it is a little less than an hour when they return. They pass his hideout, though this time, two sets of eyes scrutinise them.

Angelika and Christian return to the basement. 'Get the bat and ropes. I'll prepare the stuff.'

Over at the table, she takes the bottle containing powdered Sodium Amytal. She's guessed Johann's weight to ensure a dosage that will subdue him for the time they need. She prepares two syringes of the barbiturate and one healthy dose of amphetamine, placing that and one of the Sodium Amytal in a pouch.

Lifting the syringe, she squeezes until a drop of liquid appears at the tip. She looks at Christian, a flash in her eye. 'Ready?' He takes a deep breath and nods slowly. 'Okay, let's do it.'

Christian opens the door to the storage room and flicks the switch for the lights. Going to the cell door, he looks through the peephole and checks their prisoner. The harsh light rouses Johann from his troubled sleep; his body racked with pain and stiffness from being shackled to the wall. He longs to lie down, to move and stretch. His eyes sting: he wants to rub them. The scrape and clunk of the bolts echo in the small space. The door swings open, Christian enters and seems to fill the entire room. He has a large club in one hand, which he raises, pushing the end hard against Johann's throat.

'Don't try anything stupid.'

Johann writhes for breath. He feels the pressure building in his head. The girl appears. His eyes lock on the syringe with its glinting needle. He tries to thrash and struggle, but the club pushes harder, and with his free hand, Christian punches him in the side. 'Keep still!'

Bending down, she jabs the needle deep into his left buttock, drawing back the plunger a little; a small scarlet swirl enters the syringe chamber, mixing with the drug and, in a swift motion, she pumps its contents into his body.

Christian removes the club. Johann coughs and gasps trying to draw in air. The injection was painful, and he does not know what they have given him. They retreat, closing the door; the lights go out.

Angelika tucks away the syringe. 'He's had sufficient to sedate him heavily, so it shouldn't take long, but to be sure, we'll give it five minutes. As soon as we get him down, we must tie him up and gag him. You know what to do if he comes to or puts up a fight.' Christian nods, slapping the baseball bat into his palm.

After five minutes, they return to find Johann's head slumped forward, his body hanging from the restraints. To ensure he is not faking it, Angelika takes a needle and jabs it into the end of his little finger.

'Good, either he's totally immune to pain, or he's out of it.'

Releasing the restraints, Johann falls to the ground. Christian drags him to the other room, and they set about binding him and wrapping him in canvas.

Angelika, pumped up with adrenaline, her eyes wide, and cheeks flushed, looks at Christian. 'All right, let's go. We'll come back here later and rest up, then we're gone forever.'

Christian hefts Johann on his broad shoulder and carries him. From

Wolfgang's hideout, the eyes watch. They see the big man appear with what looks like a body on his shoulder, and as they pass, there is no doubt. A moment later, the basement door slams and the woman passes by. Wolfgang turns to Lotti and, putting his finger to his lips, whispers, 'Let's see, shall we?'

He follows them, arriving at the road just as the woman slams the side doors shut, then going around the front, gets into the driver's seat, starts the engine and drives away.

Wolfgang returns to the hideout and sits. He looks at Lotti. 'What dark business are these two about, Lotti? They come and go in the dead of night. Now they leave with a body. But is it living or is it not?'

He thinks for a bit. 'What should we do, Lotti? Is it best we not get involved? I mean, who are we? Nobody. A homeless vagrant and an old forgotten doll. Why would they believe us?' Then, in a moment, he remembers. 'Yes, of course, the paper. Now where is it?'

He checks the inside pockets of his coat and, striking a match, touches it to the candle. A halo of warm light permeates the space, and he offers the newspaper to the lightly dancing flame. 'Here, Lotti, look. There, see, there have been two murders these last weeks. Men taken to the forest, it says, killed in one place and taken to another. Just like what we have witnessed here, you think?' He lowers the newspaper. 'But don't you see, Lotti, this could be them, my God, the Forest Executioner? We will wait and see if they come back without the body, and if they do, we'll telephone the *Polizei* and tell them to come. We won't give our name. No. Just the address and what we have seen. Yes, that is good. We'll do our duty and disappear.'

With his heart in his mouth, Wolfgang returns to watch and wait. Vigilant eyes stare out: his new friend emboldens him.

The drive to the south side of Tegel Forest takes them just under twenty minutes. As they travel south down Konradshöher Straße, they are careful to check no other vehicles are about. Soon after, they arrive at the track and, turning right, bump along the unmade forestry road. She kills the lights and drives for another five minutes, where the trail ends at a parking area. All around, the tall, dark European larches press in. She positions the van in the middle of the clearing, far enough away from the trees. While she has driven, Christian has prepared Johann, lying him on his back on top of an old mattress, tightly bound with rope and chains. Into his mouth, Christian has pressed a large steel ball-bearing, tied over with a stout cloth.

Opening the back door, she looks in. 'Good, that will do it. Get the metal ready. I'll give him the Amphetamine that should bring him to.'

She slaps Johann around the face a few times. He moans, the effects of the Sodium Amytal wearing off. She administers the Amphetamine, hoping the drug will give his system a kick, raising his heart rate and breathing.

Within a few minutes, it is working. He wakes, trying to move. His eyes open, staring wildly, his pupils wide, black circles.

She looks down at him. 'Hello, Johann, or should I say, Isayev? Welcome back. It's dying time.' She slaps his face and grabs his chin. 'Can you hear me?'

He growls, moans and groans, and she senses his violence and belligerence. Angelika hops down from the van to see how Christian is getting on.

He has placed a pan on a gas camping stove. Inside are five kilos of lead taken from old roofing sheets and cut into small pieces. Within fifteen minutes, the container is full of bright silver, molten metal at a temperature of over 330° Celsius. Christian skims the scum from the top, throwing it to the ground.

He turns to Angelika. 'We're ready. Get in. I'll pass it to you; we need to be quick.'

'Okay, hold on a second; I want to make sure he knows what's coming.' She jumps back in, kneeling beside Johann, his restless eyes darting about. She slaps him hard; he looks at her with wild, wide eyes. 'Can you hear me, arsehole?'

He stares, soulless eyes blinking.

'Your friends all died screaming. They told us their real names, their Russian names; Isayev, whoever you are? You don't remember me. Do you?'

He stares, saucer eyes fixed on her.

'Like we told your friends, you should have killed us all, shouldn't you?'

He attempts to nod, moaning something, trying to jerk his body. Bending down close to his ear, she whispers, 'Before you go, I want to ensure you can never again commit rape. So, I've got a little present for you. Christian has melted some lead, and I'm going to pour it over your disgusting, filthy little cock. Enjoy!'

Johann jerks. Explosive, muffled yells filling the claustrophobic space. Going to the back of the van, she says, 'Now, Chris, I am ready.'

He gives her a thick glove and hands over the heavy pan. 'Be careful.'

She holds it just above Johann's genitals, his fevered, terrified eyes fixed on the pan, his lungs practically exploding from screams of rage and terror. Slowly, she tips the vessel, and a searing, bright silver stream cascades, flowing around his groin. The screams, though restrained by cloth and gag, are ear-splitting, and seemingly envelop the forest. There is a crack of breaking teeth, and for a while before it falls still, his tortured body writhes.

For a moment she stares with a detached, morbid curiosity at the destruction she has wrought. Worried he may have died, she checks Johann's pulse, and satisfied, hands the pan back. 'I'll give him another shot of upper; he'll come around soon. Throw the stuff in the front, but make sure the gas valve is tight shut.'

In the moments Johann is unconscious, Angelika takes a petrol can, pouring fuel onto the mattress and around his body.

They stand and wait. A few moments later, the moaning returns. Angelika leans in, almost overcome by the stomach-churning smell of burned flesh, petrol, and bilious fear. 'Time to rejoin your demon friends in Hell. This will get you used to the heat, devil-man!'

They retreat to a safe distance and, taking a Molotov Cocktail prepared earlier, she lights the rag and lobs it in. With a voracious *whoomph*, the fuel vapour erupts, and the immolation of Isayev Anastasi Stanislavovich begins. Within minutes, the gas canister detonates, blowing out the cab windows. Angelika and Christian flinch, ducking instinctively, and they watch with naïve fascination as the inferno consumes the man who took everything and became Johann Kleeman.

For a while, they stand and bear witness to the end. At last, with a twinkle in her eyes, Angelika looks at Christian. Her words are like a benediction. 'It's done. For mama, papa, and us. Thank Christ for that. Do you want to do the honours?'

He nods, takes the sign from her, and retrieving a hammer and nail from the bag, walks over to a prominent tree, and fixes it in place.

As they leave, there is a sense that the final conflagration has wiped away the sins and evils put upon them. And, as the dancing light of the funeral pyre illuminates their receding backs, they vanish into the dark of the forest, bringing their plan to a close.

'Are we free now? I feel different, but I don't know how?' Christian says.

'Yes, we did it, little you and little me.'

'What now?'

'We go back to the basement. Apart from us, no one in the entire world knows about it. No one alive, anyway. We will stay there and get some rest, lie low, then start again. We can never go back to our old lives.'

Christian glances at her with anxious eyes. 'I am sure Günther would not have told them, would he? After all, he is my friend.'

'The *Polizei* may have got him to give us up, so we cannot risk it. We have our money; we can disappear into the city and start again. You can never go back to Günther or your old job.'

They walk back along the track to the place they had stashed the car. If anyone should appear, it will be easy for them to get to cover, but it is the middle of the night, in a forest near the outer border of West Berlin, and save the company of unseen nocturnal creatures, they are alone.

Twenty minutes later, they remove the branches that camouflage the car, climb aboard and drive away. Deep in the forest, echo the sounds of the ping and tack of the van's hot metal with its macabre cargo reduced to bare skeletons of steel, charred flesh, and bone licked sensuously by the dying flames, and dense, black smoke carries away the ominous essence of what was.

21

Pleasure and action make the hours seem short

IT IS WELL AFTER MIDNIGHT when Max gets home. After they'd handed over the scene to forensics and got their burns checked out, their systems still pumped, they had met with Tobi at Beni's, a *Bierkeller* close to the office and had a few drinks to put some distance between the day's events. Earlier, he had telephoned the others, putting them in the picture and standing them down.

When Max had called Anna, she had been concerned, as she knew an event like this was bound to stir up painful memories. Like so many survivors, Max had spent the entire war either fighting or recovering from wounds. At the start, he had been only a boy and witnessed and done terrible things, dragged along in the maelstrom of misdirection and misplaced loyalty, duped by a criminal regime. He, she, and all those with a conscience carried the guilt side-by-side with the trauma and the unresolved conflict of their complicity.

She knew he had played down the events of the evening and encouraged him to blow off some steam with men that shared so much more than a career.

She waits up, and when the key turns in the door, and he steps in, smiling, fatigue etched on his grubby face, she hugs him: the kind only someone special can give. 'Max Becker, you smell of beer, smoke, and petrol. What have you been up to?'

He shrugs out of his tattered coat. 'Oh, you know, just the usual humdrum, *Polizei* business.'

Gently, taking his hand, she pulls him up the stairs, and together they climb into the shower. After, as they lie in bed, the clock showing 2 a.m., he says, 'I must get myself in a pickle more often, Dr Anna Fischer. You always knew the best treatment for a wounded boy.'

For a while, she does not reply. They lie semi intertwined, their breathing synchronised, their lives fixed together as they are meant to be.

'It reminds me of the first time we met. You remember?' she says.

'Yes, that I'll never forget. You were the loveliest, softest, most healing thing I'd ever seen; so far removed from the cold steel, filth, and wretchedness of it all.'

'You smelled just the same as you did tonight, except the beer. Your black uniform filthy, tattered, and charred. Actually, it seems to be a good look for you.'

'Why, darling, if I'd known, I wouldn't have spent all that money on that expensive suit for our wedding. By the end of the war, I had an entire wardrobe of wrecked uniforms.'

For a while, they lie in silence facing one another, eyes locked together searching, beyond mere looks but boring deep inside. 'You smell better now, though,' she whispers, her hand gently exploring his face, caressing the lines and scars; her fingers pushing through his dark hair, pulling him close and kissing him tenderly, she reaches down to his hardness.

His hand rubs gently from the base of her spine, up the curve of her back and over her shoulder, cupping and caressing her breasts, lingering on each nipple. His index finger runs down from the base of her throat, between her breasts, onto her navel and beyond, exploring and settling in the soft warmth of her.

Spent, they lie still, nothing more to be said. His life has always been, and always will be, one of a man of action, of danger, now making amends for a past that was never his to repent of. She, having touched the very essence of suffering and evil, knows its remedy and has become the ultimate healer of it: patience, wisdom, empathy, and a haven.

Aware of his alertness, she asks, 'Bastian, all right? He should have someone to go home to; he should not be alone. I wish he were not. He can't seem to move on.'

'He's okay. As he said, he's been in worse, we all have. He's tough.'

'Sometimes tough isn't enough. Keep an eye on him, won't you?'

'I do. I watch them all. I'm like a mother hen.'

'How's it going between Otti and Udo?'

'Hmm, not sure. I partnered them up today, but halfway through, they split up; said it was to get the work done.'

'But?'

'Yeah, but I'm not sure I'm buying it. I want them to work it out themselves. You're very good at wheedling things out of people. How about we invite Otti over for a meal, and you have a word?'

'Here, that's a little underhand, isn't it?'

'Well, yes, but I want to know what's going on, and I feel neither one of them is going to tell me; that's the trouble once you wear the boss hat. Barriers go up.'

'Okay, of course, but I can't promise anything.'

'If we could bottle your wisdom and diplomacy, the world would be a better place. You know something, Anna Fischer? I love you; where would I be without you?'

'Hmm, what are you really after?'

'Well, for some reason, I'm still not sleepy, so I was…'

Kissing him, she whispers, 'Sleep is for the dead.'

Three hours later, the alarm brings them back from a short, deep sleep. They've hardly moved, still entwined in one another's arms. Getting up and throwing on a robe, Max goes and knocks on the kids' doors. 'Heike, Markus, time to get up. Let's go!'

From their rooms return sleepy shouts of, 'Okay, yeah.'

He goes down and sets the kettle going, spooning coffee into the filter. He clicks on the radio, tuned into RIAS—the tail end of the news and weather.

"… *so, that's the news, now weather, light drizzle early again today, clearing up later, with a high of ten Celsius. Tonight will be mostly clear, night-time temperatures dropping to a low of five Celsius. Going into the weekend, the weather looks set to improve with a surge of high pressure and, yes, people, temperatures set to get up to fifteen, maybe even seventeen Celsius…*"

Markus comes down. 'Hey, dad, you were late back last night, working or having fun?'

'Actually, a bit of both. How was your day?'

'*Ist war prima!* I got a decent score on the maths paper.'

'*Hey, das ist geil!* I'm proud of you. Are you over at Willi's later?'

'Yeah. You going to be home early today?'

'Should be the usual time. But you know what it's like, Markus, if things come up with the investigation.'

'My friends were asking about the Forest Executioner.'

'Oh, tell them not to believe everything they read in the papers.'

'Are you after someone?'

'We've got a person or two of interest in our sights. Now come on, get some breakfast. But first, give your sister a shout, will you?'

Without moving from the kitchen and just as Anna comes in, Markus yells, 'Heike, you lazy cat, breakfast!'

Anna winces. 'Thank you, Marky. I really wanted to be deafened first thing.'

'Sorry, mum.'

Heike joins them. 'Hey, dad, why do the clothes you left in the bathroom smell of petrol and smoke?'

He gives her a hug and peck on the forehead. 'It was a wild party, sweetheart.'

She pushes him away. 'Yeah? No, you're just kidding about; I can see. What happened, really?'

'Just a minor incident at work, nothing to worry about, really. How was your day? I'm willing to bet it was more interesting than mine.'

'It was school, you know? Hey, are you free on Saturday? There's an event on at the Pregnant Oyster, isn't there, Markus?'

'Oh yes, it's a special screening of the new film, *Spartacus*. We've been studying him at school. The director is giving a talk about it, well he's not actually going to be there; it's a filmed talk before the main feature.'

Heike sits and helps herself to black bread and cheese. She and Markus exchange a knowing, mischievous glance. 'So, dad, who was Spartacus, anyway?'

Max takes a swig of coffee and smiles inwardly, aware of the game at hand. 'Well now, let me see... Spartacus... Spartacus, eh? Not sure I know a great deal about him, other than he was born in Thracia, which is now Bulgaria, about 110 BC. They were a nomadic people, skilled warriors, and at one time, he had been a soldier in the Roman army, then deserted, and later, they took him prisoner, and he became a slave and gladiator. A proud, intelligent man, he, along with a group of fellow gladiators, plotted and executed an escape, which led to a rebellion and some success against the forces that were present, which were reduced by the Third Mithridatic War and revolt in Spain, which had taken most of the troops away from Rome...'

Leaning back in her chair, Heike groans. 'Okay already, okay! Stop, for Pete's sake! Markus, you win.'

Markus grins. 'Told you he'd know.'

Heike looks over at Max. 'Dad, how come you know all that about him?'

'I probably read it in a book. But seriously, Spartacus has a strong link to communism and, in particular, German communism. Karl Marx listed him as a figure he most admired. Then there was the German Spartacus League, which led to the Communist Party of Germany. In January 1919, there was an uprising known as the Spartacus Rising. Have you not covered this in school? What do they teach you these days?'

'Honestly, dad, it sounds kinda boring,' Heike says.

Max gives her a playful nudge and laughs. 'Anyway, I didn't know they'd made a film about him. Sounds like a grand way to spend the afternoon. What time does it start?'

'2 p.m.'

'That should be all right. I'll have to go to work in the morning, but maybe if you all come to the office and pick me up at one, we can walk over, okay? Now come on, let's get our skates on.'

Thirty minutes later, Max drives to work surprised he does not feel too weary. Maybe it will hit him later. As the weather forecast had said, it is raining, with low clouds turning day to twilight. Arriving at HQ, he sees Tobi and Bastian's cars.

He enters the office to the sound of busy typewriters. 'Hey, you two, how's it going? Hope you got some sleep?'

Bastian stops typing and looks up. 'Slept like the damned, as always. I'm good, a little sore, but ready for action. Are we going after Maria today?'

'We need to speak with her, but obviously, things are going to be tricky there. I called August. He should get us a warrant to carry out a proper search of Günther's house and the business. We'll want to have a look at the other van and see if we can't pin down Christian's address; he's the key to this. As soon as Otti is in, I want you two up at the work site to talk to his men again. See if any of them know where Christian lives. She's got her firearms assessment at 3 p.m. Go with her and when she gets through, make sure she's issued a sidearm, clips, and ammo, will you?' Bastian nods. 'Tobi and I will handle Maria. We'll send the other two down to finish at the warehouse and tie up with Paul and Lutz.'

By a quarter to eight, everyone is in, and the *Stammtisch* is underway. The smell of blood is in the air; the team animated, eager to strike and hunt down Christian. Before dismissing them, Max says, 'I want you all to be careful, particularly after what happened last night. No more solo, minimum of pairs, and where possible, we don't make arrests without additional backup, got it?'

22

Is not the truth the truth?

WOLFGANG TRIES TO KEEP AWAKE, but with the cold gnawing at him, he drifts in and out. He's huddled down, head leaning against the wall, sleepy eyes watching.

The sound of muffled voices and footsteps jerks him awake; they are back. As they pass, he notes they are alone. A few moments later, he hears the basement door, leaving him swaddled in an oppressive silence.

He picks up Lotti. 'They're back, little one, and empty-handed. What has become of the corpse? That's the question.' He's not sure what to do. Does he wait and watch, or does he leave now to contact the *Polizei*? Should he telephone or go to the Kripo HQ himself? He's racked with indecision; does not want to get mixed up with the *Polizei*, happy keeping a low profile. He holds up Lotti. 'Oh, Lotti, what shall we do?'

He guesses it is early morning, around 5 a.m., still dark yet no longer night. Keen to move, he goes to find their vehicles and note down the registration numbers.

Emerging from his hideout, he walks out to the road. The Beetle is there, and he jots down the number, but no van. He walks the block but does not find it, so he goes back to watch until full daylight, and if they stay put, then he will go off and make the call.

Angelika and Christian set up their stove, make a hot drink, and eat a sandwich. Silently, they sit at their meagre repast. Having served its purpose, the basement seems alien now.

'Ange?' says Christian, 'I don't want to spend a few days here. Can't we find somewhere else?'

'I agree, it isn't good to be here, but I'm dog tired now. Let me get a few hours' sleep, then we can go off. There's a place not far where we can stay for a couple of nights. After that, we'll try to get further south and for a time move every couple of days while the dust settles, and we can look for a new apartment, all right?'

He smiles. 'That sounds good; I like that idea. I'm looking forward to starting again. Perhaps we can rent an apartment with a shop?'

Gently, she places her hand on his knee. 'Perhaps. We'll see. Now let's get some shut-eye, shall we?'

Within just a few minutes, he is asleep, his breathing steady. But for her, sleep is elusive. Tossing and turning, she cannot find a way to the deep rest she craves. Lying blinking in the darkness of the awful basement, she comprehends the enormity of what they have done, but also, she feels a sense of emancipation, taking back a part of her she thought lost.

She does not know what they should do. In truth, she longs to be free of the burden of him, to venture out, explore new worlds and, before it is too late, have something of a life. She wonders whether the *Polizei* will ever catch them, to stand trial, or maybe fight it out to the end and sweet oblivion. Perhaps in the days to come, when they have put some distance from this reckoning, she will find a way forward, a truth, a life? One thing is for sure, she is no longer afraid.

She sees little chance of it being a life without him. But then she loves him; he is a part of her and her responsibility, both burden and joy; there is and never will be anyone else.

Thinking back over the last six months, both proud and appalled at what they've achieved, she'd never thought it possible to take on such men, who in their arrogance, power, and criminality, thought themselves untouchable. She appreciates that if they can do that, really, they can do anything. They can start a small business, a café, a shop, maybe even a small hotel. She likes the idea of bed and breakfast. Christian will make an excellent breakfast cook and do all the maintenance jobs while she manages customers and the rooms. As her mind drifts off to pleasanter things, sleep takes her.

Wolfgang, now starving and needing to get going, decides he can wait no longer. They have been in there for some hours, and the morning has brought light rain. Tucking Lotti away in the inside pocket of his coat, he flips up his collar and sets off. As he gets to the end of the alley, he takes from his pocket an old red rag and ties it to a post by the entrance. Across the road, almost opposite, is their car. He peers in through the window, not sure what he is expecting to see, but there's nothing unusual.

There is a telephone booth near the Residenzstraße U-Bahn station from where he can make his call. He'll use the main free-to-call *Polizei* number and ask to talk with the detective in the paper, Max Becker. The rain has kept people at home, and as he joins the main road, an ageing bus drives by, its windows steamed up, exhaust fumes billowing from the back.

Five minutes later, he sees the yellow phone box. He has taken refuge in the like before, once spending a bitter-cold, snowy night in one. He steps in, closing the door. There is an immediate calm; the damp outside world closed off. Alone in the intimate cubicle , the smell of Bakelite, old, cheap paper from the phonebook and that faint trace of a particular, stale human odour: perhaps a subtle cocktail of the myriad people who have occupied briefly the confined space, each leaving a little of themselves. He remembers reading somewhere that every contact leaves a trace and wonders of the stories this space has borne witness to. Now, picking up the receiver, it will witness the potential end of a murderous couple hiding in a nearby forgotten basement. Hearing the dial tone—he likes the sound—strangely comforting to a man who rarely talks with anyone. As he lifts his hand, he notes it is shaking but is not sure whether it is from fear or excitement; perhaps a little of both. He spins the dial, two short sweeps, one long.

A female voice answers, '*Polizei*, what is your emergency?'

'Hello, may I speak with Kommissar Max Becker? I have information about the Forest Executioner murders. I know where they are hiding.'

'May I have your name and address, please, sir?'

Wolfgang speaks slowly. 'My name is Heinz Fremder. I have no address. I live a life of freedom on the streets.'

'You say you have information on the whereabouts of suspects in the Forest Executioner crimes?'

'Yes, yes, please, I think it is them, and I know where they are hiding. Please, may I speak with Kommissar Becker?'

'Why do you think these men are the killers? Have you seen them commit a crime?'

Wolfgang's frustration builds. He speaks briskly. 'No, not men. One young woman and a man, an enormous, powerful, tall man. I have seen them carry a body from their hiding place, and there are strange things about them. Either way, I think Kommissar Becker should know; please, put me through.'

'Sorry, sir, I'm unable to do that, but if you give me the name and location, I promise we will send out officers to investigate and will pass on your information.'

For a moment, Wolfgang considers hanging up and going to find the Kripo HQ and seeing Max himself, but that would mean they'd have him, and he didn't want that, and it would cause much delay.

'Hello, are you still there, Herr Fremder?'

Wolfgang sighs. 'Okay, I'll tell you, but you promise Kommissar Becker will be informed, yes? And you must hurry, they are there now, but I do not know for how long; they come and go, you see?'

'Yes, I promise. Now please, the address.'

Wolfgang passes on the details, including his red rag marking the alley. Concluding the call, he replaces the receiver and stands there, wondering what to do next. Should he disappear and hope they send someone, or will they think him mad and not take any notice of a homeless man's call? A loud banging on the door breaks his cogitation.

Yanking open the door, a red-faced, immaculately dressed, late middle-aged man regards him with disgust. 'Get out of here, you filthy beggar. People need to use this to make calls. It's not for you to make a home in. My God, you stink! You've stunk up this box; it is unusable. Back in my day, I would have had you transported to a camp and made to work, you jobless oaf. Get out of my sight before I call the *Polizei*.'

Wolfgang bridles. 'I fought for my country and for arseholes like you, but for what? So that I could come home to this abuse, eh?'

Outraged, the man raises his gloved hand and backhands Wolfgang across the face, knocking him aside. 'Don't talk back to me, you scum! I'll have you arrested.'

Rubbing his stinging face, the hateful words ringing in his ears, Wolfgang moves away. Save his life, he has given everything: his wife, his children, a normal life, and for what? For people like that, in their fine clothes and with money in their pockets, money they'd never share with the likes of him. All he really wants is a chance to start again, finally to return from the Eastern Front, from Russia, from the war.

Hurrying down the street, he stops at a stand and, with the last of his money, buys a coffee and *Bratwurst*. Unlike many homeless people, Wolfgang has never taken to drink. If he has enough money, he might purchase a beer, but he has always been a disciplined man and, though at times gripped by despair, believes that one day he'll find a way back.

Before the war, he had a respectable job as an electrical engineer working for the German railway. He loved to read, and his favourite thing after a day's work was to sit with his children on the sofa, one on either side, and read them stories. They'd snuggle close and listen, enthralled by tales of adventure, fantasy, and enchantment. It is a memory that both breaks his heart and fuels his hope. Aware that he has been away too long, he resolves to go back.

Mags, the operator who had taken Wolfgang's call, has been doing her job for many years. She's heard every type of crackpot and weirdo, and it is customary with cases such as this for random people to call in with confessions or sightings of killers. But there was something about the caller that rang true. His honesty about his homeless status, the precise nature of the details he gave, even his tone, but most of all, his insistence on speaking with Max.

For a few moments, she muses, drumming her fingers, then picking up the receiver, dials and waits.

Lisa Engel's phone rings. 'Good morning, KP Dehler's office.'

'Lisa, it's Mags. How are you?'

'Mags, my darling, I'm good, yes, and you? Are you over your cold?'

'Yes, much better; back to normal. Listen, I've just had a call about Max's investigation. A homeless man, name given as Heinz Fremder, though I'm guessing that probably isn't real, has given the location of two suspects, a woman and large man, currently hiding out in a basement on… hang on… wait one second while I check the notes… yes, Teichstraße. I don't know, but I think that this might be worth a look. Can you alert Max?' She listens for a while. 'Yes, yes. All right, here are the details.'

Lisa ends the call and, without replacing the receiver, dials down to the squad room but gets no answer. Hanging up, she goes and knocks on August's door.

'August, just had my sister on the phone with information on possible suspects in the forest killings. No one is in the squad room.'

August scans the proffered note. 'All right, thanks, Lisa. I'll grab some uniforms and go check it out. Get on to dispatch and see if they can track down Max, will you?'

❖❖❖

Angelika wakes with a start and an eerie feeling inside. Sitting up, she clicks on the torch; the beam cutting a funnel of light through the dark. Getting up, she goes over to Christian, shaking him awake. 'Come on,

Chris, get your things; we're leaving now.' Half asleep, he gets up. Switching on the spotlights, they gather the bags they packed earlier.

'Have you got everything? We're never coming back here.'

He nods. 'I'm ready.'

Making their way out, they emerge from the remote darkness into the damp September morning. She locks both inner and outer doors. They cross the rough ground, down the alley and out onto the street. She unlocks the car. 'Wait, you get in. I'll be back in a minute.'

As he climbs aboard, she goes back to the rough ground and throws the two padlock keys into a vast pile of rubble and weeds. They bounce twice before settling deep in the undergrowth, lost forever. Turning, she heads back, jumps in, fires up the engine and speeds away down the road.

A few minutes later, Wolfgang returns, stopping as he sees the space where the VW has been. He looks about and sighs. Cautiously, he checks the basement door and finds it locked.

He thinks, perhaps they will come back. I mean, why wouldn't they? They don't know that someone has seen them and reported it, do they? I mean, how could they?

On the point of giving up and disappearing, in the corner of the old kitchen, he spots a piece of charred wood and, picking it up, writes on the wall next to the door:

> *Kommissar Becker, it was I who telephoned the Polizei. They have gone but may return. Their car is a grey VW Beetle Reg: KB 9713. Sorry I could not wait. Heinz Fremder*

The note will have to do. If they come back, they will know of their discovery; it's a chance he'll have to take. For a while, he considers returning to his hideout and waiting, but thinks the *Polizei* will search the entire area, discovering his presence, and then what? Of course, he can pretend he's here by chance and not the man who made the call. No, he's done his duty. It is better now to get far away.

23

'tis the cunning livery of hell

AUGUST ARRIVES A COUPLE OF minutes after the uniforms, the two men waiting. Drawing their weapons, they follow the alley marked by the red rag, cross the rough ground, and arrive at the house.

While they stand on either side of the broken doorway waiting, August sends one officer round to the back. Allowing enough time for him to arrive, August, his Walther PP ready, sweeps in, checking corners as he goes, and moves through to the old kitchen. The other officer follows, covering him. Arriving at the basement door, August stops, and examines the message. He looks at his colleague, who frowns. 'What the hell? Is this a joke?'

With the barrel of his gun, August lifts the padlock, letting it fall back with a clank. 'Locked from outside, so the message might be correct, and we're too late.'

The other officer comes in from the far door. 'Rest of the house is clear, well, the bits I can get to, anyway.'

'Thanks. Got any bolt cutters in your car?'

The officers shake their heads. 'We could try the wheel brace.'

August nods. 'Go. Let's try it. While you're there, call it in and get someone out here with tools. Here, take my keys and see if there's anything in my car.'

The door defeats them. He sends the two officers around the area, checking for residents, and while they are gone, he has a good look around the house. There are signs of life, footprints and scuffs in the dust. Going outside, he explores the rough ground and, spotting the old outhouse, takes out his torch, shining it into the dark interior. Seeing it clear, he enters. Someone has been here, he thinks. Perhaps it was the man who called it in? He would have had a good view of the house from here. 'Where are you, Heinz Fremder? Or whoever you are?' August says out loud. He, like Mags, is sure Heinz Fremder is not the caller's true name. It would explain his absence now. A homeless man, possibly from the wrong side of the law, a drug addict or alcoholic? In any case, not someone wanting to talk to men from the Kripo. The shed smells old, musty, but has a lingering odour of unwashed bodies, a smell long remembered from his war days: tankers were a filthy lot. Heinz was here, probably just a few hours ago.

Coming back out to the grey, heavy morning, he walks back to his car to wait in the dry. He lights a cigarette and muses on how much easier it will be when they all have personal radios. At a recent *Polizei* trade show, he'd seen some promising new technology. He imagines resistance from older officers, suspicious of new things and a feeling of trust and old-school ethics being compromised. A *Polizei* van drives up the road, parks, and an officer gets out. August goes over to meet him. 'Have you brought bolt cutters?'

'Yes, sir. We'll get it open.' He retrieves a tool bag from the back, and the two walk over to the basement door. The large cutters make quick work of the padlock, which falls to the ground with a clunk. With a gloved hand, the officer picks it up, placing it in an evidence bag. He flips open the hasp. Standing to one side, August instructs the officer to pull the door open and as he does so, August, holding his torch and sidearm, sweeps in and down the stairs. He calls up, 'There's another door. Come down.' They repeat the process. August enters, the sharp beam of light cutting through the impenetrable black of the room. He steps away from the doorway, back to the wall, makes a sweep of the space. It reeks, with a lingering odour of vomit, faeces, and the metallic tang of blood. He notes the lights, the table, tape deck, and chairs and, in the far corner, another doorway. He trains his flashlight at the lamps, picking out the lead and following it back to the switch. He goes over and lights up the room. The glare falls on the far wall.

A voice from the doorway. 'Sweet mother, what the hell is this place?' says the officer, staring at the board, its empty shackles hanging limply yet menacingly from the macabrely stained board.

'Stay there, touch nothing,' August orders.

Going over to the other door, which is ajar, he positions himself to one side and, using his foot, swings it open, and enters. Again, he flicks a switch, which bathes the room in light. Another door. It has a peephole through which he can see light. Checking, he flicks off the switch and notes that the peephole goes dark. He relights the rooms. They locked the other door with two bolts, which glide smoothly, and he pushes it open with his foot. The interior reveals a small cell, heavy shackles bolted to the wall and, in the corner, an evil-smelling bucket of waste.

August rejoins his colleague. 'Ok, it's clear. Make your way back out. We need to get forensics in.'

Relieved to be out in the light, he walks back to the road while the officer has returned to the van and is calling in reinforcements. August lights up a smoke just as Max and Tobi drive up. Rolling down his window, Max says, 'Hey, August, what have we got?'

'Fresh bloody hell, that's what. It may have nothing to do with our investigation, but whatever it is, it's not good. Forensics are en route.' Max parks up, and as they walk to the house, August tells them that the man who called it in said that he had seen the suspects carrying a body out.

'Another body?'

'Yep, that's what he said.'

'Could it have been the last one, I wonder?'

'If not, somewhere out there is number four.'

They make their way down the stairs. 'Holy crap,' Tobi gasps.

Careful to avoid disturbing anything, Max scans the room. 'Holy crap does not describe this place.' Spotting something draped over the back of one chair, he goes to investigate. It is a small scarf. 'Hello, what's this?' Leaning over, he gives it a sniff. 'Well, well, what do you know? The sweet, spicy aroma of *Shalimar*.' Smiling, he turns to August and Tobi, who are standing at the doorway.

Tobi frowns. 'Your mystery fragrance?'

'Yes, it's the same perfume I detected in Spandauer Forest and what Lutz found traces of on the rope used to bind the first body and that, gentlemen, is good enough for me. This is their place, and I'm sure is where our victims died.'

They stand regarding the grisly scene, imagining the suffering and pain now lost to the fabric of this awful place.

'Look at the ceiling above the board. Is that a bullet hole?' Tobi says.

'Indeed, looks like it. That fits with the first body. Why did they choose to go to all this trouble to kill these men? So elaborate, thought out, and no attempt to hide the crimes, though I'm sure they did not wish us to discover this place.'

'Whatever it is, I can't see how you'd ever justify it?' August muses.

Max sighs. 'Hmm, I wonder, I wonder? All right, let's clear out and let forensics get to it; they'll have a field day here.' As he gets to the foot of the stairs, he looks back. 'Hell of a place to die.'

24

With his mouth full of news

BY FRIDAY MORNING, THE RAIN has cleared, and though still cloudy, it is dry and set fair for the coming days. Bruno Koe had spent much of the week back at the Revier-Fösterein Nature Centre, catching up on maintenance and some administration. He, along with a small team, manages the seven hundred hectares of the Tegel Forest. It was a job he'd always wanted to do, a love for nature, trees, the open air, and the freedom to manage his own time, much of which he spent alone.

Coming in early, he has a coffee and, taking his favourite Mauser 98 rifle, climbs aboard the Unimog 411 utility vehicle and sets off heading north-west along the track known as the Förster Weg. Motoring along slowly, windows down, letting the rich forest smells drift into the cab, he smiles to himself and wonders whether life could be any better.

After some six kilometres, he comes to Konradshöher Straße, the main road running approximately north-south, dissecting the forest. He waits as a few cars whip past and shakes his head at their foolishness: the forest is full of deer, and accidents are not uncommon. He's been called out on many a wet, dark night to crawl under ruined cars and dispatch some wretched creature.

From time to time he stops to mark a tree that needs attention, make a quick repair on fencing or gates, and make up job sheets for future works. By the time he arrives at the top of Freiheitsweg, it is mid-morning. Though most of the forest comprises pine, larch, and Douglas fir, this is his favourite area, an ancient oak and beech woodland, where some trees have stood for hundreds of years, sentinels to the march of time. One tree, its trunk over six metres in circumference, is his favourite. He tries to come here two or three times a month to sit under the mighty limbs, lean against the gnarled, hardened, rough bark, and bathe in its majesty. This tree, this giant of nature, is older than the city itself and Bruno likes to sit, close his eyes, and feel its potency.

Parking the Unimog, he kills the engine, takes his knapsack and jumps down from the cab. Sauntering over, he looks up at the oak they call "Fat Marie" and, with the tender glance of a lover's eye, wanders around it, one hand with fingertips extended, stroking the ancient bark. Settling down on the south side of the trunk, a light beam of pastel sunlight falls on the mossy forest floor: nature's cushion and an excellent place to rest. From his bag, he pulls a thermos, bread, and cheese and, sinking into the soupy calm of the deep forest, enjoys his meal and wants for nothing more than this moment to go on forever. His hunger satisfied; he rolls a cigarette. It is so quiet that when he inhales, the faint crackle of the smouldering paper is audible. After, he shuts his eyes and allows time to take him.

The tattering of a woodpecker wakes him. Not sure how long he has slept, he gathers his things, returns to his vehicle and heads over to the parking area near the tallest tree in Berlin—*Höchster Baum*—a larch that rises to forty metres. Once, Bruno had spent the night here and, standing by the trunk looking up, had watched the stars circle around it as though it were the axis of the universe.

Nearing lunchtime, his vehicle bumps down the soggy track and, rounding the last bend, the sight of a burned-out vehicle standing in the middle of the clearing shocks him.

There is no one about, so he stops and climbs down to check it out. It is an old van. The back doors are open, one lying on the ground where gravity had taken it as the vehicle's structure weakened. As he circles around, the bitter smell of burnt metal, rubber, and something else, sweeter, intensified by the damp, fills his nostrils. As he comes to the back and looks in, he is unprepared. For a second, he cannot make it out or perhaps does not believe what it is he's seeing, but at last, there is clarity and recognition. Turning away, he runs a few yards, collapses to his knees and is sick. For a while, kneeling, he breathes deeply; the smell and vision of deep-burnt flesh will stay with him for days.

Plucking up courage, he gets up to look again. The body lies on its back with what looks like chains holding it down. Both hands are bent upward in a grotesque gesture; the fingers, some missing, seem to claw at the air. He can't see any clothing, and beneath the corpse are twisted springs and wires. But it is the blackened skull that turns his stomach, thrust back with the mouth wide open, in an everlasting soundless scream. Bruno has had his fill and fleeing the hellacious scene, jumps in his vehicle and hastens back to base. As he drives, the forest seems to close in around him, no longer the tranquil green nurturing mother, and he needs to be out in the open. At last, he sees light ahead, the opening to the road and the route to freedom. Slewing the truck out onto the tarmac, he drives as fast as the vehicle will go and, fifteen minutes later, crashes through the office door, snatches up the phone, and dials the *Polizei*.

After, he sits for a moment, thinking, then picks up the receiver once more. 'Good morning, *Berliner Courier*,' chirps a friendly female voice.

'Can you put me through to Peter Koe, please? It's his brother.'

'One moment, please.'

There is a pause, then a click on the other end. 'Hey, Bruno, long-time-no-see, what's up?'

'I was patrolling in the forest, and at the car park near the tallest larch, there's a burnt-out van with a body in it. Do you think it is the work of those forest killers?'

'Oh crap, really? Are you all right?'

'Yes, it was a bit of a shock, but I'm fine.'

'Have you called the *Polizei*?'

'Yes, yes, of course, just now.'

'Good, I'll grab a photographer and get over there. You should go back too; they'll want to speak with you.'

Silence.

'You still there, brother?'

'Yes, sorry. It's just the thought of going back, that's all.'

'Look, I'll be there, and the place will be crawling with *Polizei*, all right? I'll see you there. Wait by the road, yes?'

'Okay.'

'Hey, thanks for ringing; it'll be a feather in my cap. The old man will be really pleased.'

Putting down the phone, he leaves the newsroom, hurrying over to the editor's office. The door's open, being closed only when someone is getting the boot. As he enters, he taps the open door. Without looking up from the copy he works on, the editor growls a curt, 'What?'

'My brother has just phoned in, found a body in the Tegel Forest. It's in a burnt-out van.'

The editor's eyes light up. 'Has he called the *Polizei*?'

'Naturally.'

'Get Bimpy and go. I want headline pictures and copy.' He looks up at Peter irritably. 'You still here?'

Bimpy grabs a bag containing two Leicas, a selection of lenses and film, and a Nizo Heliomatic 8 mm cine camera. They rush to the scene and, as agreed, meet Bruno.

Peter pulls up and winds down the window. 'Are they here yet?'

'Nope.'

'We'll follow you, and… er… don't park too close to the scene; let's keep the *Polizei* happy.'

As they come to the car park, they see it. 'That is going to look awesome on the front page,' Bimpy says.

'Come on, let's get to it; we won't have long,' Peter says.

Bimpy grabs his camera and snaps some exterior shots. Dulled by the years he spent out in Vietnam during the First Indochina War, he is unaffected by the gruesome sight of the charred corpse and, without missing a beat, clicks off shots. Taking up the cine camera, he runs the film, panning along the body and holding on the head.

Peter chats to his brother.

Bimpy calls out, 'This is going to make cool copy, Peter. Come look.'

Peter peers in through the cab, walks around, and finally looks in the back. 'Ah, shit, man, that's enough to put you off your breakfast. Look, they've tied him down and what's all that shiny stuff between his legs?'

Bruno spots the sign hanging from a nearby tree. 'Peter, look, there's something over here: a weird message.'

Joining him, Peter says, 'Curious, there's been nothing about messages at the other bodies. Those cunning bastards. I suspect they've held it back. Get some shots.'

Bimpy snaps pictures and is just running the cine when they hear a distant engine.

'They're here. Bruno, take Bimpy off quick; I don't want them to know we've got pictures. Bimpy, wait up near the road, and I'll pick you up later, but Bruno, you come back; they'll want to speak to you.'

Bruno nods and turns to Bimpy. 'Follow me.' The two of them make off into the woods and soon join a path. Bruno points out the direction. 'It's about twenty minutes to the road.'

The *Polizei* cars halt, the officers get out, don their caps and walk on over. One stops by Peter, the other goes to the van.

'Are you the one who found it?'

'No, I had come here to meet my brother. He's the one that found it. He went off into the undergrowth to take a piss. He'll be back. It's awful. Is this the work of the Forest Executioner?'

The officer takes out his notebook. 'Name?'

'Peter Koe.'

'And you say you were walking here?'

'Yes, I had come over to have a picnic lunch with my brother, Bruno; he's the head forester in this area.'

The officer looks at him, narrowing his eyes. 'Very romantic. All right, is that your car?'

Peter nods.

'Go sit in it and wait for the detectives; they'll need a statement.'

Smiling, Peter slides into his Volvo and sits watching.

Coming out at the road, Bimpy crosses over, makes his way back up to the turning and, finding a hiding place, fits a long lens to his camera and waits.

25

Home art gone

'**AT LEAST IT'S STOPPED RAINING.** Here, would you mind driving? I'm still sore from Wednesday.' Bastian throws the keys over to Otti, who plucks them deftly from the air.

She laughs. 'Sure thing, perhaps you'd like to sit in the back and put your feet up too?'

'Hilarious.'

They get in and head up north to re-interview Günther's men. For a while, they drive in silence. Bastian cracks the window and lights up.

'Didn't get enough smoke the other night, then?' she jests.

He scoffs. 'No, it was more of a raging inferno, you know?'

'Had a quick taste of Hell's fire, eh?'

'I can assure you I've been there many times.'

She nods. 'Seriously, though, are you okay? I mean, the guy was trying to kill you, wasn't he?'

'I think it crossed his mind. But, yeah, I'm fine.'

Looking over at him, she raises her eyebrows.

Bastian shrugs. 'Really! You know, if he'd seriously wanted to kill me, he'd have shot me soon as he had the chance. Fact is, I think he backed himself into a corner, got blinded by that stuff about his brother and once Max showed up, well, he was toast.'

She grimaces. 'Oh man, that's terrible.'

He laughs and holds up his hands. 'Sorry.'

She turns, smiling, enjoying the ease of his company. 'Anyway, I'm glad you're okay. I'm just getting to like you.'

He looks at her, knotting his brows.

She looks back and frowns. 'What?'

He breaks into a broad smile, warmth radiating from his hazel eyes. 'Ditto. We make a good team, don't we?'

She does not answer, suddenly checking herself and realising that her feelings for him are cloudy. For a while, they drive on in silence.

Bastian breaks the quiet. 'You did a great job at the test yesterday, very impressive groupings and timings; you're a natural. The Walther PP suits you well, too. Fancy training to join the range team?'

They fall silent again. After a bit, she says, 'Yeah, perhaps, let me get used to carrying this thing first.' She pauses, tapping a finger on the steering wheel, thinking. 'What's it like? You know, shooting someone?'

He nods and turns in his seat, puffs out his cheeks. 'Ah, I see. Good question. Well, I guess it's like this: you have a gun in your hand, a real person in your sights, and you know if you don't shoot, you or someone else are history. That bit, well, it's instinct; you'll pull the trigger, don't you worry. Then after, when they're down, you carry that with you and find a place to put it. Honestly, if what you did was just, then it'll be all right, and will sit fine in your conscience. Just remember that when someone picks up a weapon and threatens you with it, they've made a choice, and the consequences are their responsibility, not yours. Don't overthink it though, all right?'

'Is it different? You know, from killing in the war?'

'In the war? Hmm… yes. Most of the time, I didn't see who or what I killed. Except…' he pauses for a moment, 'well, there was this one time, late in '44, we had to take back a bridge the Tommies had seized. I had to dispatch a sentry, you know, stealthy-like? I grabbed him, my hand over his mouth and stuck the knife in, and he squirmed his head around and, for a moment, we locked eye-to-eye. He looked so young, scared, and shocked. Freaked the shit out of me. It was the worst experience I've ever had. I still see him, you know, in my dreams, like he owns me now.'

He stops talking, a slight shake to his hands, takes a drag from his cigarette, inhaling deeply. 'Dammit, Otti, you did it again? I've told nobody that, I…'

'Is it better? You know, out in the open?'

'Well, it's not going back into the bloody box now, is it?' He pauses, running his hand through his hair, and looks at her with smiling eyes. He sighs. 'I guess, if I'd wanted it to stay there, I'd have kept stumm, wouldn't I?'

'It's okay. I can hold secrets. You know, survivors must carry a lot of baggage about, particularly the good ones like you.'

'How do you know I'm a good one?'

'I just do. My mum's wise, always says that it's better to talk things out, you know, only carry what you can manage.'

'Well, I guess that makes sense, but perhaps it's easier said than done. Trouble is, sometimes you can't put it into words.'

'Sure, I get that.'

'Anyway, you're right about the baggage thing; not really thought of it like that before.'

They slip into silence, alone in their thoughts.

'Glad it's stopped raining, although I do like running in the rain; it's kinda cleansing,' she says.

'Just the walking for me but amen to the rain bit.'

'Do you know if these guys have been told about Günther yet?'

'I guess. Maria must have told them something when she had them down tools yesterday.'

It turned out that Maria had not told them Günther was dead, just that he'd had an accident. Conrad, at first shocked, then looking worried, asked about his job. Bastian had said he couldn't help with that. They took them one by one, noting that most of the men seemed unmoved by Günther's death. Perhaps the war had taken the humanity from them? Nothing new had come out until they spoke with the amputee-electrician, Erich Thiel.

Otti gets up and stretches out her back. 'Last one, this guy was the only one not to have an alibi for either weekend. I think you'll like him.'

'Let's get him in.'

Otti opens the door and calls in Erich, who enters and sits rubbing his leg. 'Excuse me, gets a little sore sometimes. Still feel my foot, you know, from time to time. What's this all about, anyway?'

Otti sits. 'Erich, remember me?'

'Course, pretty young woman, like you,' he notices the holstered pistol on her hip and, checking himself, adds, 'sorry, no offence.'

'None taken, Erich. This is my colleague, Detective Döhl, we just want to ask a few more questions, but first, I'm sorry to tell you that your boss, Günther, died last night.'

Erich's eyes widen, and his hand covers his mouth. 'Crap, Günther, dead? How?'

'It's a long story, but he tried to cover up evidence by destroying the old Citroën van and got caught in the fire.'

'My God, poor Günther, Maria just said he'd had an accident. You know, after the war, because of my leg, most people didn't want to give me a job, but not Günther; he didn't care about that. He was a good man. What was he thinking?'

'It's about Christian. You know him?'

'Yes, most of the men think he is a bit of a joke, you know? Although that changed a bit when, one day, we had a young cock-sure apprentice here, and he was taking the piss out of Christian, imitating him, and we were all laughing, you know like you do. Anyway, suddenly Christian just snaps, and he picks this guy up like he's nothing and hurls him against the wall, knocking him out and breaking his collarbone. After that, well, no one said anything to his face. I had little to do with him until he asked me to come and help fix an electrical problem at his apartment. To be honest, he's pretty handy, but this was an earthing problem, and the fuse kept blowing. His landlord kept fobbing him off, so he asked me.'

Otti looks up from her notebook. 'Hang on a minute, are you saying that you know where Christian lives?'

'Of course.'

'Tell us about his apartment. Where is it?'

'It's in Kreuzberg, one of those blocks, two beds, top floor, small and tidy. He lives there with his sister. I think because he's, you know, slow, or whatever, she takes care of him.'

Bastian and Otti exchange looks. 'He's got a sister?' Otti asks.

'Yes, and she's really nice, kind and quiet.'

'What's her name, and can you describe her?'

'She's called Angelika, but Christian calls her Ange. She's maybe late twenties or so, beautiful, blond hair, quite small, but sporty, you know what I mean? She's great with him, very kind and patient. She wanted to pay me for the work, but I said no, though she insisted I stay for a meal and a beer instead.'

'How long ago was this?'

'Hmm, let's see, um… maybe a year, eighteen months back.'

'Do you know what she does for work?'

'I think she's a waitress at a bierkeller in the Wedding district. Christian said he didn't like it when she worked late.'

'Did they say anything about other family or friends?'

'No, we just chatted about stuff, you know? They wanted to know about my leg and what I'd done in the war.' He laughs. 'Everybody wants to know about my leg. I should get a card printed with the story, save my breath.'

'Have you seen them since?'

'I've seen Christian, you know, at work, but not her.'

'Do you remember the address?'

'No, but I've got it written in my notebook,' he says, fishing in his pocket. 'Here,' he passes it over, and Bastian jots it down.

Bastian returns Eric's notebook. 'Thanks. Oh, you don't know what their family name is, do you?'

Erich shakes his head. 'No, sorry, never asked him that. Huh, funny, isn't it? We all know one another by our first names.'

Bastian shakes his head. 'No matter.'

'You say this is a murder investigation? Is this about those forest killings? I mean, you can't think that they've got anything to do with it, surely?'

Bastian closes his notebook. 'You're not the first person to say that, but the thing is, show me what a killer looks like, and our job will be much simpler. It takes all types, Erich. Anyway, right now, we just want to speak with Christian, that's all. If, by any chance, he turns up here, please call us and call if you think of anything else. Here's my direct line, or you can call the Kripo HQ on 71 05 71.'

They get up and turn to go. Bastian asks, 'Who were you with, you know, back then?'

'Großdeutschland, I was a radio operator, at least until this happened at Tomarovka, July '43. After I recovered, I became an instructor. You?'

'Five years a *Fallschirmjäger*.'

'Green Devil, eh? That fits, but rather you than me. If the Good Lord had meant us to jump out of aircraft, he'd have given us wings.'

'No, he just gave us the brain to make wings, great big silk ones. The jumping bit was fine; the landing in a huge shit-storm with only a sidearm, not so much. After Crete, we did little jumping.' For a moment, they regard one another, a silent acknowledgement of shared memories. Bastian nods. 'Thanks for your help, and I'm sorry about Günther.'

They jump back in the Ponton. Bastian gets on the radio asking for them to track down Max urgently. 'Let's get down there; we'll scope it out and then wait for backup.' Otti fires up the engine, and they head south. 'It's Köpenicker Straße, I'll check the map.' As he flicks through the West

Berlin street plan, he asks, 'Where do your parents live?'

'Mum lives in Charlottenburg, near the Deutsche Oper.'

'What about your father?'

She looks across at him and smiles weakly. 'I'll tell you about him another time, okay?'

'Sure, no pressure.'

'Have you family?'

'Dad's gone, Mum went to live with her sister in Dortmund, and I have an older brother, Daniel. Like me, he was in the Luftwaffe, but a pilot. Got shot down over England in the Summer of '40.'

'Oh, sorry.'

'No, he's fine. Spent the rest of the war as a POW. Toward the end, he worked on a farm and fell for one of the land girls, and they got married. They live in Sussex, near a little place called Alfriston. They have two girls, similar age to Max's kids. Alison, his wife, is lovely. He teaches maths and German at a boys' school in Seaford.'

'You see them often?'

'I've been over a few times, Christmas, birthdays, you know. They wanted me to come and join them, but *Ich bin Berliner* and I like my job.'

'So, you're not all alone, then?'

'No, we were lucky. My aunt, mum's sister, you know the one in Dortmund, she lost her two boys and my uncle.'

'What happened to your dad?'

'Gassed and wounded in the first war. He was never really in good health after and died from complications in '26 when I was still a little kid; I don't remember him.'

'So much death. Do you think that we humans can get along now?'

'Well, at least next time it'll be quick, a few H and A-bombs, and it'll be good night, Vienna.'

'Terrible thought, though.'

'Being where we are, we'll be right in the thick of it; we're the fragile line between East and West. Truth is, I don't really follow politics.'

The radio crackles into life. 'Bastian, it's Max. What have you got?'

Bastian takes up the handset. 'We've got an address in Kreuzberg for Christian and, get this, he has a sister, Angelika, young, petite, blond hair.'

'Does he now? What's your location?'

'We're en route to the apartment, going to scope it out. We'll look out for the car.'

'I'm done here for now. What's the address? We'll come over; wait for us, all right?'

'Address is Köpenicker Straße, 22-29, Apartment 446.'

'Got it. Be there in twenty, out.'

Otti glances over at Bastian. 'So, we have their hideout and their apartment; they have nowhere else to go, have they?'

'I'm sure they won't be there. Based on Günther's behaviour, he's bound to have warned them, and it's possible they have another place, perhaps with a parent? I'll tell you one thing I know: when people run-scared, they nearly always go somewhere they know well. They won't be far.'

26

Wisely and slow; they stumble that run fast

TOBI TAPS THE STEERING WHEEL. 'We're closing in. We have their basement, apartment, and vehicle description. It's just a matter of time.'

Tracing the scar on his cheek, Max thinks. 'So, let's say, for argument's sake, that Günther's told them we know who they are, right? I feel that although Christian might appear slow, it doesn't mean he isn't capable, and there's no doubt that his sister's resourceful. They've gone to a load of trouble and planning over this. When the homeless guy, Heinz, called, he said that they had carried out another body. That would be number four, but we only know about three. He also said they had two vehicles, a red Ford van and a Beetle, both missing but have only the registration of the VW.' He looks out of the side window, now tracing the scar above his right eye. 'Hmm, what do they know?'

Deciding, he picks up the handset and radios in. 'Dispatch, this is KHK Becker. I want an alert on the autobahn route border crossings, planes, and trains heading West. Arrest and detain…' he gives out the details. 'Get that dispatched immediately—Becker out.'

Tobi looks over at him. 'You think they might make a run for the border?'

'I'm just covering all bases. Question is, how clever are they? If they're cool headed, they'll stay local and go to ground, wouldn't you?'

'I would. They could go East, of course.'

'Yes, true, but they've been living and working in the West, and my bet is they won't want to give that up? And, as you know, people run where they feel comfortable. Let's assume they know the game is up. I don't hold out much hope they'll be at the apartment, but conceivably, they might have left something for us. Trouble is, they've got at least a day's head start and all of Berlin in which to hide.'

The radio crackles into life. 'Call for KHK Becker, copy, over.' Max snaps up the handset. 'Becker here, go ahead.'

'We have a report of a burnt-out van, a body inside, location Höchster Baum, Tegel Forest, officers attending.'

'Tell them to secure the scene and wait. We're attending another scene, ETA Tegel,' he looks at his *Wehrmacht* issue Silvana watch. 'Eighty minutes.'

'Officers say they are holding two witnesses: the forester, who found the body and another man.'

'Inform them to take statements, and if satisfied with their status, to let them go. We'll follow up later. Is there a report of a message at the scene?'

'Affirmative, sign found hanging on a nearby tree.' Max and Tobi exchange glances.

'Roger that. Get path and forensics out there soon as. Becker out.'

'Well, we know what happened to the van,' says Tobi.

'We'll go help access the apartment. I'll leave you and Otti there to go through things and take Bastian out to Tegel.'

As they drive up Köpenicker Straße, Bastian is waiting by the apartment building. They park and join him.

'Where's Otti?' Max queries.

'She's scouting the surrounding streets, looking for the Beetle.'

'We have another body. Once we get into the apartment, you come with me. Tobi and Otti can take care of business here.'

Shortly after, Otti appears, shaking her head. 'No sign.'

Max nods. 'All right, let's get in.'

They take the stairs and, approaching number 446, draw their sidearms. Max turns to Otti. 'You do the honours.'

She knocks, then steps to one side. '*Polizei*! Open the door.'

They wait, but there are no sounds from within. Max nods at Bastian, who takes three giant strides and hoofs the door in, the frame splintering as the old timber jamb gives way. Across the hall, a door opens, a scared face peeps out but seeing them, disappears.

They sweep in, checking each room. 'All clear. Right, Bastian, let's go. I'll catch you later, Tobi, okay?'

Tobi nods and, holstering his Walther, says to Otti, 'Let's start in the bedrooms,' then, spotting Maria's note, adds, 'Hang on, what's this?'

Putting on gloves, he picks it up and reads. He looks at Otti. 'Well, there's the proof that Maria and Günther were assisting.' He passes it over.

She looks, then pops it in a bag, leaving it on the side for forensics. She enters Angelika's room. It is immaculate, no dust or cobwebs, the bed neatly made. There are a couple of ageing pictures on the walls, and in one corner, an old sink, a slow drip from the cold tap that has worn away the enamel, leaving a rust streak down the bowl. She begins with the dresser, removing each drawer, checking underneath and behind, does the same to the bedside table, then removes the pictures. Finally, she turns her attention to the modest iron bed and, pulling back the covers, it surprises her to find a message written in red ink on a piece of cardboard, just like the others.

'Hey, Tobi? Come look, I've found something.'

He joins her and looks at the message. 'A sense of the dramatic, some humour, even.'

I LOOKED AND THERE WERE NO PEOPLE; EVERY BIRD IN THE SKY HAD FLOWN AWAY - WEDNESDAY!

'Wonder what the reference to Wednesday is about? Was that the day they left, perhaps? We'll leave it where it is, get forensics in, okay?'

'Yep, no problem,' Otti replies.

There's nothing else in either room. They carry on through the entire apartment, checking for loose floorboards and skirting, behind furniture, anywhere you can conceal something. The only things left are a few food items, the sort of provisions you'll find in every kitchen of every house. Tobi feels the kettle; it's cold. The apartment has an air of abandonment about it. In the living room, there is a bookshelf containing five books: an encyclopaedia, three novels, and a bible. They don't touch them. Tobi goes to the window. The view looks out over the Soviet sector. He can see the Spree River, the Schilling Bridge, and the Ostbahnhof, and he wonders if they've just walked or driven across, to disappear forever. Like Max, he has a couple of trusted contacts in the VoPo: he'll put a feeler out on the QT, just in case.

Otti stands looking at the sterile living room. 'Considering they lived here for at least two years, they certainly left little evidence, did they?'

'Maybe, one day, we'll find out why, eh?'

'I'll contact base to get forensics, and a carpenter sent out,' Otti says.

'Good idea. After that, we'll stroll over to the other side and have a look around the S-Bahn station, just in case they dumped the car and took the train.'

❖ ❖ ❖

After waiting for a while, the officer came and asked Peter Koe some questions, taking a brief statement. He neglected to tell them he was a journalist, but then they didn't ask. They informed him he could go and that a detective would be in touch.

As he drives out, a van comes down the track and, waving them on, he backs up to a layby. Must be forensics, he thinks. Driving out to the road, he stops, looking for Bimpy, who appears out of cover opposite and runs over. Peter winds down his window.

'I was waiting to see who turns up. Got photos of the van and its passengers. Do you want to call it and go back, or shall we hang about?'

'You go back to cover. I'll drive down and find a place to lose the car, then join you. Max Becker is the lead detective on this case. Let's see if he turns up, shall we?'

Five minutes later, he joins Bimpy, who, grinning, says, 'Just like the old days.'

A few minutes later, they hear a car approaching and slowing. It's an expensive Mercedes roadster with a middle-aged guy at the wheel. Bimpy fires off a couple of shots. Peter mutters, 'That's the great Dr Paul Schmidt, Berlin's top pathologist and former high ranking Wehrmacht surgeon. Rumour has it he treated Rommel after he received a severe injury when an allied plane strafed his car in Normandy. He's well connected, if you know what I mean?'

Paul drives on down the track, grumbling about the inconsiderate nature of murderers and pulling up behind the forensics van, takes his case and walks over to the scene. He can see Lutz, a tech, and a photographer, busy taking shots and recording details.

'Hey, Lutz,' he says joining him, 'where's the body?'

'In there, go on in.'

Snapping on a pair of gloves, a cloth mask, and glasses, he climbs in. Lutz comes over with a powerful torch, lighting up the scene for him.

Paul nods. 'Thanks. Let's see what we've got, shall we?'

He begins by looking at the head area. 'Here, Lutz, bring that light up here. There's something in his mouth.'

The area is lit up. 'Looks like a metal ball bearing.'

'His jaw and teeth are broken. Could have happened during the fire, but my guess is he bit down so hard... well... speaks for itself, doesn't it?'

'He was in agony, then?'

Scanning down the body, they pause at the mid-area. 'Hmm... that's odd; what have we got here?'

Lutz brings the light closer. 'Looks like, what would you say? Lead?'

Paul looks over at him. 'Looks to me like he's had it poured over his genitals. The PM will confirm, but that's what it looks like, and that would explain the broken teeth and jaw.'

Lutz grimaces. 'Doesn't bear thinking about. Any idea what killed him?'

'Not yet. We'll have to inspect his lungs to see if he was alive when the fire began. You smell petrol?'

Lutz nods.

Bimpy and Peter hear another car slowing, a Mercedes Ponton with two passengers. Bimpy clicks away on the Leicia.

'Got them?'

'Yeah, brother, no problem. Was that Becker?'

'Yep, the one driving. Don't know the other one.'

Bimpy takes out two *Gauloises Bleu* cigarettes, lights them and passes one over. 'Here, bro, have a decent French smoke.'

Peter takes it. 'Where did you get these?'

'Little shop in the French sector. I got a taste for them in Nam, practically lived off them, that and strong coffee and cognac.'

Peter inhales, pleased with the scoop. 'Nice. I think we're done here; let's go.'

Max and Bastian walk over to the van. 'Gentlemen!' Max says.

'Ah, Max, Bastian. Thought you two would have had enough of barbecues after Wednesday,' Lutz chortles.

Jumping down from the van, Paul tells them what they've found.

'*Quatsch!*' Bastian exclaims. 'Are you saying they poured fucking molten lead on his nuts?'

Lutz nods. 'Looks like it. Has a medieval flavour to it, doesn't it?'

'God, it makes my eyes water thinking about it. I thought I'd seen every kind of horror in the war... Holy crap!'

They have a good look around. Max points to the badge on the bonnet edge. 'It's a Ford F100, just as Heinz reported.'

Lutz says, 'Come look at the sign; it's hanging on a tree.'

The four men stop by the larch, its perpendicular trunk pointing heavenwards and hanging about two metres from the ground, a sign like the others.

WHY DO THE NATIONS RAGE? V

'Have you made anything of the other messages yet?' Lutz asks.

'No, not yet. I might put Anna on to it. She's the one for cryptic crosswords and quizzes, plus now we have four, they might make more sense.'

'I'll have a look too; you never know. Good to keep the grey matter ticking over.'

One uniformed officer joins them. 'Sir, there's a call out on the radio. It's KOK Klein.'

Max picks up. 'Hey Tobi, go ahead.'

'Apartment looks clean, save another message, which she left in her bed.' He reads it out.

'Nothing else, then?'

'No, it was like they'd never been there, really. What's it like with you?'

'Definitely them. They strapped this one down in the back of a van and poured lead on his privates and then torched him, van and all.'

'Jesus.'

'Exactly. See you back at base.'

27

There is no darkness but ignorance

ANGELIKA PARKS THE CAR A few streets away from the hotel. As with everything else, she has selected this place carefully. An establishment not bothered with registrations and with a preference for cash, which she pays on arrival: one room for two nights. The man on the reception pays them scant attention and, collecting their key, they climb the stairs to the third floor. The room, on the south-east corner, is surprisingly clean and airy, with a view out toward the Hümboldthain Park and the central station of Gesundbrunnen. But most importantly, it has a fire escape.

Christian sits down on the far bed. 'I'm starving, and I feel sad, too.'

'That's to be expected,' she says, sitting on the other bed, facing him. She places her hand on his knee. 'After all we've been through, it's going to take a bit of getting over. Hunger, on the other hand, we can fix.'

He looks up, smiling weakly. 'Good.'

'Before we go out and eat, I need you to look at this.' From her bag, she takes a copy of a Berlin Street atlas and, opening it out to page twenty-four, lays it on the bed. 'Look, we're just here, and that street is where we parked the car, right?'

He nods.

For a few minutes, she takes him through her plan of escape using various U-Bahn and S-Bahn routes and what to do if they need to split up. Taking the map, he sits studying the pages, his lips moving, his finger tracing the routes and connections. After a few minutes, he looks up. 'Look, if we take U-Bahn eight, we can change at Alexanderplatz and go off in one of three other directions.'

She smiles at him, knowing that now he has spent a few minutes taking in the maps, he'll not forget them; his memory is like that.

'Yes, it'll be hard to follow us, won't it? Let's go eat, shall we?'

'Yes, please, I could eat a horse.'

She giggles and grabs his hand, pulling him up. 'Thank God we don't have to anymore. When we get back, we'll get some much-needed rest. I don't know about you, but I'm exhausted.'

❖❖❖

He rises, screaming, his body engulfed in flames, but they do not seem to burn him as beneath the fire, his clothes and skin are untouched. She turns and runs, stumbling, her leaden legs are moving but she's not getting away. His unearthly screech increases, reaching an ear-splitting crescendo. She hears footsteps and the roar of flames, the smell of burning flesh, but she cannot turn and look, and as she feels his hand touch her shoulder, she wakes, gasping, her eyes wide. Sitting up, she tries to control her breathing. The room is still with the faint background sounds of a city at night. After a few moments, she calms down, gets up, goes over to the sink, fills a beaker with water, and drinks.

A bottle of *Shalimar* perfume sits on the shelf, and picking it up, she holds it against her cheek. It belonged to her mother, a cherished gift from her father on the last Christmas they all spent together; it's the only thing that Angelika has of hers. For years she's carried it around and, from time to time would take a sniff just to remind her. But the day they took Manfried, she wore the scent to carry her mother with her for strength. Even Christian had commented on it: "You smell like mother. I really miss her." It had made her cry, and they had hugged.

They had been lucky to have such loving and decent parents. She was always a daddy's girl, and mum, so good, so patient, had doted on Christian. Their lives had been blessed; they were not wealthy, but they wanted for nothing. And then the war came, and their world had disappeared in a vortex of violence and hate. Thinking back on them as a contented family, she has no regrets about hunting down and killing the men who had taken so much from them. She does not know how her father died, but the Ivans took him too. She looks at her brother, his colossal, powerful form filling the small bed. He's lying on his side, facing the wall, and she wonders of what he dreams.

Going over to the window, she looks out and whispers, 'Are you looking for us, Kommissar Max Becker? Where are you?' While they were eating, they'd gone over everything they thought the *Polizei* might know. Christian reminded her that Erich had been to their flat, and she had said that perhaps Günther had told them. It did not matter. Save the last message, which had been an afterthought; the *Polizei* won't find anything. They're sure that the basement will remain a secret, at least until someone is nosey enough to break the locks and look and by that time, well, who knows, it could be years.

Tomorrow she'll pick up a paper to see. Yesterday's news had reported Rolf's murder and discovery. They were still calling them the Forest Executioner: she liked the executioner part. None of the reports had mentioned the messages, and she wondered why that was. Surely, they hadn't missed them? Perhaps the *Polizei* were keeping some things a secret? In one paper, there was a good-sized picture of the lead detective, *Kriminalhauptkommisar* Max Becker, with the caption: "Ace Detective Max Becker leads the hunt." He is good-looking, she guesses fortyish, dark, tidy hair, even features, lean and carries himself well; hard to tell his height, but proportionally, he looks average.

The picture showed him walking toward the camera, his jacket and topcoat slightly open, revealing a pistol on his right hip. He wasn't wearing a tie or a hat. He was glancing to his left, and it looked like he had a scar on his right cheek. She doesn't know why, but she likes the look of him and wonders what he'd done in the war. Had he been a party member, loyal to the Führer? Weren't they all? Remembering what her father had once said: "Always best to know your enemy; try to think like them." Tomorrow, she thinks, we'll go to the library and do a little research, see what can be dug up on Max Becker.

Pulling the thin curtain shut, she places the cup back on the sink stand, takes a dab of perfume, rubbing it on her neck, and before climbing back into bed, returns the precious bottle to her bag. Shutting her eyes, she thinks of warm days before the war and happy holidays. She slips back to sleep.

'Ange, it's me,' he shakes her gently, 'Ange, wake up, wake up.'
She opens her eyes, blinking a few times. Light floods the room.
'What? What is it? Oh, yes, I'm awake, all right. What time is it?'
'It's ten-thirty. You were talking in your sleep.'
'Was I?'
'Yes, who's Max?'
'Hell, is that what I was saying?'
'You were saying, "Where are you, Max?" or something like that.'

'Oh, it's just stupid dream stuff, you know?'

'Are we going to get breakfast?'

'Yeah, yeah, why not? Do you want to go to the same place we went to last night?'

'Yes, the food was good.'

She smiles and laughs. 'You're telling me! You ate enough, my God!'

They sit at the same table.

'How long are we staying here?' he asks.

'We'll stay tonight and move early tomorrow. I'll move the car later. Try to find a dead-end road, you know, one that the *Polizei* are less likely to drive down.'

'How would they know what car we have? Anyway, you said we would not register it.'

'I'm just careful; besides, I had a weird feeling we were being watched.'

'When?'

'At Teischstraße.'

'Oh? I didn't see anyone.'

'No, it was just a feeling, and you remember that cat and the noise outside?'

'Yes, what of it?'

'Well, what if it was someone, you know, snooping around?'

Christian takes a bite from the bread roll packed with ham and cheese, thinking. 'Nah, I don't think anyone was there; why would they be?'

'We could leave the car and use public transport. We'd be tough to find then, wouldn't we?'

'I'd rather we use the car; you know I find transport difficult with all those people and the noise.'

'All right, it's fine. We'll keep the car for now. Perhaps we can change it for another in time. Now eat up. I want to go to the library; there are things I need to look up. We can walk to the Schiller from here, all right?'

It is a good day for a walk. After the midweek cold front and rain, the temperature has risen, the sun threatening to break through the light cloud. Next to reading, Angelika loves to walk. From their old apartment in Kreuzberg, it was a short stroll across the border to the Treptower Park that runs along the west bank of the Spree River, home to the grand Soviet War Memorial, nicknamed by many, *Tomb of the Unknown Rapist*. She never went there.

Sometimes, on a day off and when Christian was at work, she'd take a picnic lunch and sit in the sun by the river or the Karpfenteich Lake, watching the world go by; enjoying admiring glances from young male students, which made her smile as she was older than them—she'd never looked her age. On occasions, they would pluck up courage to ask her out to some party or dance at the University or to come and drink coffee and discuss politics. She would have liked nothing more but always turned them down, saying she was spoken for. Those days were precious, and as they amble along, she thinks that someday, when they are free, she'll go there again.

They keep to the quieter side roads, eventually coming to the busy major route of Müllerstraße and, turning right, walk the last few minutes, passing the Leopoldplatz U-Bahn station, which stands opposite a park bearing the same name and home to a Catholic church. For a moment, they stop. She regards the church. 'After we've finished at the library, I'd like to pop in there for a minute. Is that all right?'

Christian frowns. 'A church, why? We've not been to church, not since we were kids.'

'I want to light a candle for mama and papa and check something out, okay?'

They enter the Schiller Library. 'I'm going to the reference section to look at old newspapers. You look at those books you like, okay?'

Angelika goes over to the reference counter. The woman behind the desk smiles. 'Oh, hello again, haven't seen you for a while. What can I do for you?'

'Have you got Berlin papers for the last year or two on microfilm, please?'

The woman shows Angelika to a viewer and brings over a box containing the relevant film. 'You know how it works, don't you?'

Angelika smiles at her and sits. 'Yes, thanks.'

After a thirty-minute search, she finds him. It is a report about a killer called *"Der Mädchenjäger"* who had been abducting and murdering young girls throughout the summer. She remembers reading about it. There's an excellent picture of Max and a colleague, Tobi Klein. She reads the article, saying to herself, 'Nice job, Max, I like your style; he won't be bothering anyone again'. Going back further, she finds an article also about *"Der Mädchenjäger"* this time questioning what the *Polizei* are doing to catch him. There are maps showing the location of each abduction and where they discovered the bodies, none of which much interests her.

An hour later, she finds what she is looking for, an article from June 1958 titled, "Who is Max Becker? Star Detective brings serial killer to justice." She reads it through. It is full of interesting facts about what he did in the war, who he is married to, his children and, most importantly, to Angelika; he lives in Schwarzer Läufer Straße in the Zehlendorf district.

Switching off the viewer, she packs up the film and, for a few moments, thinks, drumming her fingers rhythmically on the desk.

'Here, thank you,' she says, handing back the box.

Smiling, the woman takes it from her. 'Did you find what you were looking for?'

'Oh yes, very much so. The library never lets me down.'

Leaving, they find the clouds broken and the sun is shining. 'Let's find a place for lunch, or shall we get a sandwich and eat in the park?'

He beams. 'Yes, let's do that: the park.'

28

What's done cannot be undone

AFTER COMPLETING JOHANN'S AUTOPSY, MAX and Paul settle down in his office. 'I wasn't expecting the cause of death to be a heart attack.'

'His heart was a mess, and the stress of his ordeal was enough to end it. How's it going tracking your sibling suspects?'

'We've hit a wall. We know what they're driving, at least, assuming they still are, of course. Who's to say they haven't changed vehicles, just as they did between the second and third murders? She's smart, this one, that's for sure. We don't know what their family name is yet, so we're tracking down the landlord to see if they signed a tenant agreement. In fact, one of the odd things about this case is the lack of identities.'

'Are you going to use the media to make an appeal?'

'Erich, one of Günther's men, is the only person who knows what they both look like; he's seeing a *Polizei* artist today, and hopefully, we'll end up with excellent likenesses that we can get out to the public.'

Paul takes a pull from his coffee. 'Do you think they're done?'

Max traces his scar, thinking. 'Hmm, I do. It's the message they left at their apartment; feels like a goodbye.'

'Well, I don't know about you, but I fancy getting out of here. They said on the news that we might see the sun today. You got any plans?'

'I'm going to run up to HQ. The team should be in, and I've got a good old-fashioned bit of legwork for them. After lunch, Anna and the kids are coming up to meet me, and we're off to see a new film about the life of Spartacus. Be nice to spend some time with them.'

'Good idea; step back for a few hours. Let me know if the film's worth seeing, will you?'

Walking out to his new BMW R69s motorcycle, Max dons his helmet and shrugs on his field-grey leather jacket. He switches on the ignition, opens the twist-throttle slightly and gives the starter a short, vigorous kick. The engine burbles to life, idling to the characteristic, smooth, *potato-potato-potato* of the boxer engine. Hopping on, he hefts it off the stand, blips the throttle, knocks it into first gear and smoothly pulls away. Turning north onto Tempelhofer Damm, he speeds up through the gears, relishing the feel of freedom and wishes he could point south and ride to Bavaria. The traffic is light, and he makes quick work of the eight-kilometre ride and, just eleven minutes later, climbs the stairs to his office.

The entire team is in. 'Any news on the car?' asks Max.

There's a collective shaking of heads. 'Plenty of grey Beetles, just not the right one,' Udo says.

Max gathers them together. 'They say people on the run will go somewhere they feel safe and where they know the layout. I can't disagree with that and have a hunch that they're in the Wedding district. They both worked up there; it has good transport links, and there are plenty of small, discreet hotels.'

'Yes, that would be my choice, too,' Bastian agrees.

'Why don't you think they've left the city?' Udo asks.

'Your question makes the point, doesn't it? It's the logical thing to do, get out, and Europe's your oyster. But our girl is smart, so I'm convinced she won't do what we're expecting. In addition, to get out of Berlin, they'd have to cross GDR territory, and we've put out an alert for their car and are watching stations and airports. Their features are distinctive, particularly him, so I reckon they're just too easy to spot. I think they'll lie low, perhaps split up, changing location every day or two, and when time has passed, then they'll make their move. It's what I'd do.'

Udo nods. 'Yeah, makes sense.'

'Of course, we need some luck. All of you get up to the Wedding district, drive around all the small hotels and hostels. You know the score and let's see if we can make our own luck. To cover more ground, go alone, but, and I stress this: if you find them, call for backup. Questions?'

Heads shake. 'All right, Tobi will assign your routes. We'll meet back here tomorrow morning, 9 a.m.'

With the team gone, Max picks up the phone and dials his friend in the VoPo. There is a pause, then a voice. 'Yes?'

'Walter, it's Max.'

'Max, my friend, what's happening?'

Max gives him the heads up on his suspects.

'No problem, we'll keep an eye out, if they've topped some comrades, I am sure our Russian friends won't want your suspects hiding out here, eh? Mind you, if we catch them, I can't guarantee you'll get them back.'

'It's a risk I'll have to take.'

❖❖❖

A little after 1 p.m., Anna and the kids show up. 'Hey, dad,' says Heike, 'are you ready?'

'Where is everyone?' Anna asks.

'They're all out searching the Wedding district for our suspects.'

'You sure you don't need to join them?'

'No, it's been a demanding week, and they'll be fine without me for a few hours. We're meeting back here tomorrow for a catch up.'

Markus has wandered over to the evidence board. 'Yuck, that's horrible, dad.'

'Ah, come on, Markus, you know the drill, no looking.'

'Sorry, dad.' Then he looks closely at one photo. He asks, 'Is that a message the killers left?'

Max comes and stands by him. 'Yes, why?'

'It's a quote from the Old Testament, Leviticus, I think. We've been looking at it in school, and I just remember those words. It's the bit about a person having the power to bring others to account for their sins that were committed in ignorance, or something like that.'

'Is it now? We wondered whether they might be religious or biblical, but now we know. That's a good catch, Marky, thanks.'

Heike and Anna join them and inspect the photos. Heike makes a face, Anna says, 'There's much passion here, you know, in the injuries. Do you want to check the bible now?'

For a moment, Max considers. He shakes his head. 'No, a few hours won't make a difference. Let's go enjoy the film, get something to eat, and I'll have a look later at home, all right?'

'I'll help you,' says Markus.

'Yeah, me too,' adds Heike.

'Come on, let's go,' says Anna, 'when we get home, we'll all pitch in, shall we?'

❖❖❖

Now up in the Wedding district, the team have agreed for everyone to meet at 5 p.m. at a café called Stella, on Grüntaler Straße. Bastian is last to arrive and, ordering a coffee, joins them at the table.

'What have we got left to search?' Tobi asks.

Jürgen lays out the map. 'Just this section north of the Humboldthain Park.'

'All right, let's do another hour. We've got three radio cars, so we'll team up. I'll ride solo, Udo and Jürgen, take the blue Ponton, Bastian and Otti the white. If you see something, call; otherwise, we'll meet back here at 6:30 p.m. and call it a day.'

As luck would have it, Angelika and Christian have spent a couple hours in the park, visited the church, after which she moves the car, parking it in a street the team has searched previously, and a few minutes later, they are safely back in their room.

At 6:30 p.m., disappointed, the team is back at Stella's. Max's idea seemed solid, but in a city the size of Berlin, a long shot.

Tobi buys a round of drinks. 'We'll come back first thing and widen our search.'

An hour later, Udo and Jürgen fall into step heading to the car. Jürgen says, 'We could do a couple hours more, then we can dump the car and get a few drinks. What do you say?'

'Yeah, sure, why not? Can't hurt to drive the area a while longer.'

Bastian and Otti head back to where they've parked their cars. 'You fancy a drink and a wind-down?' she asks.

'Yeah, sure, couple beers will be good, perhaps a bite to eat, too, eh?'

'I'll leave my car here and pick it up tomorrow,' Otti says. 'You don't mind dropping me home, do you?'

'No, sure thing, good idea.'

A little after 8 p.m., Christian decides he needs to get out of the room and go to the shop to buy some chocolate. Angelika is asleep. He goes alone. The nearest shop is a couple of streets away, and in just a few minutes, he has made his purchase and heads back. As he nears the hotel on Böttgerstraße, Udo and Jürgen drive by.

Christian catches Udo's keen eye. 'Look at that guy, the big one; my God, he's huge. Could be Christian. Let's pull up and see where he goes.'

Jürgen parks the car, and they watch as Christian enters the Hotel Burgermeister. 'I thought we'd checked that hotel? Still easy to miss the small entrance.'

Udo looks across, a glint in his eye. 'Let's follow him.'

'Hang on, shouldn't we call it in first?'

'We don't know it's him, do we? Come on, it won't hurt to look. We can ask at reception if he's with a woman.'

'All right, just a look, mind.'

Entering the dimly lit reception area, they see the desk is empty. There's a small brass bell, which Udo picks up and rings, a voice from the back calling out, 'I'll be there in a sec.'

A portly young man appears and looking Udo and Jürgen up and down, narrows his eyes. 'We don't allow poofs here; piss off.'

Udo thrusts his badge under the fat man's nose. 'Listen, you fat cocksucker, we're Kripo. The big man that just came in. Is he alone or with a woman?'

The man smirks and holds up his hands. 'Sorry about that, mate, my mistake. Yeah, he's with a young woman.' He leers at them and licks his fleshy lips. 'She's really tasty, know what I mean? Don't know why she's knocking around with that retarded oaf, mind?'

'What colour is her hair?'

'Blond.'

'Which room?'

'133, top floor.'

Udo holds out his hand. 'The key.'

The man hands over the master key. 'I need that back, mind.'

'Stay there and keep it shut, all right?'

He nods.

Turning to Jürgen and steering him away from the reception, Udo says, 'Come on, the two of us; we're armed. Let's go get them, shall we?'

'No, no way. We need to call it in.'

'Listen, I don't trust that fat-fuck; he'll tip them off. You go radio it in, and I'll wait and cover him, okay?'

'Okay, good idea, but wait for me. I'll be back in a minute.'

At 8:20 p.m., Jürgen calls it in, then returns to the hotel.

❖❖❖

Otti drains her glass. 'I'm whacked. Let's go, shall we?'

They get up, climb into the white Ponton, and head back. They're less than three kilometres from the hotel when the call comes in.

'Car KD1-417, are you receiving, over?'

Frowning, Bastian looks across at Otti, who picks up the handset. 'Car 417 responding, go ahead.'

'Report from KOM Jürgen, found suspects, Hotel Burgermeister, Böttgerstraße, Wedding, KOM Popp also in attendance. Can you respond, over?'

Otti mouths, *what the hell!* 'That's affirmative control, Jäger and Döhl responding, ETA three minutes. Put out a call for Becker. Jäger out.'

As she speaks, Bastian turns the car, dropping a gear and flooring it. Otti switches on the siren. 'What the hell?'

Jürgen returns to the hotel, but Udo isn't there. Desperately, Jürgen looks round. Grinning, the receptionist points up the stairs. 'He's just gone up.'

'Shit!' Jürgen pulls his Walther and goes after him.

As he gets to the top of the stairs, he sees Udo, weapon drawn, by the door and about to knock. It's too late to stop him. Just as Udo's knuckles rap on the green-painted timber, Jürgen cocks his Walther. Udo glances over at him, nods, then shouts, 'Armed *Polizei*, open up, now!'

From the other side of the door, they can hear noises and a muffled voice. Udo takes a step back and taking the key, offers it up to the lock, but before he can turn it, someone yanks the door open and Christian fills the space, taking Udo off guard. Fatefully, he hesitates, and Christian lunges forward, thumping Udo in the chest. There is a crack of splintering wood as he reels backwards scrabbling hopelessly at the air as the force from Christian's blow sends him through the bannister and over the edge. Horrorstruck, Jürgen watches as his colleague sails through the narrow gap and down three floors, with a final dull thud as he hits the ground.

By the time Jürgen has recovered himself, Christian, who has watched Udo's fall, swings round, and as Jürgen brings his pistol to bear, like a man possessed Christian is upon him and smacking his hand away, grabs him by the throat and pushes him violently to the ground.

Christian overcomes Jürgen, who hears a woman's voice scream, 'Chris! No!' Then his head meets the ground, and the world goes black.

❖❖❖

Otti points. 'There, over there, that's their car. Where are they? Have they gone in already?'

The car screeches to a stop by the hotel, and the pair run in and spot Udo lying on the ground.

'Shit! Shit!' Bastian yells.

Otti is already running up the stairs; he follows.

As she gets to the top, on the landing in front of the broken railings, she sees Christian atop Jürgen, hands around his neck and shouts, 'Armed *Polizei*, stop or I'll fire!'

Christian does not respond. She shouts again, to no effect. Taking careful aim, she squeezes the trigger and fires. The bullet hits his shoulder but seems to have little effect, and Christian continues his murderous attack. She fires again, this time hitting his thigh. Grunting, Christian releases Jürgen and, looking around, spots Jürgen's pistol. At that moment, he is eleven years old; those men are attacking and he must save his mother and sister, so he reaches out and grabs the pistol to return fire.

Arriving on the floor below, Bastian halts, evaluates the situation, takes aim and fires twice. The rounds thud into Christian's chest. Almost simultaneously, Otti fires a single shot, which strikes Christian low in the right cheek. For a moment, everything stops, the shots filling the air with the tart smell of cordite. His eyes wide and brow furrowed, Christian looks at Otti, whispers, 'Sorry.' And slumps down, dead.

A stunned Otti regards the carnage. Bastian trots up the last flight of steps. 'Come on, help me get him off Jürgen.' They check his pulse. 'He's still with us. Go down and call for help.'

Bastian enters the room, noting the open window and looking out, sees the empty fire escape. He goes back, kneeling by Jürgen. 'Wake up, buddy, come on.'

He places his ear by Jürgen's mouth and listens. His breathing is shallow. He checks to see if he has been shot, but can't detect any wounds. Checking the eyes, he notes that when he pulls the lids back, one pupil is open wide. 'That's not good,' he mutters. He checks Christian's pulse. Taking a duvet from the room, he drapes it over Jürgen, then runs down the stairs to see to Udo.

Kneeling beside him, he touches two fingers to Udo's neck. At first, he's not sure. There's a weak pulse. He rips open Udo's shirt and listens for a heartbeat; it's there, and his chest is moving.

Otti returns with the first aid kit. 'They're en route. I asked for two ambulances, won't be long. Is he still with us?'

'Just.'

'Jürgen?'

'Yes, but one of his pupils is blown. We need to get them both to the hospital quickly.'

Otto passes the first aid kit to Bastian. 'What were they thinking? I'll go check the other rooms and find out who's in.'

The receptionist is standing, mouth open, staring. Bastian shouts, 'Hey! Hey! You all right, buddy?'

The man nods.

'Okay, go wait out in the road for the ambulances. Also, make sure that no one other than *Polizei* or medical staff enters. No one! Got it?'

'What about guests?'

'No one!'

'Okay, I hear you,' he says, shaking his head and hurrying off.

Bastian goes through to the office behind the counter and finding a duvet, brings it back and lays it on Udo, then sits next to him, leaning against the wall. He takes a cigarette, his hand shaking as he lights it. 'Come on, Bas, get a grip,' he says to himself, and taking a deep drag, closes his eyes.

29

The night is long that never finds the day

MAX AND HIS FAMILY EXIT the cinema and begin walking. 'Great film, wasn't it?' Markus says. They all agree.

'It's still pleasant out; shall we walk over to Café am Neuen See? My treat,' Anna says.

Max smiles. 'Well, if you're selling, we're buying, aren't we kids?'

Markus and Heike run on ahead, Max and Anna watch them. Max offers his arm, and Anna slips her hand through. She nudges him. 'Glad you took the time.'

'I don't want to miss it all. I missed my youth, so I don't want to miss theirs. And besides, I enjoy spending time with you too, you know?'

'What are you after?' Briefly, she rests her head on his shoulder. 'Doesn't the park look lovely, the leaves all different colours?'

'Sure does.'

For a while, they walk in silence. 'Whenever I come through here, I give up a brief prayer.'

She looks at him. 'For Matti?'

He nods. Despite the years, it still hurts. 'Hard to believe that just fifteen years ago, the war ripped this place to shreds. He so nearly made it. I still miss him.'

'He was your best friend. I would have loved to have known him.'

'You would have liked him, never met a person who didn't.'

'Shame you two got split up.'

'There was a time when I thought we'd be friends forever, you know, like you do when you're young and idealist. Stupid stuff, like we'd live next door to one another, be godparents to each other's kids. Anyway, at least we had the time we did. It was fun while it lasted, lots of wonderful memories.'

After they've eaten, they walk back to HQ to pick up Anna's car. 'I'll leave the bike here and bring it home tomorrow,' Max says.

By 7 p.m., he is sitting at the kitchen table, the messages and a couple of bibles spread out. He finds the Leviticus quote, chapter four, verse twenty-five, and calls out, 'Hey, Marky, you there?'

Markus joins him. 'Yeah, dad, what?'

'You were bang on the money: Leviticus.'

'Oh, great, thanks. Can I help?'

'Sure, it's going to be a job to find the rest.'

'We like a challenge; I'll go get Heike.'

Now with three bibles to hand, Anna joins in, and they search. At 8:22 p.m., when the telephone rings, they're studiously scanning the pages.

Max picks up. 'Becker.' He listens. 'Thanks, I'm on my way.'

'Good news?' Anna asks.

'Yes, we may have found them. Don't wait up. Night kids.'

Jumping in the car, he glances at his watch; it'll be nearly nine by the time he gets there. He puts his foot down.

❊❊❊

Halfway down the fire escape, Angelika had hesitated, thinking she should go back to help him. But then, she'd heard the shots and knows he does not have a gun, so it must have come from the *Polizei*, and if they've wounded him, or worse, what now can she do for him? He told her to run, and perhaps, for the first time, he had put her needs before his. If she'd gone back and they'd caught or killed her, his sacrifice would have been in vain. At the bottom of the ladder, she'd run off down the alley, pausing at the end to see if any *Polizei* were about and, finding it clear, made good her escape.

She'd taken a chance with the car. Trying not to run, she made her way to the VW. Fumbling with the key, which she dropped twice. Eventually, the lock had popped, and she had jumped in and sat there crying, certain Christian was lost. Why did he open the door? Why did he attack them? Why did she fall asleep right at the time he needed her most? The questions had kept coming, rolling around her befuddled head.

After a few minutes, she'd gathered herself, wiping her eyes and blowing her nose. Starting the engine, she drove west, then south to find a suitable place to dump the car and lay low.

The car thrummed along, and she had soon put a few kilometres between her and the hotel. As she drove, she wondered how they had found them. It couldn't have been the car that was several streets away. In the end, she concludes that the man at reception must have given them up, have read something in the papers that tipped him off.

Getting to Spandau, she'd headed south for a bit, then cut back east, eventually reaching the outskirts of Wilmersdorf, and as she had motored down the Hohenzollerndamm, she passed the Fehrbelliner U-Bahn station and searched for a place to leave the car. Near the station, she'd turned left, driven up beyond a school and found a small car park. She'd slotted the VW into a space, killed the engine, and leaving the keys in the ignition, got out, closed the door, and walked away.

❉❉❉

Just before 8:55 p.m., Max arrives at Böttgerstraße and his heart sinks. There are several squad cars and two ambulances, both just pulling away. Uniforms have cordoned off the road, and as he walks up, they move the barrier.

Entering the hotel, he spots Bastian, who looks up and nods to him, his expression grim.

'What's happened?'

'Hey, boss, it's not good. In fact, it's a monumental shitstorm. Udo and Jürgen are both down. As far as I can tell, Udo got pushed over the railings and fell three floors. He's alive, just. Christian then attacked Jürgen, and by the time we arrived and stopped him, he'd all but strangled him. Jürgen's taken a heavy blow to the head; he's alive but in a serious condition.'

'Did they call it in?'

'Yes, Jürgen did, but for reasons that aren't clear, they didn't wait. I don't understand why? We were only a few minutes away. Christian's dead, and to make matters worse, I think that during the commotion, Angelika hopped out the window and made off down the fire escape.'

'Where's Otti?'

'On the top floor.'

'And Tobi?'

'Home, I guess. We searched until about six, then Tobi called it. Otti and I were only in the area because we'd gone to get a meal. Udo and Jürgen must have carried on looking. Shall I call Tobi?'

'No, I'll call him later. Any witnesses?'

'Receptionist has the most complete story, but he didn't witness the incident. I've got his statement. Otti has been around the rooms but as it's still early, most people are out.'

Max nods. 'You both all right?'

'Yeah. She was first up the stairs, shouted a warning but Christian took no notice. To no avail, she shouted again. She had to shoot: put one in his shoulder, and another in his thigh. It stopped him attacking Jürgen, but then he picked up Jürgen's Walther, and we fired at the same time.'

'Christ, what a monumental cock-up. Presumably, they've taken our guys to Rudolf Virchow?'

'Yeah.'

'All right, look, can you get down there and sit on them? I'll tidy up here and come over.'

Bastian nods. 'I've called Paul and Lutz; strangely, for a Saturday night, they were both in. I'll see you later, then.'

Max goes over to the reception desk. The fat man is sitting gloomily in the office.

'No one can stay here tonight. Ring round your mates and get them alternative accommodation, please.'

He throws up his hands. 'I've tried calling the boss, but he isn't answering. I don't know what to do.'

'Give them their money back; they'll understand. I'll go round with my colleague and clear the rooms.'

'What about the people who are out?'

'When they get back, officers will accompany them to their rooms. They pack and go, no arguments.'

He nods grimly and shrugs. 'The boss won't like it, but okay.'

When Tobi arrives, Max briefs him and leaves him to manage the scene, and ten minutes later, he enters the hospital and goes to find Bastian. He is leaning against a wall, deep in thought. Max breaks his reverie. 'Any news?'

'They're both in surgery.'

Max nods and leans against the wall next to Bastian. He sighs. 'I've called August. He's getting in touch with next of kin.'

'At least they made it this far. Hopefully, they'll pull through.'

'Yeah, they're young and tough. You okay?'

'Sure. Look, I'm going to step outside and have a smoke, if that's all right?'

'Yeah, course, have one for me.'

***

Exhausted, Angelika looks for a place to stay, be quiet and to think. Making her way back to the main road, she turns left and soon after passing the Hohenzollernplatz U-Bahn, spots a sign for a hotel tucked away up a side road. She checks it out. Satisfied, she walks up to the reception, where a young woman is sitting with a few academic books open beside her. Looking up, she smiles warmly. 'Hello, can I help?'

Angelika steels herself. 'I'm after a room just for tonight.'

'We haven't any singles; will a double do? It has a small shower room.'

'Yes, that'll be fine. How much, please?'

'40 DM for the room. If you want breakfast, it's fifty, though between you and me, it isn't worth the extra. You're better off going down the road to Benni's.' She winks. 'You didn't hear that from me, if you know what I mean?'

'Fine, thanks for the tip-off. Just the room, please.' She pushes the money across.

'Would you fill in the registration card, please? Just your name and address.'

Smiling, Angelika takes the card, putting on the name Gretel Weisse with an address in Düsseldorf. The receptionist looks it over and smiles back. 'My mother was from Düsseldorf.'

Angelika nods. The girl takes a key from a rack and passes it over. 'Thank you. Room 22, second floor. Do you need help with luggage?'

'No, thanks.'

'Have a good night, Fräulein Weisse.'

'I'm sure I will. Good night.'

Hardly noticing the room, she slumps on the bed and, for a few minutes, lies reflecting on what a close call it had been. Then, the thought that she'll never see him again strikes her hard. They are all gone, just her now. The tears flow, an untapped reservoir of emotion that has lain dormant for many years. Emotionally drained, she drifts off.

She is running down a long, dark corridor, more like a metal pipe with the faintest light at the end, just a pinprick. Echoing down the tube, she hears her brother's cries: "Run Ange, run! The Ivans are coming. I'll protect you. Run!" No matter how hard she tries, the light never draws closer, but his voice fades until all she can hear is her echoing footsteps and laboured breathing.

She wakes with a start. She is used to the dreams, but now she has one more demon to add to a growing list. It is still dark. Reaching out, she clicks on the bedside light, noting the time: 4:27 a.m. She gets up and goes to check the bathroom. There's a small sink, a shower and a toilet. She uses the lavatory, then splashes water on her face. Rummaging in her bag, she fishes out her toothbrush and cleans her teeth.

Stripping off, she looks at her reflection in the full-length mirror. She's lost weight, seems a little too skinny. She cups her breasts, turning sideways, then back. She's always liked her boobs, along with her hair and eyes; she thinks they're her best bits. But men's obsession with vaginas confuses her. After what happened, it has complicated the idea of sex for her. She does not trust men, though she wants to be with someone, imagining the intimacy and love and wondering what loving sex would be like.

She's always looked after herself, the one thing she can control, but lately, she's let herself go. Lifting her arm, she notes the lush growth, and her legs are hairy too. Turning front on again, she pouts and says out loud, 'To hell with it. Who cares, anyway?'

Climbing into bed, she snuggles down, wrapping the duvet tight around her, enjoying the sensation of the crisp cotton on her naked skin. Reaching out, she clicks off the lamp but does not sleep deeply, but drifts beset with bizarre dreams.

As the first light breaks through, spilling around the edges of the curtain, she sits up. She showers and puts on the last of her clean clothes. Checking the room one last time, she opens the door and trots down the stairs. There is a man on the desk. She pops the key down in front of him. 'I'm checking out.'

He flicks through the cards. 'Ah, here we are, Fräulein Weisse. I see you've paid in full. I trust you slept well?'

'Yes, thank you.'

'Can't tempt you to our delicious breakfast, then?'

'No, I must be on my way.'

'Well, come again, goodbye.'

She goes out to a mild Sunday, clouds covering the sky in a silvery blanket. There is a light breeze, and looking up, she hopes the sun will come again. For a moment, she stands, feeling lost, wondering what to do next, then remembering what the receptionist said, she heads off down the road to find Benni's.

30

To weep is to make less the depth of grief

AT JUST AFTER 2 A.M., BASTIAN drops Otti at her apartment. The adrenaline long since spent, they're both shattered, and profound, gnawing fatigue claws at them. During the drive, they've spoken little. She keeps replaying the encounter with Christian, wondering whether they could have saved him. She feels empty and just wants to climb into her bed, shut out the world, and sleep for a week.

Bastian stops the car and looks over. 'We're here.'

The car feels warm, comfortable and, in its confines, intimate. She opens her eyes and goes to open the door but hesitates. 'Quite a day. Listen, thanks. You've been a rock. I wonder if it's a record, you know, of the worst kind?'

'What is?'

'Being involved in a fatal shooting just two days after getting your licence.'

'Oh, balls to that, you can't predict when shit will happen. We had no choice, you know that, right?'

'Well, it's done now, and I am, as they say, knackered, my friend. I'll say good night.'

He smiles encouragingly. 'See you later, at the office?'

She opens the door. 'Yeah, did Max say ten-thirty? Going to be a lot of typing.'

He looks at her. In the soft interior light, there is a glint from his warm hazel eyes. 'You sure you're all right?'

She nods and smiles. 'Of course, I'll see you later.'

He holds her gaze. 'You did your job. Okay, see ya.'

She hefts the door shut, and he drives off into the night. Watching the lights disappear, she feels unexpectedly alone and realises that she should have asked him to stay. Then she thinks, don't be silly, get some control, girl. That is one place you do not want to go: work romance, in the Kripo?

No, no, and no again! Anyway, he'd probably turn her down. She climbs the stairs and wishes he wasn't so damned attractive, caring, and likeable. Though tired, she knows that if she goes to bed, she'll just lie awake, a myriad of thoughts battling. She strips off, dumping her clothes in a pile, something that used to drive her mum mad, and has a shower. After, she chucks on some sweatpants and a hooded top, she pours a generous measure of an eight-year-old Asbach brandy and, going over to the record deck, puts on The Fleetwoods album, "Mr Blue." She sets the volume low, switches off the lights, and settles comfortably, lying out on the sofa. Putting the glass to her nose, she breathes in the sweet, sherry-like aroma, swilling it around and as she sips, the dark liquid bites her tongue, mellowing as it slips down, a warm feeling in her chest and stomach. The music drifts over her, the tension eases, and she daydreams about having sex with him.

She wakes to the gentle sound of *ker-click-ker-click-ker-click* from the record player. The dark is slipping away, and threads of light herald a new dawn. Her empty glass is lying on her chest, the smell less agreeable now. She goes through to the kitchen and makes tea, searching the cupboards for something to eat. She laughs, amused that she hasn't been shopping for ages. She can hear her mother saying to her sister: "She'll be home for this and that; you mark my words." It was correct. She was still popping back with her laundry and to have a good, hot meal, saying it gave her an excuse to visit and, of course, her mother didn't mind.

She drinks the tea and decides to go and run off the cobwebs and get her head straight. Setting off from the apartment in Guerickestraße that her mother bought soon after the war, she runs up to the Landwehr Canal, following it east toward the Tiergarten. It's about three kilometres to the Victory Column, and from there, she runs back through the park. Being early, there are few people about, most enjoying a more leisurely Sunday morning. As she runs, she thinks through the events of the previous evening and wonders how her colleagues are doing. Udo hasn't exactly endeared himself to her, and she's noticed that he is often the one to challenge ideas and decisions from others. Perhaps, she thinks, that is a good thing. After all, Bastian is hardly a paragon of conformity, but with him, it is different, born from age, experience, and wisdom. Whereas Jürgen is one of those people who'd pretty much get on with anyone, what her mum would call the boy next door. It's still a mystery why they did not wait for backup. Somehow, they must have had their hand forced, or perhaps, at that moment, thought they could handle it: two young, fit, armed detectives against an unsuspecting couple? Either way, it had been a lesson to her, and she vows never to go it alone unless there is no other choice. She can see from Bastian, Max, and Tobi that their strength and effectiveness comes from their sense of the comradeship and teamwork that had seen them through nearly six years of bitter warfare. And it is thrilling that such men would accept her in their domain.

It had been a shock to use her firearm so soon and in so decisive a way, though she was glad that the decision to shoot to kill had not been hers alone. She had worried about her ability to deploy her sidearm, but it was just as Bastian said it would be, and she was content with the way they handled the situation. Though, Christian's bemused expression will take time to leave her, as will the bedevilling guilt.

Stopping by the bank of the Neuer See, she gets her breath, stretching the fatigue away. Animal calls drift over from the nearby zoo, surprising within this eccentric Northern city so far removed from the exotic places evoked by the sounds. He keeps filling her mind. She can't stop thinking about him, Bastian Döhl. She's met no one like him. 'Damn it!' she shouts out loud.

❖❖❖

Max slips into bed beside Anna. He is careful not to disturb her, glad she does not wake, so he must tell her what has happened. The body count is mounting, and it is looking bad for Jürgen. The news is better for Udo, who, remarkably, did not suffer a life-threatening head injury. A few casually discarded boxes had been just enough to soften that final impact. He has a broken back, pelvis, arm, right leg, and various other injuries, but the expectation is for him to pull through, though whether he ever gets back to active duty is another thing.

Max wakes, it is light, he's alone in the bed, the clock shows 8:45 a.m. For a while, he lies there enjoying a moment. It is rare for him to wake so late. The bedroom door is ajar. There's a knock, and Heike enters, cup in hand. Her bright, beautiful face is a tonic.

'Hey, dad, thought you'd like a coffee.'

He smiles and pats the bed. 'Thanks, sweetheart. Come sit on the bed, tell me what you've been up to.'

Handing him the cup, she sits, swings up her legs, scooching up beside him. 'What time did you get back?'

'Late, after two-thirty.'

Since the events of the summer, when she had been the target of the serial killer, Klaus Grünpeter and had helped her dad to stop him, their bond and love for one another had deepened. She knows he still feels guilty but considers that what happened has made her grow up and understand life is precious.

She rests her head on his shoulder, and he puts his arm around her. 'Everything, okay?' she asks.

'Yeah, course. Nothing for you to worry about. What you up to this morning?'

'I'm going swimming with Marky and some of the gang.' She looks at the clock. 'Hell, never enough time. I'm running late, so I'll see you later, alligator.' She kisses his cheek.

'I should be back mid-afternoon if you and Marky want to do something?'

She smiles, a twinkle in her blue-grey eyes; his eyes. 'Hey that's ring-a-ding-ding, Daddy-O.' Then, stopping in the doorway, she turns to him. 'Oh, by-the-by, we cracked those weird messages. Mum's left a note for you.'

Max beams. 'Really, that's great! Here, what's the difference between an alligator and a crocodile?'

'Ah, not now, dad.' She turns to go, then hesitates, turning back. 'Oh, go on then, what's the difference?'

'One you'll see later, the other in a while. Now go have fun,' he laughs.

She giggles. 'I like that one, better than your usual. See you then.'

He props himself up and drinks his coffee, and after a shower, goes down to get some breakfast.

As Heike said, Anna has left a note on the table:

Been called to an emergency, back later, Love A x P.S. have solved the messages!!! All to be revealed.

He tags on his own message:

Back after lunch and good news about the messages! Can't wait to hear.

Then, picking up his keys, he heads for the door.

Tobi and Bastian are both in, sitting at the *Stammtisch* table, chatting. As he passes through, he says a quick hello and, entering his office, closes the door, picks up the telephone and dials the hospital. It takes a while to be connected to the ward. He listens to the update, replaces the handset, then goes and joins the others.

'What's the news?' Tobi asks.

'Jürgen arrested in the night, but they stabilised him. It is touch and go. Udo is awake; they're keeping him sedated, but they're confident he'll recover. We need to speak to him and find out what happened.'

'Look, it was my watch, so I'll go if that's all right?'

Max places his hand on Tobi's shoulder. 'Yeah, course. It'll be good to have one of us there. His parents turned up just before I left. I think Jürgen's mum is still poorly. August said he was going over today, so you can bring him up to speed. We'll crack on and find Angelika.'

Tobi grabs his coat. 'Thanks, I've left an initial report on your desk.' He heads off.

Max turns to Bastian. 'Otti coming in?'

'Said she was, so she'll be here.'

A few minutes later, she strides in looking fresh, though she'd be the first to admit that's not how she feels. Bastian smiles enthusiastically. 'Ah, good, you're here. All okay? Get some sleep?'

She sits. 'Yes, and yes. Hi Max, how are the boys?'

'Jürgen's in a bad way, barely made it through the night, but Udo, miraculously, will make it.'

'Amazing after that fall, tough cookie. When will they know about Jürgen?'

'The next day or two, then they'll assess his brain function.'

She sighs, her eyes doleful. 'We were too late, then?'

'You did everything you could. We'll wait to talk to Udo and find out what went wrong. Tobi has gone over to see him. Anyway, in the meantime, it leaves us three tracking down the elusive Angelika. Any ideas?'

To force her hand, they agree to get the artist's impression of her in the paper and on the TV news and get alerts out to all hotels and hostels.

'Otti, you follow up on the landlord to see if we can get a tenancy agreement and some more info on her. We'll go door-to-door around the Burgermeister Hotel to see where they went and to whom they spoke.'

They're just wrapping up when August joins them. 'Hey, how are you all doing? Sorry, Max, this won't make your day any better.' He chucks a copy of the *Berliner Courier - Sunday Special* on the table.

On the front page are detailed exterior and interior shots of the burned-out van. The headline reads: "Exclusive: Cremation, Forest Executioner Style! from our on-the-scene reporter, Peter Koe." Max picks it up, scanning the article, which continues on page three, where there is a picture of Max and Bastian arriving at the scene and, irritatingly, a photo of the message, with the caption: "Killer leaves a cryptic message. What does it mean?"

'How the hell did this happen?' Then he recalls. 'Oh, shit, the guy that found the van was Bruno Koe, and the other guy was his brother Peter. So, Bruno finds the van and calls us after he has called his brother. Question is, who was taking the pictures because they couldn't have been taken after we arrived?'

'Easy enough for Peter to snap them off and hide the camera,' August says.

Otti flicks through the paper. 'Usually, they attribute the pictures, you know if it is a different person to the reporter. Look, here it is near the back, she reads: "Special report photographer Bimpy Schröder". That could be him.'

August sighs. 'Ah well, the cat's out of the bag. I know the editor well. I'll go talk to him and see what we can salvage.'

Max drops the paper back on the table. 'Let's say they owe us one. On another point, we were looking at the messages last night. Markus recognised the first as a verse from Leviticus. Anna must have carried on after I got called away, and she left a note this morning to say she had cracked them. I didn't see her this morning.'

August smiles. 'Good, let's hope they shed some light on things.'

After Max and Bastian have left, Otti has the place to herself. Sitting, she removes a form from her top drawer, feeds it into the Olympia SM3 typewriter, and taps out the report on the events of the previous evening. Finishing, she puts a copy in her filing drawer and another in Max's office and, returning to her desk, picks up the phone and dials a number.

The call is answered promptly. 'Hello, Otto Friehöff speaking. Who is this, please?'

'Herr Friehöff, I'm *Kriminalmeister* Jäger with the Berlin *Kriminalpolizei*. I'm calling regarding the request we made to track down a tenancy agreement for your apartments…'

'Yes, yes, I have the records here at home, and I am sure what you are after will be here.'

'Good. May I come over now?'

'Monday would have been more agreeable, but… very well… fine. Here's the address…'

'Thanks, I'll be with you soon.'

❖ ❖ ❖

Sliding into a booth at Benni's, Angelika orders a coffee and sits, thinking. She feels empty, needs to go where they used to go, to find him. Perhaps she can go back to the church from yesterday. It is years since she last confessed, and she almost laughs at the thought of it, imagining the priest's horror at her revelations. Maybe it's not such a bad idea. After all, isn't the confessional sacred and confidential? Perhaps telling someone will make her feel better? She could find Max's house and see what he's like. Maybe she should give herself up, then it would be over; she could rest? They'll probably catch up with her in the end, anyway. They found them last night, so why not again? And she feels so bloody exhausted.

She hadn't noticed the waiter. 'More coffee, Fräulein?'

31

If we do meet again, why, we shall smile

IT DOES NOT LONG for Max and Bastian to find the café where Angelika and Christian had breakfast. They sit at the counter ordering coffee and *Kuchen*: in Max's experience, café owners will tell you more if you buy.

Max takes a sip. 'Nice place and excellent coffee, too.'

The proprietor is stacking cups back on the shelf. 'Thank you.'

'Do you remember a young woman and a big man coming in yesterday morning?'

The proprietor stops stacking and glances at him. 'Depends on who's asking?'

Max shows his badge. 'Did you hear about the incident down the road at the Burgermeister?'

The man nods. 'Hard not to. I heard someone got shot, and some *Polizei* were injured. What of it?'

'The big guy and the woman were involved. Were they here?'

The proprietor wipes down the counter and thinks a moment. 'Yeah, yesterday breakfast and they came in the previous evening, too. He's my type of customer, if you know what I mean?'

'Where did they sit?'

The man points to a table halfway down the room.

'Don't suppose you overheard what they talked about?'

'Only when they were on their way out, he said something about going to a library.'

Bastian stubs out his cigarette. 'Schiller's near to here.'

Max drains his coffee. 'We'll check it out.' He slides some cash across to the proprietor. 'Anything else you remember?'

He takes the cash and goes over to the till. 'He ate loads. She didn't, but she's a looker, you know? If you saw her, you'd remember, and as for him, man mountain comes to mind, though he seemed kinda passive and easy. There was something about him.' He closes the till and rejoins them. 'Yeah, I know. He seemed much younger than he is, like a big kid with his mother. Anyway, if you see them, send them back; he enjoyed my food.'

Bastian laughs. 'I can see why: these *Krapfen* are excellent.'

They stand. The proprietor offers the change. 'Keep it,' Max says.

They drive up to the Schiller but being Sunday, it is closed. Leaving the car, they have a walk around, and as they come to the church, Max pauses. 'Let's go look in here.'

As they push it open, the great oak door creaks. Angelika, tucked out of sight near a pillar, sits lost in anxiety and remorse. Hearing the door opening, she glances across and is shocked to see Max and another detective. Quickly, she ducks down as though at prayer and, pulling her scarf over her head, tries to avoid being seen. The morning Mass is over, but the smell of incense hangs in the air, and there is a calming, muted atmosphere. A few people sit on pews, some fiddling with rosaries, heads bowed, others just sit quietly. Max and Bastian scan the rows. For a moment, Max looks at the bowed figure by the pillar, then shakes his head. 'Nothing here, let's go.'

They leave. Bastian lights a cigarette. 'What were you expecting?'

'Not sure, just… never mind…'

They head back to the car. 'We'll have to come back tomorrow when the library is open. Let's get back to base and see how Otti has got on.'

Following them out, Angelika stands near a column at the top of the stairs and watches them go. A short while later, they drive by. She wonders why they looked in the church, and shots of panic and exhilaration surge through her. The door creaks and an elderly lady exits, briefly looks at Angelika, then heads down the steps. Near the bottom, she pauses and turns. 'Angelika, is that you?'

For a moment, Angelika struggles to identify the woman. Then it dawns. 'Frau Mann, it has been such a long time, and you remember me.'

'Well, of course, who would forget such a pretty face? It's so lovely to see you. How are you and that brother of yours? Now, don't tell me…' She thinks and then smiles. 'Christian, is that right?'

With the mention of his name and the meeting of a trusted old friend, Angelika cannot hold back and, bursting into tears, says, 'Oh, everything has gone wrong, Gerda. He is dead.'

Remounting the steps, Gerda places her arm around Angelika's shoulders. 'Now, now, my dear. I live close by; come home and tell me everything.'

'Won't Dr Mann mind my intrusion?'

'No, he won't mind. He passed on a while back, never really got over the war, so it's just me. Please come. You look like you need to talk.'

'I'm sorry to hear that; he was a good man.' She wipes her eyes and smiles weakly, composing herself. 'Thank you. It would be good to talk. I feel so lost.'

'Come on then, it isn't far.'

❖❖❖

As Max and Bastian get back, Otti is at her desk finishing up some admin. 'Hey, boss, I've tracked down the tenancy agreement.' She hands it over.

Taking it, he reads, 'So, she's Angelika Maria Rächer, born August 28, 1930, occupation, waitress. Co-tenant: Christian Robert Rächer, born April 19, 1934, occupation, labourer. Excellent. We'll get that information and her picture out to the media. We found out that they visited a library, but we'll have to go back tomorrow.' He glances at his watch. 'I suggest we go home and start fresh in the morning.'

Before Max goes, he calls the hospital for an update and, finding there is no change and keen to get back home, he calls it a day.

On his return home, he's delighted to see everyone is in. Music drifts from Heike's room. Markus is on the sofa reading, and Anna is making dinner. Entering the kitchen, he gives her a hug, lingering a moment. 'Everything okay at work?'

'Yeah, the usual. All good. You?'

'No, not really. It all went to crap last night.' They sit, and he tells her.

Anna takes a beer from the fridge and hands it to him. 'My God, poor Jürgen. And his mother, too.'

'We don't really know what went wrong yet; hopefully, Udo can tell us. Anyway, I'm dying to know about these messages.'

She sits her eyes penetrating. 'Ah, yes. So, we knew that the first message was Leviticus 4:25, so we looked through both testaments for the same chapter-verse combination, and soon found the others! At first, it made little sense until we stopped looking at the words and focused on the numbers: 4:25. Then, taking the seemingly random letters tagged to each message as Roman numerals, we got MCMXLV, which gives us a specific date: April 25, 1945. The last message had the word Wednesday at the end, and guess what day April 25, 1945, was?'

'Hmm... let me guess... was it a Wednesday?'

'Straight to the top of the class, Max Becker. The text isn't particularly noteworthy, but there are clues. The first message references a scene where priests make a sacrifice and offer the blood to redeem the sin. The next message refers to people turning to evil ways, and the third seems self-explanatory but also references that those doing the taking will benefit from doing so. Why do the nations rage? Well, in this context, I'd say it is a war reference and ties in with the date, doesn't it? The last message we can interpret as either the end of the war and the world seemed empty or that they had run and you found nothing. The question is, what happened on that Wednesday that led them on such a killing spree?'

Max thinks. 'It was hell on earth. Berlin had been encircled, so we've lots of Soviet troops rampaging through the city, and we all know what some of them were getting up to, don't we? Everything was imploding...' he wracks his brain. 'Marky, you there?'

Markus shouts back from the living room, 'What, dad?'

Max and Anna join him. 'Have you ever covered the Battle of Berlin at school?'

'No, but I've got that new history reference, you know, the one Uncle Tobi gave me last birthday; is that any good?'

'Won't harm to look.'

They tramp upstairs, Heike hearing them, pokes her head around her door. 'What's up?'

Markus says, 'Dad's case, you know the messages. We want to know what happened that day.'

'Ooh, exciting.'

They crowd into Markus's room.

Taking down the hefty volume, they flick through the index. Anna says, 'Here we are: Battle of Berlin, pages 667-672. Look, this might be something; the date is correct: April 25, 1945, *Der Nachtwacheplatz Massacre*.' Anna scans the text. 'Doesn't say much about it other than some Soviet troops broke into the church, killing over thirty women and children.' She hands the book to Max, who reads the entry.

Heike glowers. 'That's horrible! They killed women and children hiding in a church. Who does that?'

Max sits on Markus's bed. 'War does that to people, sweetheart. That and worse. So, Angelika and her brother, or someone close to them, may have been there.'

'And were your victims there, also?' Anna says.

'Assuming they were, what did they do to Angelika and Christian? And why in hell are four Soviet soldiers roaming around Berlin so long after war's end? And why take revenge now, after fifteen years? Angelika and Christian would have been kids then. I wonder where their parents are?'

Max closes the book. 'See, kids, the more you know, the more questions you have.'

Markus takes back the book. 'I can ask my history teacher, Herr Wiener if he knows more about it.'

'Yes, good idea. Give him one of my cards and ask him to call me if he knows anything, all right?'

Anna sits next to Max. 'There's only one person who can give you chapter and verse— excuse the pun—and she isn't here, is she?'

Max frowns. 'Yes, the illusive Angelika, and right now, I don't know where she is or what she intends doing next.'

❖ ❖ ❖

Just an eight-minute walk from the church, Gerda Mann's fourth-floor apartment is in a smart building overlooking Zeppelinplatz. Angelika can hear children in the playground and wishes she could turn back time, be ten years old, pushing her little brother on the swing. Gerda joins her by the window. 'Such a joyful noise. It is one reason I chose this place. In summer, I sit, watch them play and chat with the young mothers. You see, Angelika, no matter how dark things may get, there is always a future. Now come, how about some tea, and you tell me what has happened?'

They sit, Gerda pours. 'I get the tea from an English shop; lovely and refreshing. Milk?'

Angelika nods. 'Please, a little. I never really drink tea; perhaps I should.'

'The British say that a good cup of tea will fix anything. I'm not sure about that, but I'll settle for it making things better.'

Angelika takes a sip. 'Hmm, that is good, not like any tea I've had before.' She puts down her cup and sighs. 'I don't know where to start, really.'

'How about the beginning? I have nowhere else to be, and I promise I won't judge; we're friends, no?'

'You remember that day we came to your basement hospital? Christian was badly injured?'

'Yes, of course. You had been through that terrible business in the church, your poor mother, God rest her soul.'

Tears well up. Angelika can hardly speak.

'Oh, my dear, it's all right. Please don't upset yourself.'

Composing herself, Angelika begins. 'Well, a few months ago, I was at work, I'm a waitress, you see and was waiting a table occupied by these vile men, and I recognised one of them as the ringleader of the group that attacked us in the church, so I followed him and he led me to three others who were there that day. There they were, large as life, not a care in the world, and I wanted them to pay...' Over the next twenty minutes, Angelika tells Gerda everything that had happened, up to the death of Christian the previous evening. She concludes, 'So this morning, I got up and did not know what to do. I am so alone, but I am not ashamed of what I did. Those men deserved what they got. They were malevolent.'

For a moment, Gerda is quiet. She stands, goes over to the window, and closes her eyes, thinking. At last, she turns to Angelika, saying, 'I understand, you know? I can't imagine what it has been like for you and Christian to carry that with you all those years. The trouble is, you've set in motion something you cannot control. What does your head say you should do?'

'I should go to this, Max Becker, surrender and take what is coming to me.'

'And your heart? What does your heart tell you?'

Angelika knits her brow, sighs again and shrugs. 'That's just it, you see? I can't go back and change things: what is done is done. What good will it do if I spend the rest of my life in prison? Christian saved me, gave me a chance to get away. If I betray that, I betray him, don't I? I just don't know. What would you do?'

Gerda looks at her with kind, soft eyes. 'Honestly, I can't answer that.'

Angelika thinks. 'Hmm, okay. Well, what would you advise me to do, then?'

'In my experience, if you run, then that will be it for the rest of your life. You'll always be looking over your shoulder, always be running, and may never find peace. I think that what you did came about by exceptional stress, fear, and wanting to take revenge for your parents, and for what happened to you and your brother. I know you are a good person, and I think if you carry this with you, it will destroy you. If that happens, I think the betrayal of your brother's action would lie there and not in you spending the rest of your life on the run, don't you?'

'So, you think I should give myself up?'

'It is the only way you'll ever find an end to this… this circle of violence and death. You are still young; you'll still have time after prison to have a life: a life with a clear conscience.'

'Not if they send me down for the rest of the time I have. Oh, I don't know, I really don't.'

'You may find that if you tell them everything, they'll be more sympathetic than you imagine.'

'But I think Christian may have hurt those *Polizei* officers. They won't be sympathetic about that, will they?'

'I tell you what, why don't you sleep on it? You can stay here tonight or a few nights if that's what you need. If you decide to leave, I won't stop you. But should you decide to go to the *Polizei*, I'll come with you, and I promise I'll stick by you, come-what-may, you won't be alone.'

Eyes wide, a tremble to her voice, Angelika says, 'You'd do that for me?'

Gerda smiles, nodding. Angelika hugs her, holding her tight. 'I've been so stupid.'

32

I would not wish any companion in the world but you

OTTI HAS NOT BEEN BACK in her apartment long and is sitting in silence by the window. The strident buzz of the door bell breaks her trance, but she does not move. It buzzes again, garnering her attention, and crossing the room, she throws open the door to be greeted by a grinning Bastian. 'Hey, what you up to?'

'Nothing much really, you?'

'Fancy a drink? Know I do.'

'Sure, good idea. I'll get my coat.'

On the way downstairs, she says, 'You're wearing that bloody clown tie again.'

He laughs. 'I know you like it, really.'

Being out is liberating. Indoors she'd felt detached, almost disembodied. They walk in silence for a bit as though gauging one another's spirit. Bastian breaks the ice. 'Actually, are you hungry? Because I could eat. I know a quiet place not too far from here; what do you say?'

'Yeah, that'd be nice. You know a lot of places.'

'I don't eat at home much. In fact, I'm not even sure I've ever used the oven of my cooker.'

She laughs. 'Yeah, I hear you. I'm not much of a cook either. My cupboards are bare. It drives my mum nuts. I got so used to not having food during the war it stopped being important. I mean, don't get me wrong, I love eating, just not the rest of it.'

'It must have been tough, being here at the end. I think it was harder for civilians than it was for us soldiers, you know? We had a strong sense of camaraderie and purpose, even if it was so destructive. What about your family?'

She tells him about her father, completing the story just as they reach the restaurant. Going in, they find a small table near the back, make themselves comfortable and chat while they peruse the menu and order. The food comes. Picking up his glass, Bastian says, 'Here's to us, survivors, pioneers, builders, witnesses—prost!'

'I'll drink to all that—prost!' They clink glasses, holding one another's gaze.

Bastian breaks eye contact first and sets his glass down. 'So, your father was an academic who stood his ground and paid the price? Maybe, if we'd all been that way, things would be different.'

She shrugs. 'Didn't some guy once say even a fool may be wise after the event? So, when the war started, what were you? Seventeen? You were just a kid swept along in the Nazi propaganda machine. My father was political, he was a member of the communist party, had always fought against National Socialism, and he was older, had time to find his cause. He was also a stubborn man.'

'Is that where you get it from?'

'I guess. My mother is more pragmatic. She's a language teacher, tough and smart. I think I got the best of both.'

He smiles warmly. 'I wouldn't argue with that.'

For a moment, thinking, she traces her finger down the sweaty glass. She looks up at him gazing deep into his genial, trusting eyes. She takes a quick pull of her drink. 'One day, soon after the end, we were out searching for food. Mum always took us with her when she went out; she was fearful of what could happen to us. Anyway, a small convoy of Soviet vehicles came by and stopped close to where we were queuing. An imposing-looking man stepped down from an open jeep and stood looking all around. Everyone in the queue looked away or had their heads bowed. Not my mother. A Russian speaker, she went up to him and asked him to help. She told him that not all Germans were wicked and that the Nazis had murdered her husband. My sister and I stood there, wide-eyed. That officer was General Mikhail Grikorky, Soviet military governor to Berlin. Impressed with my mother, he offered her a job as a translator and adviser. While they were talking, one of his soldiers came over to my sister and me. Bending down, he patted my cheek, smiled, then took chocolate from a bag, giving us each a bar. From that moment, things got better for us.'

'My mother used her influence to help many people. She worked for him for just over a year until he returned home. He became a regular visitor to our modest apartment, always bringing gifts of food and drink. The young officer, a Ukrainian called Mykola, who had given us chocolate, came with him. He would play with us. He said that back at home, he had two daughters that we reminded him of. He brought a violin with him and played folk songs, teaching us the words. We would dance and sing and laugh. They were moments of pure joy. I loved Mykola and got to know him well. Mum allowed my sister and I to use the facilities at the Russian barracks, doing sports, and a friend of Mykola taught us unarmed combat, which I adored and made me realise I wanted to do something meaningful with my life. I often think about him and his family and wonder how they are. My mother and Mikhail still correspond. I think they are in love, and I'm sure she took him to her bed.'

'And why not? So, that's how you know Russian and English, your mum, yes? Is she still working?'

'Yes, she teaches junior school in Charlottenburg, and says that our young are the future: they are more important than ever. Where did you learn to speak English?'

'I had some English before the war, but about halfway through, I knew we'd never win and thought we'd all have to speak either English or Russian. I vowed not to get stuck on the Russian side, so I improved my English. Max has good English and Russian, Tobi knows French. He says it is how he won his wife, Else. We are a talented lot, eh?'

Topping up their glasses, Otti says, 'So tell me about that office rumour, then?'

He scoffs. 'Which one?'

'The SS guy you put down, is it true?'

'In part. I think that two stories have got mixed up.' He pauses, taking a gulp of wine, and pulling out a cigarette, asks if it's okay. 'So, we were waiting for transport, and myself, and a friend had gone to stretch our legs, have a smoke. On the other side of the rail yard, we came across a miserable-looking crowd of Soviet POWs being herded into cattle trucks. A young SS officer, he looked about twelve, had dragged one man from the ranks and was laying into him with a baton. I just saw red. Going over, I pushed him off the wretched specimen he was beating up. In the process, he stumbled and fell, making a mess of his nice uniform. The next thing I knew was the sound of a dozen-or-so MP40s being cocked and pointed at me. The young man got up. He was bright red in the face and pulled his sidearm, shouting, 'How dare you interfere with the Führer's business? I'll have you shot.' Well, right as things were about to go south, my mate returned with our company commander, Hauptmann Steiber. He held rank over the SS guy and defused the situation. He was a good man and as horrified as I was about how the prisoners were being treated. I still got a sound bollocking, but my friend and I had a good laugh impersonating the SS guy for our mates.' He calls for the waiter. 'The *Strudel* is delicious here. You want some?'

'Yeah, sure.'

The waiter hovers, Bastian orders. '*Bitte zwei Strudel mit Sahne.*'

'So, the bit about the court-martial and all that is made-up?'

'Oh, yeah. I think the young fool had come straight from the *Hitler-Jungen*, gone through whichever lousy, brain-washing training they gave them; shoved in a fancy black uniform and sent out to mistreat defenceless people. When faced with us, I think he was too embarrassed to take it any further. In some ways, I felt sorry for him. Like he didn't know any better.'

'You probably intimidated him, a fearsome green devil, eh? What about the other story, then?'

He puffs out his cheeks 'Okay, long-story-short. I was part of the unit sent to rescue Mussolini, you know, after King Emanuelle had him arrested.'

She shakes her head. 'No, must have missed that one.'

'Never mind. The mission was successful, but we went in by gliders, and there wasn't sufficient room for all of us to be airlifted back out. My company was tasked-in with an infantry division and joined the occupying force. Often, they sent us to areas under heavy enemy assault and to plug gaps: they called us the *Führer's Firemen*. Anyway, by then I commanded a unit, and they ordered us to check out a mountain village. On entering, we took fire but soon winkled out a couple of partisans and disarmed them. We were under orders to execute resistance fighters, but as far as I was concerned, we'd done our bit, so I let them go.'

Otti raises an eyebrow and leans forward resting her head in her hand.

'The following day, we came back through the village and found an SS unit there under the command of *SS-Hauptsturmfürer* Hörtel Mentz. They had rounded up a dozen men and women and, under interrogation, had discovered what had taken place. The officer gave me an ultimatum: shoot twenty villages or take the consequences. I told him that there was no way that I or any of my men were going to execute unarmed civilians. He argued they were subversives, spies, and partisans, and the Führer commanded it to have such people shot. I stood my ground. He ordered me placed under arrest for treason and cowardice and had my men disarmed.' He takes a swig and clears his throat.

'I must have been living a charmed existence because it was precisely at that moment an artillery unit arrived to set up Flak 88s overlooking the valley. Their commander, a lieutenant colonel, had chosen it as the location for his headquarters and, seeing the altercation, had his transport stop and demanded to know what was going on. As fortune had it, he was from old Prussian military stock, loathed the SS, and had a son who was a paratrooper. He told the SS popinjay we were under his command and were wanted elsewhere, and *Luftwaffe* paratroopers were not there to carry out the SS's dirty work. A week later, the artillery unit moved out and soon after, Mentz returned, rounded up twenty men and boys and, making the rest of the village watch, had them shot. Before leaving, his men burned the village. When finally the Allies took Italy, the story of this incident, by then known as the di Tivo massacre, got blamed on my unit. A survivor had attempted to explain that we had tried to stop the killing, but it got mixed up in translation or something like that. When we surrendered, they interrogated and charged me, but fortunately, I put the record straight by naming the SS officer involved. Although I did not know the artillery officer's name or if he had survived, I could identify his unit. I had an anxious few months in prison while they corroborated my story. I don't think they ever caught up with Hörtel Mentz, and I'm always on the lookout for him. I'll never forget the people of that village; their faces haunt me.'

Otti reaches across the table, places her hand on his arm and looks into his eyes. 'Bastian Döhl, you're more like my father than you know. It must have taken courage to do that.'

'Actually, by then, I didn't really give a shit. I wish I had shot the fucker.'

'Well, you cared enough to help those people. And it wasn't your fault they died.'

Taking her hand, he squeezes and smiles briefly, a pained look in his eyes. 'Isn't it?' He sighs. 'A couple years after war's end, I got in my car, drove out to a forest and sat there, a loaded pistol in my hand. I was going to end it when there's this knocking on the window. Startled out of my trance and looking over, I saw a small boy gesturing for me to roll down the window. He told me they had been climbing trees and his little brother had got stuck and couldn't get down and could I come and help. I got the boy down, and when we were safely back on the ground, I came to my senses and got my shit together. A year later, I moved from uniform and became a detective. After a shooting contest, August spotted me and gave me a job in his firm and I've been there ever since. Max and Tobi joined a year or so later. Now, it's home and the rest, you know.'

She moves her hand from his arm and takes his hand. 'You never married again. Why?'

He grins and shrugs. 'Still looking, I'm probably not the pick of the crop, eh?'

She lets go his hand and laughs dismissively. 'Ah, man, you shouldn't be so hard on yourself.'

Paying the bill, they walk back to her apartment. There's a lightness between them; the drink and the sharing of secrets have cast a net, and when they arrive, she stops and turns to him. 'So, are you coming in?'

❖ ❖ ❖

She wakes with a start. He's still next to her, sleeping, his warmth comforting. The bedside clock shows a little after four. She gets up and, putting on a robe, goes through to the kitchen. Taking a glass of water, she sits in the dark by the window. Otti Jäger, what the hell are you doing? She thinks. She'd promised herself not to get involved with someone from work, but is she really involved or have they, in the moment, just been there for one another? No, she genuinely has feelings for him, and right from the moment she'd met him. She has only been with two other men: a young guy soon after school who had been instantly forgettable, and a longer, more meaningful relationship at university, which had fizzled out when he'd moved away.

Bastian is different. For one thing, he is older, but that doesn't matter to her. In fact, she likes it, and the sex is exceptional! Instantly felling right. Thrilling and passionate. Thinking about it makes her want to ride him again. They had spent a long time exploring one another. Going down on her, he had sent her to a place no one had done before, gentle yet intensely powerful, and she'd pulled him up and guided him in, wanting him deep inside, and as she climaxed, she felt him swell with the pulse and thrust of his cum. Lying there, silently, she had run her fingers and lips over his body marked by old scarring, a braille-like map of his brutal past, each holding a story she longs to explore.

She doesn't know where it's heading, but now it seems agreeable, and she is content to let it run. With that thought, she goes back to bed, drapes her arm over his strong back, and falls into a deep sleep.

Woken by her alarm, she is alone. On the pillow is the clown tie with a note pinned to it. Bleary-eyed, she picks it up and reads:

> Didn't want to disturb you. Thanks for a memorable night! You decide what to do with the tie. See you at work. Bas. x
> P.S. mum's the word!!

Sitting there, tie in hand, she closes her eyes a moment and holds it up to her nose. Then, getting up, she goes over to the dresser, opens the bottom drawer and, smiling, tucks the tie neatly away.

33

Speak me fair in death

GERDA RISES EARLY AND, OPENING the door to the guest room, sees that Angelika is sleeping. She leaves a note on the kitchen counter telling her to help herself to anything she wants and that she has gone shopping and will be back soon.

Angelika has slept better than she has for years. She wakes, not sure where she is and for a moment feels panicky, then remembering the previous day, relaxes. For a while, she lies in the comfortable bed staring at the ceiling, wishing to hide here forever. It would be agreeable for someone to look after her for once, and she can see that Gerda is not unhappy about having her stay, even under such ominous circumstances.

Getting up, she throws on some clothes and goes through to the lounge. The apartment is empty. Finding the note in the kitchen, she smiles, and realising she's hardly eaten anything since Saturday, has a look through the cupboards.

She's just settled down at the small table by the kitchen window when she hears a key in the door.

As Gerda comes in, she calls out, 'Hello, are you up? The coffee smells wonderful.'

'There's enough for two.'

'I'll just put the shopping away and join you.' She tidies things away, pours a cup and sits. 'How are you this morning? I hope you slept?'

'Yes, the bed is very comfortable, and I must have been more tired than I imagined.'

Gerda smiles, vivacity from her bright eyes. 'Good, sleep helps us to see more clearly. I have bought some lovely smoked trout for lunch. Do you like that?'

Angelika nods. 'Hmm, lovely.'

'All right, you take your time. There is plenty of hot water if you wish to have a bath, and there is a washroom in the basement; the machines are new. If you like, you can put your things out, and I will do them for you. I need to do some of mine, anyway, so it won't be any trouble.'

'You're so kind, thank you. A bath would be nice, but I can do my washing after.'

'Don't be silly, I insist. It's nice to be needed and useful. When you get to my age, you notice you become invisible, which sometimes is a good thing but also can be tiresome. All that age and wisdom is going to waste, and let's face it, those men who run everything aren't doing a great job, are they?'

Angelika smiles. 'No, not really. Maybe one day we'll have a woman in charge?'

Gerda guffaws. 'I expect, my dear, that Hell will freeze over before that happens.'

After breakfast, Angelika fills the bath and, stepping in, lies back in hot water. She shuts her eyes and, drifting off, wonders what Max is like. She imagines surrendering to him. Will he treat her fairly and with respect? The article said he is a family man, a war hero—if such a thing is possible—war seems the least heroic thing she can think of. As her mind wanders, she fantasises about him, his muscular arms holding her, a respected man of power and upholder of the law. She comes to, flushed and confused. The water is still hot, so she can't have been dozing long. She inspects herself and, grabbing her razor, shaves her underarms and legs, in the process catching herself just above her left shin, a ribbon of crimson liquid seeps into the water, the cut stinging. The pain feels good, making her feel alive and returning her to reality.

Wrapping herself in the warm towel Gerda has left on her bed, she dries off, combs her hair and staring at herself in the mirror, imagines the pictures in the papers and the headline: *Mass Murderer, Angelika Rächer: The Forest Executioner hands herself in, poor, stupid, little girl.*

She gets dressed and goes to sit in the comfortable lounge. Gerda comes back with the laundry. 'There we are, all done, washed and dried.'

Angelika looks at her, a wave of nauseating self-pity flows through her.. She feels like a child and Gerda's care makes her miss her mother more than she has done for years. She fights back tears, and standing, says, 'I might take a walk in the garden if that's all right?'

'You do as you wish. You are free to come and go, all right? I'll make lunch; it'll be ready in an hour.'

Angelika walks across the green space toward the playground that flanks one side. As playgrounds go, it is good: swings, slides, a roundabout, see-saws, a climbing frame, a sandpit, everything a child could want. There are a few mums with small children, too young for school. Sitting on a bench nearby, she watches them. Her head is still swimming. She'll ask Gerda if she can stay for a few days while she clears her mind and resolves what to do. Unable to hold back the emotion, she allows wet tears to track down her flushed cheeks, as the dark grip of her past, all she has lost, has done, has dreamed for, swamps her soul.

❖❖❖

Late on Tuesday morning, Jürgen dies. His mother, rising from her sickbed, is by his side, holding his hand as he slips away. Tobi and Max, alerted by the doctors, arrive earlier and are there to share in her grief and give her the words about her fallen son: his bravery, sense of duty, honour, and friendship they will miss. Words that are true but also seem hollow as the facts about what happened that night are now known to them: Udo, wracked with guilt and remorse, confessing his lapse of judgement.

Max tells Udo it was a mistake, and he has made enough himself and that Udo must put it down to hard experience and move on. Ultimately, he tells him, it will make him a better man and detective, but he knows Udo will always carry the guilt and responsibility with him, which is as it should be.

Max accompanies Frau Zeigler to the waiting *Polizei* car that will take her back home to grieve and find a way forward. Still frail, he offers an arm to support her. 'There aren't any words, really, at least none that are adequate. He was a fine young man, liked by all, and I am glad I knew him a little, though he never said much about himself.'

She looks across at him and smiles. 'He always wanted to join the *Polizei*, right from when he was small. We almost lost him during the war to that bloody man and his politics. Jürgen loved being in the *Hitler Jugend*, the uniforms, all that camping, sports, and camaraderie. He could not understand why his father and I did not see how wonderful Hitler was. He would go off to rallies, and when, you know, during the end and they were getting all those boys and old men to fight for them, he went and stood in line. They gave him a useless rusted old gun and some sort of rocket weapon and sent him out to defend the city. He fought like a man and almost died like a rat.'

She pauses for a moment, collecting her thoughts and rests; her breathing laboured. 'They paraded my son in front of that monster, outside the bunker the cowardly pig hid in while the rest of us endured. Jürgen was a good-looking boy, and Hitler stopped in front of him and, patting his cheek, told him how proud he was to have such boys to defend the Fatherland. They gave my son an Iron Cross and a fountain pen as a reward.' She laughs, but her eyes glower. 'Two days later, back on the front line, my boy was wounded and knocked unconscious from a shell blast. God be praised; a friend brought him home. The shell did not badly hurt him, but it stopped him fighting, and little by little he came back to us.'

Max frowns. 'I did not know. He said nothing to us about all that.'

'He was ashamed they hoodwinked him. Like many, he just wished to make amends.'

Max shakes his head. 'That shame was not his to carry. They seduced many, and foolishly we ignored the warning signs. Hitler always said: he alone, who owns the youth, gains the future. But for Jürgen to fight so courageously, that was something, you know? I hope he wasn't ashamed of that?'

'No, he wasn't. One day, it would have been '47, he would have been about sixteen. I surprised him in his room. He had this little box with keepsakes from his youth, you know, photographs of him and his mates in their uniforms. He also kept his dagger and medal in there; he was sitting there holding it. He looked embarrassed, but I told him we were proud that he had stuck to his belief and been so brave, if a little foolish. I told him it was okay to be a little foolish when you're young.'

'That was nice.'

'No, it was the truth. He was our boy, and we would have done anything for him.'

As they reach the car, Max holds open the door. 'I know it doesn't mean much but please let me know if there is anything I can do for you. Anything.'

Climbing in the back, she thanks him. Walking back to find Tobi, he realises that in fourteen years of *Polizei* work, Jürgen is the first officer under his command he has lost and pledges to make him his last.

Tobi is waiting outside Udo's room. Solemnly, Max nods. 'Let's break the news.'

Opening the door and going in, Udo is in bed, a cage keeping the covers from his legs and pelvis. He looks pale.

Tobi sits on the bed. 'Hi, Udo, stupid question, but how are you doing?'

'I'll get there, I'm sure.'

Max delivers the news. 'Udo, I'm so sorry, but Jürgen died a short while ago.'

Udo screws his eyes shut, his face drawn, the little colour drained away. 'Oh, God, what have I done?'

'Listen, you must get well and come back. That's what Jürgen would want.'

Udo opens his eyes, a flash of optimism. 'You'd still have me in your team?'

'Of course. Listen, when you're well enough, Anna is having you moved to her ward, so you won't be able to slack off.'

Udo looks forlorn. 'I'm so sorry. It should have been me that died.'

Max smiles knowingly. 'You know what we called it in the war?'

Udo shakes his head.

'*Das Teufelszeug*—The Devil's stuff. It's when you stand by another man and a shell goes off, and he's gone, and you don't even have a scratch. Try to reason with it, and it will drive you mad, so don't. Jürgen was your friend, and he won't want you to. Also, he failed to defend himself and is partly responsible for what happened. Don't forget that.'

Udo nods. 'Have you caught her yet?'

'No. She could be anywhere. But I'm willing to bet she won't be far. We'll get her, don't worry.'

Tobi stands. 'Now, rest, and we'll see you back at work soon, okay?'

Udo nods again, tears welling. Max and Tobi glance at one another perceptively and leave. Both have seen so much waste and senseless death they are almost immune, but somehow, this one is worse.

34

I'll observe his looks

'**HOW ARE YOU THIS MORNING?**' Gerda asks.
Angelika sits and pours coffee. 'I'm fine, much better for resting and eating well. I'm so grateful to you. And I feel less confused.'

'You look much better; the colour has returned to your cheeks. I'm happy I've been some help. It sounds like perhaps you may have determined what to do?'

'I think so, and I think I should give myself up. You were right about me not being able to live with it. Before I do, I want to see something, so I may be out late; is that all right?'

'I'll let you have a key. You do what you must, and remember, I'll be here for you.'

After breakfast, Angelika walks to the U-Bahn station on Leopoldplatz and, boarding a train, travels to Sophie-Charlotte Platz. From there, it is a short walk to the church where this began.

For a while, she stands outside looking up at the elegantly heavenward-reaching-copper-roofed-spire. The movement of the clouds gives the illusion the verdigris spike is bending, and it makes her feel giddy. She shuts her eyes, steeling herself and striding forward, turns the looped-black-iron handle, pushing open the great dark, oak door. The interior is gloomy and quiet with an air of subdued veneration. Stepping in and letting her eyes acclimatise, she looks about. It seems quite different from the day they came here to seek sanctuary from the raging battle, and an old priest had ushered them down to the crypt where dozens of fearful, war-weary women and children huddled.

Then, with nightfall, those men had come. She guessed they had stopped fighting and were looking for entertainment. At first, she had not been frightened as a few days earlier, she, her mum, and brother had been hiding in a basement, and three Ivans had come down. Silently, they had searched and, seeing that there were no soldiers or weapons, had gone away. A few minutes later, they had returned, bringing some bread and a bottle of schnapps. But the men that had come to the church were aberrant.

Closing her eyes, her head swimming at the memory of it, she almost falls; a voice from behind startles her. 'Are you all right, Fräulein?' Turning, she sees a young priest, his eyes grave, yet genial. 'Won't you sit a moment?'

She sits, leaning forward, holding her head in her hands. 'Perhaps I may get you some water?' He asks.

She shakes her head. 'No, thanks. I'm alright.'

'Would you like me to sit with you for a while?'

She nods. 'Please.'

Sensing her disquiet, he chooses the pew ahead of hers and sitting turns so that they are close, but there is a respectful barrier between them. For a moment, they remain silent.

At last, Angelika looks at him. 'May I ask you a question, Father?'

'Of course.'

'How long have you worked here?'

'Let me see; I came here four years ago, straight from the seminary.'

'Many years ago, an old priest was working here. I wonder, do you know his name?'

'Oh, sorry, I'm not sure whom you mean. How long ago are you talking about?'

'April 25, 1945.'

He raises his eyebrows, his eyes quizzical. 'How odd, that date again. You are not the first person to come here and ask about that dark day.'

She bridles, her eyes widen. 'Who else has been?'

'Two detectives came yesterday, a man and a young woman. I cannot remember their names.'

Angelika realises Max has understood the messages; it can only have been him. That's good, she thinks. She can feel his presence. She looks at the priest. 'You know about that day?'

'Yes, we celebrate Mass on the anniversary. We must never forget such events. Tell me, how do you know about this?'

She glances at her trembling hands, then looks back at him. 'I was here together with my brother and mother.' She pauses a moment and swallows. 'The soldiers murdered her.'

Shocked, he holds her gaze. 'I am so sorry. There was so much violence and pain, and I see you carry it with you still. The priest you're referring to was Father Sebastian. He too died that day. They did unto him as the Romans did our Saviour.'

Her face sets hard, eyes fixed on him. 'I know, Father, they made us watch.'

He closes his eyes for a moment. 'Oh heaven, child, how terrible for you! I understood he had tried to stop those men.'

'They were not men, Father. I don't know what they were, but not men.'

'Would you pray with me for your mother and the others?'

The air seems thick and clawing. She cannot breathe and needs to be outside. Stumbling, she runs to the door, pulls it open and keeps going until she is on the edge of the park and well clear of the building. She glances back and sees him standing in the doorway. Then she turns and heads away, sobbing.

Conflicted, the young priest watches her go. From his pocket, he takes the card the detective gave him. The name says KHK Max Becker, Department KD1 and a contact number. He flips the card over, where Max has noted down his home phone. The detectives had seemed pleasant and professional. Max had said that they needed to speak with a young woman they were concerned about and that she might come here. The woman he had just met matched her description. He can see that she is in trouble, but also in torment. Placing the card back in his pocket, he goes inside to offer a prayer and to take some spiritual guidance.

Earlier, Angelika had not been sure, but now she knows she must see for herself. She heads down a few streets to the Charlottenburg S-Bahn station. After a brief wait, the train arrives, always punctual and clean. Boarding, she settles in a seat by a window and looks out, her mind a maelstrom of raw memories. After thirty minutes and a couple of changes, she gets off at Zehlendorf. Looking at her watch, she realises it is too early and, walking down the street, finds a café.

The walk to Schwarzer Läufer Straße takes her just under ten minutes. As she enters the road, she realises they have numbered the houses using the horseshoe system. The first house on the left is 114, and the house facing is number 1. So, Max's home is fourteen down on the left. Crossing over, she heads down and passes by his house. A little further on, she sees a bus stop with a small shelter where she can wait without raising too much suspicion. His house is just before a corner, the sort of home she can only dream of. A pleasant neighbourhood with tidy gardens and well-tended streets, no doubt there is a tranquil park not far off.

After about twenty minutes, she sees two girls walking up the road. They're laughing and chatting. She guesses they're young teens, perhaps thirteen or fourteen. As they pass the bus stop, one girl looks at her, smiles, then turns back to her friend. She watches them as they walk up to Max's house and enter. She knows he has two children, so could it be them, or was it one with a friend? The girl that looked at her has Max's colouring and some of his looks, and Angelika decides the other is a friend. Thinking that if she stays any longer, she might attract attention, she heads away from his house to return later when he's home.

❈ ❈ ❈

Max opens the door. 'Come in. It's good of you to step in like this. Our usual sitter is sick.'

She steps in, handing Max her coat. 'No problem. Where are Markus and Heike?'

'They're upstairs. Kids, Otti is here. We should be back by ten-thirty or thereabout.'

'Whenever. I've nowhere else to be.'

They go through to the living room. 'Oh, by the way, just after I got home, the priest called me. Earlier today, Angelika came asking questions. Wanted to know about an old priest. She told him she was there, together with her mother and brother, and that Russian soldiers killed her mother.'

'Oh, really? Crap. That would certainly mess you up, wouldn't it?'

'He said that she told him the men that carried out the massacre weren't men.'

'Wonder what she meant by that? I mean, on one level, I get it, but why say that specifically?'

'Perhaps she's demonised them to make it possible to do those things, you know, like ridding the world of a pestilence.'

Anna comes down the stairs and hugs Otti. 'Who's demonised whom?'

Max glances at his watch. 'Come on, we'll be late. I'll tell you in the car.'

❈ ❈ ❈

Now dark and the street quiet, Angelika walks up to Max's house. She's not sure what is going to happen but wants to see him and has made up a plausible story.

There is a light over the dark blue door, and the number 101 in bright metal and a stout knocker. She raps twice. She has timed her visit well. Otti has just gone to the bathroom. A young voice shouts, 'Coming!' The door opens smartly. It is the same girl from earlier. For a moment, neither speaks.

The girl makes a face. 'Can I help you?'

'I was looking for Kommissar Becker. Is he in?'

'No, he's out. Who are you? Hey, didn't I see you at the bus stop?'

'I was told that he is a *Polizei* officer. I've just moved to the area, and I've had my car stolen.'

Heike frowns. 'What? Why don't you just call the regular *Polizei*? Dad is a detective. He doesn't really do car theft.'

'Of course, how silly of me. What was I thinking? Look, don't worry, I'll call the local station.'

'You can come in and call from here if you like? We've a list of all the stations on the wall.'

Angelika hears a flushing toilet. 'No, really, that's kind. I'll get off home. I can call from there.' Flustered, she turns and, trying not to run, heads off toward the nearest S-Bahn station.

As Heike closes the door, Otti appears. 'Who was that?'

'Not sure. It was a woman who said she'd just moved to the area and her car had been stolen, and she had heard that dad is with the *Polizei* and wanted to report it.'

'Weird, why not just call the local station?'

'Thing is, I saw her on my way back from school. She was at the bus stop just down the road there.' Heike scowls. 'Weirdly, I thought she was watching us.'

Otti's eyes widen. 'That smell, the perfume. Your dad has been going on about perfume. Can you smell it?'

'Yeah, I guess. What are you talking about?'

'Was she short, blond-haired, attractive, sporty looking?'

'Yes. How'd you know?'

'It's her, our suspect. What the hell is she doing here?'

Heike looks scared. Memories of Klaus Grünpeter rising.

Otti takes her arm and leads her to the sitting room. 'All right, first thing, let's make sure we lock all doors and windows. Where's Markus?'

'He's upstairs. Look, why don't you follow her, see where she goes?'

'I can't leave you.'

'It's important, so yes, you must. We're not little kids anymore; we'll be fine. I'll call dad, and Markus and I will go sit with the neighbours. Go on, go, or she'll get away. She's wearing a blue hooded coat and red Adidas sneakers.'

Otti grabs her coat. 'All right, tell your dad I'll call when I know where she's staying. Lock up behind me and don't answer the door to anyone.'

Running off, Otti soon falls into a steady pace. As she gets to the end of the street, she looks both ways and spots Angelika making toward the S-Bahn. By the time they get to the station, Otti is close enough to slow down. Fortunately, people are about, making her tailing job simpler.

They board the northbound S1 line as far as Berlin Steglitz, then change to the northbound U9, getting off at Leopoldplatz. Exiting the station, Angelika walks for about six minutes and, turning right into Zeppelinplatz, enters a well-appointed apartment block. Otti waits a while before entering the lobby to scan the letter boxes. She does not recognise any names. She checks for a back entrance and, satisfied that the main door is the only way in or out, exits the building and does a quick walk around.

As she returns to the front, she goes into the park to watch. Lights are showing in many of the windows. After staking it out for a few minutes, she runs back to the station and, entering the phone box, picks up the receiver and calls Max's house.

He picks up on the second ring. 'Otti?'

'Yes, boss, it's me.'

'Please tell me you found her?'

'I know where she is, but I need to get back there quick. Here's the address.'

Max notes down the details. He calls Tobi and Bastian, but there is no answer from Bastian's apartment. He telephones Malinda's.

It rings for a while before being answered. He can hear the lively hubbub of the bar. 'Malinda's…'

'Hey, it's Max…'

'Max! How goes it?'

'All well, thanks. Look, sorry to be quick; it's an emergency. Please tell me Bastian's there?'

'He's here, wait one…' Max hears a shout, 'Bastian, it's Max.'

After a brief delay, Bastian picks up. 'What's up?'
'We've found Angelika.'

35

This thing of darkness I acknowledge mine

IT IS AFTER 9 P.M. WHEN Angelika returns. Gerda is sitting reading, and relieved to see her back, looks up from her book and removes her reading glasses. 'Everything all right, dear?'

Taking off her coat, Angelika comes through and sits down. 'Yes, thanks.'

'Are you hungry?'

'I am a bit.'

'I'll make you a sandwich.'

'No, it's all right. I'll do it.'

'Don't be silly, you sit down; it won't take long.'

A few minutes later, Gerda comes back with some black bread, cheese, smoked ham, and a bottle of Rothaus Pils.

'Have a beer to wash it down. This was Horst's favourite tipple.'

Angelika tucks in. 'You must miss him?'

'Yes, every day. But I am thankful for the time we had together, particularly before the war. Did you ever find out what happened to your father?'

She shakes her head. 'No, he disappeared in the Summer of '44, you know, when they overran our troops. We lost so many, him among them.'

'I'm so sorry.'

'It's okay, it's been a long time and…'

'…. And?'

'It felt satisfying, exacting revenge. Empowering, you know?'

'Well, yes, I see that. You know, it is important now that you try to forgive.'

Angelika stops eating and looks down. 'That's going to be almost impossible.'

'I can see so much good in you, so do not carry hate in your heart, Angelika. For so long as you do, you will never be free of them and it will destroy you.'

She looks up at Gerda, pursing her lips. 'I can't turn things back, and now Christian is dead, too. I went to see him tonight, you know. Max Becker. I went to his house.'

'Oh! Why?'

'He wasn't there. I knocked, and his daughter answered. She's pretty and smart. She made me nervous, so I made up a silly story that was not very credible about having my car stolen, but she saw through me. Anyway, I panicked, ran off and came straight back here.'

'And if Max had answered, what then?'

'I think I was going to surrender myself. I thought if I did so at his house, they wouldn't shoot me.'

Gerda frowns. 'Shoot you? No, dear, they won't do that unless you threaten them, and you will not do that, will you?'

'No, no, of course not. I just want this to be over.' She pauses, sighs. 'I just don't know how.'

For a moment, Gerda thinks. 'Listen, why don't I call him tomorrow and arrange a safe place for you to give yourself up? I'll come with you.'

Angelika looks at her quizzically. 'Why are you doing all this for me?'

'Why not? You need a friend, don't you? And, if I'm honest, I wish I'd done more for you back then.'

A plump tear runs down Angelika's cheek. 'I appreciate that: the condemned should not walk alone.'

Gerda reaches across and takes Angelika's hand. 'People are seldom alone, you know? Now, would you like a cup of tea or coffee?'

'Actually, I'm rather tired; is it all right if I go to bed?'

'Of course, try to get some sleep and remember, it won't be as bad as you think.'

Down in the park, Otti stands watching and waiting for her colleagues to join her. A light comes on in one of the fourth-floor windows, and briefly, she spots Angelika drawing the curtains.

Otti narrows her eyes and smiles. 'Got ya.'

Ten minutes later, Bastian joins her. 'You've been busy. Max says you followed her here.'

'Hey, good to see you. I've just spotted her. The light came on in that window, fourth-floor, tenth from right.'

'Got you. Do we know the layout of the apartments?'

'No, not yet.'

'Well, we won't get a floor plan this time of night. How many exits?'

'There's a fire escape around the back and a basement, but the only door in and out is that one there.'

'Okay, good.' For a moment they watch in silence. 'Hey, I've got an idea. Wait here, I'll be right back.' Entering the building, Bastian scans the mailboxes and finds one that reads Herr Johnas Freitmann, *Hausmeister, Wohnung* 1001. Bastian goes and knocks. Herr Freitmann opens the door. 'Yes, what is it?' Bastian shows his badge.

A few minutes later, he rejoins Otti, grinning. 'I know which apartment she's in. I found the caretaker, and he tells me it's apartment 4004 and that window is a bedroom. Apparently belongs to Frau Gerda Mann, about seventy, who lives alone, supposedly.'

Otti looks impressed. 'You're not just a pretty face, then.'

He lights a cigarette. 'I've been called lots of things in my time but I've never been called pretty. Come to think of it, nor smart, either.'

She laughs, her eyes sparkling. 'Ah, sorry, Bas, only kidding.' For a moment, she looks at him. He returns her look, a flash in his hazel eyes. She wants so much to kiss him, but smiles and shakes her head. 'We wait, then.'

He nudges her. 'If anyone comes, we can pretend we're lovers, eh?'

She pouts and flicks her eyebrows suggestively. 'Oh, I'm sure we can manage that.'

'Oh, by-the-by, are you carrying?'

'No, I was watching the kids, wasn't expecting trouble.'

'Really? That Heike can be a handful. Besides, you should always expect trouble. Anyway, ta-da!' He lifts a trouser leg, revealing an ankle holster concealing a Smith & Wesson 42 Centennial.

She raises an eyebrow. 'You are a wicked man!'

'Well, you never know.' Taking it from its holster, he flicks open the swing-out chamber, clicks it back and hands it over. 'Five shots of .38 Special, just point and squeeze, practically no recoil. It's a quality revolver and in your expert hands, lethal; it'll get the job done.'

She takes it from him, feeling the balance, and checks it over. 'Interesting, no hammer. I like it, thanks. Let's hope we don't need it.'

'Let's hope we don't need what?' asks Tobi, joining them.

Bastian shakes his hand. 'Shooters.'

'God, we've had enough of that. You know where she is?'

'Yep.'

Max appears out of the gloom. 'Looking like a convention. What have we got?'

By the time they have formed a plan, it is a little after ten-thirty. Max is concerned that Angelika is holding Gerda hostage and using her home to lie low. Having got her number from Johnas, Max uses the caretaker's telephone.

The phone in Gerda's apartment rings; she frowns. No one ever calls this late. She picks up. 'Hello?'

'Frau Mann?'

'Yes, who is this, please?'

'My name is Max Becker. I'm...'

'Yes, I know who you are. You've found her, then?'

'Please listen. Just answer yes or no. Are you under duress or being held captive by the young woman you have at your apartment?'

'No.'

'Where is she now?'

'Asleep, I think. Listen, she told me she visited your house tonight, which probably wasn't a good idea...'

'It wasn't.'

'Please, Herr Becker, let me finish. She came to give herself up. She was worried that someone might kill her.'

'Kill her? No, Frau Mann, that's not how we do things. We don't want her to come to any harm, but this must end tonight.'

'I was going to call you in the morning and meet you, with her, at the church close by. It's where I bumped into her. Is there any way you can trust me to bring her to you tomorrow, say 9 a.m. at the church?'

'No, sorry, there's too much risk, and she may change her mind, and I don't want anyone else harmed, least of all her. Three of my team are outside your door. Please, can you open up and let them in?'

'If I refuse?'

'Frau Mann, if we do it my way, no one will be harmed. I promise we will take good care of her and treat her with respect. I am not unsympathetic, and I realise that the men she killed had done terrible things to her and her family.'

'I have your word that you will treat her kindly?'

'You have my word.'

'All right, I'll do as you ask.'

'Leave the phone connected. When you answer the door, a woman detective will bring you down to Johnas Freitmann's apartment. One last question?'

'Go on.'

'Is she armed?'

'I don't know.'

'Okay, please put down the phone and go to the door.'

Angelika, woken by the phone ringing, is listening. For a moment, her urge to fight or flee kicks in. She still has her Makarov pistol. If she goes now, she can make it down the fire escape, but to do so would damage the trust and friendship shown to her by Gerda, and they probably have people waiting for her. She walks through to the lounge just as Gerda puts down the phone. 'Wait, it's all right, I heard.' She picks up the phone receiver. 'Hello, Max, I've been wanting to meet you.'

'Angelika?'

'It is.'

'Let Gerda open the door. I promise you'll be all right. Stay on the phone, okay?'

'Fine.' She nods to Gerda, who goes to the door and opens it. Max continues, 'Are you armed?'

'I have a pistol. It's in my room, not on me.'

Otti pulls Gerda out, and they set off down the stairs, Gerda calling out, 'Please be kind.'

Following instructions from Max, Angelika shouts, 'I am unarmed!'

Tobi walks over, both he and Bastian holstering their weapons. Tobi detains her, and Bastian takes the phone. 'Okay, Max, it's done.' He hangs up.

Max is waiting as Otti with Gerda enter Johnas's apartment. 'Thank you, Frau Mann. I appreciate your cooperation. I will have some questions for you. Once we have taken Angelika to our office, we will formerly detain and question her. You may go back to your apartment, and Detective Jäger will take your statement. I would like you to come to the office tomorrow for a brief interview. I will send a car for you at 11 a.m. Is that agreeable?'

'Yes, fine, I want to help her.'

'Good, I will leave you with Detective Jäger. Until tomorrow, then.'

They place Angelika in the back of the car. All the spirit and fight have gone. She feels relieved but also crushingly depressed, knowing that her life now is in the hands of others.

The following hours go by in a blur. They process her, take her clothes and issue a prison uniform, and then lock her in a cell. The small featureless room has no window. There is a toilet and sink, and against the end wall facing the door, a metal bed bolted to the floor. She lies down, turning to face the wall and wraps the blanket tightly about her, trying to switch-off and sleep. She is cold, sleeps fitfully, troubled by stark, elemental dreams.

At regular intervals, they open the metal hatch in the cell door. She does not look but can imagine the eyes staring, checking. Checking? What are they checking for? She isn't going anywhere. Then she grasps they must be worried that she will harm herself. Harm herself? It almost makes her laugh. What more harm could she do than what they have done already? In her experience, there are worse things than death.

Right now, lying here in this cell, the people she wants are gone. She'd like nothing more than to be ten years old and for her father to gather her up in his powerful arms with his warm smell of tobacco and leather, to hold her and tell her it will be all right. To have her mother tuck her up in bed, stroke her forehead, brush back her hair and sing her to sleep. But she can't have them. She doesn't even know where they are; their bodies left to rot in some mass grave or ditch. Perhaps her mother became part of Devil's Mountain. And Christian, what of him? It's been almost a week since she fled the hotel, abandoning him to fend off the *Polizei*. She knows he is dead, but little else. She wants to ask but doesn't want to speak. What good will that do?

Fuck them, she thinks. Let them do their worst. Anything now will be a cakewalk. So, fuck the *Polizei*, the lawyers and prisons, and fuck everybody. All she has now is her silence and her story to keep locked away in her head.

36

My grief lies onward and my joy behind

WHEN ANGELIKA AWAKES, SHE IS confused and it takes a moment for her to remember where she is. As she steels herself for the battle ahead, a dispirited detachment fills her heart. They bring her a tray with coffee, bread, and cheese. She has the drink but eats nothing. After, she lies back down and turns to face the wall, closes her eyes, returning to her safe place. Later they come back for the tray. 'Hey, you aren't hungry?' She turns and nods her head. 'Cat got your tongue?' She turns her back on him.

'All right, your loss. They'll come and get you soon for an interview.' The door thuds shut, followed by the rasp of the lock and receding footsteps.

She drifts, a mellow weariness taking her. She does not care, and it's strangely relaxing. Previous inmates have scratched messages, some obscene, on the wall, and she traces the rough outline of the words with her finger. One says: *Es ist alles Hitlers Schuld!*—It's all Hitler's fault! She might put it more broadly than that but can't disagree with the sentiment. She tries to think of something to scratch on the wall, leave her mark, but for now nothing comes to mind.

Footsteps herald a visitor. The door opens. She looks up. 'All right, come on, let's go.'

They handcuff her and lead her up three floors through a squad room. She sees the men who took her, both at their desks, neither look up. She passes an office, and next to that is an interview room. They enter and sit her down. A few minutes later, the door opens, Max and the woman detective join her. She wonders if this is the detective who spotted Christian. She's not a person you'd forget.

They sit opposite, and from his pocket, Max takes a pack of cigarettes and pushes them towards her. 'You smoke?'

She shakes her head.

'I think you know who I am, and this is my colleague *Kriminalmeister* Jäger.'

For a moment, she looks at Otti searching for signs of solidarity but can't read her.

'She will take some notes, and I must remind you that what you say they can use in court, all right?'

She nods.

'Do you want a lawyer present?'

'No.'

'Are you sure? It would be best.'

'No.'

'All right, let's get started. First, you might want to know about your brother, Christian.'

At the mention of his name, her eyes widen. She nods, and he relates the story, asking if she has questions. She is silent.

Max continues. 'Last Tuesday, the officer, his name was Jürgen Zeigler, that your brother fought with, died of his injuries. The other officer suffered serious damage and may never return to work, but he will live. I want you to know that I am very sorry that your brother died in the incident; it was most unfortunate.' He pauses again, but she remains silent.

'Any comments?'

She shakes her head, does not hold back the tears. Max notes her contrition.

'While all this was going on, you got away down the fire escape. Where did you go then?'

No answer.

'We know you visited the Schiller Library to look up old newspapers, I'm guessing, since later you turned up at my house, that you were finding out about me. Why?'

No answer.

'How did you meet Frau Mann?'

No answer.

'You know that by involving her, you may have got her into trouble.'

No answer.

Max stands, walks over to the wall and leans against the cool plaster. His finger traces the scar on his cheek. 'I got your messages, you know? It took a little time, but we worked out that they referred to a day and a date that set out to explain why you abducted and killed those men. I know that you and your brother suffered some terrible trauma that day, but I don't have the full picture. Tell me your story, Angelika Rächer.'

No answer.

'You know, it's hard for me to help you if you stay silent. As things stand, you are answerable for the brutal abduction, torture, and murder of four men. Christian's boss, Günther, died covering up evidence from the van you used. Your brother is dead and one of my men, like your brother just a young man. All of this because of what you did, what you started. It's a mess, Angelika.'

He comes and sits again, leaning toward her, looking her in the eye. She looks back at him, her wet, pale blue eyes, pupils wide, give nothing away. 'I am not unsympathetic, you know. I think that somehow you accidentally came across these men, the men who had attacked all those people in the church and killed your mother.' Her eyes flicker, a brief look of confusion on her face. 'And you wanted to get them back, take revenge, settle the score. Call it what you may, it was your chance. And you know what, Angelika? I get that, I see what your motive was; you told us what your motive was with the messages. But parts are missing, and if I am to help you, I need you to fill in the gaps. Come clean, tell me everything, no lies, nothing missing.'

She remains silent and lowers her gaze.

'I want you to look at these.' He slides across a batch of photographs, laying them side-by-side.

She looks at them, pictures of the victims just as they had left them. Seeing them dispassionately in the cold light of day, she's shocked at the brutality. There are pictures of the basement, which is alarming but confirms her theory that someone saw them the day the plank fell and, perhaps later, when she had felt uneasy. She looks back up at him but says nothing. Her mind's flooded with deep, gut-wrenching sadness.

'All right, you don't want to talk, but let me tell you this: I think when you tell us your side of things, about what happened, what you and your brother went through, the court will be sympathetic. You have nothing to gain by keeping silent but everything to lose if you do. I will have you returned to the cell now. If you want to talk, just ask, day or night and I will come and listen, all right? I promise you that all I want is the truth, and that is what I want the judges to hear. Because it will go to trial, there is so much evidence against you. Also, think about getting a lawyer. It won't cost you anything, but it may save you a lot.'

Back in the cell, she searches around the bed frame and finds a thin piece of metal, part of a loop that attaches the base. She bends it back and forth until it breaks free and has a stylus to scratch out a message. Lying back on the bed, she turns on her side to face the wall, writing: *Wem kann ich vertrauen?*—whom can I trust? Rolling over, she lies on her back and stares at the ceiling, saying out loud, 'Can I trust you, Max?'

Just after 11:30 a.m., Gerda Mann is ushered into the interview room. Max stands and indicates a chair. 'Thank you for coming in, Frau Mann. I want you to know that you aren't under arrest, and you may leave at any time, all right?'

Gerda places her handbag on the table. 'Yes, I understand. How is she?'

'She has said nothing, but we are looking after her.'

'May I see her?'

He nods. 'After we have spoken, I will take you down.'

'Thank you.'

'When did you first meet Angelika?'

'In the last weeks of the war, my husband and I had set up a makeshift hospital in some basements about fifteen minutes' walk away from the church where the crime was committed. Early in the morning after, there was a loud knock on the door. She turned up with her brother, who had been shot in the leg and head. It was clear she had suffered from a terrible assaulted and was in a state of agitation and shock.'

'Yes, the autopsy on Christian revealed the historical leg and head injuries. Please go on.'

'Why did you have to kill him?'

Otti lays down her pen, saying, 'Please, may I?'

Max nods, and Otti tells her what happened.

'Pity. He was a quiet boy. He had difficulties, not sure what. He wasn't an idiot, nothing like that, just different. Kept himself to himself and communicated little. Never really looked you in the eye, if you know what I mean? Of course, the time I spent with him was after the event, and it traumatised him. Maybe that was his problem. However, he drew well, doodling on the walls with charcoal, and one time Horst found paper and pencil for him. Christian drew a picture of a man. It was brilliant, well-drafted, the features so clear. Horst asked him who the man was, and Christian said, "He killed mummy." I mean, what do you say to that?'

'Did they tell you what had happened?'

'No, not really, other than their mother had been killed and that it was a group of six or seven Ivans. While Horst tended to Christian's wounds, a nurse patched her up. She told me that Angelika had been raped and sodomised, almost certainly multiple times.' At the thought, she closes her eyes a moment. Max and Otti exchange glances.

'Anyway, they were just kids. She would have been about fourteen or fifteen, he about ten. I took pity on them.' She pauses a moment, takes a handkerchief from her purse and dabs her eyes. 'I'm so sorry, it's just struck me.'

'What has?'

'How cold and callous we'd all become, you know, back then. So much death and violence we'd become hardened and selfish; in the end, one's pity and empathy failed.'

Otti reaches out, placing her hand on Gerda's. 'But you and your husband saved them; you were helping people.'

'Oh, yes, but in the end, it was everyone for themselves. We could do little and more died than we saved. I helped Angelika while her brother got some of his strength back. By that time, it was all over, and the fighting stopped. We could come back to daylight. To the carnage. For about a month, they stayed with us and then one day, she said that they wanted to see if their home was still standing and try to find their father. I don't think they had heard from him for months. He died fighting. Such a waste. I told them to come back, but they never did.'

'How long was it before you saw them again?'

'I never saw him again. I bumped into her at the church near Leopoldplatz. When was it now? Let me see... Yes, last Sunday. She told me her brother was dead and that everything had gone wrong. She needed help, so I asked her to come to my apartment.'

'What happened then?'

'She told me what had taken place, you know, the men they abducted and killed. She wanted advice.'

'What did you advise?'

'I told her that only she could decide what to do, but it was probably better to give herself up. I said that if she did not, it would never end.'

'Good advice and heeded. Also, the fact she gave herself up helps her case.'

'She told me she had gone to your house to give herself up, said that she was afraid that you'd kill her.'

'As I said, she has not spoken to us. I have told her it is in her interest to tell her story. She trusts you, and perhaps you're her only friend. May I ask that you appeal to her on my behalf?'

Gerda regards him for a moment. 'If she confesses, what will happen to her?'

'Either way, she will go to prison. The question is, for how long? I think if we get to the truth, she will have a chance of a defence and a lesser charge. Of course, it will depend on the prosecution, but the case lawyer, Sabrina Heisig, is fair, and I am not without influence, particularly if Angelika assists us.'

'I see. So, you wish me to persuade her to talk to you?'

'It would help.'

'Well, I don't want to betray her confidence, but I will speak with her. When you take me down to see her, can you leave us alone?'

'Of course.'

They go down to the cell and usher Gerda in. 'Angelika, I have someone to see you. I will leave you. Shout when you are ready.' Max closes the door, locking it. Angelika stands and hugs Gerda. They wait for Max's steps to retreat. 'Thank you for coming.'

'I will come and see you every day, all right? Now, come and sit on the bed. I want to talk with you.'

Gerda notes the freshly scratched message and flakes of paint on the bed. She takes Angelika's hand. 'I think this, Max, is someone you can trust. He's kept his word and tells me it will help if you give him the truth.'

'Help who? Either way, I'm fucked…' she looks down a moment, 'sorry…'

'Don't worry about that. Listen, what have you got to lose? If, as you say, you are fucked, then logically, it should not matter, should it?'

'But it's all I have left. If I tell them, the world will know, and I will have nothing; I'll be empty.'

'You know, perhaps this is a story that the world should hear. It's your chance to set the record straight. I think, if it were me, I'd want to. Whatever happens, I won't abandon you, I promise.'

Angelika smiles weakly. 'Thanks. Let me think about it more.'

'Is there anything you need?'

'No, I just want to be quiet and rest.'

'I will ask if I can come back tomorrow.'

'Can you ask what has happened to Christian's body?'

'Yes, I will. I'll see you tomorrow. And do think about it, won't you?'

Max walks Gerda to the reception. 'So, what do you think?'

'She is afraid, alone, and mistrustful, which is not that surprising, really, is it?'

'No, it's not. Will she talk to me, do you think?'

'She said that if she tells her story, she will have nothing left. I think, right now, silence is the only thing she can control. Let me come and see her tomorrow. If she knows she has a friend who will stick with her, then perhaps she might cooperate.'

'Agreed. If you want to bring in some food or a book, that is fine too; just make sure the duty officer can check it over, okay?'

'Thank you.'

'Here is my card. My home number is on the back. I really want to help, you know?'

For a moment, she scrutinises him, her sharp eyes searching his. She nods. 'Yes, I think you do. She wants to know what has happened to Christian.'

'His body is in the mortuary, where it will stay until we conclude the investigation into his death. Once that's done, we can arrange a funeral. I have organised a car to take you home. I will be here on Monday. Perhaps we can speak then?'

Thanking him, she turns and heads out.

❖ ❖ ❖

Max and August go over to Malinda's for lunch. They order, carrying two large beers to their table. Taking a big gulp, Max says, 'Damn, that tastes good. Need it too.'

They clink glasses, August saying, 'Prost! And well done for getting her into custody. Otti has completed her six-month probation. Your report was impressive, or should I say, she's impressive.'

'I think she's born to this, if such things are possible.'

'She's captivated Julius, and he says he's open to more women like her joining the teams. Anyway, Monday, Otti gets a promotion and is good to go. Do you want to tell her?'

'No, you do it. It'll be better coming from the top.'

'Done, my pleasure.'

'I interviewed Angelika this morning, and she didn't say a word. Clearly, she's suffering. When I showed her the pictures of the crime scenes, she looked shocked, almost like she'd not seen them before. Gerda Mann is trying to reason with her, and I am allowing her to visit and gain her confidence.'

'We've got plenty to charge her. We should do so and hand it over to Sabrina.'

'Yes, we haven't much choice, sadly. I'll pass over what we have and see what she recommends.'

'Fine. As you know, I did a deal with the editor of the *Berliner Courier* to suppress writing anything too revealing about the body in Tegel Forest. They had a substantial set of picture and film evidence, including all the comings and goings. They must have had their photographer hidden by the entrance. The deal is that they get an exclusive once we make the arrest. I have spoken to Julius, and he has sent them a report of where we are. The story will be in tomorrow's Sunday edition, together with pictures of the victims and an appeal for anyone who knew them to come forward. We have also asked for witnesses to *Der Natchwacheplatz Massacre*. I have told them that our enquiries are ongoing and that you won't be available to comment. Julius and I will deal with the press.'

'Thanks. Anything more we can get on the massacre will help, and it would be good to find out who our victims are. So far, no one seems to have missed them.'

'Are you surprised? It is a shame she didn't come to us when she found them. We could have had them prosecuted for war crimes.'

Taking another swig, Max thinks saying, 'Hmm, for what good that might have done. I'm trying to put myself in her shoes.'

August smiles. 'You're good at that, you know? But be careful, it can be dangerous.'

37

My tongue will tell the anger of my heart

TOGETHER, HEIKE AND MARKUS COME down to breakfast. Max and Anna wish them a happy birthday. 'We'll do gifts later after school and work, all right?' Anna says, 'And I've made you each a cake to take to school to celebrate with your friends.'

'And I want you both to think about where we should go for a holiday.' Max looks at his watch. 'Sorry, I must go. You all have a great day, and I'll be back early for the party, all right?'

Away across the city, just after 7:45 a.m., Wolfgang stands opposite the Kripo building on Baggranfen Straße. He watches as uniformed offices come and go. A couple of squad cars and several motorcycles leave via the backyard. It is cold but clear; the first hint of a pale winter light and freshness cloak the city, giving that special *Berliner Luft*—Berlin air. Nothing can be worse than what has already happened, yet he feels lonelier and more miserable than he was in all the years he spent in the Russian labour camps. Deciding, he says out loud, 'Fuck it, it's now or never.'

He crosses the street and enters the imposing building; behind a counter, the duty officer is working. Wolfgang stands, head lowered, a habit of years in submissive servitude, and waits.

The officer looks him up and down. Frowns. 'What do you want? You can't sleep in a cell if that's what you're after?'

Wolfgang holds a tatty copy of *The Berliner Courier*. 'It says she's here.'

'Who's here?'

'Angelika Rächer.'

'What of it? What's your interest in her?'

Otti checks her watch as she enters the building; her mind is on admin and how to get Angelika to trust them, so she hardly notices the figure standing talking to Daniel.

Wolfgang looks the officer in the eye and says with pride, 'Angelika Rächer is my daughter. My little girl.'

His words stop Otti in her tracks. She turns. 'I'm sorry. Did I hear you right? Did you say that Angelika is your daughter?'

Wolfgang regards the attractive, tall, young *Polizei* detective. Her dark eyes penetrate, but there is a softness around her mouth.

He looks down, searching for the words. 'Angelika and Christian are my children. It was me that called in the report about the basement in Teichstraße. You see, I didn't know it was them…'

Overcome, he slumps forward on the counter and weeps great heaving sobs. In all his years, he has never cried like this. He feels all the bitter anguish of the lost years, lost family, lost everything come pouring out of him.

Otti and Daniel look at one another. She approaches Wolfgang and leads him gently across to a bench by the back wall. 'It's all right. Come and sit for a minute, let it out, then we can talk.' She turns to Daniel. 'Call through and see if Max is in, will you?' He nods and picks up the phone.

Wolfgang recovers himself a little and, looking up at Otti, says, 'I'm sorry, you must think I'm a stupid old man, but when I got back to Berlin, I'd been in Russia, a POW, you see?' He pauses, overcome with the detail of it all, does not know where to start. 'I tried to find them but failed. I thought they were all dead. Now… now it's too late. My lovely wife, Gretel, is missing. Christian gone, and Angelika in here and accused of murder. What will happen to her?'

Max appears. Otti signals for him to join her. 'Wait one minute, please. Oh, what was your name?'

He looks up, his eyes red and nose running. 'Wolfgang Rächer.'

'Herr Rächer, a moment, please; I'm just going to speak with my boss.'

He nods, composing himself, wiping his nose and eyes on the dirty sleeve of his old greatcoat, and examines the man who has just arrived, who has an air of authority about him. The detectives speak in low voices. After a few moments, she comes back. 'Come up and have a chat, and I'm sure a hot drink wouldn't go amiss, okay?'

They sit him down in the unit interview room, and Otti goes to get coffee.

Max sits. 'Herr Rächer…'

Wolfgang looks up. 'Please, call me Wolfgang; nobody has called me Herr Rächer, not in a long time.'

'I'm Max Becker, the lead investigator on this case. You say that Angelika and Christian are your children, is that right?'

'Yes, yes, sir. What will happen to her?'

Max sighs, stroking the scar on his cheek, thinking. Otti returns with a tray. 'I found a few cookies, too.' She puts them on the table and places a cup in front of Wolfgang. Instinctively, he wraps his hands around the comforting hot mug but does not drink. 'Have a cookie.' Wolfgang shakes his head. 'If you change your mind, help yourself.' He nods and mumbles a thank you.

'Wolfgang, this is *Kriminalobermeister* Otti Jäger. She is going to take some notes while we talk. I'm sorry you had to find out about your children through the paper. Your daughter thinks you're dead. I understand you were a POW in Russia?'

Wolfgang nods miserably.

'Please take your time and tell me what happened?'

He takes a noisy sip from his coffee and thinks about where to begin.

'I last saw my family on Tuesday, May 9, 1944; five thousand nine hundred and ninety-one days ago. I worked it out last night. It kept my mind off… well… you know?' He slurps his coffee. 'I was a *Feldwebel* in a signals unit attached to *Panzerjäger Abeitlung 150*. In July, Ivan overran us. It was war's end for me. They said my unit had been responsible for rounding up Soviet citizens and sending them to the Reich as slave labour. They convicted me of war crimes with a twenty-year sentence of hard labour. That's it, really. I worked, I survived, and four years ago, they released me. It was abysmal. I didn't think I'd survive; many didn't. I watched thousands of men die like animals; men like me who had done their duty and nothing more and unquestionably not the awful things they said of us. I know now that some of us did unspeakable things, but many did not. Did we really deserve to be treated like that?' Otti, who has been scribbling away on her pad, stops, looking up.

Max sighs at the endless threads of guilt. 'War brings out the very worst in all of us. But no, you didn't deserve that. I may be able to help you through my contacts as I too served on the Eastern Front, but please go on.'

For a moment Wolfgang scrutinises Max. 'You did?'

Max nods.

Wolfgang sighs and drinks more coffee. 'I guess we all did. On my return, I tried to find my wife and children, but I failed at that, too. Ever since, I've worked odd jobs, spent a lot of time on the streets, and now, this.' He lays the paper on the table, tapping at the headline. 'This disaster: I find my kids...' he trails off, tears flowing down his grimy cheeks.

Max walks over to the corner and leans against the wall. It is a sobering story and one that he had come so close to himself, but fortunately, in those last weeks, a wound had sent him to a hospital in Bavaria, surrendering instead to the Americans. For a while, it had been hard, but nothing like the experience of Wolfgang. As a fellow *Wehrmacht* soldier and war veteran, he feels great sympathy for this man. Wishing to bury the shame, postwar Germany had little time for its veterans.

Wolfgang finishes his coffee. 'I can't understand what happened. The paper says they killed those men. My daughter was such a lovely child, bright and funny. Christian was always sombre, slow and clumsy, but he was a good boy: thoughtful and kind. He had a gift for drawing and would sit for hours, sketching.'

Max sits again. 'Your daughter hasn't said a word since the arrest. She's traumatised by what has happened and her brother's most unfortunate death. As far as we know, the men she and Christian killed were all soldiers in the Red Army. Do you know what happened to your wife?'

Wolfgang shakes his head. 'My lovely Gretel. I long to hold her. But no, I don't know what happened.' He looks up at Max, hope in his eyes. 'Do you?'

For a second, Max considers what he should tell him but sees little point in hiding the truth. 'I'm so sorry, but your wife died on April 25, 1945, here in Berlin. We think killed by the same Russian soldiers your children abducted and dispatched. Your family were sheltering with other women and children in a church when a group of Ivans broke in and massacred many. We don't know how your children escaped with their lives, but we know they'd shot Christian and that Angelika took him to a doctor called Horst Mann, who patched them up, and for a while after he and his wife Gerda gave them shelter.'

Wolfgang is quiet, digesting the information. 'Gretel, dead. I had hoped that she might have survived and taken the children somewhere else.' He shuts his eyes and clenches his fists. 'But I think, in my heart, I knew she did not.'

'What we don't know is exactly what happened and why your children took such drastic action. We need to get your daughter to speak to us so that we can present the truth and help her. I know you'll want to see her, but it may be a great shock for her to learn of your return. She'll need proof. I suggest you give us some information that only you and she would know, something that would prove your identity?'

Wolfgang considers the proposal, searching his memory for something suitable. Eventually, his eyes light up. 'Ask her what happened when we went on holiday and took a trip to Lake Königssee. She'd remember that, for sure. If you give me a piece of paper, I'll write the answer.'

❖❖❖

As they make their way to the cells, Otti says, 'Well, this is a turn-up for the books. I mean, what are the chances?'

'Did they not tell you they call me Lucky Max?'

The duty officer walks with them and unlocks the door. Angelika is lying on the bunk, facing the wall, her legs drawn up.

Max waves the officer away and he and Otti enter. 'Angelika, I've got some good news for you. Are you listening?' She does not move. 'A man has come to the station; he's here now. His name is Wolfgang and claims he's your father.'

The news sends a surge of hope through her exhausted body. She turns over and swings her legs to the floor. 'What? My father? That's impossible. He fell in the war, taken by those… bastards!'

'We thought you might doubt what he says, so he has asked me a question for you, something that only you and he would know. He's written the answer on this paper.'

Her heart races. Intrigued, she nods. 'I'm listening.'

'What happened at Lake Königssee?'

She thinks back, then a flicker of a smile crosses her face. 'Yeah, we went there in, let me think, '38. The lake is famous for its echo, the sound so distinct, you see? Christian was about four and had never spoken. When he heard the echo, he shouted his name. He laughed when the mountain spoke it back to him. It was one of my happiest childhood memories. After that, he spoke more, repeating everything we said to him.' At the memory of it, she breaks down, weeping.

Max passes over the note. 'That's a wonderful memory. Hang on to it, tight.'

She unfolds the paper, recognising her father's hand, and reads:

My darling Angel, do you remember when Christy heard the echo he spoke for the first time, shouting his name over and over, then laughing joyously when he heard it back? We all laughed and were so happy to hear his voice at last. From then on, he talked more. Your loving papa—I am so sorry I have been gone for so long. xx

For a long while, she stares at the note, her tears and emotion filling the room. Otti struggles to keep her composure, wanting to reach out and console Angelika. Max, conflicted, wrestles with his conscience.

Angelika composes herself and looks at Max. 'You said he is here?'

'Yes, he's upstairs.'

'Please, may I see him?'

Max sits down beside her and passes her a handkerchief. 'You can see your father, but no more games; I need you to tell me everything that's happened, everything? No more silence. If you let me know why you and Christian killed these men, I promise we'll treat you with care and respect. If you help me, I can tell the court that you cooperated.'

She looks up at him, her protective shell crumbling. 'All right. I'll tell you everything. But please, can I see my father? It's been so long.'

We need to speak with you in the interview room so we can make a record of what you say. We can also get you a defence lawyer.

'No, no lawyers, I'll tell you everything, I promise. Now, please, I want to see my father.'

'We'll be back soon. Do you need anything to eat or drink?'

'Just some water, please.'

Max calls the guard. 'Get her some water, please?'

They walk down the cell corridor in silence. As they climb the stairs, Otti says, 'I still can't get my head around her killing those men so brutally. What the hell must they have done to her?'

'Yes, it's hard to imagine her doing that, but we must stay detached. First, we get the story, hopefully the truth, then we pass on our findings to Sabrina and let the system run. Having said that, I have an idea that may help her. I need to speak to Lutz and my wife. But first, let's talk to Wolfgang and break the good news.'

They return to the interview room and find it empty. Max scolds himself. '*Scheiße*! I can be so stupid.'

38

We band of brothers

WOLFGANG HAS NOT GONE FAR; he sits near Cornelius Bridge by the Landwehr Canal, just a few minutes from the Kripo building.

Overcome with emotion and frightened that Angelika might not want to see him, he had to get out and find some headspace. While thinking what to do, he picks up small stones from the path, idly lobbing them into the water. He wants to see her so much it hurts, but fears he'll be a disappointment.

Max sends Otti and Bastian to look for him. Max can see why Wolfgang ran. He does not know what Wolfgang did during his service, but as a *Feldwebel* in a *Wehrmacht* signals unit, it is doubtful he had done anything more shameful than that which war puts upon all men. Max considers himself an excellent judge of people, and in Wolfgang he sees a good man.

Max goes to tell Angelika that her father has left, but not to worry. He is sure he just got nervous and promises they will find him and will come and speak to her soon. Angelika asks him to call Gerda and tell her what has happened, which he agrees to do.

Sitting at his desk, ordering his mind, he picks up the phone and calls his wife.

Anna's secretary, Nadine, answers. 'Hello, Dr Becker's office. How may I help?'

'Hey, Nadine, It's Max. How are you?'

'Hi, Max, I'm good, thanks. Do you want to speak with Anna?'

'Please.'

'She's due out on her rounds. I'll check.'

The line buzzes several times before Anna picks up. 'Darling, what's up?'

'All good. I just want to pick your brains.'

'Sure. Has Angelika found her voice yet?'

'Well, we had a breakthrough; her father appeared at the office.'

'Really, her father? I thought he'd fallen.'

'Apparently not. It took the wind out of her sails, and she's agreed to tell me what happened. But before I interview her, I want to explore an idea.'

'Sure, what's on your mind?'

'Well, we know some or all the men she killed assaulted her, so I'm exploring some ideas regarding her mental state. I'm going to speak with Lutz about it, but was wondering whether any of your psych colleagues could give me their opinion?'

Anna thinks for a moment. 'Eric Stein is probably your best bet. He's a good man and up to date on the latest techniques. Do you want me to ask him?'

'Would you? I'll call you later.'

'All right, I'll see you later for the party.'

'Yes, wouldn't miss it!' He hangs up.

Max redials, calling Lutz and arranges to see him.

❖ ❖ ❖

Otti and Bastian head out on foot. 'I think I may know where to look.'

'Yeah?'

'Where would you go that's close to here where you can get some solitude?'

'The Tiergarten?'

'Yes, we'll cut over the canal on Cornelius Bridge.'

A minute later, they arrive at the canal and cross. As with any bridge, no matter how hurried you might be, you'll always glance over the side as you traverse. Otti grabs Bastian's arm. 'Stop, look down there on the bank.'

'Is that him?'

'Yes, no doubt. What do you think? Shall we go down or just watch and see what he does? Don't want to scare him off.'

'Leave this to me. Go back to the office and tell Max.'

A few moments later, Bastian walks along the path by the bank and joins Wolfgang. 'Hey, everything okay, buddy?'

Wolfgang looks up with sad eyes. 'I guess.'

Bastian takes out his cigarettes. 'Do you want a cigarette, maybe a cup of coffee?'

Wolfgang looks at him closer. 'I'll take a smoke, thanks.'

Bastian takes a cigarette out for himself and hands the rest of the pack over. 'Here, keep them.'

'Why, thanks, my friend, very kind,' Wolfgang says, taking one out, nipping off the filter and putting it between his lips. He pulls some matches from his pocket and, lighting up, takes a deep drag. 'That's good.'

'May I sit a while?'

Wolfgang shrugs. 'It's a free country.'

Bastian sits and takes a drag. 'Are you sure about that?'

'Well, usually no one bothers me.'

Bastian looks at Wolfgang's tatty *Wehrmacht* winter coat.

'That's seen some action. I was a *Fallschirmjäger*, name's Bastian Döhl,' he says, sticking out his hand.

They shake. 'Wolfgang. Pleased to meet you.'

'Look, I don't want to muck you about, but I know who you are. I work with Max, but it's all right, I'm not here to bust your balls or be the cop. I just want to talk.'

Wolfgang takes another drag and then nips the glowing end off and puts the unsmoked half cigarette back in the packet.

Bastian laughs. 'We used to do that, you know, back then. Smokes were always in short supply.'

Wolfgang looks at him critically. 'So, what happened to you after?'

'I was in Italy and surrendered to the Yanks. Spent a bit of time in the clink, then they let me go, you know, once they knew I wasn't worth the bother. I came back here and joined the *Polizei*. My wife, Lara, died during one of the last American air raids in March '45. And you?'

'Spent most of the war getting into Russia then getting out, but in the end, we got overrun, and they took me. Let me go in '56.'

'Ah, crap, my friend, that's tough. Is that why you're living on the streets?'

'I guess. Honestly, I don't know, really. I tried to look for my family, but... well, I'm sure you know the story?' He lobs a few more stones, adding, 'I'm sorry about your wife. I found out today that my Gretel died. I'm struggling to remember how she looked, you know?'

'Yes, I know, and it tears you apart sometimes. The one thing I'll never forget is the way Lara smelt, the touch of her skin: that's how I bring her back.'

'Haven't you married again?'

'No, but just between you and me, I may have met someone, you know, that makes my heart flutter, which is good because I thought I didn't have one. Trouble is, she's younger, and we work together.'

Wolfgang looks at him a twinkle in his eyes, and grins. 'Not the one I met earlier?'

'Otti, yes, but don't tell anyone, particularly not her, all right.'

'Shit, man, she is top class. Don't let that one get away.'

'We'll see, but I haven't felt this way about anyone, not since Lara.'

'You're a lucky man to find someone, you know?'

'It's early days, and then there is the stuff about us working together. I think that bothers her, probably more than it does me.'

'Don't be daft. After everything we've been through, if it's right, it's right.'

'I guess. Look, I get you're probably a bit, how should I say, worried about seeing your daughter again…'

'Worried! I'm scared fucking shitless. What if she doesn't like me anymore?'

'Well, did you have a good relationship before?'

'Yes, we were close. She's the apple of my eye. Christian was always closer to Gretel and me to her, but we loved them both the same.'

'So, why would that be any different now?'

'Ah, look at me, I stink, I live on the street; I'm a dirty vagrant, no good to anyone.'

'That's harsh. Look, first off, we can fix the presentation. You can come back to my place and have a shower, shave, and I'll fix you up with some clothes. Also, we can put you in touch with a group that helps guys like you. It's run by a friend of ours. They'll sort out a place to stay and some work. What have you got to lose?'

'Nothing, I guess.'

Bastian smiles and places his hand on Wolfgang's shoulder. 'And, crucially, I think your girl needs you more than ever because, right now, she's in the shit. You're the most important person in her life. If you bug out, you're letting her down.'

'You think so?'

'I know so. She needs you. You're her dad, and you can't just make an appearance and then fuck off, can you? Look, walk back with me. I'll tell Max that we're going to clean you up, and then we can come back later and see her. How's that sound?'

Wolfgang thinks for a minute. 'What will she think when she finds out that it was me that told you about the basement?'

'I really wouldn't worry about that. She won't ask so, for now, until you have had some time, keep it to yourself, okay? Anyway, it wasn't what got them caught.'

'No?'

'No. It was a combination of an educated guess and dumb luck. Nothing to do with what you told us.'

'All right, fine, I'll come with you.'

'Good. A new start, eh?'

❋❋❋

Max strides into Lutz's office. 'Lutz, you old sea dog.'

'Max, my brother, come sit; coffee's brewing.'

Lutz fires up his pipe, and for a few moments, they chat, enjoying the coffee.

'We would have killed for a cup like this back in '44, eh, Max?'

'I'd have killed for a clean drink of water. For us tankers, everything tasted of oil, petrol, and dirt. It's no wonder we all had the shits.'

'So, what's up?'

'Anything new regarding the basement?'

'Still waiting for the last tests, but we have a mountain of evidence: it's the smoking gun that damns her.'

'Well, although we have an excellent picture of things, what we don't know is exactly what happened and who our victims are.'

'Angelika's not singing, then?'

'Actually, we had a breakthrough this morning, at least until I screwed up. Her long-lost father, Wolfgang, former POW in Russia, came to the office wanting to see her.'

'My God, back from the dead.'

'And, to boot, it was him, not knowing who they were, that had tipped us off about the basement. Anyway, I went down to tell her, and he got cold feet and hopped it.'

Lutz grins. 'Ouch, careless, old boy, careless.'

'Yes. I've got Otti and Bastian out looking for him. I'm sure we'll find him. I feel for him. He came back in '56 and has been drifting ever since. Tried to look for his wife and kids.'

'Well, at least a smidgen of sunshine has fallen on this business. What's he like?'

'He seems solid, ex-signals, one of the many from the divisions encircled and cut off in the summer of '44. Thought we could help him through the network. What do you think?'

'Yes, I am sure we can. With whom did he serve?'

'He was a *Feldwebel* in a signals unit attached to *Panzerjäger Abeitlung 150*.'

'Well, let's get him back, and we can help. How did his daughter react?'

'Naturally, she was shocked and emotional, but it mollified her, and she's agreed to talk. I'm going to interview her later, which brings me to my main reason for visiting.'

'Intriguing, go on.'

'I think she experienced something extraordinarily traumatic. So, when she came across these men, it triggered an unnatural reaction, causing her to behave uncharacteristically. So, I'm wondering what have you for me on forensic psychiatry?'

Lutz frowns. 'Isn't that for her defence to worry about?'

'Normally, I'd agree. The trouble is, she's refusing counsel, and this isn't as clear cut as it seems, is it?'

'No, I suppose not. You don't make things easy for yourself, do you, Max? Why do you care about her so much?'

'We'll never know how many innocent civilians' lives that cursed war destroyed, but I know hers was, and it led to all this. So, I want to get this one right for her and because I think there will be a storm of media exposure.'

'I see. Well then, it is my pleasure to give you any help in my power. I know a couple of psychiatrists we can approach. When are you interviewing her?'

'First, we find Wolfgang and reunite them. With luck, first thing tomorrow.'

Lutz goes over to his desk, flicking through a Rolodex. 'Have you asked Anna about her colleagues?'

'Yes, she's suggested Eric Stein.'

'Ah, here we are.' He jots down the details on a notepad, tearing out the page and handing it over. 'Dr Seigfried Markowvitz, try him first.'

Max takes the paper. 'Thanks.'

'I'll get the final reports done ready for Sabrina. More coffee?' Max glances at his watch. 'Tempting, but best not.'

'Hey, I've got a little something for the twins, and wish them happy birthday; I can't believe they're thirteen already.' He hands over two small packages.

'Intriguing, thanks. I'm sure they'll be pleased. I'll see you soon.'

They shake hands, and Max strides off down the corridor. As he starts down the first flight of stairs, he hears running footsteps. 'Max, Max, wait, it's Otti on the phone.'

Back at Lutz's desk, he picks up. 'What's up?'

'We've found him. He was sitting by Cornelius bridge. Bastian chatted with him and found out he was worried about how he looked. Anyway, they've gone to Bastian's apartment to get cleaned up and borrow some clothes.'

'That's great. Good idea. Is he coming straight back?'

'Bastian said he'd take him for a meal first.'

'I'm on my way back. Make sure you put Angelika in the picture, okay?'

'Already done. See you later.'

'Good news?' Lutz asks.

'Yes, they found him, and he has agreed to come back.'

'I'll make some calls and see if we can find him a place to stay. I'll call you later.'

39

Hell is empty and all the devils are here

SITTING IN THE INTERVIEW ROOM, Angelika had never been so nervous and excited in her life. In just a few moments, she will see her papa again. She screws shut her eyes and tries to picture him, conjuring up his smell, the tone of his voice.

The door opens, and Otti enters, followed by Wolfgang.

Otti smiles, her eyes twinkling, and stands aside. 'I'll leave you. Take your time.' She leaves, closing the door.

He stands gazing at her, tears welling up. 'Oh my goodness, you're so beautiful, just like your mother. What a woman you have become.' He opens his arms. 'Come, hug your papa, it has been so long, and I'm so sorry I have not been here for you.'

Tears flowing, she allows him to gather her up. He feels much thinner, and some of the old strength is gone, but it is most definitely him. They hold one another tight, and for what seems like the longest time, they stay that way in silence.

Eventually, he pushes her away gently. 'Come, let's sit.'

He brings the other chair around the table so that they can be next to one another. 'I thought I'd never see you again.'

Angelika wipes her eyes. 'Me too. I thought they had killed you. Where have you been?'

Wolfgang takes her hands, looks into her eyes and tells her what happened and how he looked for them and never stopped hoping.

'How did you know I was here?'

'It was in the paper. As was the news about your brother.'

With the mention of Christian's name, she breaks down again, the guilt too much. 'I'm so sorry, papa, I tried to look after him, and I got him involved in all this business, and it cost him his life…'

'Hush, listen, slow down. Your brother wasn't a child anymore, and I am sure that he would have wanted to help you.'

'When the *Polizei* found us at the hotel, he attacked them and told me to run, to get away and save myself, but he said it was the Ivans. I think at that moment, he was back there in that church crypt, only now he could fight back. It's the only explanation.'

Wolfgang hugs her again. 'Oh my God, sweetheart, what in the hell did they do to you all?'

For a moment, she looks down, sighing. She feels shattered, the emotion quashing the energy from her. All she wants to do is hold him and never let go.

He smiles and places his hand on her cheek. 'It's all right. You don't have to tell me now. You say it when you are ready, okay?' He wipes away the tears from her cheeks with his thumb.

She looks at him with defiance. 'I did some bad things, papa, to those men, but they deserved it and I'd do it again.'

'It's okay, my love, I understand. I am so, so sorry I wasn't there to protect you.'

She shakes her head. 'They'd just have killed you, too. They weren't human, not like people I know, anyway.'

'Well, I don't care what anyone else says. I am glad that you killed them and paid them back for what happened. I'd have done the same, you know that, right? I'm proud of how strong you are, and it was not your fault about Christian. In the end, he stood up and protected you, didn't he? That was his choice.'

'He killed a *Polizei* officer.'

'I know, but I don't think he knew what he was doing. He was lost.'

'We've all been lost, I think? Gerda, who helped me, said that to move on, I must forgive. What do you think?'

'It is hard, but I think that is good advice. Maybe you don't have to forgive them, but forgive yourself. Besides, I'm here now, and I will be your papa always.'

'They're going to send me to prison for a long time.'

Placing his hands on her cheeks, cupping her face, he smiles. 'Tell them the truth, what will be, will be. You are still young, and together we can face the future, all right?'

She nods.

'You must be brave, but you are not alone anymore. I love you, and I always have. I asked them if I could give you this,' he says, taking the doll from his pocket. 'It is like the one you had as a child.'

He passes it to her. 'I call her Lotti.'

Angelika looks at him, then at the doll. 'You gave her the same name.'

'Ah, I got it right, then. I wasn't sure I'd remembered correctly. Keep her and when, in the days to come, you feel alone, take her out and I'll be with you.'

She nods. 'Thanks, papa.'

'I know it is a silly thing, but since I found her, I did not feel alone anymore. I felt like you were right with me. Of course, you and Christian and mama have always been in my heart, which got me through those dark years in captivity, but the doll made you feel closer. Trust me.'

'I do.'

There is a knock on the door. Otti enters. 'Everything all right?'

Angelika smiles. 'Yes, thanks. I'm ready to tell you now.'

'All right, I'll get Max.'

Max looks up from his desk and glances at his watch. 'I was going to do the interview in the morning, but if she's ready, we can do it now.'

They go in.

Wolfgang says, 'May I stay?'

Angelika takes his hand. 'No, papa, I must do this on my own. Come and see me after; I'll be fine.'

He nods. 'All right, if you're sure.'

Wolfgang leaves, and Max rearranges the chairs. 'Please sit.' He puts a portable tape machine on the table, the reel-to-reel tape spooled up ready. 'I want to record your story, Angelika. After, we will have it transcribed into a written statement, which you can read and add to or change before you sign. Before we begin, I must advise that you have a lawyer present…'

She shakes her head defiantly. 'No, it is fine. I want to tell you everything. The truth.'

'Okay.' He sets the machine running. 'Please begin.'

'I'm not sure where to…'

'Start from how you came to be in the church crypt before the Russians arrived.'

She nods, and clears her throat and, under the table, clutches Lotti.

'We had been hiding in the Anhalter Bahnhof, but it had become so overcrowded, and the supplies stored there had long gone, so we had to leave and look for food. Mum didn't like to go out without us. She thought it was best we stayed together. The city was ablaze, fires everywhere, the sounds of fighting all around. With all the shelling and bombing, sleep was impossible and we were exhausted, almost delirious with fatigue. We had moved about often, going from basement to basement, but while we were in the U-Bahn, you could move about the city using the tunnels, by then there were no trains, you see? We came across this woman who told us about a church near Sophie-Charlotte Platz station. So, mum walked us down the tunnel from, I think it was Gleisdreieck, it took nearly two hours, and it was mid-afternoon by the time we got there.'

'What day was this?'

She thinks for a moment. 'It was two days before, so, Monday.'

'Please, continue.'

'Well, we got to the church and knocked, and an elderly priest answered and let us in. He took us down to the crypt, where they had some bread and water and a small quantity of cured sausage. It was good. We were ravenous. There were about fifty or sixty people, all women and children; all girls, apart from Christian and one other boy. I think by then, they had taken away a lot of the boys to fight.'

'We stayed there as it was so much more comfortable than the underground tunnels. We managed some sleep and got a little strength back. We thought we were safe. We had found some leaflets that the Ivans had dropped, giving us safe passage if we surrendered. Also, a few days earlier, we had been in a basement, and some Soviet soldiers had come down. They'd looked around, wanting to know if there were any men with weapons hiding. They could see we were all starving. Later, they brought bread and some cheap schnapps. But on that Wednesday, when the others came, they were different.' She pauses, closing her eyes a moment and swallows, her mouth dry.

'It was late afternoon, I think. Mum had been getting nervous, saying that we should move early the next morning, that it wasn't safe to stay in one place for too long. I often wonder whether she had a premonition or something. During the early part of the day, there had been much fighting. We could hear the gunfire and shelling. It had blown some of the church windows in. The ground shook.' She pauses. Max and Otti glance at one another. They can see how hard this is. Angelika tries to clear her throat. 'Sorry, may I have some water, please?'

Otti stands. 'I'll get some.'

'Do you need a break?' Max asks.

She shakes her head. 'We heard the door crash open and loud voices speaking Russian. For a while, they ran around in the main church, searching and breaking things. Then it went quiet, but I could hear voices whispering. Then one of them found the crypt entrance and came down. He had a good look, then shouted, *"Tovarishchi!"* Then he yelled back up the stairs, *"Isayev, zhenshchiny, devochki."'*

Otti comes back and hands Angelika the water. She pauses and takes a sip. Max says, 'For the recording, the Russian words mean comrades, Isayev, women, girls.'

Angelika puts the cup down. 'Then the other Ivans came down, six in all, radiating aggression and malevolence. Everyone was trying to look away; they terrified us. The priest came forward and told them this was the house of God, not to harm the people, and they should leave, and they could take anything they wanted. The leader, Isayev, said to him, "We will, don't you worry!" Then they took him upstairs. One woman got up and told them that there were no soldiers here, no fighters. She handed over the leaflet. Isayev snatched it from her, looked at it, laughed, and then hit her in the face with the butt of his gun. And that was it. The others took this as a cue to begin.' She looks down, trying to find the words.

Max leans forward. 'Please take your time. Would it help if you tell me about each of the men you killed and what they did?'

She looks up and nods. 'The one we knew as Johann was the leader; we killed him last. He and a group of similar men were in the restaurant where I worked as a waitress. I could see he was the same. They made sexual advances on me and abused me verbally. It all came back, and I wanted him dead. So, I followed him, found out where he lived and within a short time he led me to the other three. I don't know where the other two are. Perhaps they are dead or back in Russia.'

'I told Christian about them and he wanted to help to get revenge. We found the basement and fitted it out, and when we had everything ready, we took Manfried Bikart. His real name is Dedov Damir Olegovich.' She pauses, taking a sip of water.

'On that day, in the church, he took me and raped me right in front of my mother and brother. Several of the others, including Johann, used me too. They went into a frenzy, going from girl to girl and woman to woman. If anyone fought back, they shot them in the head.' Tears fill her eyes.

Otti glances at Max.

'God help me. They made me and Christian watch as they raped our mother and then beat her. While the others did their business, the man called Ernst, the one we killed second, stood guard. At last, he turned to Christian, pulling him and the other boy up and taking them over to a corner he raped them; they were shouting and crying out. The other boy got away, but as he fled up the stairs, Johann shot him, the others laughing. My mother could stand it no longer and though badly beaten, sprang up and ran toward Ernst. He had a large knife, like a cleaver, which he had put down. Snatching it up, her eyes blazing, she swung at him. He held up his left hand for protection, but the blade found its mark and cut off two of his fingers. The others thought this hilarious and disarmed her. I'll never forget the look on her face, as though she knew her end had come. It wasn't fear, but rather, a reconciled serenity. For a while, Ernst lay on the floor clutching his hand. Then he got up, took the cleaver and began hacking at her. When she was down, the others joined in, clubbing her with their guns.' She stops, shuts her eyes.

'We can stop if you need a break,' Max says.

She opens her eyes, steeling herself. 'It's okay, I want to go on. Finally, Johann took a bottle of spirits, poured it over her, and set her alight. Christian was so frightened he got up and ran, heading for the stairs. I watched him go, willing him to get away, but a shot rang out, and he spun around, and then they fired again, and he fell and was still.'

She picks up her water and drinks again. Otti wants so badly to hug her, give her support but knows that she must stay professional and detached.

Angelika places her hands on the table and curls up her fingers, making fists, her knuckles turning white. 'You cannot imagine what it was like down there. The smell of fear, death, my mother's burning flesh, gun smoke, and so much blood. By this time, of the fifty or sixty of us who were there, they had killed about half, and it seemed they'd had enough. They herded those of us that were able upstairs. I had to walk past Christian thinking him dead. Manfried stayed behind; we could hear the shots, each one made me jump. They made us sit in the front pews, and when Manfried came back up they took the priest and stripped him naked. For a while, they pushed him about from one-to-another as he, eyes closed, recited the prayer for the dead. Ernst watched us. If any of us tried to look away, he'd hit us with his pistol. One woman sitting next to me broke down, and Ernst shot her. Her gore covered my face, and her body slumped across me. I was too frightened to move her. Finally, they took the priest...' she pauses, looks at Max, saying. 'I went back to the church the other day. I know you've been there; it's when I knew you'd understood my messages. The young cleric told me that the priest the Ivans killed was Father Sebastian. They took this defenceless old man and crucified him, and while he hung there above the altar, Rolf cut off his genitals, laying them on the dais. For a while they stood, admiring their handy work, laughing and passing a bottle between them. I thought they were going to end by killing us, but then, as though we weren't there, they left, and that was it.' She drinks, her face flushed, her moist red eyes, sunken.

Momentarily, the room is silent. Max says, 'If you can go on a little longer, I have a question.'

She nods solemnly.

'Do you know the Russian names of the others?'

'Yes, Ernst Bärmann was Viktor Radoslav Ivanovich. Rolf Cahnheim was Boris Artur Vacheslavovich.'

'And Johann?'

'Johann Kleeman. I knew him only as Isayev.'

'After they had gone, what happened then?' Otti asks.

'For a while, we were too terrified to move. I was in pain. They'd broken my nose, split my lip, and I was bleeding, you know, from down below. But I had to know, so I got up and went to Christian and found he was breathing. Another girl helped me carry him to a bench, and we found some strips of cloth to bandage him up. I went to check on my mother. I knew she was gone, but I had to see. I still see her like that sometimes when I close my eyes at night. She was the only one who fought back.'

'Some of the older women recovered enough to take charge and look after the younger ones. One of them told me she knew about a medic not too far away, called Dr Mann. I knew him, had met him once or twice. We thought it would not be safe to move until the morning; that was when the Ivans were too busy sleeping it off or fighting. We were terrified more would come, so we built a barricade against the door and huddled together. Waiting. In silence.'

'That night, there was a colossal thunderstorm. It was like the wrath of God. It rained so heavily, almost like it was trying to cleanse the sins, if such a thing were possible. As it subsided, we set off to find the doctor. Another woman helped me, and we found a small cart to carry Christian. When we got there, she ran off...' she pauses, frowning. 'You know, I never asked her name. I wonder if she survived? I hope so.'

'They let us in, and he saved Christian. He and Gerda looked out for us. The horror had numbed everyone, and dragged out of us our humanity.' She stops, taking another drink.

Otti says, 'I remember people standing in queues for food and water, and the shells would fall and after the gaps where people had fallen would fill up, the queue shuffling forward as though nothing had happened. I saw dead horses stripped to the bone in minutes.'

Angelika looks at her. 'You were there?'

'Yes, but we were lucky.'

Max says, 'A question for you. Until you came across Johann in the restaurant, you had no plan to take revenge, is that correct?'

'No, I had put it in the past or at least thought I had.'

'When you saw him, did you immediately want him dead?'

'The meeting stunned me, took my breath away, then the abuse started, and I could see he was the same, and everything flooded back. He wasn't a man. I don't know what he was, just wicked. There was not one shred of good in him. I saw him and his men do all those things, and there he was, living it up, and I knew I had to make him pay.'

'Do you know how they came about their German names?'

She shakes her head. 'No, sorry.'

'I think we can guess. Thank you. Is there anything else you want to add?'

'I am sorry that Christian attacked your men. When they knocked, I was asleep. He shouted to me that the Ivans were coming and to get away. I think he was confused. I yelled at him to stop, but then I heard a warning and the first shots, and I panicked and ran. I am sorry I did that.'

'All right, understandable. Why the messages?'

'Foolishly, I thought we might get away, and I wanted you to know why we'd killed those men.'

'When you first saw Johann and followed him back home, why didn't you come to us and tell us your story?'

'It didn't even occur to me. I just saw red. I was in pain, and desired revenge, not just for me but for everyone; Christian, my mother, my father, and all the others, too. We did nothing to them, were no threat, just...' she trails off. 'It's just... they took everything from us... everything!'

One last question. 'Did Günther, Maria or anyone else assist you with the abduction and killing of the four men?'

'No, it was my idea. It was just us. Günther liked Christian, and he helped us both by giving him work, money, and some self-respect.'

Passing over a piece of paper, Max says, 'Thank you, Angelika. I know that this has been hard for you, but now we know it all makes more sense. I think that is enough for today. Spend some time with your father. I will have more questions. In the meantime, if you can remember, can you write the addresses of where the four men lived?'

Nodding, her face drawn and ashen, she takes the pad.

40

To do a great right do a little wrong

AT MARKUS AND HEIKE'S PARTY, Max is subdued. Heike comes and sits by him. 'You okay, dad?'
'Yes, sweetheart, just a little tired.' He puts his arm around her. 'How's it feel being a teenager?'
Heike shrugs. 'I don't feel any different, but yeah, it's cool, I guess. Thanks for the money and gifts. I love the new Telefunken Stereo.'
'Well, you needed a better system to fill your life with music. What are you going to spend the money on?'
'Don't know yet. I will save some and fritter some.'
'That's the spirit. Come on, let's join the others.'
He tells them about Lake Königssee and the echo, and they all agree to go there for their holiday.
That night he and Anna make love: slow, deep, tender; sex that only true lovers have. After, lying in the dark, her head on his shoulder, she says, 'Want to talk about it?'
'I thought we had it bad on the front, you know. It was bad, the worst type of bad. But what I heard today was something else.' He tells her Angelika's story.
'It's a pity they did not get away. You're too good at your job.'
'They made too many mistakes. I've never had a case like this. From one point of view, it's simple: she did it. You know, I think I would have done the same, maybe even worse, if those men had done those things to you and the kids. I must make sure that we get justice for her while acknowledging that taking the law into your own hands is a mistake.'
'I think the judges will see that.'
'I'll make sure of it, but she will go down, sadly.'
'Maybe that will give her time to draw a line in the past. Do you think they will provide her with some psychiatric help, too?'
'Your Eric Stein seems very interested, and I will try to make that hap-

pen.'

'She got her father back. That's got to help.'

'Yes, I'm sure. He's got his own demons and the guilt of not being there to help.'

'They will have to help one another. It's what we did, isn't it?'

❋ ❋ ❋

Over the next few days, Angelika's father and Gerda persuade Angelika to take legal counsel, and to allow the three psychiatrists to talk with her.

Max and the public prosecutor, Sabrina Heisig, are sitting in her office. She sets the folder down on the table. 'The taped evidence is compelling, and your handling of her has been second-to-none. I have been through the reports too.'

'What do you think?' he asks.

'Two of the psychiatrists have diagnosed Stress Response Syndrome (SRS), and the third's saying Situational Disorder.'

'Okay, that's good. Can we work with that?'

'Well, there's a caveat.'

'Oh, go on.'

'Well, usually, a diagnosis of or acceptance that a patient is suffering from SRS only applies for about six months after the events that caused the trauma. In Angelika's case, it's been fifteen years.'

Max frowns. 'What the hell does that mean?'

'It suggests that if the symptoms are still present, it was a pre-existing condition and not the result of the trauma.'

'Oh shit, really?'

'However, the doctor your wife put us on to, Eric Stein, has been looking at some cases with war veterans, and he thinks that this isn't correct and can prove that these men were all perfectly fine before their exposure to the events that caused their condition.'

'And what about Angelika?'

'Well, I've suggested that the defence appoint him and that we won't be offering any counter psychiatric evidence. If he can show that she is suffering from this disorder, we'll accept it.'

'And?'

'For a guilty plea, we can offer *Totschlag* with a sentence of nine years.

If she takes the help and keeps her head down, she'll be out in five to six.'

'Manslaughter, then. If you can do that, it sounds fair, I guess.'

'It's a brilliant deal. I will have to get the nod from my boss, but that should be fine. Surprisingly, Julius is taking a personal interest in this case, and they are old buddies. Anyway, we'll put it to her defence team, and I'm sure they'll play ball.'

'Thanks, Sabrina. I know this is the right thing to do.'

She smiles and stands. 'Yes, me too.'

❖❖❖

Later that day, as he climbs the steps to his office, he meets Eric Stein coming down.

They shake hands. 'Have you seen her again?'

Eric nods. 'Yes, an interesting and disturbing case. It has decided me to examine more civilian casualties, see if I might find out more about this disorder.'

'Can you cure her? If that's the right word.'

'Well, we can't rewind the clock, but we'll use therapies to work out the issues and give the patient ways to deal with them. They acknowledged this problem way back in time. I believe the Spartan general, Leonidas, accepted that some of his soldiers reached a point when they could not fight anymore and had to be dismissed. Shakespeare describes such a disorder in his play Henry IV Part 2, and there's the line from Macbeth. Let me think, how does it go? Ah, yes: "Canst thou not minister to a mind diseased… Pluck from the memory a rooted sorrow?" Yes, that's it. Fits nicely with this case.'

'The prosecution is suggesting she will get nine years. Do you think she can handle prison?'

'Essentially, she's resigned to it. Having her father back to support her makes a big difference, as does Gerda. I will continue to treat her, too.'

'That's wonderful. Well, let me know if I can do anything, and I hope your research goes well.'

❖❖❖

August joins Max in his office and places a copy of the *Courier* on his desk. 'Hey, have you seen this?'

Max picks it up. While he reads, August goes off, returns with two coffees, closes the door, and sits opposite.

'Bloody hell, where did all this come from? Who's leaked?'

August lowers his voice a little and leans forward. 'Julius.'

Max makes a face. 'Julius leaked this? What's his game?'

'He never ceases to surprise me. When I came in this morning, he was sitting in my office, well that's never happened before. He told me that enough time had elapsed, and with her hearing due in a few weeks, he had, and I quote, "exercised a little propaganda." Cunning, eh?'

'Propaganda, is this what he calls propaganda?'

August nods. 'Yes, I think it might be.'

Max grins. 'The crafty old bugger.'

'He said that it was time to open an old wound that has been festering for a long time: civilian victims of the Soviets.'

'Ah, I see.'

'Of course, this is strictly in confidence and goes no further, but I suspect Julius has colluded with the mayor.'

'Brandt is in on this? I thought they hated one another.'

'Politics can make strange bedfellows. Anyway, I think it might kick up the dust in East-West relations.' He taps his nose. 'So, mum's the word, okay?'

❋❋❋

Within a few days of the publication of the *Courier* article detailing the events of Angelika's ordeal and the ordeal of German civilians, there began a storm of media interest in the many atrocities carried out against them during the closing months of the war. Victims emerged, recounting their traumatic experiences, and within a week, Angelika and her story gained notoriety, the media calling her "Angel Avenger".

On the morning of Wednesday, December 7, 1960, they hear her case. Eager spectators pack the courtroom, and thousands more have come out onto the streets. There are chants of "Angel Avenger", "Free the Avenger", and "Our Guardian Angel". Some women, victims of similar crimes, hang from their necks signs written in red marker with the letters: AA, which becomes a symbol of the cause and the ensuing media storm carries Angelika's story to the world.

Below the court, Angelika's lawyer, Hendrika Baumhoff, sits opposite her client, who carries a bemused, distant stare. Hendrika smiles. 'It is a circus up there. Are you ready?'

Solemnly, Angelika nods. 'Yes, let's get it over with.'

Hendrika leads her up, and as she arrives in the courtroom, the crowd erupts, shouting words of encouragement. It takes several minutes to calm the room. They usher in the five judges, who are no sooner seated than several people shout, 'Free the Angel! Free the victim!'

Angelika sits passive, a faraway expression on her angelic-looking face.

Regaining order, the senior presiding judge says, 'We will have no further outbursts in this court. One more, and I will have the room cleared. Now, let us proceed…'

Angelika pleads guilty to the abduction and killing of the four men, and the court allows the psychiatric report to be submitted. Max speaks up for her, giving evidence of her cooperation and to her surrendering herself. They do not charge her with Jürgen's death or the injuring of Udo.

Following a court adjournment to consider the evidence and read the reports, they bring Angelika back on Tuesday, January 24, 1961. Customarily, Max does not attend such hearings, but this is different and like no other case he has ever worked on. He and Anna go together, and sitting with Wolfgang and Gerda, await the ruling.

In the once more packed room, Angelika looks small, delicate, and overpowered by the event. It is hard to associate her with everything that has happened. When they deliver a sentence of nine years on each count, to be served concurrently, she remains passive. Perhaps the merest hint of relief flashes across her face at the sentence she had been told to expect and come to terms with, is what she gets. The public benches break out in booing and shouts of 'wronged!' and 'too harsh!', but court officials whisk Angelika away, the shouting and noise receding as they go down to the basement and take her to a waiting van, which drives to Hakenfelde Women's Correctional Centre to serve her sentence.

Max and Anna walk arm-in-arm across the Tiergarten. 'Are you all right, darling?'

'Yes, I'm glad it is over. At least she can move forward now; we all can.'

'Some of the press have been very unkind to you; you don't deserve that.'

He shrugs. 'I represent the state. They need someone to kick. It's fine. It'll blow over.'

'It really upset the kids.'

'That's the worst part, isn't it? I don't know how I can save them that. It will pass. People will find another cause.'

'Perhaps, one day, your part in all of this will be told.'

He chuckles. 'Yeah, I'll write a memoir, eh? After I retire. Can you imagine?'

'You should. You don't have a dull life.'

'You can say that again.'

They walk for a while, the cold fresh air tinged with a low wintering sun, the trees haloed, their dark limbs scratching at the ashen sky. 'Sometimes, I think I should quit and open a bike shop, leave all the crap behind.'

'You'd just get bored and fat, drinking too much beer with your buddies. Besides, I think what you do makes a difference.'

❖❖❖

For months, determined journalists dug deep to report countless stories of horror, and the interest and support for Angelika continued to simmer away. Until, on the morning of Sunday, August 13, 1961, West Berliners awake to find barriers being erected, dividing their city. It had taken almost everyone by surprise and is a masterclass in East German deception and control.

❖❖❖

February 1961

Following the death of Jürgen and incapacity of Udo, Julius Grob, seeing that he has a top team of investigators, designates them KDXV—*Kriminal Department Extreme Verbrechen*—handling only the most serious crimes and cold cases.

Now just the four of them, Max has turned his office into the evidence room with the small *Stammtisch* table and display boards, moving himself out to the main squad room, where he feels more comfortable. Sitting at his desk, he's reading Otti's report on Der Fuchs' murder.

'So, Lutz has linked Johann's fingerprints to the photographs that were left at the scene?'

'Yes, they couldn't get any prints off Johann's body, so they matched them with the prints in his apartment. There were multiple sets on the photographs: yours, Johann's, Der Fuchs', and an unidentified set, and I think they belong to our assassin.'

'You don't think Johann killed him, then?'

'No, because Lutz matched the mystery print with another at the scene, but there was none of Johann's present.'

'Great, we'll see if Dieter Welk can come up with anything.' The phone rings. Max frowns and picks up the receiver. 'Becker.'

'Max, it's August. We have a report of the body of a woman left near Buchbinderweg in the Rudow district.'

'Have Paul and Lutz been called?'

'Lisa is calling as we speak.'

'Okay then, we'll be there in thirty minutes.'

As he puts down the receiver, the others are looking at him.

'Get your coats. We've got a customer!'

41

Now let us go hand in hand, not one before the other

Berlin: Thursday, March 11, 1966

WINTER REFUSES TO LET GO as cold grips the land and light rain falls from dank skies. The ageing bus stops at the junction of Martens and Hakenfelder Straßen, and a solitary passenger gets off. With a hiss of brakes and a belch of smoke, the bus pulls away. Wolfgang watches it disappear. He lifts his face to the sky and breathes in the air, letting the icy rain fall on his skin and, smiling, begins the ten-minute walk to Hakenfelde Women's Correctional Centre. For a little over five years, he has been here many times, but today will be the last. As the road bends sharply to the left and runs along the eastern edge of Spandauer Forest, where almost six years earlier Angelika and Christian had left their first victim, is the prison entrance: a modern, concrete, functional facility, a pair of imposing gates and to one side a small blue door marked: *Besucher! klingeln und warten!*—Visitors! ring and wait!

He looks at his watch: 6:45 a.m. He is forty-five minutes early but does not mind, as being late is not an option. He takes shelter under the branches of a tree. A few minutes later, he hears an approaching engine. A small red coupé stops and backs into one of the designated spaces. The driver kills the engine, steps out and waves to him. 'Hey, Wolfgang, I'm glad I'm not late.'

Initially, he does not recognise the young woman, but then it clicks and waving back, he says, 'What are you doing here?'

'I'm here to give you and Angelika a lift home. Dad asked me to. Look, come and wait in the car out of the rain.'

Gladly, he joins her. 'This is so nice of you and your dad. How did you know?'

'Dad seems to know everything, or at least likes us to think so. He knew it was going to be early and the buses out here aren't regular, so he asked me to play taxi for you. We would have given you a lift here, but he's not sure where you're living now.' She laughs. 'There, you see, he really doesn't know everything, does he?'

'Well, I'm lost for words. Angelika will be very grateful, as am I. I haven't seen you for... what is it?'

'Must be three years. Mum was working, so I went with dad to that veterans' dinner. To be honest, it was kinda boring,' says Heike. 'All those drunk old men banging on about the old days. Ugh, never again.'

Wolfgang laughs. 'What are you doing with yourself these days?'

'I'm just starting my degree at the Free University, and then I'm going to join the *Polizei*. I want to be a detective.'

'Wow, that sounds like a plan.'

'Yeah, I know, bit corny and not very original, but it's what I want to do.'

'I understand.' He says, nodding. 'You want to follow in your father's footsteps, eh? You two were always like two peas in a pod.'

'Well, yes, but actually it was more to do with Otti, you remember Ottilie Jäger, who works with dad. She's so brilliant and loves what she does. She's going to mentor me through college, and I hope to join the team once I graduate. Dad's got another few years to retirement and reckons Otti stands a good chance of taking over from him.'

He smiles. 'It's good to have a positive role model. You've got it all worked out, yes?' Briefly, a flash of sadness masks his face. 'Perhaps if my Angelika had... well, if things had been different, you know?'

Placing her hand on his arm, she squeezes. 'Things will be better. From today she's free and you have one another and deserve to live a little. Grasp it with both hands and look forward, not back. The past is done with.'

'You have a lot of your father about you. I think you will make a brilliant detective. You have empathy and wisdom, particularly for one so young.'

'Have you made any plans?'

'The media interest blew Angelika away, and she realised the power of the pen. A publisher has asked her to write her story, and she wants to be a journalist and has been taking courses, and a university has offered her a place to study.'

'That sounds great. I'd love to read her story, for sure. Things are changing for us girls, you know. You sure you want to stay in Berlin?'

'Yes, this is where we are from. We buried Christian here, and somewhere…' he looks out through the windscreen, gesturing. 'Somewhere out there is my darling Gretel.'

'Well, if there is anything I can do to help, ask me. Anything.'

He nods, smiling. 'Thank you.'

For a while, they sit silent, listen to the light drumming of the rain. The windows fog up. Heike starts the engine and setting the heater going, the compact car soon warms. Looking around the interior, Wolfgang says, 'This is a nice car. What is it?'

'It's an Opel Kadett. It was an eighteenth birthday gift from my parents, which was so cool and generous. Mum said she was sick of being an unpaid taxi driver.'

He laughs. 'How is your brother, by the way?'

'Markus? Oh, he's doing great. He's so bloody clever; trouble is, he knows it. He got a place at the Technical University in Munich. It's like the top place in the country for sciences.'

'Your parents must be very proud of you both. I know I would be.'

For a moment, she checks herself. 'We've been so lucky… so lucky. I never forget that.'

'Luck, my arse,' said Wolfgang. 'You get out of life what you put in. You deserve what you have, no doubt. Never be apologetic for that.'

They chat, time passes, and at precisely 7:30 a.m., a small door by the main gate opens, and Angelika steps out, the door slamming behind her. For a moment, she looks lost, almost fearful of the open space. Leaping from the car, Wolfgang runs across, gathering her in his arms, and dropping her canvas bag, she hugs him as if she'll never let go.

-Das Ende-

If you enjoyed this book, please leave a review, it really helps to know what readers think. Also I have a bonus for you on my website…

Your Free Book is Waiting. Read on…

It Was Our Destiny
A Max Becker Thriller

A discovered trunk concealing a silent history leads to a deadly confrontation.

Berlin, 1960.

After his kids discover an old trunk that contains gear from his days as a Nazi soldier, Max realises he was wrong to keep his past hidden.

Interrupted by the telephone, he is called away to the discovery of a young girl's body. The eerie crime scene unsettles him, fostering a suspicion that she is not the killer's sole victim. Embarking on a relentless investigation, destiny leads him to a fateful rendezvous with an armed man.

Unarmed and cornered by a deranged thief, can Max summon all his wits to outmaneuver the gunman?

It Was Our Destiny immerses readers into the heart-pounding world of the Max Becker German historical crime thriller series. If you love morally complex characters and meticulously authentic settings Tim Wickenden's gripping novella promises an unforgettable experience.

Subscribe to my newsletter and get it FREE today at:

www.timwickenden.com

Also by Tim

Girl Hunter
A Max Becker Thriller

A nation scarred by echoes of war. A devious serial killer who has slain nine girls. There are scant clues, and the killer seemingly unstoppable, until forced into a terrifying choice…

Find out more and how to buy at:

www.timwickenden.com

Appendix A

Translations & Notes

Used throughout the book:

Straße or *Starßen*—Street or Streets - often in German nouns are compounded, so many street names are joined with the word, street. The German ß character denotes a double 'ss' in English.
Platz—Place
S-Bahn—Berlin's overland/surface railway service
U-Bahn—Berlin's underground railway service
Frau—Mrs
Herr—Mr
Fräulein—Miss or Ms
VoPo—Volkspolizei—The East German People's Police
Polizei—Police

Characters:

The German police ranks translated into UK and approximate US equivalents:
Kriminalhauptkommissar—Detective Chief Inspector/Captain Leitender *Kriminaldirektor*—Commander/Colonel
Kriminalrat—Detective Superintendent/Major
Kriminaloberkommissar—Detective Inspector/Lieutenant
Kriminalhauptmeister—Detective Sergeant/Sergeant
Kriminalobermeister—Senior Detective Constable/Detective
Kriminalmeister—Detective Constable

Chapter 2

Achtung! Sie verlassen nach 40m West Berlin—Attention! You will leave West Berlin after 40m.

Das Demokratische Berlin—The Democratic Republic of Berlin

Chapter 4

Krapfen—filled doughnut(s)—a Berlin speciality
Panzer—Armoured vehicle
Kuchen—cake

Chapter 6

Für die Soziale Revolution—For the social revolution
Die Rosa Muschi—The Pink Pussy (Here 'Pussy' is a slang term for vagina).
Liebesmädchen— (Love girl) prostitute
Currywurst mit Pommes frites—Curry Sausage with French Fries/Chips (UK)
Mein Herr—Mister

Chapter 8

Skat—A popular German three player, trick-taking card game - almost a national obsession. No relation to the American card game called Scat.
Klinkerwerk—Clinker Factory/Brick Works—a part of Sachsenhausen concentration camp.
Die Berliner Welt—The Berlin World

Chapter 9

Teufelsberg—Devil's Mountain is a famous landmark in Berlin. Easily spotted as you fly into Tegel Airport.
Tante Ju—Aunt Ju (Also known as Iron Annie) was the nickname given to the three engined, WW2 Junkers Ju52 Transport aircraft.
Bierkeller—Beer Cellar. The German word for a pub or tavern is Die Kneipe.

Chapter 10

Stammtisch—Regulars' Table. A Stammtisch is an informal group meeting held regularly, and also the usually large, often round table around which the group meets. A Stammtisch is not a structured meeting, but a friendly get-together. Some German Bierkellers/bars/restaurants have a Regulars' Table. It is like the local pub where frequent customers might have their own table or spot - like the American TV sitcom, Cheers, where everyone had their place at the bar. A Stammtisch sign often has the quote: *Hier sind sie die immer hier sind*—here they are who are always here.

Schwanz—slang word for penis

Chapter 16

Wetwork—A euphemism for murder or assassination that refers to the spilling of blood. Can be traced back to the late 19thc. Sometimes: wet job, wet operation, wet affair, though these are primarily Russian terms.

Chapter 15

Hallo bitte, hilfe, hilfe!—Hello please, help, help!

Chapter 19

Wehrmacht—Regular Armed Forces. It comprised The *Kreigsmarine* (navy), *Luftwaffe* (airforce), and the *Heer* (army). Prior to the rise of Nazi Germany, it had been called the Reichswehr. It was separate to the *Schutzstaffel* (SS)—Protection Sqaud—but closely co-operated with it and with the *Einsatzgruppen* (SS Task forces of which there were four working behind the advancing German forces' front lines. They were tasked with ethnic cleansing, chiefly eliminating Jews and other people considered subhuman or enemies of the Third Reich). Günther Alsbach's unit, the Pioneers, were military engineers. Despite this they were core combat troops and often sent in first.

Scheißekuchen-mit-Senf—shit-cake-with-mustard.

Chapter 21

Ist war prima—it was great/swell

Das ist geil—that is awesome/amazing. Like the modern phrase: that is sick.

Pregnant Oyster—Due to the way it looks, Berliners coined this nickname for the House of World Cultures, which opened in 1957, a gift from the American people

Chapter 22

Bratwurst—A German sausage made from pork. The name comes from the Old High German word Brät, meaning highly chopped meat, and Wurst, meaning sausage.

Chapter 25

Fallschirmjäger—Paratrooper
Ich bin Berliner—I am a Berliner

Chapter 26

Quatsch—This curse word stems from the verb *quatschen*, which means "to chat." It's one of the most used terms when expressing disbelief or anger. Despite there not being a literal equivalent in English, in essence it means "Nonsense!" or "Bullshit!"

Chapter 27

Mädchenjäger—Girl Hunter. Title of the first Max Becker book.

Chapter 31

Das Massaker am Nachtwächterplatz—The Massacre at Night Watchman Square

Chapter 32

Die Fallschirmjäger—The paratroopers. Also known as The Green Devils, the German Airborne forces (part of the *Luftwaffe*) were some of the most fearsome and effective troops of WW2. Known as the Führer's Firemen, they were often moved about to reinforce areas where the enemy was making ground. *Hauptsturmführer*—Head Storm Leader. This was an SS rank equivalent to captain. Some of the most infamous Nazis held this rank, among them: Dr Josef Mengele (Doctor at Auschwitz), Klaus Barbie

(The Butcher of Lyon), Josef Kramer (Kommandant of Bergen Belsen at the time Ann Frank and her sister Margot were there, both of whom perished), and Amon Göth (who committed multiple atrocities in Poland and ran the infamous concentration camp, Kraków-Plaszów as appeared in the film Schindler's List).

Luftwaffe — Air Force -literally, Air Weapon.

Bitte zwei Strudel mit Sahne — Two Strudels with cream, please.

MP40s or Maschinepistole 40 — is a German sub machine gun.

Hitler Jugend — Hitler Youth. The paramilitary organisation for German teen boys. In the latter part of the war, many of these boys played an active role as part of the *Volkssturm* (people's storm). There was a junior version for pre-teen boys, called *Deutsches Jungvolk in der Hitlerjugend (DJV)* – German Youngsters in the Hitler Youth, and a group for girls, *Bund Deutscher Mädel (BDM)*. Many members were indoctrinated with the Nazi ideology and were ardent Hitler supporters.

Chapter 37

Scheiße — shit (with emphasis).

Chapter 38

Feldwebel — Sargeant Panzerjäger Abeitlung — Tank Destroyer Unit

Chapter 40

Totschlag — Manslaughter (is the intentional killing of another human and is punished with five to fifteen years in prison or imprisonment for life in particularly severe cases).

Kriminal Department Extreme Verbrechen — Criminal Department Extreme Crimes

Appendix B

Chapter headings: Shakespeare Quote References

From which play or sonnet:

Chapter 1 — The Tempest
Chapter 2 — Julius Caesar
Chapter 3 — A Midsummer Night's Dream
Chapter 4 — Much Ado About Nothing
Chapter 5 — Hamlet
Chapter 6 — Othello
Chapter 7 — Timon of Athens
Chapter 8 — Julius Caesar
Chapter 9 — Henry VIII
Chapter 10 — As You Like It
Chapter 11 — Sonnet 54
Chapter 12 — Hamlet
Chapter 13 — The Tempest
Chapter 14 — Hamlet
Chapter 15 — Richard II
Chapter 16 — Richard III
Chapter 17 — Othello
Chapter 18 — King John
Chapter 19 — Antony and Cleopatra
Chapter 20 — Richard II
Chapter 21 — Othello
Chapter 22 — Henry IV Part 1
Chapter 23 — Measure for Measure
Chapter 24 — Measure for Measure
Chapter 25 — Cymbeline
Chapter 26 — Romeo and Juliet
Chapter 27 — Twelfth Night
Chapter 28 — Macbeth
Chapter 29 — Macbeth
Chapter 30 — Julius Caesar
Chapter 31 — Julius Caesar
Chapter 32 — The Tempest
Chapter 33 — The Merchant of Venice
Chapter 34 — Hamlet
Chapter 35 — The Tempest
Chapter 36 — Sonnet 50
Chapter 37 — The Taming of The Shrew
Chapter 38 — Henry V
Chapter 39 — The Tempest
Chapter 40 — The Merchant of Venice
Chapter 41 — The Comedy of Errors

Creating Max Becker

Author's note

IT TOOK SOME TWO YEARS to create Max Becker, a detective character that I thought interesting. In researching Max Becker and his colleagues, as well as visiting and reading books about Berlin, I read many biographies of German wartime veterans and was taken with their stories and the impossible circumstances that they found themselves in. Many, particularly regular *Wehrmacht* troops (regular German armed forces), who made up most of the German combatants, once recruited, were sent off to face years of the most appalling warfare, slogging it out against an Eastern foe that seemed to have unlimited human resources backed up by a ruthless regime every bit as depraved and criminal as their own.

While they fought and died, the Nazi machine put its extreme ideology into practice, and while the plight of the millions of Jewish victims is well documented, other groups targeted by the Third Reich are less well known. It is estimated some six million Jews died, but a further five million from other minority or vulnerable groups were also exterminated: homosexuals, political enemies, Gypsies, the disabled, to name a few, and many of these people were German.

After the failed assassination attempt (on of many) on Hitler in July 1944, Germany imploded as it crumbled under assault from two fronts, lack of resources—most notably, fuel and war materials. Millions of civilians died or went hungry and homeless as the allies carried out remorseless bombing campaigns, often on soft targets. *The End, Hitler's Germany 1944-45* by Ian Kershaw, published by Allen Lane, is an exceptional book detailing this time, which sets out to explain why Germany fought on for so long against overwhelming odds.

As the Red Army swept into the Eastern part of Germany and on toward Berlin, some elements carried out terrible atrocities against the civilian—mostly women and children—population. It has often been stated that they did this to take revenge on what German forces had done to them, but there are accounts of Soviet troops slaughtering and raping other nationals, even concentration camp victims. In my research, I came across such an event that took place on October 21, 1944, in a little village called Nemmersdorf, and it was this that led me to weave my tale about Angelika and her family as innocents caught up in the depravity of war. Interestingly enough, soon after completing this novel, I read a war memoir of a machine gunner, titled: *Blood Red Snow - The Memoirs of a German Soldier on the Eastern Front* by Günter K, Koschorrek, a Greenhill book, who was at Nemmersdorf the day after the Soviets had left. The following is a quote from his journal for October 22, 1944, "It is impossible for me to describe all the terrible sights we have witnessed in Nemmersdorf. I can't find the right words, and it is repugnant to have to talk about the horrific acts perpetrated on innocent women, children and old people." He was deeply affected by what he saw, and although the primary purpose of my book is to entertain, it also deals with the deep moral issues that war brings and how it affects those that experience it. In a scene not dissimilar to Bastian's story in my novel—which at the time I wrote it, I wondered whether it was credible—Günter's Koschorrek's outstanding and honest account details a time he was ordered to execute some Italian partisans, which he refused to do. On being ordered to carry out the execution, he and a friend took the partisans behind some rocks, shot into the air and then let them go. It was joyful to find Günter's account confirming my suspicion that many ordinary German soldiers were incapable of committing such acts. In other memoirs that I have read and studied are many examples of the fundamental moral fortitude of the regular German troops. Though parts of my book are dark and the level of violence may seem extreme, I have tempered much of what really took place and which I thought too shocking and brutal to put in a work of fiction.

Many of the soldiers, men like my characters, Max, Tobi, and Bastian, came back from war to find out what had been going on, themselves now reviled and shamed. Many such men kept their peace but happily, as they grew old, decided that they should be able to tell their side of the story, and I realise history has not been entirely fair to them.

While my Max Becker stories are exclusive works of my imagination, the countless human stories from that time back them up. While researching the character of Max's wife, Anna, I came across a Red Cross nurse, Elfrieda Wnuk, who was the inspiration for Anna. Elfrieda lost her leg during an air raid on the Eastern Front and was the second woman to be awarded the Iron Cross 2nd Class. Despite her wounds, she continued to serve and was clearly, an exceptional person. I hope one day to find the time to go to Germany and search out her story. If Elfrieda had been British or American, she would probably be better known and held up as an icon of her time, but as a German, few people have ever heard of her. The role that many women on all sides, played in the war is breathtaking and when planning Angel Avenger, I needed strong female characters to help carry some of those stories and create a balanced narrative suitable for a modern readership. In writing the book, Angelika and Otti, with the roles of Anna and the young Heike supporting them, became the core of the story on which the male characters hang.

The character, August Dehler is entirely fictional, but his name belonged to a real Panzer commander, described in Otto Carius's war memoir, *Tigers in The Mud*, Stackpole Books. Otto was very fond of him, and his character struck me. The real August died in a tragic accident in January 1943. To protect their tanks from the extreme cold of night, they would dig them in. August had motioned for his driver to back the Panzer III out when he slipped on the frozen ground and was caught by the tank track. Otto writes, "… it grabbed him without his driver noticing it. The tank was immediately brought to a stop… he was killed immediately, without ever having uttered a sound."

I must also thank Otto's memoir for giving me Max's "saved by a cigarette" story as he had a similar experience (I adapted the account, but it is clearly Otto's), and it brought home to me the randomness of war, in that a moment of change could have so drastic an impact. Like Max, when Otto bent down to take a light from someone else, it saved his life, enabling him to tell us his story and to grow to old age. I must stress that Max is entirely fictional and isn't based on Otto or any other living person, but as with most invented characters, he is a tapestry of many.

Most of the locations mentioned in the book (though some street names have changed since 1960) are real. The location of Max's office on the corner of Kurfürsten and Baggranfen Straßen was the location of the headquarters of The 3rd Panzer Division, which is the Division that Max joined just before the war (2 volumes titled, *Armored Bears* details their history). If you go to Tegel Forest, you can find the tallest tree *Höchster Baum*, and the massive oak, *Dicke Marie* (Fat Marie), though hopefully not a burnt-out van with a dead Russian inside! Berlin is a magnificent city full of fascinating history and culture, and I recommend it highly!

Acknowledgements

MY SINCEREST THANKS TO FIONA Bailey, Jim and Delia Stokes, and to the author, Patricia Watkins, all of whom offered advice, read early drafts and encouraged me to keep writing. Jim suggested I be bolder in the basement scenes, as initially, I had played those down. My friend and fellow author, Patricia, gave me lots of practical advice about publishing. My thanks to Helen Culyer for proofing and editorial work. My thanks and love to my wife, Clare, who gave me space and moral support to keep writing, and as I sat hammering away on my keyboard brought me many cups of tea. Most importantly, if you're reading this, it means you've probably read the rest, and for that, I thank you hugely.

T.W.

Author Bio

TIM LOVES TO WRITE, AND reads with a passion: the one sets him free, while the other allows him to walk in the shoes of others. We are nothing without stories. Tim's began in Zimbabwe. He spent his childhood there, in Hong Kong, and then Germany.

Aged five, a serious accident left a deep impression on him, and after his well-meaning parents packed him off, aged eight, to boarding school in England, he suffered abuse and neglect, all of which have become grist to his mill and essential inspiration with which he infuses his characters and their stories.

Tim now lives in South West Wales and when not writing, he walks the coast, goes paddleboarding, loves to read, and listen to music.

Printed in Great Britain
by Amazon